The Wild Adventures of Doc Savage

Please visit www.adventuresinbronze.com for
more information on titles you may have missed.

THE DESERT DEMONS
HORROR IN GOLD
THE INFERNAL BUDDHA
DEATH'S DARK DOMAIN
PHANTOM LAGOON
THE WAR MAKERS
THE MIRACLE MENACE
THE ICE GENIUS

(Don't miss another original Doc Savage adventure coming soon.)

DOC SAVAGE

DEATH'S DARK DOMAIN

A DOC SAVAGE ADVENTURE

BY WILL MURRAY & LESTER DENT
WRITING AS KENNETH ROBESON

COVER BY JOE DeVITO

ALTUS PRESS • 2012

First Edition — October 2012

DESIGNED BY
Matthew Moring/Altus Press

SPECIAL THANKS TO
*James Bama, Jerry Birenz, Nicholas Cain, Condé Nast,
Jeff Deischer, Dafydd Neal Dyar, Rick Lai, Dave McDonnell,
Matthew Moring, Ray Riethmeier, Art Sippo, Howard Wright,
The State Historical Society of Missouri, and last but not least,
the Heirs of Norma Dent—James Valbracht,
Shirley Dungan and Doris Lime.*

COVER ILLUSTRATION COMMISSIONED BY
Mark O. Lambert

Like us on Facebook: "The Wild Adventures of Doc Savage"

Printed in the United States of America

Set in Caslon.

For the incomparable Steve Holland—

**Who personified
the Man of Bronze
as no other....**

Death's Dark Domain

Table of Contents

Chapter I

THE UTTER BLACKNESS

FIANA DROST WAS the first one to encounter the terrible black thing that could not be seen, touched, felt or explained.

The thing was in fact not known to be black, but was only supposed to be black. Rather, a smothering impenetrable darkness was the predominant sensation of those who came into contact with the impossible darksome thing and lived to speak of it. Or perhaps it was, after all, black. No one could say—not even those who stared directly into the blackness and heard the beating of its leathery wings.

It was confusing to say the least.

The incredible affair began in a confusing fashion, too.

In the last moments before the nebulous shadow of terror fell upon the disputed piece of Balkan real estate that was called Ultra-Stygia, Fiana Drost stood looking at the evening sky on the balcony of an old fortified church that had been converted into a drafty inn for the benefit of the swarm of newspaper reporters who had come to witness the world's latest war. There was no war. Not yet. One was expected momentarily, and so the press had descended on the picturesque stone inn perched on the rocky bluff overlooking Ultra-Stygia from the Tazan side. Tazan was a coastal country, presently holding its collective breath. Its neighbor on the northern side of Ultra-Stygia, Egallah, was massing tanks and soldiers in anticipation of a land grab. Ultra-Stygia was the object of their hoggishness.

That, at least, was the viewpoint of the government of Tazan.

From the Egallah side, their diplomats pointed out that Ultra-Stygia had been theirs for centuries, and was therefore rightfully the property of its hereditary people. It was their perfect right to take it back—by force of arms, if necessary. In fact, it was their solemn duty to do so.

The unnerving situation had been thus for nearly a month now.

The representatives of the fourth estate had arrived to find Fiana Drost already ensconced in a modest suite. Since the war was late getting underway, they had taken to badgering the mystery woman for comments to sprinkle in their cabled reports. Fiana Drost showed good sense. She put off all interview requests.

It was after the dinner hour, and no war having materialized, the reporters were loitering about the inn, seeking diversion. Fiana Drost being the most diverting thing around, it was only natural that she began thinking of herself as a jar of honey that had attracted too many bears.

Fiana had fled to the bell tower to get a breathing spell from all the unwanted attention. She stood there looking at the rising moon over Cateral, which was the name of this bleak frontier town.

The reporters had proven persistent, and it was suspected that a few of them had designs beyond their stated intentions. One wanted Fiana to run away with him. Two were threatening to shoot themselves if she didn't accept their matrimonial proposals. She had that effect upon susceptible men.

Fiana Drost was no frail flower of womanhood. She did not appear delicate. Nor did she flutter her eyelids at men who chanced to enter her personal orbit. That was not Fiana Drost.

She was on the tall side, her unblemished skin was on the pale side, and her intelligent eyes and long hair were both of such an intense black that they shone. The combination was quietly stunning, especially by moonlight.

None of this exactly explained her fascinating quality; rather it was probably a combination of things that people noticed. She did not fit any preconceived notion of femininity. Her features were sensitive, but there was an underlying strength to her every facial expression, even in repose.

It was difficult to lay a finger on what kind of woman Fiana Drost was. She was entirely unique.

Moreover, Fiana Drost was an enigmatic creature. She had been in this frontier region some weeks, but little was known of her past. She might have been native to Tazan. No one was certain. She had no noticeable accent. A few of the more imaginative scribes ventured the opinion that Fiana Drost was a spy in the pay of Egallah. It was commonly supposed after all, that some guests of the hotel were presumed to be clandestine agents of Egallah.

In truth, Fiana Drost might have been anything—including what she appeared to be: an exceedingly attractive young woman with both time on her hands and money enough to allow her to lounge about a disguised military outpost while she waited for a war to commence.

Fiana had been at the bell-tower window staring out into the excessively quiet night when she started. Her slim hands, touching the cool wood of a balustrade rail set before the open window, clenched. There was a very modern anti-aircraft gun emplacement situated in the inn's garden, concealed by sandbags heaped about. But that was not where her dark, doe-like gaze was resting.

A strained sound emerged from between her pale, uncolored lips.

The sound was not loud, but it carried. And it brought a man stepping into the bell-tower, which served as a kind of makeshift balcony, alarm on his handsome face.

The man was young, athletic and wore his worry like a hair shirt. When he had introduced himself to Fiana Drost, he had called himself Simon Page, with the Associated Press. He hadn't been a pest like the others, so Fiana tolerated him in her strong, self-contained way.

Naturally, Simon Page had promptly fallen in love with the mystery woman. She didn't seem to be in love with him, although Simon had told her he had hopes.

"What is it?" Simon blurted anxiously. "I heard you cry out."

The girl did not move or reply. She simply stared out into the night, with her small knuckles going white as her fingers gripped the rail.

"What's wrong?" Simon Page asked.

Fiana Drost did not respond. But her hands came away from the rail. She folded her slim arms, clutching her elbows, as if to still them.

Simon Page knew this girl—not as well as he would have liked, it was true—but close observation led him to suspect that she would not frighten without a compelling reason. He began to wonder what she could be looking at.

His eyes searched the area below the stone inn. It was an expanse of darkness, whose flatness was broken only by a low depression, not far off. A few bats wheeled about in animated flight.

After a tense period, not knowing what else to do, Simon decided to give her some information she had asked him to get. He still didn't understand why she had wanted this particular information.

"You were asking yesterday about this fellow they call Doc Savage," Simon said. "Remember? To-day, I looked up some dope on him. To tell the truth, what I found out amazed me. If this chap is half of what his reputation indicates, he's remarkable!"

He paused, hoping Fiana Drost would say something. She didn't.

Page reached out to touch her shoulder, hoping to break the eerie spell that the Tazan moon—he supposed—had wrought on the strange young woman. "I learned quite a bit, if you care to hear it."

Fiana Drost shook his arm off, casually.

"I'm not interested in Doc Savage now!" she said suddenly. She turned abruptly, pale fingers becoming fists. "Simon, will you do something for me?"

"Of course, darling!"

"I want you to come with me."

"Eh?"

Fiana Drost's eyes became great dark pools holding an imploring light. "Just accompany me, please. No questions."

Simon Page hesitated only a moment.

Minutes later, he was leading the way down the winding road that led from the old inn to the great dusky expanse that was Ultra-Stygia.

A few nettles carpeted a low patch of ground before the inn. After Simon Page got a flashlight out of his car, the two made their way down to the depressed area, as if descending into the bottom of Ultra-Stygia. Simon Page seemed distinctly puzzled. Darkness did not seem as intense as it had earlier. He had difficulty keeping up with her.

During the descent, Simon continued his interrupted recital.

"Doc Savage seems to be what physical culture experts and learned men have dreamed about—a man that was reared from the cradle by experts and developed into a physical marvel and a mental genius. This man, I was told, is devoting his life to the career for which he was trained. Believe it or not, this career seems to be traveling over the world, righting wrongs and punishing evildoers."

This discourse produced no response from the determined woman, so he gave it up.

When they reached the bottom, Simon Page evinced a surprised start.

Here was a no-man's land of charred landscape. In both directions, barbed wire was strung as far as the eye could perceive.

There were trees—broken hulks with no leaves clinging to them. The ground had been turned so that no grass or shrubs grew. Of course, it was winter, so little could grow.

The heavy smell of wood smoke hung in the still air. It smelled exactly like a house that had burned up would after a long rain. Their throats became scratchy. It made for a doleful atmosphere.

There were no soldiers, no sentries picketed in the bleak desolation. The government of Tazan had not wished to create a provocation that might serve as a pretext for an invasion, so it had done the next best thing. It had scorched the earth closest to its border so that snipers and enemy forces could not creep close without being seen.

No life was visible below. Yet Fiana Drost had seen something down here. She raced forward, heedless of the dead nettles that tangled the shallow wash.

"Watch your step!" Simon cautioned. "Thorns abound, my rose."

Fiana rushed on. Simon Page followed, calling, "Wait!"

Hesitating, Fiana Drost turned to face Simon Page. "I have changed my mind. Turn back, I beg of you."

Simon caught up. He lowered his voice. "But—why?"

"Don't be such an American fool. I am being—grave. I—I'm afraid you will think I am—superstitious."

"Nonsense!"

Fiana Drost paused, seeming to be debating whether to make explanations. She had become paler still. Her lips—they were exquisite in spite of the strain—parted slightly.

"No matter what happens to-night," she said earnestly, "don't breathe a word to another soul. And above all, don't print any of it."

Simon Page swallowed hard. He nodded his head wordlessly.

They hurried on—a strangely perturbed girl and a vastly puzzled young man. By now Simon Page could see that Fiana Drost had become overwrought concerning something; he didn't know what. He couldn't understand it. Back in his mind, striking him now and then, was the knowledge that no one really knew anything about the girl. She was a beautiful stranger in Cateral.

Simon asked, "Where are we going?"

"It must be around here!" Fiana said tensely.

"What?"

"The thing I saw a moment ago."

"What thing?"

Fiana's doe-black eyes raked the night. "I do not know what it is—but it was very large and incredibly black," she said distractedly.

"How could you make out something black at this hour of night?"

"The black thing," Fiana Drost imparted, "was blacker than the night sky. Blacker than the primordial night that preceded the world's first dawn." Her voice sounded as thin and chill as the night wind blowing over Ultra-Stygia.

Simon Page had trouble finding words. His mouth felt dry. This was a superstitious country, this disputed slice of land. Wild things were said to be abroad in the night. Evil creatures for which science had no name. Simon Page felt suddenly cold.

The girl reached feverishly for the flashlight and he let her have it. She ran forward, twitching the ivory beam around, searching.

"I do not understand," she murmured. "The black thing alighted right here, on this very spot."

Simon Page noticed that the flash ray was shaking and saw the reason why. Fiana Drost's slim hands were shaking nervously. In fact, the moon-pale skin of her bare arms was trembling like disturbed water.

Observing closely, Page studied the obvious terror which she was registering. He reached out and gathered her close to him. This impressed him as a highly satisfactory act, so he put his other arm around her. A delicious warmth leaping through him was the result.

She must have known how astonishment wracked him—paralyzed him—for she went quickly on with the blazing flashlight, still searching.

Once, she paused and lifted an arm at the heavens, changing her position slightly—as if fixing in her mind the direction from which some object had come out of the north. After this, she moved on, toward a stunted travesty of a tree.

There, they came upon a dying man.

THEY understood that the man was dying in the first glimmer of awareness that the crumpled form was indeed human.

For one thing, the man was too pale. Lilies have a pallor that is pleasing to some eyes. The man had that kind of coloration, but it was not pleasant to behold. Living human flesh should not resemble a lily.

His lips were the same waxy color as the surrounding skin, and that was white. Ghosts are possibly paler than the dying man, but not by very many shades. He was seated on the ground, his back up against a dead gray husk of a tree which had been blasted by lightning and scorched by man.

Simon Page stared, astounded. He had been with the Associated Press since leaving college. Dealing with the unvarnished realities of life normally encountered by newspapermen had made him very level-headed, so he was greatly startled by anything he did not understand.

The dying man had thin yellow hair atop his head and blood was running in scarlet strings from between the fingers of his left hand. The hand was clamped to the side of a chalk-white neck, trying to hold the corpuscular fluids in his body.

It was too late. A great deal of it had obviously leaked out. What remained was a turgid desultory bubbling, like a freshwater spring gurgling up its last moisture.

Oddly, there was not much scarlet on the surrounding ground. And only a cupful on the victim's clothes. He made Simon think of a hapless fly after it had fallen out of a spider's web.

"He's badly hurt," Simon Page whispered. "Must have crawled here."

The flashlight's questing beam, however, disproved this notion. There was no trail of red drops leading away from the dying man. Nor were there drag marks. The charred earth was of a texture to take footprints, but there were none. It was impossible to imagine the man having walked to this spot where he had sat down to die under his own power.

He might have been deposited there by a great winged… something.

"Who are you?" Simon asked the bloodless one. "How did you come here?"

The dying man showed his teeth in agony. That simple act seemed to be an effort.

Fiana splashed light into his face. Her eyes grew very wide for a minute, then narrowed.

"You are Zoltan, who disappeared," she breathed.

The crimson trickle from the dying man's neck seemed to be slowing.

"I thought—I thought the thing was carrying me off to Hell itself," he muttered, his words thick spaced sounds.

"What thing?"

"The black winged thing that stole my—eyes."

The man's eyes were still in his head. They were half rolled upward now. If he could see—which was doubtful—it was only dimly. The natural light that gives the human eye the impression of life was fading.

"Can you see?" Fiana demanded.

"It slaked its thirst after it devoured my eyes," the man went on, "and I could feel my veins grow thin and flat as the vital fluids were sucked away. When it had enough, it dropped me here… to die…."

That last word escaped him with a leaky creaking.

A CHILLY silence descended. Other than the skeletal rattle of spindly tree branches, no noise disturbed the night air.

Simon Page moved his head slowly, as if cudgeling his brain to accommodate such notions as a strange man falling out of the night sky, and telling the fantastic story that he had been carried here by a black creature that stole his sight and drank his body dry of its natural supply of blood.

It was, of course, utterly on the ridiculous side. Level-headed Simon Page sniffed loudly, skeptically, then turned to the girl—only to observe in the flashlight glare that Fiana Drost was stark, with rigidity seemingly fixed all through her.

"What is it?" he demanded.

"Look—on the ground!"

Simon shifted his gaze. Her pointing finger helped him. It indicated a disturbed patch of earth.

"Looks like something took a scoop out of the ground with a shovel," he observed.

"No shovel did that," said Fiana. "A pitchfork, perhaps." Her voice was very queer.

It was true. The markings suggested pointed tines—or the mark of a claw clutching at the earth. Simon appropriated the flashlight and searched for more.

"Over here," Fiana cried suddenly. "Another of the awful marks."

Simon followed her about three yards, where there was a nearly identical earth disturbance. He swept the flash ray about, but failed to locate a third mark. Or more ominously, any sign of footprints belonging to the hypothetical pitchfork wielder.

"If—" Fiana started, swallowing twice, "if a great creature had deposited him here, it would have alighted on this very spot."

"No bird grows so large," Simon pointed out.

"The black thing I saw—thought I saw—was large enough to leave such marks," Fiana said hollowly. "With its talons."

"Talons?"

Fiana shook off her queer mood and stamped back to the wretched one they had discovered under the lightning-blasted tree.

The dying man had been huddled, and now he slackened weakly. The crimson seepage from his neck had ceased. His staunching hand fell away. He moaned a little, then his moan became words.

"Tell them—tell them Ultra-Stygia is accursed!" he shrieked. "It is the roof of the pit of Hell itself! I know. The roof opened and I looked—into—the—pit."

"What did you see?" Fiana gasped. "What did you see—in the pit?"

"I saw," the dying man rasped, "the eyes of the damned ones."

"Eyes?"

"Eyes without faces. Eyes floating in the darkness without bodies to support them. But that is not the most horrible part. The disembodied eyes stared at me—as if there were a malign intelligence behind them."

"He's raving," Simon scoffed. "He needs a doctor."

"Hush," Fiana breathed, kneeling before the wretch. She had the flashlight now and was spraying it liberally on the man's face. "Tell me more, Zoltan. What was the black thing?"

"It was—*black*. There is no other description for it than *black*. It was composed of a blackness more hideous than mortal mind could conceive. Hell is paved in cobbles of such unholy material."

"This is not rational talk," Simon interposed.

Abruptly, the man expired. He gave a series of rattling jerks, and seemed to collapse within himself. One hand, clenched, fell open and something tumbled to the ground with a clatter.

Fiana scooped the object up. She straightened, holding the thing up to the rays of her flash.

"Oh!" This, from the girl, was a gasp.

"What is it, Fiana?" Simon demanded. Then he saw what it was. A black bat—not real. A small emblem of enamel, not unlike a brooch—not that any woman would wear such a ghoulish bit of adornment. The wings were not fully spread, and curled inward, as if the creature were using its claw-tipped membranous wings to fend off a predator. Noticing this, Simon Page tried to think of what could be so terrible that it struck fear into a bat, itself a nocturnal predator.

Then he noticed the bat's eyes. Or lack of them, rather. They had been obliterated. Gouged, he saw, by some sharp tool.

"Blind—as a bat...." Fiana murmured.

"What?"

"There is an expression—to be as blind as a bat. This bat had been blinded in a horrible way." Fiana shuddered. "Come—quickly."

Fiana Drost did not wait for him to respond. She started back. Simon leaped after her, casting frequent glances over his shoulder at the brooding darkness of Ultra-Stygia.

CATCHING up with the hurrying girl, Simon noticed that she walked with the flashlight lighting her way. The other hand was open and empty. He wondered vaguely what she had done with the tiny black bat without eyes. He got in front of her.

"But—I don't understand, Fiana darling. What about that poor man?"

"There is nothing that can be done for him now," Fiana snapped. "He is dead."

The coldness of her tone so stunned Simon Page that he stood rooted and speechless, staring at the lunar-white countenance of bewitching Fiana Drost.

Impatiently, she pulled his arm. "Come. We cannot stay here."

And because she was so anxious, so insistent, he followed her. They reached the top of a rise, heading back toward the inn, before Simon spoke again.

"I can't—I don't believe what just happened. Was it—as

strange to you as to me?"

The girl walked faster. "Remember. You mustn't mention this. Ever!"

Simon Page gripped the girl's arm and stopped her. "Look here! I think you should give an explanation. Who was that man? How did you know his name?"

The girl did not answer immediately. "I'm sorry," she said.

"What do you mean—sorry?"

"I mean that I am sorry that I dragged you into this!" she said sharply. "You, of all people."

"I don't—"

Her doe-dark eyes regarded him sternly. "Simon, you must forget this! Forget everything you have witnessed. Do you understand?"

Simon Page seized his flashlight and directed cold glare upon Fiana Drost's stark features.

"I don't see why I should forget this," he complained. "You seemed to know that—man."

Fiana fixed him with her intense gaze. "You saw Zoltan, saw how he looked. He witnessed something once, and failed to forget. Let that be a lesson to you."

The memory of the lily-white man was distinct enough to make Simon Page's epidermis feel as if it were crawling.

Simon mumbled, "He must have been mad—that stuff about a black, blood-sucking creature as big as a house."

The girl shook her head. "There is much you would not understand, more you would not believe. Trust me. Forget all that you saw."

She started to hurry on.

"Doc Savage!" Simon Page called suddenly after her.

Mention of the name "Doc Savage" brought the girl to a halt and around to face the flashlight. Her lips parted. Her eyes grew very wide. Their color was a fathomless black.

"Why did you say that?" she demanded.

"You're acting very strangely, Fiana," Simon accused. "There's some kind of infernal mystery here that's more than a little incredible."

"But why say *Doc Savage?*"

"Because of what I heard about him. He seems to follow the strange profession of helping other people out of jams."

The girl bit her lips. "I still don't see why you mentioned his name."

"Didn't you ask me about Doc Savage?"

"Oh, that!" Fiana Drost shook her head. "That had nothing to do with this. I was just curious, having read an article about him."

"Stranger and stranger," Simon Page declared grimly.

The young woman threw up her chin and seemed about to fling something biting. But she whirled, instead, and ran toward the inn.

"Fiana!" Simon shouted. He ran after her. She proved to be fleet and uncannily sure-footed in the dark.

He caught her at the entrance to the inn, took hold of her arm.

"Listen, I do not understand. You've changed. You've become positively cold-blooded."

The words had tumbled out, and Simon Page soon had cause to regret uttering them.

Fiana Drost faced him indignantly. "You're insulting! I don't want to see you again!"

"But—"

She flounced inside, slamming the door behind her.

Simon Page, wearing an expression as much puzzled as hurt, started to follow, then reconsidered. He decided against bothering her.

Simon paused outside the great stone church, and smoked his way through two cigarettes furiously.

Then he went to his room and paced for a time. There were

telephones installed in the converted inn rooms, and Simon considered asking the front desk to connect him with Fiana's room. He decided against this course of action. He had come all the way from Boston, Massachusetts to report on the war everyone expected. Without a war, there was nothing to wire back to his editor. If no war came, he would be recalled or sent elsewhere, and that would mean never seeing Fiana Drost again.

It was that last unappealing realization that decided him.

Simon was going to find the black thing. "Already wasted too much time!" he muttered. "Should have done it earlier!" He seemed tempted to go to Fiana Drost at once, and demand a closer look at the tiny black bat ornament. "I'll do it later!" he said aloud. Despite the fact that it might be none of his business, Simon Page had plainly decided to take an active part in the mystery.

Simon loaded a revolver he extracted from his travel bag. There was no telling into what peril a story might lead him. He went out into the night with the gun in his pocket, and his flashlight in one hand.

Overhead in the night sky, flapping bats were returning to the hollows of dead trees to rest.

MINUTES later, Page had returned to the scorched spot where the dead man lay. Zoltan was still there. Now he no longer resembled a human being, but the discarded victim of some parasitic creature—a dried shell that had once been a man, now tossed aside after all the vital juices had been drawn off like sap from a healthy tree.

Gun in one fist, flash in the other, Simon Page crept on.

He walked some distance. Only his feet treading the burnt earth made noise. It was a monotonous, macabre sound. Simon might have been the only living thing for miles around.

Simon began to feel vaguely that something was wrong. He did not immediately place what it was. Then suddenly he knew. The bats! Instead of roosting peacefully, the bats were fluttering around as if they had recently been disturbed.

Then he heard the wings.

The moon was, by this hour, very high in the night sky. Simon Page looked upward, and saw the lunar orb. Around it floated a sea of stars.

From somewhere among those silvery lights, the whirring of wings seemed to come. Craning his head back, Simon attempted to make out the source of the growing sound. He could not.

Pressure of wind stirred his hair. The ashy ground cover under his feet lifted, disturbed by unseen beating pinions.

The sound was coming closer. Simon Page thumbed the safety on his pistol. He waved it skyward, as if in warning.

Cinders rose in a noisome cloud about his legs. Far over his head, a field of stars was blotted out. Simon fired toward that anthracite patch. His revolver barked twice.

Abruptly, the whirring sound seemed to plummet. Simon had presence of mind enough to run for his life. He imagined a great dark creature dropping to the earth, mortally wounded, and had no desire to be crushed under its bulk.

So he ran. Oddly, the whirring, beating sound pursued him. He used his flashlight to pick his way around the shattered trees that dotted the landscape. The pressure of beaten air rolled across his back. The thing was gaining!

Just when Simon Page was about to give up all hope, his flash ray went out. It was a shocking thing to happen. The batteries were fresh. The light had not seen much use. They could not have died. It was impossible!

Turning, he tried to spy the thing bearing down on him—and he received another shock. Simon could no longer see the stars! Nor the moon. The midnight sky was impenetrably black. Was the creature that huge, after all, that it could blot out the *entire* night sky?

Seized by fear now, Simon ran. He tucked his elbows close to his ribs and put all his churning might into escape.

Without light, he could not see an inch before his wide staring eyes. All the world had become black. And the beating wings were following relentlessly.

Abruptly, Simon changed direction. He fled west. And suddenly, he could see again. After a fashion. The sky was full of stars once more and the moon was there, shedding its platinum effulgence.

Most astonishing of all, his pocket flashlight was again spraying illumination!

Heart racing, Page ran on. And the beating wings caught up again. As did the darkness. The night sky was doused of light. The flashlight, hard in his fist, issued no discernible light. He could see nothing. And so ran into an obstructing tree.

He bounced off, shaken. Finding himself in the dirt, Simon Page attempted to rise.

Then the hairs on the back of his neck stood up stiff and straight.

The thing was directly overhead now. He could feel its smoky breath. The darkness was smothering. It was difficult to breathe.

As he lay there, something seized him with an irresistible grip. Simon Page struggled, fought. The thing that had him felt like horn. *Talons!* But what sort of creature possessed talons large enough to take hold of a full-grown man?

Then, something sharp like fangs sank into his shoulder and, in spite of himself, Simon Page screamed.

The horrible blackness overtook his frenzied brain.

Chapter II

THE DAMNED ONE

WHEN SIMON PAGE awoke, he did a strange thing. Under the circumstances it might not have been so strange, but the speed with which he did it was peculiar. It showed a remarkable presence of mind.

His eyes snapped up, and he beheld the night sky. He saw the spectral magnificence of the lunar disk and surrounding stars.

Simon blinked twice. Then he brought his hands up to his chest and felt of his heart.

It was still beating. Only after receiving that steady reassurance indicating he still walked in the world of the living, did Simon Page take stock of his surroundings.

He lay flat on his back and in his throat was the smoky air of the scorched patch of land known as Ultra-Stygia. He tried coughing some of it out of his lungs. It came out in visible plumes. The winter air felt cold.

Then he sat up. The act of sitting up brought to his attention the throbbing pain in his left shoulder. Then he remembered the fearsome sensation of sharp fangs sinking into that shoulder.

Simon Page reached up to look at the cloth over the shoulder. He could see no cloth. No shoulder. In fact, he could not see his hands when he held them before his face.

It was a shock. He looked up, and there was the reassuring light of the stars, but they held an inimical twinkling now.

Simon Page found his feet shakily. He was sore in a number of places and his skin felt icy to the touch. It was only then that he realized that he was naked.

He went in search of his clothes. By wan moonlight, he could make out shapes of spidery, leafless trees, not much else. He began to flounder for his flashlight, but that was not to be found, either.

After some difficult minutes, Simon gave up the search, and began walking back to the stone church faintly visible on the bluff.

He gave silent thanks for the fact that he had awoken while it was still dark. It might be possible to slip into his room without loss of dignity.

Simon had walked an uncertain distance when he saw the eyes.

They were blue—a very sharp crystal blue. They were visible to his left, and they floated approximately six feet above the ground, supported by nothing that he could discern.

More unnerving, the eyes were plainly regarding him. Staring, rather. They were unnaturally round, like billiard balls. Their lidless regard stabbed through the darkness.

Holding his hands in a modest manner, Simon Page returned the frank stare. The sight of the disembodied eyes was so starkly unbelievable that no terror accompanied the vision. Perhaps, Simon reflected, all terror had been squeezed out of his soul by the evening's terrible events.

Simon decided to hail the owner of the eyes.

"Who are you?" he called. "Why are you looking at me like that?"

The eyes continued to stare.

A voice directly behind him was startling in its cold frankness.

"Forgive him his staring, for he is newly dead."

Simon gasped, "Dead?"

"He has been condemned to walk this terrible desolation for

his sins, as have you."

Simon turned. "My—sins?"

"You know their names," said the chilly voice. And in the direction from which the sepulchral tones were emanating, floated a pair of eyes. Only the whites could be seen. The center of the white orbs were identical in hue to the surrounding blackness, so it looked as if the optics had been cored, apple-fashion.

The effect was uncanny in the extreme.

Simon Page was not a superstitious sort. He did not avoid black cats, especially, felt no qualms about walking under ladders, and when the thirteenth day of the month coincided with Friday on his calendar, he hardly took notice.

But standing out in the utter darkness of Ultra-Stygia, being scrutinized by accusing eyes attached to no mortal shells who had pronounced him dead, Simon Page felt his strong heart quail.

"What—what makes you say I'm dead?" he demanded.

"It is plain to see that you have shed your earthly cloak of flesh," said the cold voice. "You exist only as a soul, condemned to look upon the world with eyes that only the damned can see."

"You mean—you mean I'm just like you?"

"Just as we are—dead."

"It's not true!" Simon shrieked.

"Your body," said a third voice, "lies back to the north, where you left it."

Simon whirled. And beheld another set of eyes in the darkness. These optics were gray.

"I'm not like—*that!*" he gulped. "I can't be."

The discarnate voice intoned, "You were seized by a great vampire bat, which discarded you when it had drank its fill."

"No—no!" Simon screamed, thinking of the clutching black thing.

"Do not return to the land of the living. There is no place for you there."

The three sets of accusatory eyes began converging upon him. Simon began backing away, walking on his bare feet. His shoulder ached. His eyes burned in his head—if he still possessed a head, which he had begun to doubt.

The floating orbs bored at him in round-eyed silence.

Then one spoke his name.

"Do not leave this domain, Simon Page."

The sound of his own name coming from the uncanny soul beings was scary enough to send Simon Page running out of Ultra-Stygia as fast as his legs—or whatever provided him with locomotion now—could carry him.

He ran without looking back. He ran without heeding the terrible cold fear deep in the pit of his stomach.

WHEN the stone church on the bluff came within sight, Simon Page slowed down. He cast his gaze about for something to cover his nakedness. Finding nothing, he crept cautiously to the side entrance.

The lobby was well lit, but there was only one person at the front desk, the desk clerk who was busy reading a newspaper whose headlines screamed of war.

Simon Page saw that he could not cross the spacious lobby without being seen. And since he had no clothes, he hadn't pockets to carry his room key. He would need a key.

The electrified lighting system, although new, was of the type in which the current-carrying cords were exposed. It had proved impossible to bury ordinary wiring into the clammy stone blocks that made up the former church. It was simple enough to trace the exposed cord to the single switch that controlled the electrical lights.

Simon did so, creeping low. One eye on the front desk, he suppressed the lobby lights by turning a switch.

A startled exclamation came from the desk clerk. Putting

his paper aside, he came stamping toward the switch. In the dark, he could not see Simon Page pass by, utterly naked.

Simon found the cubbyhole with the hook containing the spare room key. As it happened, it was the third from the left on the topmost row. He discovered the cubby by feel and, as a precaution, grabbed the keys on either side of the one he was certain belonged to his room.

Creeping to the elevator, Simon slipped into the tiny cage. He had a piece of luck. The cage stood empty. He ran the doors closed and sent the cage toiling upward.

When he emerged on the attic floor, it was likewise quiet. He slipped to his door, tried the keys until the lock turned, then stepped in.

"Whew!" Simon breathed. Turning on the light, he stepped into the washroom.

Simon Page washed his face in the sink and considered taking a hot bath. His exposed skin felt dry and scratchy and he was chilled to the bone.

Looking up from the sink, he stared into the mirror. His eyes looked back at him, red-rimmed and tired. Then his green irises widened, pupils dilating in shock.

For the orbs floated in the mirrored surface without any mortal meat surrounding them!

THE human mind is a remarkably adaptive organ. Confront it with certain stimuli, and it will react according to prescribed boundaries. Should a man stumble across a man-eating tiger in Central Park, for example, he would naturally turn and flee from the danger first, only then to consider the improbability of there being man-eating tigers in Central Park.

Simon Page was no different. He saw the eyes in the mirror and his first impulse was to flee. He might have done so, except that the A.P. man remembered that he was without benefit of clothing. His natural fear instincts were momentarily over-whelmed by other instincts just as compelling.

The thought of running out into the hotel hallway and attracting the attention of Fiana Drost kept him from risking it.

Not that every nerve did not cry out for flight. Simon grasped the white porcelain edge of the hotel room sink in an effort to keep himself from fleeing.

After a suitable interval in which he got control of his nerves, Simon looked up into the mirror.

The eyes were his own. Frightening realization, but there was no denying it. They were very wide and exactly the verdant color of his own—emerald shot with darker lines so that they resembled peepholes into some jungled realm.

When Simon leaned closer to the mirror's surface, the green eyes moved toward him. And when he narrowed his eyes, the detached orbs mimicked the operation. How they managed this was a puzzle.

Simon, by forcing himself to experiment, grew accustomed to the spectacle, nerve-chilling as it was.

He closed one eye. And miraculously the mirror mate to the eye he shut disappeared!

He was staring at one eye now. Just one. He opened the other and there were two again. When he closed the opposite eye, once again, a single forest-green orb stared back at him, a few inches to the side of the one which had vanished.

Trembling, Simon Page lifted hands he could not see and felt of his face. He detected eyelids, lashed and tangible. Yet somehow, when he closed his eyelids, his orbs winked out of existence.

What did that mean? he wondered, heart beating high in his throat.

Simon pressed a hand to the glass. In a moment, the misty outline of his fingers and palm took form, created by the natural warmth of his flesh.

Did that mean he was not dead?

Simon walked back into the room and sat down on the side of the made bed. The mattress gave under his weight. He had weight! He looked down. He could see nothing of himself, but the bed cover was a smooth hollow where he had planted the seat of his pants—had he been wearing any such.

In the fashion of a drowning man whose mind insists upon recalling the dominant events of his life, a great many thoughts rushed through Simon Page's brain in those moments. In this instance, Simon was reliving the hours leading up to the events that had brought him to this sorry disembodied state.

Then one thought came uppermost, burst from his unseen lips like a single bubble of oxygen breaking the surface of a pond.

"Doc Savage!" he said. "Doc Savage is the man to help me!"

He scooped up the room phone. It was a French-style phone, with the receiver and mouthpiece molded in one unit. He clicked the switch hook until the desk clerk picked up.

"I wish to place a long distance call," Page blurted breathlessly. "To New York City."

"What is the number in New York you wish to reach?"

"I don't know the number," Simon said, ragged-voiced.

"Then I do not think the call can be completed."

The long-distance operator was of the same opinion after Simon Page was put through to her over the clerk's sullen objections. She spoke good English, as her job required.

"Get me Doc Savage in New York City," clipped Simon.

And that stilled the long-distance operator's objections. Such was the power of the famous name.

In less than ten minutes—the time necessary to set up the connections—the hotel room rang and Simon Page picked it up.

He got a distant ringing—the sound of a telephone in New York as transmitted over a great transatlantic cable, Simon knew.

There came a click. And a voice, remarkable even over the thousands of miles of seafloor-laid cable.

"This is the headquarters of Doc Savage," the remarkable

voice said.

"This is Simon Page! I'm at the Cateral Inn, in Tazan. Something incredible is— "

Unperturbed, the remarkable voice continued speaking.

"There is no one here at present, but this recording device is equipped to record your voice if you wish to leave a message."

It was a recording! Simon began blurting out his story when the door to his room opened. It creaked. It was an old door. But Simon failed to hear the creaking over the sound of his own voice.

At first, it seemed as if there was no one at the door.

Then eyes winked into being. Two pair. One very blue and the other of a sinister black quality.

A voice, low and cold, intoned, "Simon Page. You have wandered into the land of the living in defiance of our warning. We have come to take you back—where you belong."

Simon turned. He shot off the bed. The phone receiver clattered to the floor. A hissing came from the earpiece. Evidently, whatever had depressed the switch hook had failed to sever the connection.

Simon felt hairy things like paws fumble for his bare arms. There was some confusion. He could not see the outreaching paws, nor could the floating eyes perceive his invisible form. The fight that followed did not even look like a fight, except that there came the meaty slapping of hands, blows. And scuffling. A lamp upset, bulb shattering.

And Simon Page cried out, "The eyes! The disembodied eyes are in my room!"

Came a swish, a hard sound, followed by a thump. The green eyes that belonged to Simon Page rocketed backward and seemed to land on the floor like matched dice.

They stared upward, glazed and unseeing. Then, together, they winked out of existence.

Hovering over them were the floating eyes, two blue and two black, regarding with cold unconcern the spot where the green eyes had vanished.

A detached voice said, "We will bear him to his rightful place."

And from the telephone, the curious voice of the long-distance operator asked, "Did you wish to be disconnected now?"

Chapter III

SECRET SANCTUARY

A BITTER WIND was howling among the ice floes of the far reaches south of the North Pole.

Laden with snow, it swirled around the crevices of a rocky islet set in the metallic blue mural of the Arctic Sea. Driven flakes, like the fallen dust of long-dead stars, beat against an obdurate shape that might have been a crystal ball. Except the ball was blue and opaque, and sunk to its gleaming equator in the heaped snow of the remote isle.

A hundred foot high blue agate standing on an Arctic isle, and as big around as a Manhattan city block.

The ticking of hard snow particles was a constant refrain against the Strange Blue Dome. It went on for hours, seemed to have been going on for days, and promised to continue for weeks if not months to come. Grit, scoured off the outthrust crags of rock ringing the isle, was picked up to be commingled with the remorseless, biting snow.

The grit was driven with a force that would have quickly clouded exposed glass with myriad scratches. Yet the glassy surface of the blue dome withstood the onslaught, showing no sign of abrasion. In fact, the sandpapery wind might have been the handiwork of Mother Nature, proudly polishing a mighty azure gem thrust up from the center of the earth.

The Strange Blue Dome was no freak of nature surrendered by an upheaval of the earth's crust, however.

For a man, head bent before the wind, bundled up in a parka

and sealskin boots, approached the object. The vast dome dwarfed him. It was utterly featureless, yet the figure stamped toward it as if it were an otherworldly sanctuary prepared to receive him.

The man walked with a stick. It was no twisted bit of wood or branch. It could scarcely be any such thing. No trees grew for hundreds of miles in any direction. The tree line was far to the south of this distant spot, across ice-cake choked waters. The man did not lean on the walking stick, as would a cripple. Instead, he carried it in one felt-gloved hand, employing it to knock apart humps of snow obstructing his path.

As he approached the blue phantasm, a strange thing transpired.

A portal opened in the featureless shell of the Strange Blue Dome.

It was uncanny. Looking at the thing, an observer would have sworn that no such portal existed. There were no cracks, no lines, nothing to indicate the dome was anything but a single shimmering piece of some unfathomable substance.

Yet the portal had swung open. It smacked of magic.

The man stepped through, and after a moment, the portal swung back into place. When its edges once again conformed to the curve of the Strange Blue Dome, the great blue gem of a structure once more presented the appearance of utter and complete solidity.

The howling wind continued to abrade the shimmering blue half-sphere that was obviously hollow—and inhabited.

No sound of wind penetrated the arching agate dome as the man with the cane stood stamping caked snow off his sealskin boots. He shucked off his parka hood, revealing a face denoted by an eagle-like handsomeness. Snow clinging to his hair was perhaps a shade lighter than the crisp hair itself. But probably not.

His stamping done, the white-haired man proceeded to divest himself of his parka. He did this without laying aside his stick, which, shaken free of clinging snow, proved to be a dark cane of very good wood.

The removing of the parka became something of a production, inasmuch as the white-haired one seemed completely loath to surrender the stick. It switched back and forth between gripping hands until the parka had been doffed. Then, the man removed his boots and climbed out of his soft bearskin leggings.

"Jove!" he muttered at one point.

After the entire complicated and cumbersome operation had been completed, the man stood in immaculate morning attire, complete with pearl gray vest and striped trousers.

Given the fact that he had stepped from the howling wilderness of the North Polar wastes, the man now presented a picture that was nothing if not comical.

Evidently, one other thought so, for no sooner had the faultlessly attired individual finished brushing the clinging remnants of snow from his attire, than howling laughter filled the space in which he stood.

This came from a ridiculously wide mouth belonging to an individual who more resembled a caveman than a modern specimen of manhood. His bullet head, sloping shoulders and bowed legs might have been donated by a gorilla. Rusty red fur coated every visible portion of his anatomy, other than his broad, amused face.

"Haw, lookit that!" he exploded. "Ham Brooks, Eskimo Barrister. Ain't you a sight!" The speaker's voice was disconcertingly squeaking, almost childlike.

"Listen, Monk, you homely baboon," the one addressed as Ham snapped. "I come from the finest Pilgrim stock."

"You've come a long way, then," Monk said. "What you're trying to tell me is that you're blue-blooded?"

Ham scowled at Monk malevolently. "Exactly."

"You may be so blue-blooded you can give a transfusion to a fountain pen," Monk said. "But what does it prove? To me, you're—"

Abruptly, Ham let out a screech. His dark eyes were fixed

on a button that was hanging from his coat by a single thread.

"Drat!" he complained. "I've pulled a button loose. And I have no spare coat!"

"Fashion plate!" Monk snorted. "You should hire yourself a tailor for a valet, and have him follow you around with needle and thread."

"I wish my New York tailor were here," Ham grumbled.

"I wish he was here instead of you," Monk assured him.

Ham Brooks, in addition to being an avid pursuer of the title of best-dressed-man in the country, was also Brigadier General Theodore Marley Brooks, who had a reputation as one of the nation's leading lawyers. Ham's brain was as sharp as the faultless creases in his pants.

Monk was better known as Lieutenant Colonel Andrew Blodgett Mayfair, an industrial chemist of remarkable renown. His resemblance to a simian cave-dweller would have caused a big-game hunter and an anthropologist to grab him by opposite wrists and have a tug of war over possession of the trophy.

If Ham could get Monk locked up in jail, he would probably do it. Monk would do likewise. Theirs was that kind of friendship.

Angling off to the left, Monk prepared to resume some task which Ham's arrival had interrupted. He reached a radial-type airplane motor. Beside this stood a wheeled cradle. Apparently, Monk's immediate problem was to get the motor on the cradle.

He bent over and grasped the engine. He heaved. Cats seemed to arch their backs under his coat fabric as enormous muscles swelled.

The motor hardly budged. It was too heavy.

Monk gave it up, straightened, and looked around. At the far end of the hangar stood a lifting crane.

"Guess I gotta rig the crane up to handle this motor," Monk grumbled.

He started away. A voice halted him.

"Just a moment, Monk."

The voice was remarkable for its qualities of tone. Neither loud, nor particularly emphatic, the voice conveyed an impression of restrained yet unbounded power.

The speaker dropped from the cabin of a nearby plane.

At first glance, the man might have been mistaken for a statue of bronze metal. The bronze of his hair was slightly darker than that of his skin, and the hair lay straight and smooth as a metallic skull cap.

Many features about this man were arresting. His eyes, for instance, were strange. They were like pools of flake-gold—a dust-fine gold which was swirled about continuously by tiny whirlwinds.

That this bronze man possessed fabulous strength was evident from the tendons which cabled his hands and his neck. These resembled nothing so much as the rounded backs of steel files, except that they were the hue of forged bronze.

Doc Savage wore a crisp white shirt, open at the throat, which hardly concealed his incredible physical development. The play of bar-like tendons at his neck, the confident ease with which his rippling muscles flowed as he moved, hinted at phenomenal strength in reserve.

And that he was actually the muscular Hercules which he seemed, was demonstrated when he grasped the motor, the weight of which had baffled apish Monk. The bronze man did not appear to put forth extreme effort, but the muscles which had bunched under Monk's coat suddenly seemed small compared to those which arched across the bronze man's shoulders.

Doc lifted the weighty motor and placed it on the cradle.

The pleasantly ugly Monk stared, his small eyes popping a little. He knew how much strength it had taken to lift the engine. He was amazed, although he had seen this bronze man perform remarkable feats of strength on other occasions.

"Thanks, Doc," Monk said, his tones mixing awe with gratitude.

Ham approached, elegant cane tucked jauntily under one arm.

As Ham came near the bronze figure of Doc Savage, a surprising phenomenon occurred. Ham seemed to shrink in stature, as compared to Doc. This was due to the fact that Doc Savage was a giant in size, yet his sinews were developed with such general thoroughness that his proportions were entirely symmetrical. At a distance, he seemed no larger than other men.

Ham wasted no words.

"Long Tom in New York, has been gathering information for you, Doc," he said briskly.

Doc Savage replied nothing. His unusually regular bronze features did not change expression.

ALL the world knew of the remarkable individual known as Doc Savage. His fame had spread to every corner of the globe. Journalists did their level best to keep the legendary Man of Bronze before the public. His discoveries in science, in medicine and other fields of endeavor commanded headlines.

Greater still were his exploits as an adventurer. No common soldier of fortune, Clark Savage, Jr.—to give his full name—had for years been roaming the globe, solving the ills of the world where ordinary methods failed. He never took pay. But if a person came to him with troubles vast enough, Doc waded in.

This, too, the public knew.

Yet for all of his feats of daring and philanthropy, Doc Savage was known by another title the press hung on him. The Man of Mystery. Everyone knew that Doc held forth in the top of New York's greatest skyscraper. Here, he received those who came to him for assistance. Or turned them away if they were undeserving. The philanthropy of Doc Savage lured many to his portals.

From time to time, the newspapers reported rumors to the effect that Doc's work was supported by great wealth, which he derived from some secret source. No one had ever been able to unearth that supposed trove. So these rumors remained just that. Rumors.

Thus far, no one had ever gleaned the amazing truth: that the mysterious bronze man controlled a gold mine that would have staggered any of the rulers of the ancient world. Hidden in a valley deep in Central America, guarded by descendants of the Mayan empire. Whenever Doc had need of funds, he had but to radio his Mayan friends, who dutifully sent out a burro train of gold to civilization. The gold was deposited into a bank account in the bronze man's name.

Deeper than this was another secret, that of the place in which they now stood.

It was called the Fortress of Solitude.

Whereas most of the general public had an inkling that Doc Savage possessed some inexhaustible source of funds, no one suspected the existence of the Fortress of Solitude.

It had been built at the suggestion of his father, the man who had placed Doc in the hands of the scientists who had made him the superman that he was and who later discovered and bequeathed to the bronze man the Mayan gold, as a place where Doc could repair for intensive study and reflection.

Originally, the Fortress had been carved out of the hollow cone of an extinct Arctic volcano. It was ringed by fumaroles exuding poison gases and could only be reached by autogyro— the only craft able to alight upon the ice lake atop the crater.

But an accident in landing there had caused the bronze man to redesign the Fortress.* It was during his last extended period of study at the old Fortress that Doc had developed the uncanny weldable glasslike substance with which he had built the Strange Blue Dome.

It had seemed like a good idea at the time. Perhaps it was.

But as he surveyed the strange retreat, the bronze man could not help but reflect on the events of the preceding weeks.

A man had come to this desolate isle, a cruel devil who called

---

* *Python Isle.*

himself John Sunlight. He had been a prisoner of a Soviet prison camp until he had broken free, taking with him an assortment of human flotsam and like-minded rogues. In a stolen ice-breaker they had ventured into the Arctic Sea until, starved and desperate, they had stumbled across the great blue dome in the frozen wastes.

The Fortress, as it now stood, had been constructed so that only Doc Savage—or one entrusted with certain magnetic keys—could enter the apparently seamless dome of bluish glass. To one who did not know its secrets, the Fortress would have seemed impenetrable.

But John Sunlight had been no ordinary man. He had divined that the Strange Blue Dome was the product of the human mind, and from that simple fact, had reasoned that it was possible to fathom its mysteries.

John Sunlight had become the first human being other than Doc Savage—the first white man rather, since the tribe of Eskimos who guarded the retreat were allowed entry to get to certain provisions stored there for their continued well-being—to pass into the fabulous Fortress.

More than merely a laboratory and a place in which the bronze man could plunge into study and reflection, the Fortress of Solitude was the impregnable vault where Doc Savage stored an assortment of weird devices of a scientific nature which he considered too dangerous to be allowed to fall into untrustworthy hands. Some were inventions Doc had perfected himself. Many times in the course of his adventures, Doc had seized scientific machines of a nature too diabolic to be put to any practical use, but which were too advanced to be destroyed. Doc often spent weeks studying these devices, in the hope that the principles displayed could be turned to good use.

John Sunlight had come upon these murder machines, and with them had initiated a reign of terror, first using them to annihilate in ghoulish fashion those he deemed to be his enemies.

Once that was accomplished, John Sunlight, fiend that he

was, had sent the word out to certain nations that these death-dealing devices were available for purchase.

Representatives of many nations had come here to the Arctic to bid on these things. So too had come Doc, Monk, Ham and another aide, Long Tom Roberts, in disguise, to put a stop to the horrible auction of death.

In the violence that followed, most of the terrible weapons had been lost. At least one that the bronze man was able to ascertain, had been carried off by a dignitary named Baron Karl, the representative of a particularly rapacious Balkan country.

Of John Sunlight, they found tracks leading deep into the blinding wastes—tracks that ended in a confusion of snow, some blood, a rifle and rags of clothing.

Polar bear tracks had led away from the spot where the footprints of the most evil creature ever cast in human form had ceased to impress the polar crust.

It was assumed by all concerned that the wickedness that was called John Sunlight had been consumed by the Arctic bruin. Assumed, that is, after an extended search of the surrounding wastes produced no sign of the devil who had been willing to ignite wars for his own profit. Nor, oddly enough, of a full-bellied bear.

Neither was there any trace of the cache of war weapons stolen from the secure vault where the bronze man had kept them from the world. This last was very disturbing.*

It was now some weeks later, and Doc Savage along with Monk and Ham, were completing the necessary repairs to the Fortress of Solitude, which had been severely damaged when the bronze man had crashed a plane into the great hangar door in order to regain entrance, after John Sunlight's minions had locked themselves inside.

They stood now in that hangar. Above their heads, the top of the structural dome, as seen from below, was fashioned in such a way as to permit the night sky to be seen. The glassy blue

---

* *Fortress of Solitude.*

substance, which could be welded and repaired so as to create the semblance of a seamless hemisphere, was made so that it was possible to see out, but one standing outside could not penetrate the outer surface with his vision. The principle was not unlike that of so-called Argus, or one-way, glass.

Doc Savage stood looking up at the wheeling stars, his bronze mask of a face resolute.

"It is time," he said.

"We goin' home?" Monk squeaked.

"We are," said Doc.

"I guess that means John Sunlight is dead for sure," Monk offered.

"It is," Doc Savage said with just the slightest trace of brittle emotion in his controlled voice, "fervently to be wished."

Monk and Ham exchanged startled glances. Doc Savage held human life in high regard. The taking of it was prohibited to members of his tiny band. Doc seldom wished ill of any man, and death to none. He did not believe in the edict of an eye for an eye.

But many men had died—innocent men—as a result of John Sunlight gaining the horrific weapons that had been cached in the Fortress of Solitude. Indirectly, Doc Savage was responsible for those deaths. The knowledge weighed heavily on his noble soul.

With a stash of those weapons still unaccounted for, only two possibilities presented themselves. That they had been cached in the frigid waste by John Sunlight for later claiming. Or that he had escaped to civilization with them.

Doc Savage knew, as did Monk and Ham, that it would be far, far better if John Sunlight had indeed perished. Otherwise the world was not safe. And the ultimate goal of John Sunlight, they had come to understand, was nothing less than complete and total world domination.

Doc stood looking up at the stars another few moments. Then as if snapping out of a trance, he climbed into the waiting plane. It was an amphibian of unusual design. There were features that were many years ahead of the current aeronautical developments. This was an experimental aircraft Doc kept at the Fortress, on which he tested new ideas before building them into his fleet of work planes.

Doc Savage made, very softly so that it was hardly audible within the big silenced plane, a small trilling sound. The note was exotic, as weird as the song of some tropical bird, or the vagaries of the wind in a waste of arctic ice pinnacles. Most peculiar quality of the trilling was the way it seemed to come from everywhere, rather than from any definite spot; it was distinctly ventriloquial.

The sound was a small unconscious thing which Doc Savage made in moments of mental stress, or when he was contemplating unusual action, or was very puzzled.

He was thinking that somewhere in the great globe that was the Earth lay more death and destruction than humanity had ever faced. And it was entirely his fault.

Doc spoke with brittle earnestness. "Our next job, fellows, is to recover those infernal machines, and this time, we will *destroy* them."

Monk and Ham clambered aboard. They took their places.

Doc started the engines. The motors ran up revolutions, their cannonading in the cavernous hangar side of the Fortress of Solitude strangely muffled. The acoustics of the place were remarkable. A whisper at one end could be heard at another. Yet the glasslike material possessed sound-absorbing qualities that drank up the plane thunder.

A trip of a switch caused the radio-controlled hangar doors to separate and valve open.

The bronze man ran the amphibian out onto the howling snow. Visibility was not great. But it hardly mattered. Under the accumulating snow, the isle was a flat hump of bare rock. The edges were thorny with rock, but at this side the stone ran smooth and sloping to the water's edge, a natural ramp.

Doc ran the plane into the water, let it settle on its floats and then jazzed the throttle.

The plane beat across the water, the wings found purchase, and it was soon airborne.

As the plane banked southward, Monk and Ham attempted to peer through the snow for a last look at the strange azure blister on the Arctic that was the Fortress of Solitude.

"I ain't gonna forget that place any time soon," Monk said in tones bordering on awe.

For once, Ham Brooks did not disagree.

They settled down for the long flight home.

Chapter IV

THE MUSHROOM MAN

LONG TOM ROBERTS—MAJOR Thomas J. Roberts was his full name—was probably the least impressive-looking member of Doc Savage's intrepid band of adventurers. He was neither tall nor physically imposing. The term "sawed-off" might have been applied to Long Tom had anyone felt brave enough to do so to his face. In actuality, the undersized electrical wizard was reputed to be able to lick his weight in wildcats. His complexion gave the distinct impression that he had grown up in a mushroom cellar, yet he had never been known to become sick. Colds and other such diseases seemed to go out of their way to avoid him.

This verged on the miraculous, given the long hours that Long Tom spent in his private experimental electrical laboratory, an elaborate wine cellar he had snapped up very cheaply just before Prohibition had been repealed. The dank place, typically strewn with transformers, capacitors, and other apparatus of his profession, no doubt contributed to Long Tom's mushroom pallor. He was considered a magician of the juice who would one day rank with Edison and Steinmetz.

Long Tom had participated in the terrible ordeal in the North Pole involving John Sunlight. At the end of it, Doc Savage had come into possession of a number of individuals who had escaped with John Sunlight out of the Siberian prison camp, and who, for reasons of their own, had thrown in their lot with the vile monster in human form.

They were not evil. Not all of them. Some were simply weak-minded, and others easily led. Still, they had participated in the deviltry of John Sunlight and deserved punishment.

It was not the way of Doc Savage to turn over to lawful authorities those transgressors who had fallen into his hands. He did not personally believe in the punishment of prison or electric chairs or gas chambers or gallows. In fact, he was against killing, except in self-defense.

Doc Savage had years ago created a place where the wicked could be sent for rehabilitation. It was a secret place. Doc knew that society would not understand his methods, so far advanced were they.

It was to this unknown institution in the wilds of upstate New York that Long Tom Roberts had ferried his charges. There, they were turned over to surgeons Doc himself had trained, to undergo delicate operations on their brains. Their memories were wiped as clean as a blackboard is cleaned of chalk with a wet rag. They would know nothing of their vicious pasts, be reeducated, taught a useful trade and finally returned to society with sufficient funds to launch them on a new start in life.

Countless miscreants had been put through Doc Savage's "crime college." All had been successfully returned to society. None, so far, had ever gone back to crime.

The underlings of John Sunlight were now in the early stages of their rehabilitation.

Long Tom had returned to Doc Savage's headquarters in the tallest skyscraper in the heart of Manhattan after discharging his responsibility. He was there now, orchestrating the worldwide search for John Sunlight, who was widely presumed to be dead. But Doc Savage left nothing to chance and so Long Tom was very active by transatlantic telephone.

He was on the instrument when a call came in. There were many telephones scattered about the headquarters, each with their own line. Long Tom ignored the insistent buzz while he completed his own call. He knew if it were his bronze chief reaching out from the Fortress of Solitude, Doc would not—could not—employ a telephone, there being no telephone cable going to the North Pole, communicating instead by short-wave radio. So Long Tom completed his call.

Among his responsibilities was the monitoring of the difficulties in the Balkans. John Sunlight had been actively selling devices appropriated from Doc Savage's Fortress of Solitude to both sides of one of the simmering Balkan feuds that threatened every so often to boil over in armed conflict.

In this case, a scientific weapon had been sold to a representative of the bellicose nation called Egallah, upsetting a balance of power that had existed since the end of the Great War. The representative was a smooth snake popularly known as Baron Karl—actually Baron Sig Karlis—who enjoyed the confidence of his prime minister and functioned as a sort of high-profile spy. He had no sooner returned to his homeland with the pilfered device than John Sunlight had summoned the ruler of Tazan—Egallah's chief Balkan rival.

The "playboy prince" they called him. He was by reputation a gay fellow, but he did not smile when he received the news from John Sunlight that his rival now possessed a terrible war weapon. John Sunlight offered a comparable weapon to the playboy prince. The prince—king, really—had no choice but to purchase the offering, a death device infinitely more awful than the one sold to Egallah.

Unfortunately for the playboy prince and his now-helpless nation, neither he nor his purchase survived their encounter with Doc Savage. Turning over the mangled remains of their departed ruler to the Tazan embassy in New York had been one of Long Tom's responsibilities.

So now Tazan, bereft of its ruler—not that anyone missed the jolly rogue—lay helpless before the new power of the Balkans, Egallah.

The long-simmering situation had not come to a full boil as

yet. But it was expected. This was the war the world fretted its collective fingernails over.

Invasion might be a better term for it, as Long Tom was learning.

"You say your agents understand that Egallan military forces are poised to grab up a hunk of Ultra-Stygia?"

"*Da,*" said the thick voice over the transatlantic line. He was a high-ranking official of the Soviet. His government was very grateful to Doc Savage for his quashing of the John Sunlight threat. Sunlight had employed one of his death machines—now smashed, miraculously enough—to assassinate the Soviet official who had sent John Sunlight to Siberia in the first place.

"It is understood by our operatives in Pristav, the Tazan capital, that Ultra-Stygia will be overrun soon. The Minister of War in Tazan, who is named General Consadinos, now runs the country. He will no doubt send his forces to counter-attack."

"This is bad," Long Tom muttered.

"It is not good," the Soviet official admitted. Then, in a voice that was pitched low with disquiet, he asked, "Has the body of the black devil Sunlight been discovered yet?"

"No," said Long Tom. "And if a polar bear did eat him, there won't be anything to discover. Not recognizable, anyway."

The presumed fate of John Sunlight was too grim to offer much relief. It was believed that he was consumed while helpless and still living.

"Have you dug up any more dope on Sunlight?" Long Tom wondered.

"The files on this man were in the prison camp that was burned to the ground when the terrible Sunlight escaped," the official related. "It is not known what his true name is, even."

"John Sunlight was not his true name?"

"*Nyet. Nyet.* He is—was—called 'Sunlight' because of the terrible black moods into which he would fly. It is a humor, *da?*"

"A joke, you mean."

"*Da.* A joke. But it was no joke the day John Sunlight was born into this world."

"Right," said Long Tom, and disconnected.

Long Tom got out of the chair in which he sat and walked along a forest of test tubes and electrical equipment comprising one of the greatest experimental laboratories in existence, out a door, and passed through the remarkable library crammed with ponderous tomes until he reached the reception room which housed Doc's ingenious message recorder.

Long Tom played the record back.

It was a grisly recording, with his long pauses and fight sounds. But what seemed to electrify the slender wizard of the juice was the mention of Tazan.

Long Tom immediately put through a call to the Cateral Inn in Tazan. While he waited for the connection to be established, he attempted to raise Doc Savage at his Fortress of Solitude by short-wave. There was no answer. Clearly Doc had departed the Fortress.

There was fierce static to boot. So when the phone rang with his overseas connection, Long Tom snapped off the short-wave set.

In swift order, Long Tom Roberts established that the caller, Simon Page, had mysteriously disappeared from his hotel room after placing a call to New York City. That was all the long-distance operator could offer.

"I am on my way to Tazan," Long Tom snapped.

He tried once more to raise Doc Savage on the latter's aircraft set, failed, and went to a window, where he wrote on the glass with what appeared to be a piece of chalk. The chalk, oddly enough, left no discernible mark. Long Tom seemed unperturbed by that, and hastily quitted the eighty-sixth floor by elevator.

He was en route to the world's latest place of discord. And there, he would find trouble—a carload of it.

Chapter V

COUNTESS OLGA

THE ATLANTIC PASSENGER liner *Transylvania* was casting off its lines when Long Tom Roberts piled out of a taxicab at the South Street seaport docks. He looked very little like the world-famous electrical expert. He stood fully an inch taller than normal, thanks to special built-up shoes, and his pallid epidermis had been reddened by an astringent solution, calculated to mask his mushroom complexion.

He tipped the cabby only a nickel, thus establishing his identity to anyone familiar with the penurious Long Tom of old.

Carrying his luggage under each arm, Long Tom hiked to the gangplank just as they were getting ready to raise it.

"Walter Brunk," he announced to the purser.

The worthy took his ticket, which Long Tom had carried in his teeth. His gold front teeth, of the buck variety, were masked by porcelain shells.

"Welcome aboard, sir," he was told.

Long Tom climbed the gangway just as the great funnels began belching smoke.

Tugboats nosed in, pushed the liner out to open water.

By that time, Long Tom had been shown to his berth, which was on a middle deck and of moderate price. Unpacking revealed that he had brought along only such clothes as were necessary for the crossing. The rest was in the nature of electrical equipment, along with one of the supermachine pistols with which all of Doc Savage's men were equipped. These were intricate mechanisms, the product of the bronze man's inventive skill, capable of unleashing a variety of shells with blinding speed. Several drums of ammunition, looking like small canisters of home-movie film, were packed with the unusual weapon.

Night fell. Long Tom dined late. Taking an after-dinner tour of the promenade deck, he stopped to look at the stars, which were out in full force. It was then that he began having the unsettling feeling that he was being watched.

It struck him as preposterous. His disguise was clever, and there was no reason for anyone to think that Long Tom Roberts was on this vessel. He had told no one, leaving only a message for Doc Savage on a headquarters window, which could be brought out by application of ultra-violet light. And his disguise was good enough to pass muster. Long Tom had resorted to it not because he was concerned about being shadowed, but because his fame was such that ordinary passengers, had they recognized him, would no doubt pester him with questions about his work with the world-renowned Doc Savage.

Still, the feeling persisted. It added to the chill of the evening.

Pretending not to notice, Long Tom sauntered about the after deck, keeping his eyes peeled.

It was during this circuit that he laid eyes on the striking woman with the very pale skin.

She was as tall as any man, but carried herself with a kind of spectral elegance. Long Tom was no connoisseur of femininity, but this specimen caused him to stop dead in his tracks. She wore a slinky evening gown that shimmered, and a chic turban the hue of polished emerald. Not a tendril of hair coiled out from its tight confines. Nor were the color of her eyes discernible at a distance. The length and thickness of her eyelashes accounted for that.

In spite of himself, Long Tom drew near her. There was something eerie about her, lounging at the rail, that seemed to invite attention.

Other men were eyeing her, as if considering whether to make an approach. Long Tom gave that no consideration. He merely observed the woman.

Then she sidled up to him and started a conversation.

"Good evening," she said coolly.

"Nice night," Long Tom returned vaguely.

"It is very cold out here. In the Atlantic." Her voice had a touch of accent Long Tom could not place. "Cold as the grave." She shivered in her sleek gown.

Long Tom couldn't think of a suitable reply, so he volunteered, "Name's Walter Brunk."

"I am Countess Olga. Pleased to make your acquaintance, Valter Brunk. Vat is your destination?"

"Southampton," Long Tom said cagily. It was no lie. The liner docked at Southampton before going on to the Continent.

Countess Olga nodded. "It is good that you are disembarking at Southampton. Europe is not a pleasant place these days. There are troubles brewing. You can read it in the clouds. They remind one of var clouds. It is better to disembark at Southampton, than it is to travel on to unpleasant places such as... Ultra-Stygia."

Under the constant rushing of water against the hull, Long Tom swallowed his surprise.

Ultra-Stygia was the strip of disputed land between the kingdom of Tazan and neighboring Egallah. Both nations claimed it as their sovereign territory.

"Ultra-Stygia," said Long Tom in his Walter Brunk voice, "is probably the last place I would want to visit."

"That is very vise," replied Countess Olga. "For many who go to Ultra-Stygia are buried there. You have been varned."

"Warned! See here—"

But Countess Olga began to drift away like a languid specter of womanhood.

Long Tom let her go. But he watched closely as she departed. Then, deciding that there was more here than met the eye, he attempted to follow the unusual woman.

His puny size made Long Tom an excellent shadower of men. He could duck out of sight or behind the trumpet-mouthed ventilators easier than a larger man might. His light weight made it a simple matter to muffle the sound of his footsteps.

Still, Countess Olga managed to elude him.

It was very strange, the manner in which Countess Olga evaded Long Tom Roberts. He had been stalking her along B Deck, staying well behind and otherwise acting nonchalant.

He lost sight of the statuesque woman only once. That was when she turned a corner.

When Long Tom caught up, rounding that same corner, there was no sign of the elegantly tall countess.

There was only a man lounging at the rail, idly smoking a cigarette. The man looked up as Long Tom came into view, then looked away with a disinterested expression. He had the smooth-faced look of a man who shaved twice a day, but was otherwise unremarkable.

Ignoring him, Long Tom followed the deck to its terminus, found no trace of Countess Olga. He went to the rail and looked overboard. He had not heard any splash, and peering into the Atlantic rushing by saw no disturbance in the water. He returned the way he had come, ruddy features faintly puzzled.

In the interim, the lounging cigarette smoker had vanished.

A reconnoiter of other decks produced no sign of Countess Olga, so Long Tom reluctantly retired for the night.

OVER the next two days, Long Tom kept his eyes peeled for the mysterious countess. But she never showed herself, nor did he manage to spy her at meals. It was very strange. It was as if she had gone overboard.

On the third night out, with Southampton less than a day's steady steaming, Long Tom's luck turned.

He was circumnavigating the decks, the mystery of Countess Olga still uppermost in his mind, when he heard weird music.

The music sounded like nothing he had ever heard before. It was muffled, but even so there was an unearthly quality to it that pulled and impelled, as if the melody exerted a magnetic attraction.

Sail-like ears hunting, the slender electrical wizard made for the sounds which seemed to be emanating from a cabin on B Deck.

Going from door to door, Long Tom laid an ear against each one until he discovered the correct cabin.

Bunching knuckles, he knocked.

The music continued its unearthly sweep. But there was another sound discernible. A busy clattering. It, too, was muffled. It reminded Long Tom of a typewriter, except that the keystrokes continued seamlessly, mechanically, without pause or change in rhythm.

Knocking hard, Long Tom raised his voice.

"Steward!"

That failed to elicit a response. The music continued and the clattering as of a busy typewriter went on unceasingly.

Cabin doors are not of the type that can be unlocked with a lock pick, so Long Tom didn't bother. It was possible that the combined sounds masked his knocking. Not likely, but possible.

Noting the cabin number—B-12—Long Tom withdrew to a safe point of vantage. Settling into a deck chair in the shade of one of the great horn-like deck ventilators, he pretended to read a magazine.

After a while, the cabin door opened.

Out from it stepped a rather wolfishly lean man. Long Tom took him in. It was the smooth-faced fellow he had seen lounging on the lower deck the night he had lost Countess Olga in the maze of passageways that was the *Transylvania*.

Something about that coincidence caused him to get up and follow the lean man when he passed by. Long Tom was no believer in coincidences.

Keeping a discreet distance, the ruddy electrical wizard stayed on the man's heels a fair part of the way to the dining room—the man's evident destination.

Rounding a corner with caution, Long Tom walked into the barrel of a long-nosed automatic of foreign make.

The smooth-faced man spoke tersely. "You are following me. No?"

"I am following you, yes," admitted Long Tom, deciding to get the preliminaries out of the way.

"Why?"

"To keep in practice." He proffered a business card that said: WALTER BRUNK, PRIVATE INVESTIGATOR. Long Tom added, "It's how I make my living. I'm on my way to England on a hot case. Following strangers keeps me in shape. Nothing personal. Guess I'm not doing so hot to-day, eh?"

The man's eyes narrowed. It was evident that he did not take to that explanation.

"You lie," he said smoothly.

Long Tom elected to shift tactics.

"O.K., I'm following a suspect. Maybe you can help me out."

"The name of this suspect?"

"Countess Olga. A jewel thief. I was following her the other night, lost her on B Deck."

The other nodded. "I remember you, Brunk. You looked puzzled that evening."

Long Tom shrugged thin shoulders negligently. "Yeah. She gave me the slip, all right."

The other regarded Long Tom speculatively. "What if I told you that I know what happened to her?"

"Go ahead and tell me," invited Long Tom.

"I warn you. You will scarcely believe my tale."

"Tell the tale and let me worry about the believing part," countered Long Tom.

The man waved his cigarette. "The lady in question passed by me. I noticed her. She appeared very beautiful in a ghastly way."

Long Tom said, "That was her. Pale as a glacier."

The other nodded. "She looked lonely, so I started to follow her myself. Around a corner she went, I was not far behind her. Then I beheld the most uncanny thing."

The man hesitated.

"Out with it," suggested Long Tom.

"I rounded the way just in time to witness her depart from this Earth."

The lean man allowed that to sink in.

"She didn't jump," Long Tom said flatly. "I would have heard the splash."

"No, Walter Brunk. She did not jump. I reached the spot where she stood in time to see—not the woman—but a hideous squirming mass of black vapor where she had been. Vapor that drifted slowly away in the wind, and left nothing. The woman had died in some incredible fashion. Right before my eyes."

Long Tom searched the man's face for signs of lying. He found none.

"Why didn't you report this to a steward?"

The man made fussy gestures with his hands. "I considered this. But first I needed a cigarette. That was when you happened along. That decided me. If you, who were not a few yards from the very spot where a woman had perished in so inexplicable a fashion, did not witness to the fatality, of what use would my testimony be? The authorities might—how you say—finger me for her disappearance."

"So you said nothing?"

The man inclined his head slightly. "I have said nothing. But neither has anyone else." His cigarette waved vaguely. "Look around you, do you see any search parties? Any commotion or alarm?"

"No," Long Tom admitted.

"Neither do I. But I made discreet inquiries. And do you know what I discovered?" He lowered his voice conspiratorially. "There is no such passenger registered as Countess Olga."

"Olga wouldn't be her last name," retorted Long Tom.

"No Olgas. No *contesas*. No missing woman passengers. What do you think of that, Mr. Brunk?"

"It's ridiculous!" snapped Long Tom.

"No more ridiculous than a woman turning into a sable black ghost and drifting away with the ocean breeze."

Long Tom had nothing to say to that. He made a jaw, rubbed it thoughtfully.

"I'll check out your story," he decided at last.

"Which I will deny," smiled the man. And pocketing his pistol, he took his departure.

Long Tom grabbed the first steward he chanced upon.

"The other night I talked to a tall woman. She called herself Countess Olga. Where can I find her?"

"Never heard of her," said the steward. "What last name?"

"Don't know." Long Tom flashed another business card. "She's on the lam. Jewelry heist. I'd like a look at the passenger manifest."

Long Tom was taken to the ship's captain, who heard his story out. A passenger list was produced. His identification stood up to the scrutiny of a transatlantic telephone call. The private investigation organization was run by Doc Savage, and was legitimate. It had a worldwide reputation. Long Tom studied the list and found no one by the name of Olga.

"Any passengers not accounted for?" Long Tom inquired.

The captain advised, "There have been no reports of persons overboard, if that is what you mean."

"I guess that's what I mean," muttered Long Tom, frowning thoughtfully.

Taking his departure, Long Tom made his way to the cabin

from which the strange music had been emanating.

When he reached B Deck, he piled into a commotion. There was a quantity of gray smoke coming out of the cabin. Quite a bit of it. Persons hung back as if terrified by what might be burning in the cabin.

"What's going on?" Long Tom asked a flustered steward he yanked out of the knot of milling crew and passengers.

"A passenger walking along heard frightful screams emanating from that smoking cabin," he was told. "Black smoke was pouring from the edges of the door, which was shut. Suddenly, the electric lights dimmed. Horrifying sounds came from within. Rushing here, the passenger saw a fantastic thing—a man, lying rigid and apparently afloat in midair, with a horrible expression on his face. A fixed grimace. And there was nothing visible to support him in the air. Then the body of the man became a squirming, intensely black mass of vapor, which slowly vanished before his eyes, until there was nothing remaining."

Long Tom absorbed this in shocked silence. He shook it off, rushed into the cabin, batting away the pungent gray smoke. There was nothing unusual within. No radio. No musical instrument. Not even a typewriter.

Long Tom stuck his head out of the cabin.

"This smoke is gray. You said black."

"The witness said it was black. Evidently it is thinning."

"Where is this witness?" demanded Long Tom.

The steward looked around wildly.

"I—I do not see him at present," the steward stammered.

"Well, describe him to me then."

The steward did. Long Tom listened to the description in its entirety, then rushed off in search of the man.

But he found no sign of anyone fitting that exact description. And when the smoke finally cleared, the occupant of Cabin B-12 was nowhere to be found.

Rummaging about the cabin, Long Tom failed to discover

any source for the weird music that combined qualities of a wailing wind and a moaning specter. Neither did he find anything that could have produced the machine-like clacking.

Nor was the missing passenger discovered for the remainder of the passage to Southampton.

It was something to chill the blood.

Chapter VI

THE LEATHERY HORRORS

AT SOUTHAMPTON, ENGLAND, Long Tom Roberts disembarked with his luggage, which he refused to allow a porter to carry. This was not purely penurious, but practical. The equipment contained within was too valuable to risk loss or damage.

Seeking out a waiting room, Long Tom entered the washroom, and locked the door. There, he swiftly changed clothes, tore the labels off his luggage, and emerged wearing a porkpie hat and thick-lensed glasses. Changing shoes, he reverted to his normal height. But he added several inches to his waist by tying a bladder around his belt, which he inflated by blowing into a tube. Soap had removed the uncharacteristic ruddiness from his face.

When he emerged, the pale electrical wizard looked no more like Walter Brunk than he did Long Tom Roberts.

Using the name Ned Foy, he purchased a fresh ticket, grumbling at the loss the unused portion of his original ticket represented, and re-boarded the liner via a pier shed.

Long Tom was unpacking in his new cabin when the *Transylvania* was warped out of its berth, to the tooting of tugboat horns. His face wore a look of perpetual puzzlement. It was an expression he had worn since the disappearance of the mystery man who had occupied Cabin B-12.

The vanished man's name, as it turned out, was Emile Zirn. Not much was known about him. A world traveler, if the labels pasted on his steamer trunks were any indication. No one questioned had much to volunteer about him. Socially, he had been friendly enough, but reserved.

As for the individual who had discovered Zirn's smoking cabin and reported the grisly manner in which the missing man had perished, no trace of him was uncovered, either. He could not be identified by description. The crew had gone to great lengths to count all passengers. This they did twice.

The results were reported to Long Tom Roberts by the ship's purser.

"We are short only one passenger."

"Emile Zirn?" Long Tom had hazarded.

"Precisely."

"Three missing passengers, but only one can't be accounted for?"

"Correction. Three reported missing, but only one actually so."

"Doesn't make sense," said Long Tom, scratching his head.

The purser spread his hands helplessly. "But there you have it."

And so Long Tom had gotten off to shed his Walter Brunk disguise. He hoped that by doing so he might flush out his quarry.

As the *Transylvania* plowed from the Atlantic Ocean into the Aegean Sea on its way to the Black Sea, Long Tom prowled the decks and found exactly nothing.

In his frustration, he managed to slip into the cargo hold. There, with the titan throb of the ship's brawny engines ringing in his ears, he prowled among items ranging from mountainous sacks of mail to a flashy red roadster being shipped abroad. The slender electrical wizard found the latter unlocked, methodically examined its interior and trunk, all of which proved to be untenanted.

Long Tom summed up the results of his painstaking searching with a low growl of disappointment. "Ahr-r-r!"

On the last night before landfall, he heard the haunting strains again. It was coming from a distance. It was almost as if it were drifting out from the midnight waves. But he tracked it to A Deck just in time to hear the eerie chords trail away like the keening of a dying banshee.

Long Tom stood watch for over two hours, hoping that the music would repeat. Reluctantly, he returned to his cabin disappointed in that respect.

MORNING found the liner pulling into Pristav, Tazan. From a distance, the city showed qualities of the medieval and the modern. As the rising sun burned off a morning mist, more and more it seemed solidly twentieth century in its skyline.

Long Tom could spy a castle on a knob of a hill. Tazan was a principality, and still ruled by royalty. Black funeral flags chattered in the wind. All visible national flags flew at half mast. The nation was still in mourning for their ruler, the former playboy prince, who had perished in the Arctic during the grim affair orchestrated by John Sunlight, whom Long Tom Roberts fervently wished moldered among the dead of history.

When the gangplank was lowered, Long Tom stationed himself on the port rail where he watched every passenger disembark. He counted them carefully, for he had a hunch.

As hunches went, it paid off beautifully—at first.

As the last group of passengers crowded the top of the gangplank, bundled up against a biting winter wind, Long Tom counted and recounted their number. On the third recount, he was certain of his findings.

The number of passengers who had left New York—including those who had either disembarked or boarded at Southampton—was the same! In other words, there was no missing passenger—never mind three!

Long Tom shoved forward, began searching the faces. Many men wore their hats with the brims pulled down and not a few wore their overcoats with lapels lifted against the coastal winds.

Recognizing individual faces was not an easy thing.

But Long Tom had excellent eyes and soon spotted his man.

It was Emile Zirn! He was stepping onto the gangplank. Zirn wore a Borsalino hat, wide brim pulled low. The generous collar of his camel hair overcoat stood up, not quite concealing his close-shaven cheeks. He toted only one item of luggage. It resembled a portable typewriter case, but was far bulkier in heft.

Pointing, Long Tom shouted, "Stop that man!"

Instead, two stewards rushed up to arrest Long Tom.

He got disentangled from them and produced a business card—his real one. This brought forth apologies and offers of assistance.

By then, Emile Zirn—if that was the man's true name—had been bustled into a waiting sedan by two men who were there to meet him. One accepted the typewriter case and there was a great deal of congratulatory handshaking. The sedan whined away, its tail pipe expelling cold fumes.

Long Tom hailed a taxi and said, "Follow that sedan!"

The taxi man understood English. Some, at any rate.

"Which sedan?" he asked politely.

"Never mind," said Long Tom, exiting the hack. "Shove over."

The driver resisted Long Tom's attempt to take the wheel from him, so the puny electrical wizard gave him a quieting sock on the jaw, which had the added benefit of throwing the hackie into the seat opposite.

Long Tom shut the driver's door behind him, took the wheel. The cab surged out of the waiting area, and away into busy traffic.

Long Tom had managed to keep the other sedan in sight and fell in behind it.

Traffic was a confused clot of machines. Many were older models. Most drove decorously, owing to a recent dusting of snow which, under the steady pressure of tires, was turning to a slippery brown slop.

Long Tom kept the sedan in sight as it wended its way through the picturesque city. He passed three statues of the late king. All were draped in black crepe.

The sedan's destination was not long in coming.

It was the Naxa—a new luxury hotel situated near the government zone.

"Luck for a change," Long Tom muttered.

He didn't think so when he barged into the modernistic reception area and confronted the startled clerk.

"Three men just checked in, one named Emile Zirn. What room did they take?"

The clerk said stiffly, "No one by that name is registered in this hotel. And who are you?"

Long Tom hesitated. He did not want the local press to know that he was in Tazan; hotel staff are notorious tipsters.

"Walter Brunk," he clipped out, producing his card. "Investigating an international jewelry-smuggling ring. Now about the three men who just checked in—"

"Room 44. I can provide you with a spare key…?"

The man took the key off a brass hook and dangled it out of reach. Obviously, he was angling for a tip.

Long Tom produced a five-dollar bill from his billfold and the frown that descended upon the clerk's long face exceeded his own. Long Tom switched to a ten, but this produced no facial alterations.

Reluctantly, the electrical wizard parted with a twenty-dollar bill and the key found its way into his outstretched palm.

After Long Tom disappeared from the lobby, the clerk picked up a telephone and asked the switchboard to connect him with a certain room. When he had his connection, an excited exchange commenced. Had Long Tom Roberts overheard it, and understood the language being spoken, he might have reversed his course and hastily exited the Naxa.

For the conversation was couched, not in the language of

Tazan, but rather in the tongue of Tazan's Balkan rival, Egallah!

Unsuspecting, Long Tom took the stairs to the fourth floor and crept along a well-carpeted corridor redolent of some floral scent. He turned toward the battery of elevator shafts, and halted sharply after a single step.

The stretch of corridor was dark. Illumination was furnished by indirect wall lights. These were dark.

Reaching into a pocket, the slender electrical wizard produced a small flashlight. This operated by a spring-generator, which required winding at intervals. Long Tom had given the device a brisk wind before entering the hotel. He thumbed it on, raced it around.

The carpet underfoot was a rich, expensive purple, with a nap that felt inches deep.

Long Tom stopped quickly, picked up the glittering object which had caught his eye. He turned it curiously in his hand, tingling with sudden interest.

It was a penknife, the uselessly small gold-handled variety that snaps on the end of a watch chain. It lay close beside the door through which Long Tom had just passed. Anyone going up or down the corridor could have dropped it there accidentally.

But the single blade had been melted off for half its length. It was stained a metallic blue as if it had been exposed to terrific heat.

Immediately above the spot where it had lain was a wall socket into which the hotel chambermaid probably plugged the vacuum cleaner used to tidy up the corridor carpet. The receptacle was burned about the edges.

Long Tom dropped the knife into his pocket. It was obvious that someone had thrust the blade into the wall socket. That would blow out the fuses—and put out the lights.

Dousing his flash, Long Tom proceeded, displaying even more caution than previously.

Coming to Room 44, he halted, ears sharpening.

The unearthly music the slender electrical expert had twice heard aboard the *Transylvania* came floating out from behind the closed door!

Moving cautiously, Long Tom sidled up to the door, placed an oversized ear to the panel.

Inside, a clattering came through the thick panel. It was mechanical and went on and on, as a kind of counterpoint to the music, whose wavering strains suggested a dying thing from another sphere. It brought the gooseflesh rising on Long Tom's forearms and prickled his scalp. He rubbed the back of his neck as he contemplated his next move.

Long Tom's ears were large enough to be serviceable. But the sounds emanating from the hotel room occupied one ear entirely. The other one, he was not focusing on. His weight lay against the panel, so eager was the electrical wizard to capture every sound within.

Consequently, Long Tom failed to hear the panel directly behind him fall open, and a shadowy figure begin creeping up behind him. The deep nap of the carpet absorbed all footfalls. The absence of lights also aided the stealthy one.

Thus it was that when two hands seized him, Long Tom Roberts was caught entirely unawares.

"Hey!" he howled. "Wha—?"

Something made a swishing sound and Long Tom saw stars. *"Ahr-r-r!"*

Dazed, Long Tom was hauled backwards, and snatched through the open door of the room from which his attacker had stolen. The door clapped shut and many hands caught at him, snatching and grabbing roughly.

THE room within was blacked out in some manner. It was a warm box of ink. A steam radiator could be heard clanking. Long Tom plunged into it and the door clapped shut behind him.

Scrambling to his feet, the electrical wizard was momentarily disoriented.

The sounds of the music and the accompanying clattering came, muffled and indistinct, as if from far away. He peered about. Discerned nothing.

But Long Tom could sense that he was surrounded by shadowy figures. They pressed close. There was something about them that evoked a palpable aura of malevolence.

Fishing into a pocket, he found his flashlight, drew it out. His thumb felt for the button.

Abruptly, the flash was knocked from Long Tom's hand!

Long Tom was no slouch in the pugilistic department. Even though he could not see, he lashed out with a fist and connected to a jaw. It felt human enough, but there was the strange sensation of his knuckles skidding off tough hide.

That foe fell backward, making a weird flapping pelican sort of sound.

Suddenly, Long Tom smelled leather. To his mind came the familiar aroma of old boxing gloves.

Several figures closed in. Long Tom lashed out. This time his fists impacted things that were not jaws. They, too, felt smooth and leathery.

The huddling things swallowed him in an embrace that felt like bundled wings. Great leather wings.

Reaching for his supermachine pistol, Long Tom never got it out of its armpit holster. Hands clutched at him. They felt like claws. They tore at his hat, his hair, seized his arms and wrists. Before he knew it, Long Tom was being pushed to the carpet by unseen horrors that flapped and breathed weirdly in their exertions.

In a normal fight, Long Tom could whip a half-dozen men before breakfast. A full dozen after his morning eggs.

But under these circumstances and handicapped as he was, the weird things smothered him into helplessness.

"What—are—you—birds!" he jerked out.

But the only reply was horrid, eerie music that penetrated his brain as if it, too, were attacking him.

Something—it felt like a webbed hand—covered his mouth and nose, shutting off oxygen.

Long Tom fought back, wrestled hard, but there was something in the unhuman hand. Something unpleasant. It filled his straining nostrils. Chloroform! He felt his last senses ebbing, and the darkness that surrounded him soon became absolute....

Weighted and pressed to the floor, Long Tom's undersized form gave out a last spasmodic jerk, then relaxed.

One by one, the leathery attackers climbed back to their feet.

In the darkness, a steamer trunk was produced and Long Tom was thrown into it. The lid dropped over his slender form with the finality of a coffin closing.

By then, the faraway uncanny music had faded into silence.

Chapter VII

PAT GUESSES WRONG

A **SILVER-COLORED AIRCRAFT** dropped out of the sky over the upper Hudson River. Silent as the wind, it skimmed over the rushing water rather low, then hiked around to drag the river once more.

Finally it alighted, floats smashing water, motors reversing, and ran over to the concrete ramp of a vault-like warehouse built on a pier on the Hudson side of Manhattan.

Engines revving anew, the pilot guided the craft up this ramp under power. Riverward doors opened and the amphibian surged up into the confines of the long brick structure.

The door closed. On the side facing land was an old sign. It read:

HIDALGO TRADING COMPANY

When the amphibian came to a rest, a hatch popped and out shouldered Monk Mayfair, followed by Ham Brooks. They were arguing, as usual.

Monk batted Ham's cane out of his ribs.

"Did I poke you?" the dapper lawyer asked innocently.

"You sure did," snarled Monk. "And I just want to tell you, I've been promising the Devil a man a long time, and you certainly do resemble my promise."

"I have always suspected you of being an overgrown imp from the lower regions," sniffed Ham.

Doc Savage emerged last.

"Want me to refuel this ark?" asked Monk.

The bronze man shook his head. "We will take the new transoceanic. Prepare it for a hop to Europe, or any other spot on a moment's notice," he stated.

"Gotcha, Doc," said Monk. He ambled off.

It could be seen that the vault-like interior housed an amazing array of ultra-modern craft. There were other planes, ranging from a small racer that was all motor to a big twin-engine flying boat. There was also a cabin autogyro, a strange-looking submarine in a dry dock and, most amazing of all, a dirigible hung under the rafters. This was Doc Savage's fleet of globe-girdling craft.

Monk got to work on the big flying boat, which alone of the fleet was painted bronze.

Ham set to refreshing the stores of ammunition and other equipment that had been expended during their last adventure. Boxes of supplies came out of a storage locker.

During this activity, an electric light began flashing and a shrill whining came from a far corner.

"That's the telephone," Ham announced.

Doc Savage moved to the closest instrument, picked it up and said, "Hello, Pat."

A surprised female voice exclaimed, "Have you added psychic to your list of talents? How did you know it was me?"

"A new device I am testing," explained Doc. "It is rigged so that when a known number rings this line, the light flashes in a prearranged rhythm. This flashing is intermittent and excitable, which told me it was you."

"Are you implying that I am of the excitable persuasion?"

"At this moment, your voice is," returned Doc dryly.

"It so happens that I have a mystery for you to solve. It landed on my doorstep."

A touch of concern entered the bronze man's well-modulated voice. "Say again?"

"Someone sent me a package. I imagine they thought it would get to you through me faster than if it was expressed to your headquarters."

A repressed urgency threaded the big bronze man's tone. "What type of package?"

"Oh, it was a steamer trunk. The usual thing. It landed at my beauty salon—"

"No, what was in the package?"

"A raccoon coat."

"That is all?" queried Doc.

"No, sitting on it was Eloise."

"Eloise?"

"I think," Pat suggested, "you ought to swing by and see Eloise for yourself."

"We will be right there. In the meantime, don't touch anything!"

"Too late."

"I mean it, Pat."

But Pat Savage had already hung up. She was Doc Savage's cousin, and a frequent horner-in on his adventures, much to the bronze man's unalloyed displeasure.

Doc Savage called to the others. "Monk. Ham. There may be trouble at Pat's place."

"What kind of trouble?" inquired Ham, giving his slim dark cane a spin.

"Package from an unknown party."

Monk growled, "We'd better haul our freight over there."

Doc Savage went to a gunmetal gray sedan with a long nose and a generous wheelbase. He climbed behind the wheel, Monk and Ham jumping aboard as Doc got the car in motion. The bronze man was wasting no time.

The doors facing the street rolled up as if by magic, and the sedan slid into traffic. A radio signal from the vehicle had actuated a mechanism, which impelled the electric doors to open.

All of Doc's machines were thus equipped.

PATRICIA, INCORPORATED, was an establishment off Park Avenue catering to the upper crust of Manhattan womanhood. It was a combination beauty salon and gymnasium. There, a woman of means could have her hair coiffed, her face encased in a mudpack and unwanted pounds taken off with various machines designed for that exact purpose. It was all very highbrow.

Doc Savage pushed into the modernistic lobby and a polished blonde receptionist stood up, her mouth dropping open.

"M-Mr. Savage! Wh-what are you doing here?" she blurted out. "I mean, I will fetch Miss Savage."

Although it was no secret that Patricia, Incorporated, was owned by Doc Savage's cousin, the bronze man was not known to enter the establishment, as a rule. So his arrival occasioned quite a flurry and fluttering among staff and customers both.

Doc followed the receptionist to Patricia's private office.

A bronze-haired girl with a coat of tan to match stood up from her desk and beamed perfect teeth. Her eyes sparkled with a golden glint that caught the attention. This was Patricia Savage. Her beauty made all others resemble wilted flowers.

"Doc!" she hailed. "Meet Eloise!"

Sitting on the desk was a hairy creature which regarded them with gimlet eyes.

"Hey, it's a monkey!" howled Monk.

The monkey took one look at the apish chemist and placed both hands atop her head as if encountering a long-lost relative. She gave out a sharp squeak and dived under the desk.

Pat reached down and pulled Eloise out by her tail, which nature had decorated with raccoon-like rings.

"Pat," Doc said sternly. "Set the monkey down."

Pretty Pat made a face. "Why, Eloise doesn't bite. Or at least she hasn't yet." Doc Savage removed his coat and used it to gather up the monkey.

Eloise was not happy. She struggled, but the bronze man made his metallic hands into a vise to keep her from escaping.

Ham Brooks moved in and scrutinized the struggling creature.

"Reminds me of my pet ape, Chemistry," he sniffed.

"Maybe you can marry them off and I'll get some peace," grunted Monk.

"You nitwit! At least I possess a pet suitable for a gentleman. Not a pig."

The dapper lawyer was not calling the apish chemist a pig. Rather, Monk had a pet porker. He carried it everywhere he went.

"What are you looking for?" Pat was asking Doc Savage.

Doc said nothing. His face had fallen into lines of vague concern—vague because emotion was something he was schooled to suppress. Doc rarely displayed outward feeling. He was showing a little now and to those who knew him well, it was as if a siren was going off.

Doc reminded, "You mentioned a raccoon coat."

Pat went to a closet and produced the coat. It was a long thing of the species college students had been wearing a few years ago, but the fad had abated and now they were rarely seen.

"It doesn't fit me, and raccoon is passé, anyway. I wouldn't be caught dead in such a fur. Notice that it's ringed like Eloise's tail. I deduced there must be a connection. Why else would they be sent together?"

"Was there a return address?" asked Doc, golden eyes steady.

"No, only this." From a desk drawer, pretty Pat produced a folded sheet of paper. She unfolded it and showed it to Doc, who never released his grip on the squirming ring-tailed monkey.

The note read:

THESE TWO ITEMS, IF UNDERSTOOD PROPERLY, WILL REVEAL A RIDDLE AS OLD AS TIME.

It was unsigned.

A trilling emerged from Doc's parted lips. It careened, displaying a wondering quality, then keyed up into a sound resembling apprehension.

"Pat," Doc said gravely, "place the note on the desk and please wash your hands thoroughly."

Pat frowned. "Why?"

"Germs."

Pat made a face. "That monkey doesn't look very germy to me. In fact, I think you should apologize to Eloise for insulting her that way."

"Pat," said Doc sternly.

"Oh, all right." Pat went to a washroom and the sounds of rushing water came.

"I think it would be advisable if we all took a ride," Doc announced upon her return.

"Where to?" asked Pat, growing suspicious.

"It would be best not to say."

Doc spoke to Ham in Mayan, the language they used to converse with one another, but which Pat did not know.

Frowning darkly, Ham availed himself of a telephone and placed a call.

"Are we all going to the circus?" Pat wanted to know. When no one smiled, she added, "That was my idea of a joke."

"This is no joke, Pat," Doc told her in a grave voice.

"I am," she returned seriously, "beginning to believe you."

Pat Savage wore an astonished look on her face when a private ambulance pulled up to the curb and two white-coated attendants were inviting her onto a gurney.

"What is this!" she said huffily. "I am not ill!"

Doc advised, "You can go under your own power. But you are going, young lady."

"My fair foot!"

Ham interjected, "Do you fail to realize how many people have mailed bombs or death devices to Doc's headquarters, only to be intercepted before they can do harm?"

Pat eyed them skeptically. "A raccoon coat and a ring-tailed monkey? The worst that could come of this is a dose of fleas."

Doc grasped her arm, said quietly, "Better to take precautions now than to have regrets later on."

"Oh, all right."

Pat walked out to the ambulance and got onto the gurney of her own free will. With grim efficiency, the internes strapped her onto the thing. This was shoved into the back. The door slammed shut and the machine pulled away, its gong clanging disconsolately through mid-town traffic.

Doc followed in his gunmetal sedan. Once out of Manhattan, the ambulance driver shut off his gong and settled down for what proved to be a protracted drive north.

THE trip took two hours. During the long drive, Pat Savage craned her face so that it became visible at the rear window and, knowing that Doc Savage was an expert lip reader, mouthed the words, "Am I being kidnapped?"

Behind the wheel, Doc Savage shook his head in the negative. He was an expert lip-reader.

Into the trunk, Doc had placed the raccoon coat and the ring-tailed monkey. He hadn't liked doing that, but it was necessary. Eloise finally quieted down after some twenty minutes.

It was dusk when they pulled into a gated fence surrounding a cluster of gray stone buildings huddled under the shadow of an immense rocky hill.

This was Doc Savage's "crime college." Nestled in the foothills of a wilderness mountain range, this facility was a secret just as great as Doc's Arctic sanctuary. Here, criminals captured by the bronze man were spirited, to be reeducated and taught a new trade.

Heart of this complex was a hospital, where the unique brain surgeries were performed by a team of specialists in Doc's employ. These delicate operations removed any criminal proclivities by correcting a malfunctioning gland the bronze man had determined governed bad behavior.

Three men stood waiting for them at the hospital portion of the institution. They were garbed in green surgical gowns and caps, swatches of cloth pulled tightly over their lower faces. With only their eyes showing, they looked forbidding.

"We'll take her from here, sir," they told Doc Savage as Pat Savage was rolled out. She jumped to her feet, having undone her straps along the way.

Pat demanded, "Doc, what's going on here! Who are these Dr. Frankensteins?"

Doc said, "Pat, go with them."

Pat stamped her foot. "Not until I know more."

"This is in the nature of a private hospital," explained the bronze man. "You will be subjected to tests to determine whether or not you need to be quarantined."

Pat placed brown fists on hips with stubborn resolve. "I get it now!" she flashed. "You want to hog this mystery all for yourself. Well, I won't stand for it!"

"It is nothing of the sort," returned Doc, with just a touch of indignation. Pat was always accusing him of not wanting her involved in his affairs. It was the truth. But the bronze man rarely resorted to subterfuges—and then only when he believed Pat's life was at risk. She was his only living relative.

"Is that so?" countered Pat. "What about the time that you—"

Pat let out a gentle sigh and her eyes began fluttering. For, unbeknownst to her, one of the surgeons had inserted the needle of a syringe into her shoulder. Surreptitiously, Doc had signaled for the action to be taken.

Pat's knees buckled. To her credit, she swayed, out on her feet, somehow managing not to fall.

Doc caught her gently, and bore her into the grim gray building.

An examination room had been prepared, and Pat was laid out on a table.

Swiftly, the bronze man donned surgical mask, gown and gloves. He ignored his cousin and immediately opened the case in which Eloise the ring-tailed monkey had been carried. Monk had toted it from the car.

Doc Savage took his time. Using gloved fingers, he spread the monkey's fur, exposing the pale skin and examining carefully. When he was done with the tiny scalp, he moved down the body, finally scrutinizing the ringed tail.

His trilling piped up, profoundly disturbed. With a glass pipette, he took a sample of what he found and bottled it.

Next, he turned his attention to the raccoon coat. This received the same kind of examination. Once again, Doc found something of interest and removed a particle of matter with a pipette. It resembled a tiny white snowflake.

"This coat is too dangerous to keep as evidence," Doc told one surgeon. "Burn this in the incinerator."

"At once, Dr. Savage."

The coat was returned to its box and carried away.

DOC turned his attention to a microscope of good quality. This reposed on a work table. He placed a sample from one pipette onto a slide and examined this.

His trilling started, stopped, started again, as if the bronze man were attempting to throttle it, but his mind would not stay on the task.

The second sample was examined next, then Doc turned to the attending doctor.

"I am afraid that this monkey must be destroyed."

"I will attend to it," said the surgeon, placing the limp form in the valise and bearing it away.

Doc had changed gloves each time—and now he was donning new ones.

He checked Pat Savage's scalp, found nothing, and turned his attention to her arms, rolling up both sleeves and examining the skin. Finding nothing remarkable, he removed her shoes and checked her feet.

The big bronze man was tense as he did so, but as his examination progressed, he seemed to relax slightly, in stages, while still remaining intent upon his work.

A few moments later, Doc stripped off his mask and gown, placed them in a laundry bag—gloves last—and emerged.

"Burn this bag," he told an orderly.

Monk and Ham rushed up, faces worried.

"What's the word, Doc?" asked Ham.

"Pat will have to be quarantined for a week," Doc directed. "It will be wise to keep her under observation for an additional two months to be certain that she is not infected."

"What's she got?" Monk muttered.

"Let us hope," the bronze man said, "that she will develop no symptoms of what she was exposed to. For it is invariably fatal."

Monk and Ham raced one another to turn as pale as shocked ghosts.

The dapper lawyer found his tongue first.

"Were there germs on the coat or the monkey?"

Doc nodded. "I found specimens of the agent of death on both."

"Blazes!" gulped Monk.

Ham wrung the barrel of his cane in gloved fingers. "I am thinking that this was not an attempt on Pat's life," he ventured.

"Precisely," said Doc Savage. "Someone wished to assassinate me and, knowing the kind of precautions I normally take, employed a more circuitous route."

Smacking one furry fist into an open palm as big as a catcher's mitt, Monk growled, "And, mystery-hound that she is, Pat fell for it like a ton of bricks! I'd like to get my hooks on the necks of them that perpetrated this scheme."

Ham worried his stick distractedly. "Doc," he said, "do you think this could be the handiwork of...."

"It is diabolical enough to be John Sunlight's doing," admitted Doc. "All available evidence was that he was consumed by a marauding polar bear up in the Arctic. But we cannot afford to ignore any possibility, or fail to follow any trail."

The bronze man's words were cold, resolute. It was clear that this attempt on his life, through the agency of infecting his cousin, had shocked him to his core.

"So what type of germ was employed?" asked Ham worriedly.

"No germ. A spore."

"Spore!" Monk exclaimed.

"A bacteria spore," said Doc Savage. "Anthrax was the agent of murder."

Chapter VIII

SITUATION VERY BLACK

THE TIME WAS three days later.

Doc Savage entered the quarantine room to which Pat Savage had been removed. She sat up in bed, looking frosty of eye. Her color was healthy, Doc saw.

Doc smiled. "How are you feeling, Pat?"

"Madder than a mud hen!" flared Pat.

Doc consulted a chart at the foot of her bed. "I see that your appetite is good."

"I have had," Pat rejoined, "better food in one of those joints where I had to put a nickel into a slot in order to get my apple pie."

"The food here is nutritious," Doc pointed out.

"And that's another thing. Where exactly *is* here?"

"Upstate."

The bronze-haired beauty eyed Doc. "I know that. I could see the evergreens flying past during the ambulance ride. Is this one of those charity hospitals you run on the sly?"

"That is a very good guess, Pat."

"Fibber!"

"What makes you say that?" Doc asked, shining a penlight into her clear golden eyes.

"The orderly who served me my breakfast."

Doc turned off the light. "What about him?"

"I recognized him from last year's news reels. He was wanted for bank robbery in five Midwestern states. The police never caught him. But there he was, dishing up eggs and ham, content as can be."

"You may be mistaken."

Pat said archly, "I noticed you said, 'may.' Not 'are.' Having trouble with your fibbing?"

"Let me see your tongue, Pat," invited Doc.

"I am beginning to suspect that I have been consigned to that special 'university' you run for crooks. The one that you made me swear never to breathe a word about."

"Your tongue."

Pat obliged by sticking out her tongue and making it vibrate in the style of a tart Bronx cheer. When she ran out of steam, Doc employed a tongue depressor and examined the extended organ carefully.

"No coat."

"That reminds me," Pat said around the wood tool. "What happened to my raccoon coat?"

"Burned," said Doc.

"Just like that. No 'by your leave?'"

"It was dusted with anthrax spores," Doc Savage said gently.

Pat retracted her tongue and absorbed this information. Her eyes got rounder than usual. She folded her arms.

"Now I'm afraid to ask after Eloise."

Doc disposed of the tongue depressor. "Best you forget Eloise."

Pat heaved a forlorn sigh. "So that note was a lie, after all. The one about revealing the greatest riddle."

Doc Savage regarded her with steady gaze. "No, in a sense, it told the truth. Had you become infected, you would have seen revealed the great riddle of life."

"You mean what is back of beyond?"

Doc nodded soberly. "One way of putting it."

Pat let her bronze-haired head drop back on the pillow, laid a shapely forearm athwart her brow and asked in a mock-fatigued voice, "How long have I got?"

"About a week."

Pat snapped erect. Horror twisted her lovely features. "You mean to tell me—?"

Doc shook his head. "No, you will need to remain here another week, just in case. But I am certain that you have passed the point where symptoms would have appeared, had you become infected by the spores."

"If I remember my youthful days in the great out of doors, breathing problems and black spots on the skin are the first signs of anthrax."

"You have neither of those," the bronze man assured her.

"That's a relief." Her voice became conspiratorial. "So who is gunning for you this time, cousin?"

"That remains to be seen," replied Doc. "But we are endeavoring to discover the assassin's name and motives."

Pat bent a level eye on Doc Savage. "I suppose it would be asking too much to be let in on the action."

"By the time you are released," Doc told her, "we will have left the country."

Pat brightened. "International intrigue! My favorite flavor."

Doc shook his head gravely. "Too dangerous for a woman."

"And me, who nearly succumbed to the anthrax meant for you."

"Your death was not the objective, you know. The assassin hoped that you would expose me indirectly."

Pat shuddered deliciously. "Murder by blood relative...."

MONK MAYFAIR poked his bullet head in, gave Pat a grin that would have frightened a bulldog, and addressed Doc Savage.

"Doc! A radio-telegram came to our headquarters! From Long Tom. Ham just brought it."

"Excuse us," Doc told Pat and exited, shutting the door behind him.

Doc accepted the radiogram. It had come from the *S.S. Transylvania*. It read:

COUNTESS OLGA TURNED INTO COAL GHOST. HER SMOKE EVAPORATED. ONLY WITNESS EMILE ZIRN REPORTEDLY DID SAME. NEXT WITNESS VANISHED. BIG BLACK MYSTERY. TRYING TO GET TO THE BOTTOM.

Monk whistled. "More than ten words. Must be big to get him to spring for the extra dough."

Ham interposed, "Doc, he is describing the effect of the electron-stopper John Sunlight stole from your Fortress, the diabolic device which freezes atomic motion, with the end result that the victim dissolves into a cloud of hideous black smoke."

"Yeah," agreed Monk. "But you destroyed it up there. Didn't you?"

"I did destroy the device," confirmed Doc.

"Could someone have built a new one?" wondered Ham.

"Not without first disassembling the original and memorizing its inner construction," advised Doc. "A possibility, if remote."

"So what's the explanation?"

"I do not yet know," Doc Savage admitted. And the lines into which his bronze features fell bespoke of the gravity with which the metallic Hercules viewed this latest development.

DOC SAVAGE went to his private office and began making transatlantic telephone calls. In short order, he learned that the radio-telegram had come from the liner *Transylvania* just before it docked in Southampton. It was sent by Walter Brunk, an alias Long Tom sometimes used. "Brunk" had abruptly disembarked at Southampton, despite having purchased a ticket to Pristav, Tazan.

Doc contacted the private detective agency for whom the fictitious Walter Brunk purportedly worked. They scoured the seaport city, and made inquiries in London and elsewhere.

No sign of "Brunk" or Long Tom turned up.

Doc asked Ham to contact the steamship company who owned the liner and to get passenger lists.

Ham was busy with calls for nearly an hour.

"Copies are being expressed to our headquarters and will be there when we return," he reported.

"Better I take them by phone," said Doc.

Ham extended the telephone receiver. After some preliminaries, the bronze man fell silent as he listened to the passenger lists being read off to him. Doc took no notes. None were necessary. His amazingly retentive mind was absorbing the names, and if a year from now—had the necessity arose—he could recite them back without missing one.

Doc thanked the other and hung up. He continued with his open line of investigation.

After several more hours were consumed, receivers were replaced upon cradles and Doc stood up.

"We will return to headquarters," announced Doc.

"What about Pat?" asked Monk.

"If we take the time to say our farewells, she will no doubt badger us with entreaties to join in this affair. It is far too dangerous. We came close to losing her. Besides, she is in good hands here."

"And out of the way, too," Monk grinned. "I get it."

Doc's tone and manner were so grim, neither aide took up an opposing point of view.

They left the secret institution by sedan and blended with the sparse traffic of the mountainous region.

On the long drive cityward, Monk and Ham took turns puzzling out the matter.

"It is obvious that the secret message Long Tom left at our headquarters about the missing reporter, Simon Page, ties into this new mystery," announced Ham.

"Sure," agreed Monk. "But how?"

"There is no question that Long Tom believed that the disappearance of an American in the region where John Sunlight attempted to foment a war was justification enough to set off for the Balkans," mused Ham. "But it appears that he encountered unexpected trouble before he reached his destination."

"Three passengers go missing in the middle of the Atlantic," grumbled Monk. "Wonder why the papers ain't reported any of that?"

"You homely gossoon!" Ham flared. "They always hush up these things if they can. It's bad for business, murder on a transatlantic liner."

Monk eyed the bronze man. "What do you think, Doc?"

Doc Savage usually kept his opinions to himself, but the strain of the last few days, coming on the heels of the terrible events up in the Arctic Circle, had caused his habitual self-possession to become slightly unglued.

"No Countess Olga was listed on the passenger manifest," he stated. "Although she was seen by many prior to her vanishing. Emile Zirn disappeared before docking, and the unnamed witness to his demise has never turned up. I have all this from the captain of the liner, to whom I spoke."

Ham frowned. "So what does it all mean?"

"It means that it would be advisable to reach Pristav as soon as possible," said the bronze man.

"What about John Sunlight?" pressed Ham.

"We have our worldwide detective agency searching for him. The matter of the darkness machine now in the possession of Baron Karl's country, Egallah, is our other priority."

Monk piped up, "What do you suppose got into Long Tom?"

"No doubt Long Tom arrived in Tazan. One of the passengers who boarded in Southampton was Ned Foy. This is another alias of Long Tom's."

"You'd have thought he'd telegraph us when he arrived," said Monk, scratching one rusty wrist.

"That is the disturbing part of this extended mystery," agreed

Doc. "Long Tom has been in Pristav for three days and a checkup of every hostelry in the city shows that he never registered at any establishment under any of his known aliases."

"He mighta thought up a new one," suggested Monk.

Doc shook his head. "Long Tom knows our standard procedures—to check into foreign hotels under false names known to all of us, so as to leave a trail easy to follow."

"I admit that it does not sound good for Long Tom," Ham said slowly.

Doc Savage fell silent and compelled the sedan to break speed limits all the way to the city. He employed a siren to force traffic to make way. There was a great urgency in his driving.

Chapter IX

EXPEDITION TO DANGER

TAZAN, IN THE Balkans, is no pleasure hop. Reaching it meant crossing the Atlantic Ocean to the British Isles to take on aviation fuel, before proceeding across Western Europe to the Balkans.

Doc Savage took the most direct route. Most transatlantic aviators fly north to Nova Scotia and take on fuel there, before embarking upon the arduous voyage over the waves, the distance between Nova Scotia and the British Isles being the shortest direct route. But Doc decided against that. He made no stops for gasoline after he topped off the tanks in New York. The bronze man kept the two throttles controlling the engines of his big speed plane against the open-pins most of the time.

Doc's giant amphibian was a high-wing job. From boat-shaped hull to motor cowls and exhaust stacks, it was streamlined to the finest degree. The ship was fitted with wheels for landing on earth. These cranked entirely out of sight.

The remarkable plane had a cruising speed in excess of two hundred and seventy five miles an hour. But stubborn headwinds retarded its progress significantly.

This was a larger craft than the one Doc had flown from the Arctic. It was his latest ship, and came equipped with features he had lately developed. From streamlined nose to stabilizer, it was painted a distinctive bronze color.

Below, the heaving Atlantic Ocean became a monotonous corrugated field which heaved and wrinkled at intervals, like the jeweled hide of some sparkling blue dragon. High above, clouds galloped along in magnificent herds.

"We are running low on fuel," Doc Savage announced, his eyes flicking to the fuel gauges.

"We can try refueling in Ireland," Ham suggested.

Doc nodded. "Monk, get on the radio and see if you can locate the closest fueling depot."

"Gotcha, Doc." Monk leaped for the short-wave, began fiddling with the dials.

After several minutes of this, he let out a howl.

"Blazes!"

Ham glowered. "What is it, you ape?"

"I was fishin' around the radio broadcasts from the Balkans, and picked up something strange. Doc, listen to this."

Monk unplugged the telephonic headset, allowing the transmission to come out the cabin loudspeaker.

It was a kind of music. Low, unreal, it wavered weirdly, seemingly being the product of musical instruments not found upon the earth. An eerie wandering thing, the melody—if such an utterance could be so described—plunged and climbed, thrilling the nerves.

"What is that?" Ham wondered.

Doc Savage listened for some time, face expressionless.

"Did I pick up a transmission from the moon?" Monk muttered uneasily. He liked his music loud and brassy. This was patently not of that order.

"What station is broadcasting that?" asked Doc.

"One of the Tazan commercial stations," supplied the hairy chemist.

They listened for a time and the weird strains trailed off, to be replaced by ordinary band music.

"Monk," said Doc at length. "Find us fuel."

Plugging the jack back into its receptacle, Monk got back to work. The cockpit settled down into a calm atmosphere, in which the muted drone of the two radial engines seemed somehow far away.

Monk was busy some time. Finally, he seemed to obtain results.

"Where can we meetcha?" he asked excitedly. "Great Blasket Island? We'll find it."

Monk snapped off the radio. "I found an Irishman with a bargeload of aviation fuel. He says he can meet us at Great Blasket Island, which is just about the westernmost point of Ireland."

Doc nodded. He changed course slightly, taking the monster speed plane southward.

"Bally good luck there should be a quantity of fuel there," Ham sniffed.

"Luck of the Irish, I calls it," Monk said, beaming.

IT was somewhat past midnight when Doc dropped his plane in Dingle Bay, off the western coast of Ireland. Great Blasket was the largest of six isles, looking like a pod of whales bathing in the moonlight. The streamlined hull knocked up sheets of spray, carving a wake that collapsed on itself.

"The worst leg of this daggone trip is behind us," Monk muttered sleepily.

"I'll wager the worst prospects lie before us," Ham rejoined, flourishing his ever-present sword cane.

The pig, Habeas Corpus, crawled from under Monk's chair.

Ham gawked. "What is that insect doing here!"

Monk shrugged. "Sleepin', I guess."

"But you agreed to leave him behind if I left my Chemistry back in New York!"

Chemistry was Ham's pet—a runt ape of no discoverable species he had picked up in South America.

"I did," Monk said innocently. "Somebody musta forgot to tell Habeas."

Monk scooped up the pet pig, and began scratching behind its wing-like ear. "Habeas, I guess you don't hear none too good," he said amiably.

Ham looked mad enough to unsheathe his sword cane and wrap the fine blade around Monk's nearly non-existent neck. Instead, he settled for guessing out loud how many cuts of meat the scrawny porker might produce if the opportunity ever came to butcher him for food.

Monk clapped both hands over Habeas' long inquisitive ears.

"Don't listen to him, hog. He don't eat pork anyway. He just likes to rag on his betters."

The porker opened its mouth and seemed to say, "Shoats are superior to shysters in any book."

At that humorous example of ventriloquism, Ham purpled and stamped around in the cabin, fuming, until Doc Savage announced, "We will refuel as rapidly as possible."

Doc Savage, handling the controls, ruddered the plane in toward Great Blasket Island's northeastern shore. When he blooped the powerful motors, they threw off streams of air, which in turn scooped up great fans of spray.

In the water, a low shape showed—a barge. Amidships this craft was decked over. On the deck stood numerous metal drums.

A man stood amid these drums. He was alone on board. Lifting arms, he waved them in greeting.

Doc piloted the big plane toward the large seagoing platform. It glided to a point very close to the barge, reversed engines, and dropped a sea anchor electrically. A splash near the nose told of the anchor entering the water.

Doc shoved open his window, waved once.

The dark shape in the barge called out, "Faith, are ye the party what wants gasoline?"

"We are," Doc admitted.

"Wonderful luck! For I have all you need!"

The son of Erin stepped into the floodlights. He wore a cloth cap and a Mackintosh coat that fit him like a swaddling blanket.

Ham threw open the hatch.

"Monk," Doc suggested, "see if his gas is all right. If it is, we'll patronize him. The time we'll save makes it worth the cost."

With monkeylike agility, the homely chemist sprang to the barge. He carried a bottle, which he filled with gasoline from a drum. Then he sprang back to the plane, entered the cabin and for possibly two minutes was very busy analyzing.

"It's good gas," he told Doc.

The Irishman—he introduced himself as Patrick Allerton van Shaughnessy—had a hand-force pump on his barge. It was of large capacity. With it he rapidly transferred fuel to the big plane tanks.

"Fill 'em up," Monk said. Doc remained in the cockpit. He was too conspicuous and they were soon to be flying into what might turn into a war zone. No point in stirring up the press. Doc always avoided publicity.

"Goin' far?" the Shaughnessy inquired cheerily.

"Clear to Russia," lied Monk.

"Brrrr! Be cold up there."

Monk was standing atop the broad wing.

Ham stuck his head out the cabin door. "Why don't you give him a hand, you lazy ape?"

"It's his gas, his pump, let him earn his fee," snarled Monk.

They fell to arguing, with the result that Monk Mayfair reentered the cabin to make sure Ham had not locked Habeas the pig into a valise, with the intent of dropping him into the water.

After a bit, Monk returned to his post, saw that the Irishman was in the middle of exchanging drums and said, "Shake a leg, Paddy. We're in a powerful hurry."

"I be goin' as rapidly as I am able, sor," the Shaughnessy

returned.

Monk nodded, sat on the wing, and proceeding to whistle impatiently. Whether it was Monk's ferocious appearance, or the whistling, the Irishman pumped furiously.

After two more barrels of fuel had been drained, the Irishman removed the nozzle of his hose and beamed, "'Tis done! It's be wantin' my pay, I am now."

Monk clambered down and peeled out a number of large bills from a fat wad he extracted from one pocket. "There you go, my good man."

"Think nothing of it, sor," said the Shaughnessy.

Returning to the cockpit, Monk said, "Let's get this crate in the air, Doc."

Doc Savage was watching the Irishman. The latter ducked behind the drums stacked in the landward side of the barge, disappearing from sight. The flaky gold in Doc's eerie orbs became agitated whirlpools.

"Hold on," Doc said. The giant bronze man flashed to Monk's chemical equipment. Monk had a portable laboratory, which he had perfected himself. He never went on an expedition without it. From Monk's paraphernalia, Doc drew a fat syringe and a glass vial.

Grimly, Doc siphoned gas from the fuel tanks. Next, he introduced selected chemicals from Monk's assortment. What the bronze giant discovered caused him to hastily cork the glass tube.

"This fuel has been contaminated!" he rapped.

"What's wrong with it?" Ham demanded.

"Toward the last, the fellow must have pumped a tank of chemicals aboard," Doc explained. "The chemical additive is of a nature to clog the fuel lines. The vibrations of our motors, for instance, would cause the stuff to mix with the aviation fuel, with the result that we would run out of fuel—or seem too—after an hour or two of flight."

Ham howled, "On our present course, we would have gone

down over the water!"

"That shamrock shyster!" Monk growled. "I'll murder him for this! I'll—"

Monk swallowed the rest.

Abruptly, Doc Savage left the plane, ran onto the wing and made a leap for the barge. Other than the drums, it was empty.

Doc slipped into the water. His hair soon vanished beneath the waves.

Monk waited. When Doc came up, Monk intended to yell and ask the bronze man if it would not be all right if he went along. Monk hated to miss action.

But Monk did not see Doc Savage reappear.

DOC SAVAGE came up many yards from the floating plane, and only a short distance from shore. Two or three silent strokes put him on land.

The Irishman was not on shore. Doc had not expected him to be.

Doc's spring-generator flashlight, which gave a thin white rod of a beam, was waterproof. He thumbed it. The flashbeam spouted illumination. The fellow who had planted the chemical clogger had evidently taken no chances and fled the vicinity.

There were footprints. Doc traced them with his flash ray.

The bronze man worked to higher ground, and into a coastal forest.

The forest was not deep. On the other side of it there appeared to be a village. There were no lights at this late hour, and the peaty smell of hearths came to his sensitive nostrils. At this time of year, people went to sleep with their furnaces lit for warmth.

Deciding that he stood little chance of overtaking the Shaughnessy on foot—given the other's familiarity with the forest—Doc kicked off shoes and socks. A substantial tree made an efficient ladder. Doc went up this.

Perched on a high bough, he sighted a nearby limb, gave a

leap. He caught the other limb easily and swung atop it. The footing swayed and bent under him as he ran along it. A moment later, Doc was in another tree.

Going even higher, the bronze man found a forest lane of the aerial type—although a man accustomed to city sidewalks might have sworn progress was impossible.

Aided by the brilliant moonlight and the uncanny acuity of his eyes, Doc swung from tree to tree. An experienced circus aerialist could have managed most of the leaps, but the idea of doing them under such conditions would have turned him white-headed.

The village came into view. It was a dark cluster of thatched roofs. From branch to branch Doc dropped downward, finally reaching the ground.

Doc waited there. The bronze man was confident he had distanced the Irishman. The fellow should be coming out of the woods in a few moments.

A twig snapped. Another. This was all the trained ears of Doc Savage needed to ascertain the other's steady course.

Using increased wariness as he drew near, Doc came within a few yards of the procession of snapping sounds. He could hear a man breathing heavily. The breathing was rasping, labored.

Doc headed for the spot where the man should exit the forest. Pressing himself to the bole of a particularly large tree, the bronze man laid in wait.

Footfalls approached. Someone coming. In the murk, he was a bear-like form in a Mackintosh coat.

Doc Savage stepped into his path with a suddenness that was breathtaking. One moment the path ahead was clear, and the next there was a metallic Atlas blocking the way.

The Shaughnessy leaped backward with cat-like speed. Fingers were suddenly about his throat, squeezing. He was being pressed to the ground. The Irishman squirmed on the woodland path. He went to the verge of unconsciousness. He gulped great quantities of air in and out of his mouth.

Doc relented, withdrew his terrible corded hand.

The other's hand dived into his coat pocket. He did not draw the gun which was apparently there, but pointed it at Doc without removing it from his pocket.

"Who are you?" he demanded.

Doc's golden eyes gazed piercingly. The moonlight was faint here.

"Doc Savage," said Doc. "And you?"

"Sure, and my name is Patrick Allerton—"

"Your *actual* name," Doc pressed.

"Zirn. Emile Zirn," said the other.

"Which Emile Zirn are you?"

"Why, I am the genuine Emile Zirn, naturally." His Irish accent had faded away like so much blarney. He stood up.

"Let's state it more clearly," Doc said. "A man named Emile Zirn disappeared from the passenger liner *Transylvania* en route to Southampton, England."

"I am that Emile Zirn," the other admitted. The man had not removed his gun from his pocket—or his hand either. "Only I was not on board the liner when she left Southampton. My enemies seem to know everything that was going on. I feared they would try to kill me aboard the liner. So I disembarked at Southampton."

"You must have come to Ireland by boat," Doc said dryly.

"I did."

"And how does it happen that you are here in the Irish coast hawking gasoline?"

"I fled to Ireland to escape my enemies. I heard your radio call, and knew that you were Doc Savage. I knew also that you must be traveling to Egallah, a terrible place. Knowing that you are a champion of humanity and knowing that Egallah is a place to which men go and never return, I decided to save your life the best way I knew how."

"By doping my fuel?"

"Precisely. I gather you have deduced the truth."

"Our plane might have gone down over difficult terrain—or water—with fatal consequences," the bronze man pointed out.

The other shrugged. "But you are a superior pilot. You would have landed safely. You are a wizard of death-defying escapes. You are a genius, a modern Prometheus. Why, Thomas Edison has nothing on you. Einstein is scarcely your equal. You are renowned for roaming the world and setting difficult matters to rights."

After this long speech, Emile Zirn drew a full breath into his lungs. That distracted his mind slightly. There was a blinding flash of bronze in front of him. He felt a terrific wrench of his arm. Cloth tore loudly.

Emile Zirn stared. His gun was now in Doc Savage's hand. The big bronze man seized it before Emile Zirn realized what was happening.

Emile Zirn rubbed his eyes. He had just seen a man move so fast that it was like magic.

DOC SAVAGE looked at Emile Zirn's gun. The weapon was an automatic with a barrel the size of a fountain pen and almost twice as long. It was a gun which fired a bullet of small diameter but great velocity and carrying power.

"I do not like to have a gentleman point a gun at me while I talk to him," Doc said.

Emile Zirn shrugged, said nothing.

Doc used his powerful flashlight, trickled the beam over Emile Zirn from head to foot. He clicked it out.

"Emile Zirn was reported killed," Doc advised.

"I am alive, as you can see," asserted the other. "Not dead."

"We will accept that for the present," Doc told him.

"How do I know that you are in fact the famous Doc Savage?"

Before the bronze man could reply, Emile Zirn struck out with a balled fist.

The immediate consequence of this was that the metallic giant barely reacted while Emile Zirn tucked his throbbing fist under one arm and made expressions of agony.

The midriff he had hit had felt like ridged stone.

"Why did you contaminate my fuel tanks?" Doc asked after the worst of the other man's pain had subsided.

"It—it was to save you from the Dark Devil that I did as I did," gasped out Emile Zirn.

"What is the Dark Devil?" Doc questioned.

Emile Zirn made a violent gesture with his undamaged hand.

"Heaven alone knows. It is something sinister. Some power. I do not even know whether it is human. But there are rumors that it has something to do with the terrible things transpiring in Ultra-Stygia. To be truthful, I know of only one person who might be able to tell you something of this Dark One."

"Who is that?" Doc asked.

"A notorious adventuress, Fiana Drost."

Doc Savage looked his question.

Emile Zirn absently plucked at his sleeve. Something re-sembling fear came into the eyes which were like black buttons on either side of his thin-bridged nose.

"Fiana Drost is nothing less than a spawn of the Nether-world," he spat.

"What?" said Doc.

"You heard me. Hell itself birthed her. She may be one of the things that prowl Ultra-Stygia by night. One of the Undead."

"I see," said Doc Savage, reserving further comment.

Emile Zirn said, "If you please, I would appreciate the return of my pistol."

"I doubt that you will need it," Doc told him and kept the weapon.

Taking the man by the collar, the bronze man marched him back to the anchored plane.

When they reached the big speed ship, Monk Mayfair shoved

his blunt head and shoulders out the cabin door, and called out boisterously.

"Hey, Doc! I think I fixed the gas!"

"Is this possible?" blurted Emile Zirn.

"Monk is one of the world's leading industrial chemists," reminded Doc.

Doc hauled Zirn on board the amphibian.

"Who is he?" asked Ham Brooks, pointing with his elegant cane.

"He says his name is Emile Zirn," said Doc, surreptitiously motioning with a hand not to react to the familiar name.

Monk and Ham appraised Zirn with skeptical eyes.

"What happened to the Irishman, van Shaughnessy?" asked Monk.

"Zirn was Shaughnessy," stated Doc.

"So what do we do with him?" asked Monk, cracking furry knuckles.

"He claims to have wished to preserve us from meeting death in Ultra-Stygia."

"Jolly decent of him," said Ham dryly.

"Since Mr. Zirn was originally en route to Pristav before threats upon his life caused him to change his travel plans," said Doc, "perhaps he would enjoy safe conduct with us."

Monk howled, "After what he done!"

Zirn interjected, "I only wished to—"

"Stow it," said Monk. "Doc, I mixed some counteractant stuff into the gas. Should be safe to take off now."

Doc nodded. "We will do that."

"Wait!" said Zirn. He looked uneasy of eye. "I—I have never flown in an airplane before. Is it safe?"

"Unless we lose a wing or get shot down," said Monk blandly.

Zirn swallowed several times. "I do not think I wish to fly with you gentlemen."

"Consider yourself our prisoner then," advised Doc.

"In that case, I must have a parachute. If I have a parachute, I think I will feel safer."

A parachute pack was produced and Emile Zirn donned it. He seemed to have no trouble figuring out how to buckle the webbing straps.

Selecting a seat near the exit door, he settled in.

Doc Savage dropped into the control bucket and snapped the two radial engines into life. They began howling like the proverbial Irish banshees, driving the big plane along. The sea anchor was withdrawn electrically.

The amphibian scudded over wavetops, bouncing and jarring. Soon, they were in the air, hammering in the direction of Europe.

Endless water cascaded under their wings. Emile Zirn sat quietly and looked uneasily out the windows. His dark eyes were sunken with a kind of unease.

Their course took them over Western Europe, and before long they were flying over the nation of Calbia, whose military planes provided Doc Savage with an escort all the way to the border of Tazan.

This caused Emile Zirn to stir from his long, uneasy silence. "Why do the Calbians offer you such a courtesy?"

"Ain't you heard?" boasted Monk. "A few years back, Doc stopped a revolution down there. For a reward, they tried to crown him king."

"There was a princess included in the arrangement," added Ham. "But Doc would have none of that."*

Emile Zirn made no reply. He looked slightly airsick.

At the border, the Calbian warplanes broke off and Doc flew on into the middle of Tazan. His course took him south, in the direction of the Black Sea.

THE noonday sun was climbing higher when they sighted the skyline of Pristav on the far horizon. It was yet far away, but

---

* *The King Maker.*

owing to the amazingly clear sky, the spires of its medieval churches could be discerned.

Doc Savage slanted the plane downward.

Monk Mayfair was at the radio set, endeavoring to contact the administrative tower of the main air field serving the city. He was having trouble finding the correct frequency.

Out of the loudspeaker came a weird vibration. It made their eardrums sing and their hearts want to skip a beat.

"That dang funeral music again!" Monk muttered.

"It is the death march of the Jagellon Dynasty," Emile Zirn said thickly. "It is played whenever a Tazan king dies."

"How do you know that?" asked Ham sharply. "Are you a native of Tazan, or Egallah?"

"I refuse to answer," he muttered.

Monk listened briefly to the eerie strains, then found the air-field wavelength.

"Doc-1 callin'. Requesting permission to land."

"Permission denied," a voice snapped back in thick English.

"Wait a minute! What do you mean—permission denied? Don't you know who you're talkin' to? This is Doc Savage's bus."

"That makes it a different matter, then," the voice said reluctantly.

Monk grinned. "See? Doc's name opens doors better than Aladdin ever did."

"It was unwise to announce ourselves like that," Ham murmured.

"It worked, didn't it?" countered Monk.

Doc was taking the plane around in order to approach into the wind. It was high noon. A brilliant winter day. No clouds. A bright sun. Visibility was perfect.

Abruptly, a smothering supernatural darkness clamped down. The interior of the cabin became as the inside of a lump of coal. India ink filling the cabin would have done no better job of obscuring their vision. It was impossible to see anything.

"What happened?" howled Ham.

"Never mind what happened!" yelled Monk. "How the heck are we gonna land in this soot?"

"It is the Dark Devil!" screamed Emile Zirn. "We are doomed men!"

Chapter X

TERROR IS BLACK

THE ENTIRE WORLD had turned into a smothering ball of absolute *black*.

The black ball began spinning, which added to its horrible qualities.

Doc Savage rapped out, "Monk! Ham!"

Pawing at his eyes, Monk squawled, "It's the darkness maker! They turned it on us!"

Displaying unbelievable controlled calmness, Doc said, "Find your parachutes! Hurry!"

"Find my parachute?" complained Ham. "I can't even see my fingers!"

"Habeas!" Monk bellowed hoarsely. "Where are you?"

In the weird supernatural blackness, a piggy squeal came. It sounded wretched, tortured. Monk lunged in that direction.

There was a mad scramble for pig and parachute packs as Doc Savage struggled to hold the great twin-engine amphibian level.

This was not as simple as it might seem. Pilots retain their orientation in the air by keeping one eye on the horizon and the other on the altimeter. It is very easy, when doing extreme aerial maneuvers, for example, to lose sight of the relationship of an aircraft to the earth. A simple thing to become disoriented.

Doc Savage's training had included several weeks blindfolded in a school for the sightless. This was when he was younger. He learned many tricks to use maneuvering in intense darkness, how to sense air currents on the face, or discern slight sounds that could enable an alert man to navigate a maze in utter darkness without visual clues.

None of these skills were useful now. His feet were not on solid ground and there was no air coming to his face. Doc was at the wheel of a massive aerial behemoth that any minute now might plow into the ground, plunge into the ocean or—worse still—collide with a mountain. For this was mountainous country.

Doc Savage's vibrant voice grew urgent. "Bail out. Now!"

Suddenly, the door opened. Slipstream came rushing in—cold, bracing and terribly frightening in the lightless confusion of the cabin.

Ham cried, "Doc! What about you?"

"I will follow directly."

Monk exploded, "Hey! Where's Zirn?"

Doc called out, "Zirn was the one who opened the door. He jumped out."

"That took nerve," barked Ham, scrambling for the door by feel. The cold air helped guide him.

"Aw, he was just chicken," returned Monk, finding Habeas in the unrelieved murk.

Holding the frantic shoat under one burly arm, Monk felt his way to the doorframe. There he paused, eyes bugging sightlessly from their gristle pits.

"Hey! How do I know which way is down?"

Shoving up behind him, Ham Brooks gave the apish chemist an encouraging kick to the seat of his pants, saying, "Gravity will guide you."

Howling, Monk tumbled out. Ham followed. He still clutched his sword cane. No doubt he would carry it to his grave.

They plummeted through an abyss of cold, black nothingness, knowing the helpless plight of the blind. They *were* blind. It was terrifying. Monk clung to Habeas, and Ham to his cane. After counting to ten, they yanked at their ripcords and hoped for the best. Only the sound of their chutes cracking told them they had deployed successfully. Then they were two human pendulums falling into an endless void.

Above, came the moan of the amphibian going off somewhere.

They listened hard. It was the only faculty left to them. Their optics were useless.

Ham said, "I don't hear Doc's chute cracking...."

"Sure hope he got out," Monk moaned.

Then it was all they could do to prepare themselves for landing. In the weird darkness, they had no way of knowing if they were about to land on dirt or water, or someplace infinitely more dangerous....

IN the cockpit of the amphibian, Doc Savage struggled with the controls.

His sense of equilibrium was unsurpassed, but it was of only theoretical use now. So much of what a man knows about his relationship to the earth comes from the visual senses that, under these weird conditions, Doc wasn't certain whether he was flying level or not.

It felt as if he were, so Doc trusted that feeling. Yet it was unnerving. No light came to his flake-gold eyes. They no longer operated as nature intended.

Doc's immediate concern was to get the plane on the ground safely, if that were in any way possible. For when he told Monk and Ham that he would be along, he did not mean that he intended to parachute out. To abandon the aircraft to its fate would risk it landing on occupied buildings with horrific results.

The bronze man was not prepared to relinquish control of his plane, lest it become an instrument of blind death.

As best he could, Doc Savage flew in the direction where he believed open water lay. He had experimented by trying to circle. When the air coming through the open door smelled of salt water, that gave him an approximate heading. Unfortunately, there was no way to be certain that he was flying true to the Black Sea.

Doc flew and flew. In his mind, he knew that if he could keep the lumbering plane aloft and on course, he could steer it far out into the sea and completely eliminate all risk to life and limb—excepting his own, of course—but such was the compassion of the mighty bronze man that he placed himself last.

The amphibian droned on. The minutes whistled past. Light was a thing not present in any form.

After a time, the distressing lack of vision ceased to make Doc's heart pound, and his adrenalin subsided.

Without warning, Doc flew into a zone of bright sunlight. The stabbing sudden light came as a shock to his unprepared eyes. They squeezed shut, involuntarily.

Once again, Doc had to fight with the controls—now being blinded by natural light.

But after several seconds, the bronze man could see that he was skimming over wavetops. His altitude was much lower than he expected to be, and this came as an unwelcome shock.

Lifting the bawling plane by its control yoke, Doc regained altitude.

After a while, normal vision returned.

Doc Savage brought the amphibian swinging around, back in the direction of Tazan. This time he dropped his airspeed to allow for the possibility that the zone of blackness would be encountered on the return leg. But it was not. The device that produced absolute darkness was no longer in operation. This was a tremendous relief.

Circling back, the bronze man flew until he came to a forested area where Monk and Ham had bailed out of the leviathan speed plane. The black was definitely no longer present.

He spotted the white bells of their collapsed parachutes blowing along the ground. They were being hauled along a grassy area by playful winds. Doc's golden eyes, sharp as those of an eagle, searched for Monk, Ham and Emile Zirn.

The bronze man spotted Zirn first. Over a field of brown grass, he was being carried off into a thick stand of evergreens, arms and legs waving wildly. Vainly, the man was struggling with his captors.

But there were no captors to be seen!

Doc banked, came around. He dropped the amphibian's altitude. Made another pass.

This time, Doc saw clearly that Emile Zirn was being held aloft by—absolutely nothing!

The man was fighting to get free. His fists were lashing out, pounding at his captor, but the thing or things conveying him into the forest were invisible! Horror twisted his features.

One pass was all the bronze man needed to ascertain that fact. There was no mistaking the phenomenon. A full-grown man was being borne away by an unknown force.

Myriad footprints were appearing as if magically around Zirn as he was carted off. It was as though the unseen creature possessed multiple feet!

Then out from the trees charged Monk and Ham, superfirers in hand. They trained their weapons in the direction of the footprints, began firing. The weapons seemed to vibrate and become blurry, so rapidly did the mechanisms operate.

This caused a remarkable change in the behavior of the creature below.

As if enraged, it stopped. The footsteps ceased their centipede progression and began stamping about in place, mashing the dead grass crazily.

Emile Zirn's arms and legs suddenly stretched out. He threw back his head, and his mouth opened in what must have been a howl of sheer agony.

The meaning of this became apparent. The creature was attempting to tear Emile Zirn's arms and legs off his body!

Grimly, Doc searched for a spot to land. There was none nearby. All was tall pines.

The bronze giant flew on until he came to a lonely highway. It was not an ideal landing spot, but he made the best of it.

Dropping his wheels, Doc lowered the flaps, reduced airspeed and made a first approach. The road was not empty of vehicular traffic, but it appeared to be a country road and therefore not very busy.

Doc came in, centered on a stretch of road that ran more or less straight, then chopped power to the two mighty motors.

Doc's aircraft was a flying boat, so the wheels came down from the keel-like hull. This feature made landing on anything other than a regulation airstrip extremely perilous.

Fortunately, the road was blacktopped, the grade relatively flat.

Doc set the big bronze bird down with a low rumble and only two distinct jars, when wheels encountered shallow chuckholes.

A motorcar, rounding a corner, suddenly slowed. The vehicle backed up, scooted around, and tore off in the opposite direction—no doubt to give warning.

Doc braked one wheel—the starboard—throwing the great aircraft into a moaning turn. It went up on a low dirt embankment, and jerked to a stop.

Cutting power, Doc plunged out. The cabin door had not been closed after the bailing out of Monk and Ham. He ran toward the stand of firs.

The hooting of supermachine pistols came distinctly.

It was nearly a mile to the scene of the amazing action. Doc redoubled his speed, took to the trees and made excellent time, jungle-fashion.

When he emerged from the forest, only Monk and Ham were in evidence, the muzzles of their machine pistols still smoking. They were administering first aid to Emile Zirn, who lay sprawled on the ground, arms and legs extended like a beached human starfish.

Monk whirled at sight of the bronze man.

"Doc! You made it!"

"What happened here?" rapped Doc.

"We landed O.K. and went lookin' for Zirn here. But before we got to him, we heard a commotion. Lots of caterwauling."

Ham added, "We discovered this man Zirn being carried off by something very large and invisible. It was covered with multiple orbs."

Doc's trilling wavered out. He stifled it.

"Yeah," added Monk. "They didn't look human. What I mean, the eyes didn't come in pairs. They were all separate, looking in every direction at once. And they were round and staring, like cue balls."

Doc knelt to examine the writhing Zirn.

"This man's arms have been pulled out of their sockets," he announced.

Monk grunted, "Blazes! Imagine the strength of that blamed thing! It must have been the size of a dang elephant!'

Doc addressed the distraught man. "Zirn, what attacked you?"

But Emile Zirn only moaned and squirmed, his arms flopping helplessly in agony.

Doc grasped one wrist, set a foot into the man's sturdy ribs, and exerted a sudden yank. Something popped.

When the bronze man stepped back, Emile Zirn's right arm was back in its socket.

Doc moved around to repeat the operation on the other arm, but the pain was so terrible that Zirn shrank from his touch.

"Steady," Doc said. He took hold of the other arm and repeated his strenuous performance.

After that, Emile Zirn hugged himself and rolled over and over, moaning.

Doc addressed his men. "Did you hit the creature?"

"We couldn't tell!" Ham said wildly. "Our drums were charged with mercy bullets, so we aimed low to avoid striking Zirn, hoping to hit its legs."

"Yeah," seconded Monk. "The daggone monster began thrashin' about and makin' enraged sounds, but it wouldn't go down. Not to mention the fact that we weren't exactly eager to get any closer and arouse that snortin' centipede of a thing."

Doc directed his attention to Emile Zirn, who was slowly subsiding. "Zirn, what can you add to this?"

Emile Zirn struggled to get control of himself.

"It—it had more arms than a tarantula!" he groaned. "All of it covered with bristling hair."

Doc looked at him. "Your story sounds unbelievable, Zirn."

"Doc, we all saw it," interjected Monk.

"Or didn't, rather," admitted Ham.

Doc Savage passed up the opportunity for an argument. He began searching the immediate vicinity. He spotted the footprints in an area where the soil was still soft enough to take them. They were unshod. They reminded him of human footprints, bare, but their ends were fringed—as if the feet were covered on thick bristles.

"Reminds me of gorilla footprints," mused Ham. "Monk leaves similar tracks, after his Saturday night bath."

Doffing shoes and socks, Monk made a footprint next to one of those uncanny ones.

"Hairier than me," he decided.

"That is saying a great deal," quipped Ham.

Doc Savage followed the queer footprints into the forest, Monk and Ham trailing cautiously, eyes alert, muzzles of their supermachine pistols aimed at the way ahead.

They penetrated far into the trees. It was a thick place, vaguely unsettling even in bright afternoon sunlight. Dead grass showed signs of trampling. Habeas Corpus, the pig, placed his long snout over these spots and sniffed curiously.

"Big as a truck," Ham breathed.

"Bigger!" insisted Monk.

They trailed the uncanny spoor as far as they could. Rocks in the terrain began to multiply. Footprints became sparse. Doc led them onto the rocks, as if reading invisible sign.

"This dang thing is intelligent," muttered Monk. "It's tryin' to throw us off the scent."

Mention of scent caused Ham Brooks to look to the bronze man. Knowing that Doc's senses were trained beyond those of an ordinary mortal, he asked, "Can you smell the creature, Doc?"

The bronze man nodded. He had been using his nostrils all along.

"I do not recognize this odor," he admitted.

Monk began sniffing the air around him. Next to Doc, he possessed the most acute sense of smell. "Smells kinda like polecat."

Ham inhaled a long draught of air, made a face of disgust. "I am forced to agree with this ape, this once. It is a skunky smell, but rather faint."

While Doc was searching among the rocks, they heard a terrible shrieking from the direction where they had left Emile Zirn.

Reversing course, Doc sprinted back the way he had come.

Monk and Ham charged after him, Ham waving his unsheathed sword cane.

"It musta doubled back!" Monk howled.

THEY came upon Emile Zirn spread-eagled upon the brown turf, sprawled in a growing lake of scarlet. The area around his Adam's apple was as raw and red as a beefsteak.

"Throat cut!" Ham snapped.

Doc knelt, examined the man. A scarlet crescent at his throat bubbled, releasing life fluid.

"Zirn, what did this?"

A single gurgling word escaped the injured man's encrimsoned lips.

"P-poly—"

"What did he say?" demanded Ham.

Monk scratched his rusty head. "Sounded like a girl's name. Polly."

"Speak up, Zirn," urged Ham.

But Emile Zirn would never speak again. Life was departing his jittering body. It gave a final convulsion, then subsided. The frantic light in his eyes began to dim. Then it died.

Doc Savage noticed something lying on the ground, almost hidden in the warm life fluid that was beginning to flow more sluggishly.

Using a handkerchief, he lifted it into view.

"Whatcha got, Doc?" asked Monk, squinting tiny eyes.

Sharp-eyed Ham answered for him.

"A bat!"

"A medallion in the shape of a bat," clarified Doc Savage. "See the broken chain? It had been worn about someone's neck and used to slash this man's throat."

Doc turned the grisly thing around in one hand. The wings were scalloped, after the fashion of a bat, and the eyes were mere hollows.

"The wings look sharp enough to do a bloody job," Ham breathed.

Doc nodded grimly. "The points of the ears are long, like stilettos. This is a murder tool."

"Where the heck did it come from?" asked Monk.

"Could Zirn have been wearing it around his neck?" wondered Ham.

Before that question could be answered, Doc Savage raised himself up and began looking for fresh spoor. He found fresh foot impressions.

"It went back into the forest," he decided.

Monk brandished his mercy gun. "Let's hunt it down!"

Just then, an unearthly howling came from the forest. It was a many-voiced caterwauling, indescribably discordant. It sounded as if a chorus of demons had commenced mourning one of their own.

"I don't like the sound of that," murmured Ham uneasily.

"Don't sound human to me," agreed Monk.

"To overcome this thing," said Doc Savage slowly, "we will need special equipment from our plane. Gas bombs. High powered rifles with mercy slugs of sufficient size to bring it down."

"What if it gets away?" asked Ham, anxiously.

"It will not get away," said Doc, turning in the direction of the plane.

Monk and Ham wasted no time in following their Herculean bronze chief. They had no stomach for confronting the unknown monster without their leader.

Chapter XI

COLD-BLOODED WOMAN

SPRINTING, DOC SAVAGE reached the road well ahead of his two aides. For all his colossal size, the bronze man could move like a hurricane. His speed gave lie to the theory that the fleetest sprinters were wiry of build.

A motorcar came whipping around the turning of the road near where Doc's aircraft rested in the sun. It was a cream-colored convertible machine, the canvas top folded down, and looked rather expensive.

A woman crouched behind the wheel. Seeing the big aircraft blocking the way, she flung the wheel to one side. The roadster lifted onto two wheels, balanced precariously. It appeared to be out of control.

The grille, like the open mouth of a steel-fanged shark, veered toward Doc Savage by the side of the road.

Doc leaped out of the way, landing in the shadow of one broad wing.

Careening, the car flipped over. The sound of crunching windscreen glass was heard. The auto came to rest like an upended beetle, its windscreen mashed flat. Glass shards were strewn everywhere.

Doc Savage put on speed, reached the overturned vehicle. Its tires still spun. Steam began hissing from the cracked radiator. Scalding water pooled underneath.

Doc made a rapid circle of the vicinity. There was no sign of the driver. Plainly, she was pinned beneath the vehicle, no doubt trapped behind the wheel.

Doc Savage moved in, wrapped metallic fingers around the molding of the driver's compartment. Powerful shoulder muscles bunched and writhed.

Without outward strain appearing on his metallic features, Doc began lifting the one-ton roadster!

Monk and Ham turned up at this point, faces concerned.

"Lend a hand," Doc rapped.

Monk lent his strength to Doc's own. He reached out hairy hands, helped heft the vehicle higher. Perspiration popped out on his minuscule forehead.

For his part, Ham Brooks set his sword cane aside and ducked under the machine while Doc and Monk kept it elevated. His dark eyes widened.

"It's a girl!" he cried out in surprise.

"What are you waitin' on?" Monk roared. "Haul her out!"

Frowning, the dapper lawyer dug around, found her arms and pulled the woman free. Carefully, he laid her out on the grass. She was entirely insensate. A rill of crimson fluid trickled out of her scalp.

Thinking that they were done with the roadster, Monk released his grip. But Doc Savage did not. He raised both arms and by main strength upended the mangled vehicle, pushing it back onto its wheels. It jounced in place, rocking on its springs.

"Whew!" said Monk, who was no slouch in the muscles department.

Reaching the girl's side, Doc Savage gave her a cursory examination. The wormlet of blood crawling from her hair entered one ear, but she appeared otherwise uninjured. From a pocket, the bronze man extracted a vial, unstoppered it and waved it under the girl's nostrils.

Reaction was instantaneous. Eyes fluttering, the girl began rousing back to life. She wore a winter coat of woolly sheepskin, of the type called Caracul. Her hair was so very dark that it might have been spun from ebony silk.

Her eyes—a very intense doe-black—focused on the tower-
ing Man of Bronze.

"You are Doc Savage," she said suddenly.

"Yes."

"I rushed here to warn you. The soldiers sighted your airplane.
They are coming to arrest you!"

"Why?"

"How can you ask that? Do you not know where you are?"

"Tazan," said Doc.

"No, you are in Ultra-Stygia, which is disputed land. If you
are arrested, you and your men are subject to being shot as
spies."

"Blazes!" squeaked Monk. "Doc, we'd better get back into
the air."

Doc Savage reached out to pick up the woman with the
intention of bearing her to the safety of the plane.

She pushed his hands away, flared. "Unhand me! I can walk!"

Surprise flickered in Doc Savage's eyes—a thing which rarely
happened. On other occasions Doc had encountered young
women with nerve. He had even considered some of these
remarkably brave. They were, however, shrinking violets in
comparison with this steely specimen.

She jumped to her feet. "What are you all waiting for? Irons
to clamp on your wrists?"

"What about you?"

"It would be better for me if I were not discovered where
you had landed," the dark-eyed woman admitted.

Doc Savage said, "Follow us, then."

They clambered aboard their craft, closed the door, and
brought the large aircraft back to life.

Turning about on one moaning engine, port brakes applied,
Doc got the amphibian lumbering back onto the road.

Pointing her into the wind, the bronze man advanced the
throttles. With a throaty song of power, the plane surged ahead.

The air wheels bounced more than usual, owing to the unevenness of the country blacktop.

Air flowing under the broad wings lifted the thundering amphibian off the road. The aircraft cleared the furred treetops of the forest, wheels cranking up into their hull wells.

Doc climbed to a safe altitude, and set course for Pristav.

"You have no conception of how dangerous was the territory you have just put behind you," the woman intoned.

"On the contrary," said Ham. "We just witnessed a man being carried off and murdered by a giant creature of prodigious strength."

The woman took that statement in stride. "Was—was this creature invisible?"

"It was," said Ham levelly. "Are you familiar with it?"

"Not 'it.' *Them*. We of Tazan call them by many names. The Invisible Ogres. The Hairy Ones. Polyphemes. *Ciclopi*."

For four or five seconds following that announcement, Doc Savage's weird trilling sound came into being and penetrated to the far corners of the cabin. Having no tune, yet melodious, inspiring without being awesome, the fantastic note seemed to come from everywhere.

The woman evidently did not realize whence it emanated. She looked around wonderingly. She remained wide-eyed with wonderment even after the sound died.

Doc Savage said from the cockpit, "Did you say *Ciclopi?*"

"Yes. Otherwise, Cyclopes."

"Jove!" cried Ham. "I remembered reading about them. Ulysses encountered one during his famous Odyssey. Polyphemus was the fellow's name. He was a one-eyed giant many times larger than a man!"

"This creature," Doc Savage interjected, "possessed several eyes."

"There are many species of *Ciclopi* dwelling in Ultra-Stygia," returned the woman. "Some are small and the size of an ordinary human. Others are gigantic, and boast many heads, eyes and hands. Only these orbs can be seen. Otherwise, their unhuman nature defeats the eye. They cannot be discerned under any light."

"What is your name?" Doc asked abruptly.

"Fiana Drost," she said.

Doc Savage did not show by his metallic expression that he had heard the woman's name spoken by Emile Zirn. He had not mentioned this exchange to his men. Instead, the bronze man asked, "How did you come to encounter us?"

"I am a citizen of Tazan. I was in Ultra-Stygia, searching for my American friend, Simon Page, who went missing."

"Page!" snapped Ham. "That was the man Long Tom went to find!"

"I do not know this Long Tom, but I have discovered no trace of Simon Page, who is said to have been captured by strange things that prowl Ultra-Stygia."

"By these creatures?" asked Doc.

The woman shrugged. "By them, or others. There are ghouls living in the caves of Ultra-Stygia. Things that fly at night that look like bats, but are the size of vultures. Men are found drained of their life's blood. Vampires do this, some say."

"The man who was with us had his throat cut," Ham offered.

Fiana Drost drew her long woolly winter coat more tightly about her slender form.

"For Ultra-Stygia," she imparted, "that passes for a normal death. I speak of those who are discovered without blood, showing the mark of the Undead on their throats. Two puncture wounds. Or their jugular veins slashed as if by a cruel beast. It is very unpleasant. I have seen this with my own eyes. A man named Zoltan, a countryman of mine, vanished. He was found in this condition. He subsequently died."

The cabin fell silent. Doc Savage and his men had encountered many strange things in their eventful and far-ranging careers. They were not credulous men, but they had learned not to be too skeptical. Especially where death was concerned.

At length, Fiana Drost spoke again. "This man who was found with his throat cut. What was his name?"

"Emile Zirn," supplied Ham.

The woman was silent for a space of seconds. "This Emile Zirn, what did he look like?"

Doc Savage gave a concise description of the man, omitting nothing important.

"I do not know this Emile Zirn," Fiana Drost said at last.

"He knew of you," Doc interjected.

Fiana waved a dismissive hand, saying, "Pah! Many men have tried to make love to me. Or wish that they could."

Ham, ever alert in his lawyerly mind, turned to the woman and asked, "Do you know another Emile Zirn?"

She fixed him with her unfathomably liquid eyes.

"Why do you ask me this question?"

"We have heard of an Emile Zirn who disappeared from a liner crossing the Atlantic, on his way to Pristav," said the dapper lawyer.

"I do not believe I know that Emile Zirn either," Fiana Drost returned thinly.

Monk and Ham exchanged glances. It was usually their way, when finding themselves in the company of an attractive young woman, to start tripping up one another in an effort to dominate the attention of the bit of femininity in question.

But this one time, the cold-blooded manner of this woman seemed to cool their usual ardor. They maintained a reserved decorum. Even Habeas the pig, always happy to hop into the lap of a young lady, spurned Fiana Drost.

Fiana volunteered, "I do not recommend that you fly directly to Pristav, where you will not be welcomed. For war appears to be in the offing and perhaps you will be dragged into it, in the event of a surprise attack by Egallah."

"Is such an attack expected?" asked Doc.

Fiana nodded firmly. "At any moment."

"We do not normally take sides in conflicts between nations," stated Doc quietly. "But we have business in this region."

"What manner of business?" inquired Fiana, arching one pencil-thin eyebrow.

Doc Savage failed to reply. He appeared busy with the controls and unhearing. It was a habit of his, not responding to a direct question if he preferred not to answer it.

Noticing this trait, she pressed Monk and Ham. "Why do you men come to this troubled land?"

Ham offered, "As Doc Savage said—business."

Fiana Drost gave up. Her dark eyebrows drew together and she fell solemnly silent once more. Despite the electrically warmed cabin, she seemed cold. For she drew her coat more tightly about herself.

Monk Mayfair spoke up. "Doc, do we start lookin' for Long Tom, or tackle the other problem?"

Doc Savage said, "Time is of the essence. We will split up. You and Ham will go in search of Long Tom. I will attend to the other matter personally."

Ham was on the radio and listening intently through headsets. After a time, the dapper lawyer jerked erect in his seat.

"Doc—that unnerving music again!"

"Cut it into the loudspeaker circuit," directed Doc.

Ham yanked the plug. Over the cabin loudspeaker, uncanny cadences came.

Hearing this, Fiana Drost gasped.

"What do you know of this?" demanded Ham suspiciously.

"It is the funeral march of the late King Vladislav of Tazan," she said. "Always it is heard over the radio these days."

"This is coming from Tazan?" asked Doc.

"Yes. They—we are in mourning."

Doc said nothing. He cocked his head to listen closely. At length, he said, "It does not follow the identical melody as the last time we heard it."

Fiana hastened to explain, "It is an improvised piece, you understand. A medley. It is not always the same each time it is performed."

"I don't recognize the instruments being played," Ham said slowly.

Fiana said, "There is only one instrument. The electric harp."

"Never heard of it," said Monk.

Doc offered, "The so-called electric harp is capable of unusual orchestral effects. It is sometimes employed in motion picture films to achieve musical atmosphere."

"It makes me want to shiver all over," admitted Ham.

"That is the point," said Doc.

They volleyed along for a time. Doc was flying north, to landlocked Egallah. The great expanse of Ultra-Stygia, which still bore signs of having been a battlefield during the Great War, unrolled below. Sunlight showed evidence of frost heaves here and there.

"Picturesque lakes," commented Ham.

"Those," corrected Fiana, "are bomb craters filled with water from a recent rain. Everything that you see below remains contested territory, even twenty years after the Armistice."

"Tazan controls it currently, do they not?" asked Ham.

"And has since the war ended. But Prime Minister Ocel of Egallah has sworn to repatriate it. He is a very determined man."

"So we've heard," said Monk.

"There have been many skirmishes there. Soldiers operating in Ultra-Stygia. But that is not the worst of it, of course. Things are a-prowl in the disputed area, things that cannot be killed by bullet or bayonet."

"So we saw," said Ham.

"Or didn't see," countered Monk. "All I could make out were the brute's eyes."

Ham suddenly asked, "Why are those beasts called *Ciclopi* when they have so many eyes? I fail to understand that part of it."

"It is rumored," said Fiana, "that the *Ciclopi* possess several separate heads, each equipped with one orb."

"That make sense, I guess," muttered Monk.

"It does not!" snapped Ham contrarily.

Doc Savage asked, "Did either of you notice the color of the creature's eyes?"

"Brown," asserted Ham.

"No, they were black," insisted Monk.

"Which is it?"

Fiana answered that. "One of the unpleasant things about the *Ciclopi* is that each head contains eyes of a different color. Some have seen blue eyes. Others, brown, gray, green. Even yellow has been reported."

Monk asked, "What do you make of that, Doc? It does kinda sound like we're dealin' with a Hydra-headed monster."

But Doc Savage declined to reply. What he thought, the bronze man kept to himself.

NOT many minutes later, Fiana Drost began fidgeting. She took to examining her nails distractedly, looking out the window often and exhibiting other evidence of internal worry.

"What is the matter?" asked Ham.

"I am unused to this flying," she admitted.

"It's perfectly safe," Ham assured her.

Fiana began glancing about the cabin. "I do not see any parachutes...."

"We kinda used them up gettin' this far," Monk admitted.

"I think we have one or two left," suggested Ham gallantly. "Would you feel better wearing one?"

"I would. Thank you."

Ham offered to help her climb into the parachute harness

and pack, but the woman refused assistance, going instead to the washroom where she donned the rig.

"Modest, I guess," muttered Monk.

Fiana returned, wearing the harness under her Caracul coat. Once she settled back into her seat, the dark-haired woman seemed to relax. For the first time, she began to make casual conversation.

"What manner of aircraft is this?"

Monk beamed. "It's Doc's personal bus. He designed it himself."

"It is a warplane?"

"No, Doc don't believe in armin' his birds."

"Remarkable! He is flying over disputed territory, and he goes unarmed."

"We can handle anything thrown at us," inserted Ham Brooks. "This ship is swifter and more maneuverable than any aircraft ever built. It is easily ten years ahead of its time."

Doc Savage did not contribute to this discussion. He was by nature reserved.

Fiana inclined her head in the direction of the unresponsive bronze man. "I imagine only he knows how to fly this remarkable aeroplane."

"Naw," said Monk. "Me and Ham are pilots, too."

"That is a relief to hear," drawled Fiana.

"Why is that?" asked Ham.

"I was worried what would happen if he were incapacitated. I have heard of pilots who have suffered heart attacks while flying. Catastrophe always follows."

"Flyin' out here, we each took turns in the control bucket," reassured Monk.

"You flew all the way from America in this aircraft?" Fiana sounded genuinely impressed.

"It was rough, but we made it," admitted Monk.

"May I inspect the controls?"

"Sure," said Monk, climbing out of the co-pilot bucket to allow the dark-eyed woman to take his place.

Fiana addressed Doc, "Mr. Savage, you must be the bravest of men."

Doc ignored the compliment.

"You have a reputation for being very capable. No doubt you will locate your man, Long Tom. And whatever other business you have here, it will be accomplished masterfully."

Her hand drifted out to touch his shoulder.

Doc Savage did something very natural for him. He colored with embarrassment. He turned his head, pretending to study the rugged terrain unreeling below.

Fiana Drost withdrew her hand. Unseen by the others in back, she slipped that hand into the fur-trimmed collar of her woolly coat.

In a flash, it came out, holding a hypodermic syringe. Setting the needle's point against the bronze man's shoulder, she used her thumb to press the plunger home, discharging the contents of the syringe into Doc's bloodstream.

Doc Savage reacted. His head jerked around. Whirling eyes fell upon the woman. Shock seemed to freeze the minute flakes in his animated irises. A long breath escaped his parted lips.

Then those eyes rolled up into his head, and Doc slumped over the controls.

Venting a shriek of horror, Fiana Drost jumped out of her seat.

"Look! He has fainted!"

Monk and Ham leaped from their seats, eyes wide and unbelieving.

"Blazes!"

"Great Scott!" howled Ham.

No longer under control, the amphibian slid off one wing, falling into a tailspin.

After that, all was chaos in close confines.

Monk and Ham battled to be the one to reach Doc. Fiana was in the way. This complicated rescue operations. Ham pulled her aside—not gently, either.

Fiana Drost retreated into the cabin of the plane, huddling by the cockpit door. Her eyes were fierce.

Monk and Ham got themselves untangled from one another. Only Monk was strong enough to haul Doc off the controls. He did so.

Ham dropped into the co-pilot seat and seized the dual controls. He began wrestling with the yoke, while working control pedals with his feet.

It took some time, but the dapper lawyer got the big amphibian straightened out. Soon, it was flying level.

Once the craft had been righted, Monk and Ham took stock of the situation.

It was the apish chemist who noticed the glass tube sticking out of Doc Savage's shoulder.

"For the love of mud! Doc's been doped!"

"That infernal woman!" howled Ham.

Just then cold slipstream filled the cabin, causing their heads to jerk around.

Monk and Ham were just in time to witness Fiana Drost's feet exit the cabin by the gaping door.

"Not again!" wailed Ham.

Chapter XII

EXECUTION ORDER

MONK MAYFAIR WAS bellowing, "She jumped!"

"What did you expect her to do—wait to be handcuffed?" snapped Ham. "She stuck Doc with that needle!"

A horrified expression roosted on the apish chemist's homely face. "Do you think it's poisoned?"

"How would I know?"

Monk reached over. With a hairy paw, yanked the syringe out of Doc's arm. He held the tip to his nose, sniffed curiously.

Ham asked, "What does it smell like?"

"Sedative," Monk decided.

"Not poison?" blinked Ham, relieved.

"I said it smelled like a sedative!" Monk yelled back. "I can't say for sure without runnin' a chemical analysis. And keep your eyes on your flying. We don't need to crash right now."

Neck reddening, Ham turned his attention back to his course. He banked the big plane, banked again, bringing it around in a great sweeping turn.

Laboriously, the giant amphibian began circling back.

"What are you doing?" demanded Monk.

"I want to see where that devil woman landed."

"Good thinking, for once. Why didn't you keep an eye on her?"

"Why didn't *you?*" Ham shot back waspishly.

"I thought you were watching her," Monk growled. "You sat

119

closer to her than I did."

After that, they were too busy raking the terrain with their eyes to argue the issue.

Ham sank the airplane lower, to aid in their reconnaissance.

They were skimming over open rolling hills. These looked peaceful. It was a beautiful winter's day. The skies were clear and the exact hue of blued steel.

"I don't see any parachute bell," Monk muttered. He had produced a pair of binoculars and was using them to sweep the ground below.

"She must have landed all right," Ham decided.

Monk shook his bullet head. "Not at this altitude. It would take longer. And there's no sign of a chute draggin' along in the dirt. Or hung up a tree, for that matter."

Ham gasped in horror. "Perhaps it failed to open."

"Would serve her right." Monk craned his blunt head around. "But by now I'd see the bell. And I don't."

Suddenly, Ham spoke up. His voice was thin and unreal.

"Look up," he said.

"Huh?"

"I said, 'Look upward,'" repeated Ham.

Monk Mayfair crabbed his upper body around and endeavored to gaze in the direction Ham was indicating.

There were two things fluttering up there in the clear blue sky.

One was Fiana Drost's Caracul coat. It was falling. No one was wearing it.

The other was the dark-haired woman herself.

She was a sleek black apparition. From head to toe, her body gleamed like wet skin. Stretching from each wrist to her ankles was a ribbed wing of some leathery kind. Another similar membrane connected her legs, which were flung wide.

Employing these appendages, she was holding herself loft.

"She looks like a big vampire bat!" Monk howled. *And she's flyin'!"*

Not flying perhaps, so much as gliding, they saw in the fleeting moment the aircraft swept under her. She appeared to be flapping her leathery wings. But it was difficult to tell. They caught only a glimpse of her.

What was certain was that instead of falling to earth, Fiana Drost was swooping along as if the open sky were her natural environment.

"No wonder she kept her coat buttoned up all the time!" Monk said, aghast.

"Could she—she—" Ham stuttered.

"Don't say it," muttered Monk. "All my life I ain't believed in vampires, and I don't want to start changin' my mind now...."

Ham flew on, face rigid, apparently stunned by what he had witnessed.

Monk shook him hard. "Ain't we gonna follow her, shyster?"

"What? Oh, yes!" said Ham, snapping out of his trance of incredulity. He began turning the great bronze bird around.

THE dapper lawyer was destined never to complete that turn, for out of the sun dropped a trio of monoplanes. Gray smoky lines ran past their windscreen. They resembled long cobwebs.

"Ain't that—?" Monk started to say.

"—Tracer bullets!" yelled Ham, throwing the amphibian into a sideslip.

Slamming the control yoke forward, Ham attempted to evade the attackers from above. He jockeyed about in the sky, performing chandelles, Immelmanns, and other acrobatic maneuvers that slammed them about in their seats.

Other aircraft climbed up to meet them. Two flights of modern fighters.

Soon, they were surrounded on both sides by formidable-looking warplanes. They were painted in the national colors of Egallah, whose night-black flag was emblazoned on their stabilizers.

"Better get on the radio before they shoot us out of the sky," Ham warned.

Monk rushed to the radio and worked it frantically. Normally fearless, his concern was for his insensate leader, Doc Savage, who lolled in the control bucket, helpless and unaware of their predicament.

"Doc Savage plane to Egallah fighters," he chanted. "This is Monk Mayfair transmitting."

A crisp response crackled out of the headphones, *"Doc Savage plane, do not resist. You are prisoner of the Republic of Egallah. You will follow us to military air field."*

Monk repeated this to Ham, "They want to lead us to an air drome."

Ham scowled back. *"Do we have any choice?"*

"I guess not," mumbled Monk. Into the microphone, he said, "Lead the way and we'll follow. We got a wounded man on board."

"Who is wounded?" demanded the voice.

"Doc Savage."

"We will have an army surgeon meet us at the air field."

Ham fell in behind the squadron of warplanes, his handsome face wearing a worried frown.

ONE of the reasons Doc Savage painted his super-speed planes a distinctive bronze was not ego, but to identify them when flying over foreign countries. The uniform metallic color made them unmistakable in the air, or when spotted from the ground. This precaution was because the bronze man was sometimes forced to fly over disputed territory, as was the case here.

The bronze hue was to signify that this was not a warplane, but an unarmed aircraft. Possibly, this precaution had kept them from being shot down from the beginning.

In any event, it was possible that they had been intercepted in order to avoid misunderstandings.

"They sounded reasonable," Ham said to Monk as they approached the air drome.

"Yeah. Let's hope they stay that way." He was pulling on Habeas' long ears absently.

The amphibian came in smoothly, wheels dropping electrically. Ham taxied the big plane to the far end of the field where a knot of soldiers in mud-brown uniforms were assembled. They stood with rifles at the ready.

"Welcomin' party," Monk grunted.

Ham snapped off the engines while Monk threw open the cabin door.

As the Egallan warbirds began landing one by one, an officer came aboard and introduced himself.

"I am Captain Bela, commandant of this air drome. Where is Doc Savage?"

"There," said Monk, pointing to the bronze man, who had been laid out in the aisle.

Captain Bela proved to be the base surgeon, for he began making a careful examination of Doc Savage.

"He is not dead!" Captain Bela sounded surprised.

Monk supplied, "He's doped or something. A woman did it. Name of Fiana Drost."

Interest flickered in the surgeon's dark eyes. He seemed to know the name; possibly he was only searching his memory.

Sticking his head out the cabin door, Captain Bela called for a stretcher to be brought.

"Doc Savage will be conveyed to the military hospital in Danla," he said firmly.

"Where is that?" Ham demanded.

"Nearby. He will be in excellent hands."

They stepped outside the plane. An ambulance wheeled into view. It was rather out-of-date, but the orderly who took possession of Doc Savage seemed efficient. It took four of them to lug the bronze colossus out of the plane and into the open ambulance bed.

Ham addressed the commanding officer. "We insist on going with him."

"That will be quite impossible," returned Bela. "You must be interviewed first. There is the matter of your flying over sovereign Egallan territory without official permission."

Ham explained, "Our friend, Long Tom Roberts, has disappeared in Tazan. We were on our way to locate him."

Monk added, "That's right. Only we ran into engine trouble and had to set down."

The captain nodded. "Yes, in Ultra-Stygia. This has been reported. A detachment of the Tazan Elite Guard was sent to seize you, but you apparently escaped."

"Could be," said Monk. "Thanks to Fiana Drost. She warned us. Then she up and did dirt to Doc."

Captain Bela gestured to a low building. "We will talk in my office. I assure you that your leader will be in good hands."

Having no other real or reasonable choice, Monk and Ham followed the commanding officer to his office. It proved to be in the building that also served as the operations shack. It was not a big air drome. There was more runway than anything else.

Arriving warplanes were lining up on either side of the tarmac. There were a lot of them. None were very old. So these were not surplus planes bought from other nations.

"Expecting a war?" Ham inquired.

"Maneuvers," returned the captain crisply. "We must be prepared in the event General Consadinos and his Tazan dogs attack."

"We understood that Egallah was preparing to invade Ultra-Stygia," said Ham, frowning.

"Here in the Balkans," said the captain, "the wind changes direction several times a day."

IN the commandant's office, they were served hot coffee and invited to tell their stories.

Ham took the lead. He left out a lot. The unbelievable matter of the invisible things of many eyes and presumed heads was one morsel the agile-tongued lawyer chose to keep to himself. Ham did not wish for his credibility to suffer.

Captain Bela listened intently to it all before commenting. "Fiana Drost, you said the woman's name was?"

"Yes," confirmed Ham. "We know nothing about her, other than the fact that she presented herself to us as a friend."

"But she stabbed us in the back once we got into the air," added Monk.

"And you say that she jumped from your aircraft after stabbing your leader." The commandant snapped his fingers. "Just like that?"

"She appeared to be a cool customer," allowed Ham.

Monk put in, "If you search, you might find her parachute. Or her body."

"We have searched," returned the commandant. "And I regret to inform you that we found neither."

That was all they said about the cold-blooded woman. Monk and Ham left out the apparent fact that she had turned into some kind of human bat after leaving their amphibian. That, too, was a gesture toward maintaining their credibility.

At the end of the interview, Monk and Ham were told, "We must detain you until we ascertain if your story checks out in all particulars."

"Say, who do you think—" Monk started to say.

Ham elbowed him sharply. "This is a reasonable request, commandant," he said smoothly. "We only ask that we be permitted to see Doc Savage as soon as practical."

"Rest assured, you will join your bronze chief before the night comes on."

Monk subsided. He had brought Habeas Corpus along with him. As they were escorted from the office, he toted the shoat by one oversized ear. Habeas seemed not to mind at all. Actually, seemed to enjoy it.

Armed guards arrived to escort them to another building. And only when they saw iron window bars did the pair understand that it was what passed for a stockade or brig.

"Is this necessary?" Ham demanded sharply.

The commandant returned in a reasonable voice, "We hardly have hotel accommodations here. And besides, there is someone you would like to meet who is also our guest."

"And who is that?" asked Ham.

The captain smiled under his brush mustache.

"I do not wish to spoil the surprise," he said smoothly.

THE surprise—and it was a very big one—was that once they were thrown into a cell, they heard a familiar voice call out to them. It came from a cell farther along.

"Monk—Ham, is that you?"

"Long Tom!" hissed Ham.

"You skinny runt! What are you doin' here?" demanded Monk.

"Search me. I was following a bird named Emile Zirn."

"We know the guy," offered Monk. "He tried to contaminate our gas supply in Ireland. But we got him."

Ham added, "We brought him as far as Ultra-Stygia, then he bailed out."

"Got away, huh?"

"Not quite," said Ham thinly. "Something attacked him in the woods."

"Wolf or beast?"

"I wish it was either—or both," said Ham fervently.

Monk growled, "Let's skip that part, Long Tom. How'd you wind up here?"

"As I was saying, I followed Emile Zirn—"

"Must be a different Emile Zirn," murmured Ham.

"Will you let me tell it!" snapped Long Tom.

The others fell quiet.

"I followed Emile Zirn to a hotel," continued Long Tom.

"The clerk gave me the runaround, but I got the better of him. Found the room where Zirn was supposed to be. At the door, I heard strange music coming from inside."

"Strange?" said Ham.

"Like the organ music of Hades."

"We heard some of it, too," said Monk. "Over our plane radio. It's spooky-soundin'." Pursing his lips, the gorilla-like chemist assayed a few bars of the composition. "Like that."

Long Tom nodded. "I heard a similar tune on the liner, as well. Anyway, I was eavesdropping at the hotel room door and someone slipped up behind me and pushed me into another room. After that, I found myself in darkness fighting... things."

"What kind of things?" asked Monk.

"Dark leathery things. They seemed to have wings. They outnumbered me. I couldn't fight them all. Before I knew it, I was out cold. When I woke up, I was here. Jugged."

"Wait a minute! You were knocked out in Pristav, but you woke up here in Egallah?"

"Is that where I am?" Long Tom sounded dazed.

"You must have stumbled upon a nest of Egallan spies operating in Pristav to wind up here," suggested Ham.

"Nest is right," murmured Long Tom. "I don't think those devils were human."

"Hmm," mused Ham. "I imagine you were spirited here."

"How would I know?" said Long Tom peevishly. "I was dead to the world."

Monk interjected. "We happened on a woman named Fiana Drost. Name ring a bell?"

"Never heard of her," admitted Long Tom.

"She stuck Doc with a sedative, then jumped out of our plane. Only she never cracked her chute."

"Dead?"

"Last we saw of her," said the hairy chemist, "she was flappin' away like a harpy out of the hot place. Had big bat wings, and all the trimmin's."

"I saw the same apparition," Ham Brooks admitted.

Long Tom made a sound of disgust. "You are describing the leathery things that waylaid me. It was dark so I could not see them clearly. But when they moved, their arms rustled like wings."

"I was afraid you'd say that," Ham rejoined. "By reputation, this region is the birthplace of the vampire legends."

"Feelin' anemic, Long Tom?" Monk asked carefully.

"Bunk!"

Having ridded himself of that vehement expostulation, the pale electrical wizard was silent a very long time. They took a few moments to absorb everything they had heard.

After a while, Long Tom thought of something to contribute to the general gloom.

"That is not the worst of it," he intoned. "I am to be shot at midnight as a spy."

That statement took only a half second to sink in.

"Midnight?" exploded Monk dubiously.

"Not sunrise?" asked Ham, looking at his wrist watch.

"They do things differently in Egallah," Long Tom said dryly. "Anyway, I was wearing a disguise, so they decided I must be a spy."

"If they plan to shoot you," Ham said slowly, "it stands to reason that we are slated for the same fate."

"There's nothing reasonable about being stood up against a stone wall and perforated!" Monk objected.

"I will not argue that point—for once," returned Ham. "But if they are going to shoot us without due provocation, or legal justification, what are they going to do with Doc Savage?"

"Probably put him to work," said Long Tom.

"Say again?"

"That's what they tried to get me to do. I wouldn't play ball, so it's a blindfold and a last cigarette for mine."

"What kind of work?" asked Ham.

"I suspect that it had to do with the darkness-making machine Baron Karl got away with," Long Tom said slowly.

Monk grunted, "We know. They turned it on us the minute we flew within range."

"That's the funny part of it," Long Tom said. "I got the idea that these people have been experiencing unexplained blackouts. So they know something strange is going on, but they don't know what's causing it. They wanted me to devise a protection."

"That don't make sense," Monk muttered.

Ham Brooks broke in. "Sounds as if that Baron Karl has not yet surrendered the device to his regime."

"Can you blame him?" Long Tom retorted. "Egallah has experienced a grisly wave of political killings these last few years. He may need to control it to stay alive."

"As long as it ain't the work of that danged John Sunlight," Monk offered.

Another prolonged silence followed. Mention of the dreaded name of their nemesis, the arch-devil who had caused all their recent troubles, further suppressed their spirits.

Monk broke the gloom. "I just noticed something."

"What is it?" asked Ham.

"That shadow on the wall over there. It looks exactly like a gallows."

Ham made a gesture as if to whack the simian chemist with his cane, but realized that he had prudently left his stick back in the plane.

"You would think of something cheerful like that!" he complained.

Chapter XIII

A SPY RESCUED

DOC SAVAGE CAME to returning consciousness, not in the promised hospital ward, but in an infirmary room of another type of building entirely.

He saw the iron bars. They were very thick. The window was constructed out of blocks of stone and looked very old, if not ancient.

Doc arose, took stock of his surroundings. The chamber had the appearance of a very modern hospital room. His head felt all right. He examined his person for damage, found only some bruising here and there. A bandage had been applied to the puncture mark on his arm.

Getting out of bed, Doc went to the window and scrutinized his surroundings.

To all appearances, he was in a high room in a stone castle that might have been built around the time the Huns were sacking Pristav.

A rattle of a doorknob indicated someone about to enter.

Doc moved to the door, set himself at one side.

A doctor entered. His eyes fell on the empty bed. Then he felt great metallic hands clamp around his throat, stifling any outcry he might vent.

Retaining his chokehold, Doc lowered the man to the stone floor while closing the door with his foot. His amazing vitality had returned. There was none of the giddiness of the effects of prolonged sedation.

"Who are you?" asked Doc, in the man's own language.

"Dr. Bronislaw. At your service."

"Where is this place?"

"Castle Groava."

"In Egallah?"

"The very same," the doctor allowed.

"Where are my men?" asked Doc.

"Under guard. Elsewhere. It is not my station to know."

Doc Savage placed a reassuring bronze hand on the physician's shoulder, and performed a chiropractic maneuver on a nerve center. The man promptly lost consciousness.

Doc caught him and laid the man out on a couch. Harvesting and donning the other's white doctor's smock, Doc cracked open the door and set one golden eye on the corridor without. He saw military guards. They were armed. They failed to notice him. One yawned widely; the other followed suit.

The metallic giant went next to the window and tested the bars. They were strong. But the mortar holding them fast was aged. It crumbled here and there.

Using nothing more than his muscular strength, Doc Savage began twisting the bar that appeared sunk in the loose mortar. Soon, it began grinding and complaining as he rotated it in place. With a firm yank, Doc broke it free, tossing it onto the bed where it made no noise landing.

The second bar proved more stubborn.

Doc felt about his person. He had not been wearing his vest of gadgets, nor his alloy-mesh union suit undergarment that would normally have protected him from the syringe attack. Both were too cumbersome to wear during a transatlantic hop, and further represented significant risks should he have to ditch over open ocean. So Doc lacked many of his gadgets. But his shoes were beside the bed. He went to them, picked up both. Removing the heels, he extracted two vials. Uncorking them, he poured their contents on the second bar. Then the third.

A bubbling hissing commenced. Doc withdrew and covered his mouth and nose with a pillowcase to protect his lungs from the violent fumes.

He used a pillow—which he vised in one hand—to wrest loose the acid-burned bars and deposited them on the bed, where they continued smoking malodorously.

Levering himself out, Doc used his finger strength to find purchase. He peered up and then down. Up looked more promising.

Fingertips digging into cracked and broken mortar, the mighty bronze man ascended the thick stone wall until he reached the crenellated roof combing. Going over this was a simple matter.

From this vantage point, Doc could see the air drome some miles distant. An Egallan flag chattered in the cold wind. There was little other activity visible.

Doc reconnoitered the roof, keeping low, and peered from between the merlons. He quickly learned that the castle stood on a prominence and that there were any number of ways down to the ground, provided he was not spotted.

Doc chose the wall that overlooked a number of parked vehicles sitting in a cinder-strewn patch of ground.

Dropping one leg over the notch between two merlons, Doc began his descent. It was smooth going. He could climb many New York skyscrapers in just this fashion, and their surfaces were much smoother, being composed of polished granite with very narrow edges and inset mortar lines.

These rough stone blocks were like steps. Doc reached the ground without incident. He eased to the line of motorcars, his feet making almost no noise traversing the cinders, selected one and tried the door. It opened to his touch.

Slipping behind the wheel, Doc placed a finger on the starter. He hesitated.

Years of training had taught him that escaping tight spots is rarely as easy as it seemed. This smacked of being too convenient.

Doc hesitated. He ducked behind the wheel lest his giant form be seen.

The parking area stood at the top of an inclined road. That gave Doc an idea. Releasing the clutch, he exited and gave the machine a flowing shove.

The car began backing out of the space.

Rushing back behind the wheel, he took control, and began steering.

Soon, gravity and momentum were carrying the freewheeling sedan backwards down the winding road. Doc steered with the help of the rear-vision mirror.

The road wound in such as way it was impossible to know what lay around the next corner. An oncoming car would prove inconvenient, if not dangerous.

As he maneuvered, his flake-gold eyes ever alert to his surroundings, Doc Savage spotted activity in one corner of the castle.

A line of soldiers were exiting a side door with what appeared to be a prisoner. They were led by an officer. Rifles were carried military-style, resting against their shoulders. The soldiers wore brown uniforms the hue of Missouri mud.

Doc braked, bringing the car to a smooth, noiseless halt.

Something about the prisoner evoked a memory of familiarity.

Doc Savage's eyesight was unusually acute. It took only a moment for him to ascertain the identity of the prisoner.

It was Fiana Drost!

ENGAGING the hand brake, Doc left the vehicle at once. Despite what had come before, he was not about to leave the cold-blooded woman to an unknown fate. Furthermore, she could be the key to some of the strange things that were happening in this complicated corner of the Balkans.

Moving low, Doc reached a decorative hedgerow and hunkered down, listening.

It soon became clear that this was a firing squad.

Under command of the officer, Fiana Drost was placed before one of the castle's outer walls in the customary manner. She looked resolute, but resigned. Her composed expression might have been that of one preparing to face eternity.

The officer spoke up.

"You, Drost, have been found guilty of plotting against Egallah!"

The dark-haired woman winced. Her chin lifted in defiance, however.

"And for this you have been sentenced to death. Have you any last words?"

Fiana shook her head. She swallowed hard. Her eyes were hot with pent tears.

A cigarette was offered from a silver case. Fiana refused it without a word.

The obligatory blindfold was tied over her doe-dark eyes. Her hands were already bound behind her back. Her entire body stiffened.

The order to present arms came. Rifles snapped to brown shoulders.

Doc Savage picked up a rock, hefted it and let fly.

It sailed gracefully over the intervening space and knocked the commanding officer off his shiny boots. His nose broke when it struck the flagstone courtyard.

Consternation seized the firing squad. A man blew a whistle.

Doc Savage popped up from concealment, letting them have a good look at him. They obligingly charged in pursuit, cursing fervently in the language of Egallah.

Doc led them on a chase to the waiting vehicle. He ducked inside. This time, he engaged the engine. It muttered to life. Doc depressed the gas pedal, and reeled away along the winding approach road.

The firing squad reached the roadside and someone took

charge. He barked out an order to kneel and fire. It was obeyed.

Evidently, the riflemen forgot for a moment that they composed a firing squad, for six men pulled triggers and were rewarded by six futile clicks.

The seventh soldier's bullet ripped out of its muzzle and spanked off the rear bumper, scoring chromium.

Doc abruptly sent the car into a screeching turn and accelerated up the road, straight at the kneeling execution squad.

Consternation ensued. Muddy brown uniforms broke in all directions. Doc flew past them, reached the courtyard and leaped for Fiana Drost.

At the sound of the solitary rifle discharge, the woman had apparently fainted or something.

Doc scooped her up and deposited the dark-haired woman into the passenger seat. Clamping the driver's door shut, he took off again.

On the lower road, the firing squad was reassembling itself. A whistle blew shrilly. Men were digging into uniform blouse pockets for spare ammunition.

One hit pay dirt. He got his rifle reloaded, brought it up, fired once.

Doc Savage blew through the scattered men like a hurtling juggernaut.

In passing, a bullet smacked the rear window, shattering it. The slug lodged in a car seat, all but spent.

Remarkably, that was the extent of the attempts to inhibit the bronze man's escape.

Doc reached the roadway below and turned south, in the direction of the military air drome where he had spotted the bronze glint of his great amphibian from the castle's roof.

There, he hoped he would find Monk and Ham.

Chapter XIV

ESCAPE

MONK MAYFAIR AND Ham Brooks—not to mention Long Tom Roberts—had no intentions of waiting for Doc Savage to come out of his narcotic coma. It was often on such occasions—and there were many—when one of the aides was unjustly imprisoned, allowing the Man of Bronze to straighten out affairs was the prudent thing to do. He could cut through red tape like no one's business. Failing that, the bronze man was a genius at defeating capture. His men often suspected him of having gleaned the secrets of the great escape artists of the past. But Doc never spoke of that.

This was one time when they were left entirely to their own devices.

Monk put it best. "No tellin' how long Doc will be in whatever hospital they shipped him off to."

"That sedative's effects could last for days," admitted Ham glumly.

From somewhere up the cell corridor, out of their sight, Long Tom put in, "So you two are saying that if we want to escape that firing squad, we have to fend for ourselves."

"That's what I'm sayin'," said Monk. "Got any ideas, Long Tom?"

"It just so happens I was planning on busting out of this hoosegow around supper time."

Ham perked up. "You have a plan?"

"Better. I have a half-dollar."

"That won't buy us much," muttered Monk.

"No? Watch this."

Lifting his voice, Long Tom called out, "Guard! Guard!"

No one responded, so Monk and Ham joined the chorus. They yelled and complained loudly, taking off their shoes, using them to pummel the cell bars. This produced no results.

"Anyone know the local word for guard?" asked Ham, restoring his footwear.

None of them did, so they changed their yelling to screams of pain and distress.

Eventually a warder showed up, key ring jangling at his hip.

"What is the matter?" he demanded in a suspicious voice.

Monk pointed to the adjoining cell. "Our buddy, Long Tom. It's his stomach. It's always actin' up."

Lying on his cot, Long Tom clutched his belly and bayed like a hound dog in gastric distress. It was a very convincing performance.

The guard looked concerned. "What is wrong with him?"

"Damn jail grub," groaned Long Tom. "Gave me ptomaine."

"He needs better food than he is getting," Ham suggested hopefully.

Turning away, the guard grumbled, "He is to die soon. He does not need any food."

"No last meal?" asked Monk, looking disappointed. Monk liked his food.

"Perhaps some bread and water later."

"Look here," moaned Long Tom. "I have a half a dollar, American money. Will that buy me some decent chow?"

The guard looked suddenly interested. He whirled from the door through which he had been planning to exit, approached the cells, eyes avid. He was mentally computing how many meals fifty U.S. cents could purchase—for himself.

"Show money," he undertoned.

Reaching into a pocket, Long Tom said laconically, "Here."

The other made an impatient gesture. "Toss coin to me."

Sitting up, Long Tom attempted to throw the half-dollar. It fell short, falling inside the cell itself.

"I cannot reach," complained the guard, who got down on one knee and stretched his arm through the iron bars as far as he could manage.

"Hold your horses," said Long Tom, levering himself up on his cot with evident pain writhing over his pale features.

Standing up, the undersized electrical genius made his way to the coin. With one toe, he gave it a nudge. It skidded a little, just within reach of the eager guard, but still remaining within the jail cell.

Lunging eagerly, the guard went to grab for the coin. Long Tom clicked his heels together just as the guard's grasping fingers touched the coin. He failed to see the thin trailing wires which snaked back to Long Tom's shoe heels.

When the guard's fingertips brushed the coin, he began doing a jig on his knees. He howled, moaned, and made frantic contortions with his suddenly-rubbery body.

Long Tom separated his copper-plated heels. The electrical charge coming from tiny dry-cell batteries secreted in each shoe heel cut out. The guard's convulsions instantly ceased. To the accompaniment of a long groan, he folded up into a heap.

Satisfied that it was safe to do so, the slender electrical wizard stepped up and clouted the guard on the jaw by shooting one rock-hard fist between the door bars.

The guard collapsed. It was a simple matter to confiscate his key ring.

"Trick coin, eh?" Ham said, who had witnessed some of it.

Long Tom pocketed the device. "Yeah. Been waiting for a chance to use it on someone."

Monk grinned. "I use 'em myself."

"I will take that as a confession of guilt," sniffed Ham. "You've been winning too many coin tosses lately."

"Luck, I call it," Monk said brightly. "Runs in the family."

Long Tom unlocked his cell door, showed himself. He looked as if he had just crawled out of a coffin—which for the puny electrical wizard was perfectly normal.

Fumbling at the lock for some moments, Long Tom finally got Monk and Ham loose. They stepped out.

The guard had a sidearm. Monk and Long Tom made a grab for it. Long Tom won. Monk decided not to challenge him for possession. Long Tom's temper was nothing to fool with on a good day. Facing the prospect of a firing squad, he was undiluted poison.

They reached the passage and tumbled out, uncaring who or what they encountered. The trio were in no frame of mind to be cautious. Escape was uppermost in their thoughts.

Long Tom led the way, revolver jutting from his fist. He stretched his pale head around a corner and hastily withdrew it.

"Two guards," he whispered. "Both armed."

"I'll fix 'em," Monk decided.

Suiting action to words, the hairy chemist bounded around the corner and fell upon the unsuspecting guards with all the enthusiasm of a bull gorilla harvesting coconuts.

In this case, the coconuts were the heads of the two unprepared guards.

Normally, Monk liked to howl during an ambush. But that would be unwise in this case. So he simply charged around the corner and grasped heads, got them firmly in the crooks of his hairy arms, and began conking the heads together. Ten seconds of this made the hapless men as loose and unresisting as puppets. Monk dropped them and grabbed up one fallen sidearm. Ham got the other.

They took a minute to break open the revolvers and count ammunition.

"Enough for a start," Monk decided, snapping his pistol back together.

"Let's go!" hissed Ham.

Habeas trotted after them. He had been sleeping in the corridor. The pig had a way of never getting very lost.

They traversed two corridors before they heard sounds ahead. Everyone drew to a skidding stop. Except Habeas Corpus. The long-legged shoat's hoofs failed to find traction on the polished stone floor and he went skidding around the corner ahead of them all.

Habeas was spotted at once. He made an abrupt about-face and retreated, ears straining out like wings.

SHOUTS, the sounds of weapons slithering from holsters, rifles being cocked came distinctly. In full cry, men came running in their direction.

Monk, Ham and Long Tom considered resistance, decided against it.

Instead, they dropped to the floor and laid themselves out in a row.

The soldiers charged around the corner and began tripping over their outstretched forms, making a confused pile of arms and legs.

Pistols abruptly left hands, yanked by upward-snatching fingers. Fists reached up, connected with jaws and noses. Monk rapped a man on his skull with his own gun butt. They began flinging the fallen off them.

In a trice, the scrappy trio were on their feet, holding the weapons on the captured soldiers. They positively bristled with arms.

"I didn't think that old gag would work," Long Tom observed.

"It always works," boasted Monk, grinning.

The soldiers lifted their hands above their heads—an easy thing to do when one is prostrate upon a cold stone floor. They looked astonished, if not down right embarrassed, at their plight.

Ham asked, "What do we do with them?"

"Their uniforms might fit you and Long Tom, but not me,"

decided Monk.

Long Tom nodded. "That's good enough." They began exchanging clothes.

When that operation was completed, Monk Mayfair enthusiastically brained each and every conscious man with a pistol butt.

"That settles that," he said with undisguised glee.

A minute later, Monk was being marched out of the place, hairy hands held high, at the rifle points of Ham and Long Tom, each wearing Egallah brown.

Habeas trotted along, ears erected, playing prisoner.

It was a bold plan, but plans born of desperation are often thus. They did not speak the local language, except Ham who could muster up a smattering of the tongue, but probably not enough to get them by most situations.

So they settled for boldness and confidently marched the hairy chemist out onto the tarmac.

They were not spotted at once as they exited. It took three or four minutes for the apish form of Monk Mayfair trudging along to draw attention.

A voice called out. It was gruff, questioning. They understood none of it.

Ham waved at the man, said nothing.

Another cry came.

This time, Long Tom waved them off angrily, as if it were none of their business.

Ham threw in a stray word or two of Egallanese, which he recalled meant, Mind your own business.

That gained them a few yards of marching.

When they spotted their amphibian plane on the side of the tarmac, they decided to make a run for it.

That brought howls of protest from all directions.

Monk pulled two pistols from his belt, where they had been concealed. He fired wildly in all directions, not caring whom he hit. Monk was blood-thirsty that way.

Ham and Long Tom were more cautious. Ham sighted, unloosed discouraging lead and kept going. He was a fair sprinter.

In this fashion they reached their plane. Monk got there first, hauled open the door and they piled in. The door slammed behind them, just before a bullet drummed against it.

Ham got the motors going. The self-starters were designed for cold weather such as this. The engines were kept warm by a circulating chemical.

Releasing the brakes, Ham got the amphibian rumbling onto the runway and moving fast.

"Where was the prevailing wind?" he asked frantically, eyes searching the field for the tell-tale wind sock.

None of them had taken the time to notice.

"Just get us upstairs!" Long Tom yelled.

Rifle bullets began arriving. Lead spanked off hull and wing surfaces. Doc's planes were all bulletproofed. But there remained points in vulnerability. The tires, for example. They could be shattered by a high-powered rifle slug, properly placed.

"If they hit the wheels with a lucky shot," warned Ham, "we might not get her off the ground safely."

"Fly this bus and leave the defendin' to us," called Monk from the door, which he had flung open. He was blazing away with a supermachine pistol he had extracted from an equipment case.

The apish chemist had not taken the time to see what kind of drum the fearsome weapon was charged with. It turned out to be demolition shells.

Monk discovered this when he fired a single test shot at a military truck from which two men were firing.

The truck jumped into the air in a jumble of smoke and noise. Fire tongues spurted. All firing from that quarter ceased.

"My lucky day!" enthused Monk, grinning from ear to ear.

Setting the tiny weapon to constant fire, he began hosing buildings, warplanes and everything else that could be used to block off the tarmac, or follow them into the air.

The air shook with prodigious detonations. They were thundering. It was as if volcanoes were going off all around. Uniformed men fled in every direction, seeking escape, but finding additional explosions. One man lost his head. Literally.

"Knock it off!" Long Tom yelled back. "Some of that shrapnel could wing us."

Monk cut loose with a final punishing blast and slammed the door shut.

The rumbling tail wheel was lifting off the tarmac by now. Immediately, they were vaulting into the lowering sky.

Monk and Long Tom hastily took seats.

"We sure fixed their wagons," chortled Monk.

"Yeah, that we did," said Long Tom, slapping his thin hands together, signifying a job well done.

"There's only one problem," murmured Ham, climbing the plane.

"What's that?" wondered Monk.

"I think we just declared war on Egallah."

Monk placed his homely face to a window, looked back and saw the ruin that was the military air field.

"If we did," he decided, "we won, hands down."

Ham frowned. "But they're the one with the blackness machine we're trying to recover."

"We'll worry about that later. We found Long Tom, got him busted loose—"

Long Tom flared up. "What do you mean—got me loose?" snarled the irate electrical wizard. "Who had the shocking coin?"

"True. But you couldn't have broke out all by your lonesome. It took Ham and me to haul you out of there. We had the getaway plane, don't forget."

"Glory hog," accused Long Tom.

Monk shrugged carelessly. "Anyway, we're free and clear. Now we gotta find Doc."

"So where do we look for him?" asked Long Tom reasonably.

The expressions on the faces of Monk and Ham plainly told that they did not have an inkling.

"This," grated Long Tom, "is going to be complicated."

Chapter XV

STARTLING SURPRISES

AS IT TURNED out, Doc Savage found them.

Driving in the direction of the military base, the bronze man spotted the explosions. These were hard to overlook.

His eyes went to the titanic eruptions and he recognized from their violence and the extremely black color of the resulting smoke that they were created by the high-explosive demolition shells from one of his superfirers.

So Doc was not greatly surprised when the bronze amphibian lifted into view, angled off, and picked up a heading in his general direction.

The direction of flight was not perfectly aligned with Doc's route, however. He braked, jumping for the side of the road. Normally, he might have employed his pocket radio transceiver or a smoke grenade to attract attention. But he had none of these on his person.

So Doc collected several very large stones and arranged them in the grass so that they spelled out a word.

D O C

It might work, or it might not.

To insure that it did, the bronze man rushed back to the waiting car and found a spare can of gasoline and some matches in the glove compartment.

Pouring the gas over the arranged stones, Doc rasped the match alight and set fire to the stones. They erupted into leaping yellow tongues, like fiery devils dancing.

That seemed to work. The plane overflew the burning stones, turned and wobbled its wings. That was a signal that they had spotted him.

Doc pointed up the road. The pilot obligingly veered in that direction.

Returning to the sedan, the bronze man drove along, seeking a stretch of road where the aircraft might land safely.

One showed itself a mile up the thoroughfare. Doc pulled over to the shoulder of the road to signal that they attempt a landing.

The landing went well enough, Doc recognizing the sure hand of Ham Brooks at the controls from the way the wings held steady as they settled down prior to touchdown.

The amphibian coasted to a halt and Doc approached, Fiana Drost draped in his arms. He had scooped her out of the passenger seat.

Long Tom popped the hatch open.

A flicker of surprise crossed the bronze man's usually impassive countenance.

"Hi, Doc. I just broke Monk and Ham out of jail. Don't let them tell you different."

"What was all that commotion a minute ago?" asked Doc.

"Explain later. We practically decimated the Egallah air force back there."

Doc nodded. The bronze man handed Fiana Drost up. Long Tom reluctantly accepted the woman and the bronze giant climbed aboard.

Locking the door behind him, Doc charged for the control cabin.

"Where'd you find her?" asked Monk, jerking a thumb at Fiana Drost, whom Long Tom had deposited on a seat, strapping her in for safety's sake.

Doc replied, "In front of a firing squad."

"Must be firing squad day in Egallah," declared Ham.

Doc let the comment pass for the moment. He seized the controls and booted the craft around and into the wind.

The big bird took off with a remarkably short amount of runway. Doc made it look easy. The high wing possessed superior aerodynamic lifting power.

CLIMBING to cloud level, Doc Savage said, "Your story, please."

Long Tom went first, filling the bronze man in. He began with his encounter with the mysterious Countess Olga on board the *Transylvania,* her subsequent vanishment, as well as that of Emile Zirn, who also vanished for a time.

"But I smelled a rodent," Long Tom concluded, "and picked up his trail. All I got for my pains was to be chloroformed in the dark and abducted to Egallah."

Doc Savage listened to Long Tom's account in silence, then requested, "Describe Zirn."

"Smooth faced sort," Long Tom said. "Average height. Continental clothes. Nothing special."

"That doesn't sound like the Emile Zirn we encountered," Ham mused. "Besides, he is now dead."

"How did he die?" asked long Tom.

"An invisible monster pulled him apart, then cut his throat," said Monk carelessly.

Long Tom looked to the hairy chemist for signs of humor, and found none.

"The Emile Zirn we happened upon in Ireland," added Monk, "claimed that he was the same guy who vanished off the liner."

"Ridiculous!" Long Tom snapped.

"I take it you never located that missing reporter, Simon Page," inserted Ham.

"Rub it in, why don't you?" Long Tom said querulously.

Doc Savage asked, "The smoky residue that followed the

apparent deaths of Zirn and Countess Olga. You say it was gray in color?"

"Right."

"Not black?"

Long Tom shook his head vehemently. "No. I was told that it was black by witnesses. But when I saw the stuff, it was gray."

"Sounds like the electron-stopper," Ham murmured. "Men turn black as coal, and fall apart in a haze of the same hellish hue."

Doc Savage reserved comment.

"There was another thing," added Long Tom. "Just before he disappeared, that queer music was coming from Zirn's cabin. There were sounds like a typewriter, too. But when the cabin was searched, no typewriter was found. Not even a radio. I heard the same combination of sounds coming from that hotel room on Pristav, where I was waylaid before I could barge in on that Emile Zirn." Long Tom rubbed his jaw thoughtfully. "Come to think of it, Zirn carried what looked like a portable typewriter case when he disembarked the liner."

Doc Savage regarded the slender electrical wizard steadily.

"Was there anything unusual about the sounds coming from the supposed typewriter, Long Tom?"

"Only that the typist—whoever he was—rattled away like nobody's business."

Monk muttered, "Wonder what the connection could be?"

"Search me," said Long Tom. "But if you want my opinion, that weird music didn't sound like anything that any broadcast station would ever put out over the air."

"Do you think that the infernal melody had anything to do with Zirn's disappearance?" wondered Ham.

"I don't know what to think," admitted the pale electrical wizard.

Monk and Ham next told their tales, placing great emphasis on Fiana Drost's apparent transformation into a human bat, and her subsequent escape.

"You could be describing the things that waylaid me in that Pristav hotel I trailed my Emile Zirn to," reminded Long Tom.

"What did they look like, Long Tom?" Doc inquired.

Long Tom scowled. "It was darker than the inside of a bat," he said, "but the things that attacked me felt and smelled like old leather."

"Anything else?" pressed the bronze man.

"Yeah. They flapped like pelicans when they fought."

Monk glanced back to the slumbering Fiana Drost.

"Don't look now," he said, "but that dark-eyed dame back there may be kin to them leathery horrors."

Long Tom puckered his sour face. "If what you said about her turning into a devil-bat is half true," he said, "I vote we dump her out and let her find her own way home."

Doc Savage took all this in stride. He asked no further questions, but seemed very thoughtful as he piloted the thundering amphibian.

Doc recited his experiences last, from awakening in an Egallan hospital room, his subsequent escape, and his discovery and rescue of Fiana Drost from a firing squad.

"It was fortunate that a part of my training is to imbibe minuscule portions of chemicals that might be expected to be used against me by enemies, thereby building up my tolerance against such attacks," he concluded by way of explanation for his swift recovery against the sedative that had been used to overcome him.

They sat in silence for a moment, digesting it all.

"The action ain't let up once since we hit town," Monk offered at last.

That was an understatement, to say the least.

Doc Savage spoke up. "Now that Long Tom is safe, our next job is to recover the darkness machine stolen from my Fortress."

Monk grunted, "That's gonna be tough, since it's in the hands of the Egallans. They already turned it on us once."

"Or did they?" Ham ventured. "Do not forget, we were attacked while flying over Ultra-Stygia—which is Tazan territory."

"Ham has a point," Long Tom added. "In espionage, secrets can change hands overnight. It's possible that the Tazans stole it from Egallah."

Monk grumbled, "Or maybe that double-dealin' snake, Baron Karl, is holdin' out on his iron-fisted dictator."

"During that time," Long Tom elaborated, "they tried to talk me into helping them figure out a defense against the darkness. I overheard talk that Baron Karl was nowhere to be found. They were very worried about him."

Doc Savage asked sharply, "You say Baron Karl never turned the device over to Prime Minster Ocel?"

"That was the trend of the talk," Long Tom added glumly.

Ham turned to Doc. "What do you think?"

Doc Savage advised, "I brought along sufficient funds to purchase the dark-making device, if we can obtain a fair hearing from whoever has possession of it."

"And if not?" wondered Ham.

"Then we will take it by force, if necessary."

Monk grinned broadly. "I got me a feeling that we ain't yet seen half of the action that lies ahead of us."

"Amen," said Long Tom. It sounded as if the puny electrical wizard was looking forward to it, which conceivably he was since he had been cooped up in a military prison over several days.

Doc stated, "Since it is unsafe to remain in Egallah, we will fly on to Pristav."

"Do you reckon we'll be welcomed there?" asked Monk.

"Inasmuch as we appear to be returning one of their spies alive," sniffed Ham, "I fail to see why not."

All eyes went to Fiana Drost asleep in a cabin seat. She was wearing an outfit of plain homespun cloth, which might conceivably have been her prison garb. In repose, she looked beautiful, in a glacial way.

Monk decided to check her for bat wings. He found none. He brushed her very dark hair off her ears next.

"What are you looking for?" demanded Ham.

"Pointed ears like a bat or the Devil might have," said Monk. "But she ain't got either."

"Check her tongue," drawled Ham. "Maybe it has a fork in it."

Monk decided against that examination. He reclaimed his seat, drew in a deep breath and let it out slowly.

"It's just hit me," he said.

Ham eyed him warily. "What did?"

"We were almost stood up before a firin' squad back there. And I was gonna have a last meal of bread and water."

"So?"

"It reminds me that I'm hungry. When we get to Pristav, I'm having me a steak."

"Out here, it might have to be a venison steak," reminded Ham.

"Venison will do," Monk decided, smacking his lips noisily. "Just as long as it's red and raw."

LANDING in the Tazan capital proved to be a surprisingly simple and uncomplicated affair, given their previous experience with the seemingly supernatural darkness.

Doc Savage flew a direct line to the coastal seaport of Pristav, while Ham Brooks handled the radio.

"I have a high official of the government," Ham reported.

Doc instructed, "Request permission to land."

Ham did so.

Back crackled the reply. *"What is your business in our country?"*

Doc told Ham, "Inform them that we are returning a native,

who was recently a prisoner of Egallah."

Monk grinned. "That ought to do the trick. Right, Habeas?" The pig grunted happily.

Ham related that to the government official, then listened to the response.

"Who is this lost person?"

"She calls herself Fiana Drost," Ham replied.

There was a short pause, during which noisy static rushed and hissed.

"We will be pleased to receive Miss Drost," the official said promptly.

"It's all set, Doc," reported Ham, turning off the transceiver.

Doc nodded, adjusting the controls for approach.

Monk turned to the seat behind him where Fiana Drost dozed. He grinned.

"Boy, is she gonna be surprised to be home safe."

As it happened, Fiana began stirring. She blinked sleepily and unfolded herself.

"Where are we?" she asked, sleep draining from her thick voice.

"Approaching Pristav airport," imparted Ham.

A slim hand flew to her open mouth. "Oh!"

"This time, young lady," said Ham Brooks sharply, "you will land with the rest of us."

"You are doubtless wondering about me," Fiana Drost said thinly.

"We didn't exactly figure you for a creature of the night," Monk grunted.

"I am not what I appear to be," Fiana allowed thinly.

"I'll tell a man," snorted Monk.

Before the conversation could get interesting, Doc Savage announced, "We are landing."

The changing of the engine sounds corresponded to that alteration in course. Doc drove the amphibian downward, ever downward, lining up on the main runway of the Pristav airport.

Fiana Drost asked dully, "Are—are we expected?"

"Are you kiddin'?" Monk asked. "You're our passport to land."

Fiana Drost's gaze grew clouded. She looked about her person, then searched the cabin with troubled eyes.

"Where is my parachute?"

"We're fresh out," Monk lied. "And don't get any cockeyed ideas. We're almost on your home soil."

Fiana Drost possessed an unusual natural pallor, and it was difficult to imagine her growing any paler. But this she did. It was as if all human hue had drained from her face, her neck, her hands. Her rouged mouth became consequently redder by contrast.

Flinging out of her seat, Fiana made a desperate dive for the cabin door.

"Not again!" howled Ham, lunging for her. He missed.

But Monk Mayfair, seeing what was coming, reached the door in time, blocked it with his wide body.

Fiana snarled, "Out of my way, dolt!"

"You're not wearin' a chute," returned Monk, taking her shoulders into his big hands.

Fiana began clawing. Her bared teeth lunged for Monk's throat. There was not much neck there, so the homely chemist was in little danger.

Using both hairy hands, Monk shoved her back. Fiana fought back like an energetic wildcat. She employed her long nails for the most part. Monk acquired some scratches to add to his proud collection of facial scars, but that was the worst of it.

Doc Savage banked the aircraft sharply, throwing the woman to the cabin floor.

Finally, the simian chemist pinioned Fiana's wrists with both paws. She subsided reluctantly. After that, Monk hoisted her up off the floor and onto her seat.

Fiana sat there, pale and fuming.

"Were you planning to turn into a bat again?" queried Ham, genuinely alarmed.

"I was prepared to die...."

"Blazes!" said Monk. "Doc, you better get this bus onto hard ground—fast! I think this she-bat's suicidal."

Doc Savage did just that, slamming the amphibian downward, then lined up on the approach runway. The air wheels touched, bumping along busily until the tail wheel finally made contact with the tarmac asphalt.

Soon, they were coasting to a slow stop. Doc cut the whining engines, one by one. Monk flung open the cabin door.

They began piling out.

A CONTINGENT of Tazan soldiers were assembled to meet them. They wore uniforms the approximate color of dusty limes. Their steel helmets were dark gray.

This welcoming committee was headed by a tall man in a resplendent military uniform, with a long curved sword hanging in a scabbard by his side. He stepped forward, smiling so generously the points of his mustaches bristled.

"Allow me to introduce myself. I am General Basil Consadinos, War Minister of the principality of Tazan. At your service." He actually clicked his heels when he executed his snappy bow.

Doc Savage nodded. "We have just arrived from Egallah, where we were held prisoner of the government there."

"Yes, yes," Consadinos said briskly. "So our loyal spies informed us. I understand that you have brought us a pretty present."

Ham Brooks escorted Fiana Drost from the plane. She came reluctantly, eyes sunken.

"Here is your lost lamb," he said, gesturing with his cane.

Under his breath, Monk muttered, "More like a fugitive bat."

The general's mustaches spiked like cat whiskers. "Excellent. Men, seize her!"

Soldiers swiftly surrounded the woman. She seemed unsurprised by this turn of events. Ham was shoved roughly aside.

"What is this?" demanded Doc Savage sharply.

General Consadinos smiled suavely. "We are grateful to you, Savage, for surrendering her to us. For this woman is an Egallan spy."

"Ridiculous!" snapped Ham. "We just rescued her from an Egallan firing squad."

Doc Savage interposed, "General, how do you know that she is a spy for Egallah?"

"Our spies in Egallah have so informed us."

Soldiers began hustling Fiana Drost to a waiting limousine. She made no effort to resist. Her shoulders sagged, all fight knocked out of her by the abrupt turn of fortune.

"What is to be done with her?" asked Doc Savage.

The general shrugged negligently. "What is customarily done with spies? She will be interrogated and shot."

"We object," said Doc.

General Consadinos' voice became oily. "You are honored guests of Tazan. It is improper for you to object. Now, what is your business in Pristav?"

Doc Savage watched the limousine doors open and close, swallowing Fiana Drost. The machine started off. Fiana Drost cast a fleeting, forlorn glance out the rear window. The expression in her dark doe eyes was that of a doomed person.

"We have reason to believe that a terrible new war weapon has fallen into the hands of Egallah," Doc started.

Consadinos nodded briskly. "No doubt. Egallah is a cauldron of terrible things. Not for nothing is it known as the cradle of vampirism. They are our hereditary enemies."

"That weapon was stolen from us," explained Doc. "We seek its recovery."

Consadinos began toying with one quirked mustache point. "This is very interesting news. Now, then, we have made arrangements for you all to stay in the royal suite of the Kronstadt, our finest hotel. Come with me. We will discuss this nasty matter like old friends."

Reluctantly, Doc Savage agreed.

"If Fiana Drost is a spy, as you say," he said quietly, "we would like an opportunity to interrogate her. She may have knowledge of this fearsome weapon of war."

"I will consider this. First, let us repair to the hotel. You will find it very comfortable."

Having no other choice, Doc and his men allowed themselves to be packed into another limousine. It flew the colorful flag of Tazan, at half mast.

THE royal suite of the Kronstadt Hotel was everything that might be desired. Marble floors. Damask draperies. Solid gold faucets. Other luxuries. Even Ham Brooks was impressed.

"Rather elegant," he said admiringly, twirling his cane.

"I am pleased that you are pleased," purred General Consadinos. He clapped his hands together. "Now—tell me of your adventures in Egallah, that benighted land."

Doc Savage said, "Your respective nations appeared headed for war."

Consadinos frowned heavily. "There is a portion of Ultra-Stygia that both countries claim as their birthright. We call it Monti Alb. To the detestable Egallans, it is the Marea Negra— the Great Black. By any name, it is a section of Ultra-Stygia that has remained a bone of contention stuck in our respective national throats down through the ages."

Doc asked. "These lands have traded hands many times over the centuries. Why has it become such a tinderbox now?"

"That," said Consadinos, "you will have to ask of the Prime Minister of Egallah, the tyrant, Boris Ocel. For it is his tanks that are massing. His black warplanes have been filling the skies. A strike is expected soon. Very soon."

"I see," said Doc.

"We are in hopes that this Fiana Drost will provide us with valuable intelligence that is more correct than guesswork, you see. But we will speak no more of her."

His tone was so definite that Doc Savage decided to drop the issue for now.

"There is another matter of interest to us," said Doc, changing the subject.

Consadinos cocked a gray-shot eyebrow. "Which is?"

"An American reporter named Simon Page vanished from a hotel in the frontier town of Cateral a few days ago. Before he did so, he contacted my headquarters. One of my men, Long Tom Roberts, traveled to meet him, but fell victim to what appeared to be agents of Egallah's espionage service."

The general made a firm mouth. "Ah, Simon Page. I know of whom you speak. But he is not missing. Simon Page is our prisoner."

"Prisoner?" interjected Long Tom.

"We caught him in Ultra-Stygia under very suspicious circumstances."

"Which are?" asked Doc.

"He was often seen in the company of the spy, Fiana Drost. We therefore concluded that he was in league with the devil-woman."

"Why do you call her that?" asked Ham, sharply.

Consadinos smiled broadly. "All spies of Egallah are devils. It is that simple."

Doc said, "We would like to visit Page, to learn his story from his own lips."

General Consadinos frowned anew. "I do not think that is a very good idea, Savage. For he is in a very bad way."

"Injured?"

"Worse than that."

"What could be worse?" asked Monk, low brow wrinkling.

General Consadinos was a long moment in replying. His

face worked thoughtfully, as if weighing matters. He worried one mustache point, then the other.

"I have changed my mind," he announced, smoothing down his mustaches with two fingers. "You may visit your American friend, after all."

"Where is he?" asked Long Tom.

"A very ancient castle, close to here. Come, Savage. We will go there now. Your men must remain here, however. I understand that they have had a very difficult time of it. And this consultation is not for underlings."

Doc Savage did not object to this suggestion. It made sense.

The others were content to remain behind and take advantage of room service. They were very hungry after their imprisonment, especially Long Tom.

THE drive to Jagellon Castle, as it was called, was not long. Winter showed few signs of having arrived. No snow, only some frost, touched the ground. The air coming through the open windows was not very cold. It might have been late Fall.

The general attempted some conversation. "This war weapon of which you speak. What is its precise nature?"

Doc declined to answer directly. "It is too terrible to contemplate. Let us say that no nation can withstand its operation."

"I see..." mused the War Minister of Tazan, who went back to fussing with his mustache points. When they pulled up to the pile of ancient stone that was Jagellon Castle perched on a knobby hill, Doc Savage was escorted within. There was no moat, no drawbridge. This was a Balkan fortress, the former seat of a cruel count, according to the history books.

There was a cellar, however. Really more in the nature of a dungeon. Doc Savage was led down to it. The way was lit by bare bulbs hanging by electrical cords from the stone ceiling. The wattage was very feeble. It was difficult to see. They walked single file, Consadinos in the lead, his green-uniformed soldiers taking up the rear. A long-faced turnkey accompanied them.

Coming to a halt, General Consadinos clicked his heels smartly, and announced, "Here."

The dungeon cell—there was no calling it anything but that—was sealed by an iron-studded door built of heavy oaken timbers. A latticed panel was sunk into the center of it. It looked very old, but possessed a sturdy appearance as if it were originally constructed to resist a battering ram.

Consadinos opened this grilled artifice, and invited Doc to look inside. The bronze man did.

The chamber was very dark. There were no interior windows, of course. Nothing could be seen of any prisoner.

The general said, "Mr. Simon, you have a distinguished visitor."

Something stirred within. A disagreeable odor wafted out. Doc Savage recognized it, but withheld comment.

A distinctly American voice spoke up, "Who is it?"

General Consadinos said, "A famous fellow countryman, Doc Savage."

"Doc Savage—! Here?"

Something stirred noisily and the weak voice seemed to gather strength.

"Have you come to release me?" Page asked anxiously.

"Not quite," purred Consadinos. "Mr. Savage merely wishes to confer with you."

The general signed for the turnkey to open the door. This was done. Hinges groaning, the thick door was swung open ponderously.

Consadinos waved Doc in, saying, "It is not permitted that he be allowed to leave, not in his unfortunate condition. So you must conduct any conversation behind this locked door."

Doc Savage hesitated.

"Merely a matter of form. You understand protocol?" Consadinos challenged. "Yes?"

Doc nodded, stepped within.

The door was immediately clapped shut behind him. A key

turned in the lock, making an unpleasant squealing. It had not been oiled in a long time, evidently.

"Page," said Doc, attempting to discern the man in the gloom.

"I am here."

"Where?"

"Directly in front of you."

Doc Savage's eyes began adjusting to the murk. Slowly, a pair of lizard-green orbs began to resolve themselves. They were lidless, grotesquely round, like serpent eyes. The serpentine suggestion was enhanced by the fact that the orbs hovered barely a foot above a tangle of dirty straw in one corner of the dirt floor.

The straw stirred. Slowly, two eyeballs began rising in an eerie fashion, coming level with his own.

Doc fixed the position of the man, moved toward him.

As Doc approached, the eyes steadied, became clearer. But the man remained elusive. Not even his outline showed.

Abruptly, those uncanny emerald eyes blinked. When they did so, they disappeared entirely.

With both hands, Doc Savage reached out. His hands encountered nothing that felt human to him.

"Page!" rapped Doc. "What has befallen you?"

Simon Page sobbed, gave a low, despairing cry. "I have become a beast...."

Chapter XVI

THE ARGUS

DOC SAVAGE'S EERIE trilling saturated the gloomy dungeon cell interior, an evanescent thing permeated with a quality of wonder. His corded hands began exploring the formless figure before him. He found no clothes, only a natural coat of something that reminded him of boar bristles. He located the man's head, brought it to the grille, where a little light leaked in. The looming green orbs appeared to be encased in an unseen tangle of fur.

"Close your eyes," directed Doc.

The staring green eyes winked out.

"Now open them again."

The uncanny emerald orbs reappeared.

Doc found the top of the man's head. What he encountered was not human hair, but something coarse and bestial. He turned the man's head this way and that. Each time he turned it, the twin eyeballs moved. The whites showed almost all the way around. It was a grisly thing to behold, even to the bronze man, who had performed autopsies in the past.

Curiously, when the head was turned more than a quarter of the way around, the eyeballs ceased to be visible. It defied understanding.

Doc released the head. He asked sharply, "What happened to you, Page?"

"I was out in the Ultra-Stygia when everything went black. Everything! The entire world was doused."

161

"Go on," encouraged Doc.

"Something huge and winged descended upon me. I felt a great claw catch me up. I guess I blacked out. When I came to, I encountered men with eyes—but no bodies. They told me that I was dead. Am I?"

"No."

A sigh of relief filled the malodorous atmosphere of the dungeon cell. Page resumed his account, his voice ragged.

"I fled, returning to my hotel. When I got to my room I discovered that I had become like *them*. A pair of eyes in an empty void. They came again, dragged me away, claiming that I had fallen victim to a marauding vampire bat. They kept insisting that I—and they—were lately deceased. It was all too much for me, I'm afraid. I passed out, waking up here. I have been a prisoner for many days. I lost all count. But with each day that passed, I grow hairier and more bestial."

"Who brought you here?" demanded Doc.

"I do not know," Page admitted. "I have no idea where this is. Am—am I in Hell?"

"No, you are in the dungeon of Jagellon Castle, outside of Pristav."

"Why would the Tazan government imprison me?" bleated Simon Page.

The polished voice of General Consadinos came through the door grille. "My dear man, do you not recall the series of slanderous articles you once wrote, denigrating our late king?"

Page's voice grew startled. "But—that was years ago."

"And his late majesty has never forgotten. This is his revenge. From the grave, if you prefer." The polite clicking of heels came again.

Doc Savage went to the latticework door grille. "Holding an American citizen prisoner will get you in a lot of international hot water," he advised.

The War Minister of Tazan laughed shortly. "I quite imagine so. However, I promised King Vladislav that should Simon

Page ever fall into our clutches, the royal dungeon would be his fate."

Doc Savage said, "This man is almost completely invisible."

"Yes. That is the condition in which he came to us. It is very sad."

"He is also covered in a growth of hair that is more animal than human."

"Perhaps," clucked Consadinos, "Simon Page encountered— how you say—a werewolf in the wilds of Ultra-Stygia. Some of our own citizens have been severely infected by such beasts, becoming beasts themselves."

"You will release us at once," Doc Savage ordered.

"I am afraid that is not in our national interest. For you see, you know about Mr. Simon's unfortunate condition. I cannot have you telling the world of this. And you have stirred my interest with your talk of a new Egallan war weapon. I must look into this."

Doc Savage lunged for the door. He put his massive shoulder into it. The hinges groaned, creaked, but they held.

One by one, the lights began going out behind the grille. They were accompanied by retreating footsteps.

Doc Savage waited for the corridor door to bang shut. A long silence followed.

"You are trapped here, with me," Simon Page said dispiritedly.

"Never mind that," said Doc. "Is it true that you antagonized the late king?"

"Yes. He was called the playboy prince in those days. He was quite the rogue, and a hand with the ladies. I gathered a lot of data on him and wrote it up for the international press."

"He became a laughing stock for a time," stated Doc Savage.

"The king seemed to enjoy his sordid reputation. I saw no harm in building it up." Page sobbed loudly. "Now look at me."

Doc Savage made a circuit of the dungeon. The walls were

wet with groundwater seepage. No doubt recent rains had filtered into the ground and made their way through the great stone blocks of the castle foundation.

Emerald eyes followed Doc's every move.

"This place is a fortress," Simon Page said flatly. "You are wasting your time. I have been through every square inch of this space."

Doc Savage said nothing. He was not particularly interested in the walls. He merely wished to ascertain how the dungeon was constructed.

Next, Doc went to the door. This he began feeling with his sensitive fingertips. The door was composed, he discovered, of stout timbers. Very old, rather dry in spots, but also wet in others. The combined age and dampness had made the wood punky in several places.

The hinges were of iron, or felt like iron. There was the inevitable rust, but they were firmly screwed into the wood, Doc's metallic fingers told him.

The peephole grille appeared modern and was the weakest portion of the portal. It could be forced out of its frame, but to no useful end, Doc decided. The lattice frame was too small to permit escape.

Doc Savage sat down to rest.

"Page, tell me about the disembodied eyes," he said. "Did they appear human?"

"They came in pairs, like normal eyes."

"Did you gain the impression that the beings supporting those eyes were of normal proportions?" pressed Doc.

Simon Page gave this some thought before replying. "I imagine so. I hadn't thought of it before. Why do you ask?"

Doc Savage did not reply. His flake-gold eyes studied the door by what little light trickled in. He was thinking.

Finally, the bronze man imparted, "In another hour or so, we will be leaving."

"How?"

"By the door," explained Doc. And that is all he would say until the hour elapsed.

ABRUPTLY, the bronze man stood up and faced the portal. Once more his strong fingers moved over the rough-grained wood. He found a spot where the wood was dry and began excavating it. The wood gave way before his metallic fingertips. A normal man might have made some progress, but Doc Savage was no ordinary individual. Fingers dug and probed, picking and wrenching the wood like steel chisels. Piles of debris began collecting on the floor.

"I can hear you working," Page gasped. "What are you doing?"

Doc Savage said, "The wood on the edge of the door by the upper hinge is bad. It is crumbing to the touch."

"Touch! It sounds like you've taken a crowbar to the door!"

Doc continued working, until he had the moist part of the door around the upper hinge dug away. Then came a weird sharp squeal of metal.

"What was that?" Page asked, alarmed.

"The hinge," returned Doc.

It could be heard falling to the dirt floor.

Simon Page sat up. A thread of light picked out one solitary eyeball hanging in space like a detached stare. "Can you get the other hinge loose?"

"Not likely. That portion of the wood is in better shape."

"Then what—?"

Then came an ungodly noise. A combination wrenching, squealing and splintering.

Sufficient light existed for Simon Page to get an idea of what was happening.

Doc Savage was tearing the portal off its remaining hinge! The lock proved stubborn. The metal tongue did not want to give way. But the mighty bronze man persisted and turned the door in both hands, as if extracting a gigantic tooth. Finally, it surrendered.

Doc set the portal to one side. Reaching back for Simon Page, he pulled him along.

"Free!" Page exulted.

"Quiet," said Doc, moving along the corridor in darkness, nostrils working, eyes trying to see where little light shone.

Soon, Doc led Page to the corridor door. It proved to be unlocked. Carefully, the bronze man eased it open.

A tiny squeak came. Reaching into his coat, Doc removed something small and brassy, applied it to the hinges. The smell of lubricating oil came. Doc emptied the tiny oilcan and tossed it aside.

Finishing his opening of the door, Doc Savage stepped out into a corridor that was lit by hanging lights. Weak as they were, they stabbed the optic nerves blindingly after the hour or so of enforced darkness.

Doc looked both ways and picked a direction. He paused to glance behind him and as trained as his senses were, he almost gave a start.

For Simon Page was only a set of green eyes hovering at the height of a normal man. There was nothing more of him to be gleaned!

"Stay close," Doc cautioned.

"Right."

They passed along the ancient passageway, which turned left twice. The bronze man moved with calm assurance. Retracing the way that led him into the dungeon area, he knew that a flight of stone steps lay just ahead.

In the wan light, Doc almost missed the sentry.

A scent came to him first—rank and skunky—like a dog that had rolled in something foul.

Doc halted. Page followed suit, but not before bumping into the bronze man. Page felt unnervingly like a cactus on legs.

The sentry consisted of two disembodied eyeballs—a yellow one and a brown one. They floated in the air directly ahead, staring unblinkingly.

Doc's trilling seeped out, but he caught it in time.

Doc studied the orbs. They stood approximately three feet apart—far too wide to belong to a human head. But they occupied the same plane, suggesting they belonged to a single invisible cranium. The mismatched eyes regarded him with a stark roundness that was unnerving.

The shocking sight brought to the bronze man's retentive mind stories of the many-eyed Argus of Greek myth—a guardian giant who possessed so many orbs that four peered in every direction. This creature seemed to have only two, however.

Carefully, Doc Savage advanced.

The weird orbs drifted toward him, moving in unison. The noise of hairy feet shuffling on stone accompanied the steady approach.

Lifting his fists, Doc set himself. He aimed for the spot where a chin would be in a human face, between and below the eyes. Doc Savage shot out a bronze fist.

His knuckles failed to connect with anything!

Doc pumped out the other fist. It, too, passed through empty air. It was uncanny. It was as if the floating orbs were detached from any mortal mounting.

Abruptly, the eyeballs separated!

Worse yet, they were veering at him from opposite flanks.

Behind him, Simon Page choked back a groan of horror and retreated to a wall.

A set of hairy hands clutched at the bronze man's forearms.

Doc shook one off. Then it returned. It felt strong. Humanly strong, not inhumanly so.

Testing its strength showed that the bristling beast was no match for his own trained muscles, so Doc began twisting, broke the thing's grip.

Out of nowhere a third hand seized him. Then a fourth. They were coarse-haired, like bear paws.

A growling voice spoke up in the language of Tazan.

"Another human for the pit."

"Yes," said a second voice. "He will make a good serf."

Doc Savage listened to the two voices, placed them in space and wrestled free.

This time, bronze knuckles cracked out and found fur and bone.

Strange sounds came. Gurglings. A heavy body hit the floor with a mushy thud. The brown eye fell like dropped marble. It failed to bounce.

Now only one eyeball floated in sight. The yellow one. It glared hideously.

Doc Savage made for that, reached out with both hands and took firm hold on what seemed to be a thick-haired neck.

His usual trick of pressing nerve centers in order to produce unconsciousness rarely failed him. But the thick bristles defeated that part of the operation that required sensitive feeling for the correct nerve. No matter how he probed, Doc could not recognize the spot.

Coarse-coated fists began hitting him in the face. Prudence demanded a retreat. One cannot effectively fend off fists that cannot be seen.

Doc retired to a corner, sheltering Simon Page. He lifted his great arms, held them before his face, in case the thing advanced.

The single yellow eye closed, vanishing utterly.

Realizing that this meant an imminent attack, Doc Savage propelled himself out the corner, in the general direction of the vanished eyeball.

A bronze battering ram, he encountered an upright form and bore it to the ground.

The thing went "Oof!" in a sick voice that told that it weighed considerably less than Doc Savage's more than two hundred pounds.

Doc held the thing down, feeling along the bristles—it appeared to be nude and encased in thick, wiry hair—until he encountered a head. No time to find a jaw for cracking. Doc instead grabbed at the top of the thing's rough scalp and rocked the head back and forth until repeated pummeling against the stone floor elicited a groan. The thing collapsed, losing all animation. The yellow eyeball popped open, then slowly closed again, signifying unconsciousness had set in.

Doc Savage stood up, metallic expression slightly odd.

Simon Page's voice rang out, "You defeated it!"

"Both of them."

"Both—?"

"Two creatures, pretending to be one."

"What are they?"

"Later," said Doc, driving the man forward.

Together they reached another door. Doc poked his head out, saw nothing, then motioned for Simon Page to follow.

Working along the stone-flagged passage that smelled of must and mold, they began to hear voices talking excitedly, urgently.

"What do you know?" one dominating voice demanded. "Speak!"

Silence.

"Then tell us what Baron Karl has planned for the invasion."

"I do not know," a female voice returned.

Simon gasped. "That sounds like—"

Doc Savage signed for quiet with a sharp chop of one hand. Signaling for Simon Page to remain behind, the bronze man advanced carefully.

His going was stealth itself.

Turning one corner, then another, Doc came to a room where light showed around the edges of a very modern door. The voices were coming from the other side. They were growing more rancorous.

THE harsh male voice of General Consadinos was saying, "You are a spy for Egallah. Admit this!"

"I admit nothing," said Fiana Drost wearily.

"Doc Savage brought you to us, with a wild tale of a new weapon of war. What do you know of this thing?"

"I pray," said Fiana firmly, "that this new weapon will prove to be the one thing that can defeat your unholy forces."

"What do you mean?"

"You know full well what I mean. The things that are abroad in the night."

"There are many things abroad in the night in Ultra-Stygia," returned Consadinos smoothly. "It is a haunted land."

"We both know this," Fiana spat. "We are in a new era of warfare, fighting with new forms of terror machines."

"If you have nothing to contribute to our defense," said General Consadinos, "then there is left for you only the execution wall."

"I have already stood before such a wall today," spat Fiana Drost. "Such trifles mean nothing to me. Do your worst, you cur."

The meaty sound of a hand slapping flesh sounded clearly.

At that, Doc Savage wrenched open the door.

His appearance, so bold and unexpected, caused every head to turn and eyeballs to pop from their sockets. Mouths opened. Jaws dropped. No one spoke.

In those fleeting seconds, the mighty Man of Bronze was plunging across the room where a Tazan soldier was belatedly recalling that he possessed a sidearm in a belt holster. He failed to snatch for it in time.

Bronze fingers snared the still-holstered weapon, and yanked. The web belt supporting weapon and holster tore loose—gun, steel buckle and all. When the guard got hold of his balance, he was staring stupidly at the muzzle of his own pistol.

Doc had removed it from the holster, tossing the latter aside.

General Consadinos said suavely, "It is understood that Doc Savage does not shoot to kill. It is against his well-known code of ethics."

Doc dropped the muzzle, fired, placing a bullet in the wood directly in front of Consadinos' booted right toe.

"Bullets do not have to kill," he pointed out. "They can maim."

Consadinos grew so white his mustaches seemed to darken. Words hung on his tongue unuttered. No one moved.

The bronze man shifted to the chair where Fiana Drost sat trussed hand and foot. He began unraveling knots. They were good stout knots, but under his strong fingers they came apart easily.

Standing the woman up, Doc Savage told her, "We will go now."

Fiana blinked doe-dark eyes doubtfully. "How?"

"Yes. How?" echoed Consadinos stiffly. "You are in my nation. Alone. There is no escape."

Doc Savage strode up to the general and seized him by the throat. Bronze fingers moved along the flesh, found the nerves they sought, and put the man to sleep on his feet.

Doc lowered him to the floor, one-handed. This display of casual strength brought gasps from onlookers.

"Remarkable," breathed Fiana Drost.

Doc saw a key ring on a table and, recognizing it as the key ring that opened the dungeon cells, reasoned that one of the keys might fit this door. So he took it.

"You will shoot them now?" asked Fiana eagerly.

"No," said Doc.

Her fierce eyes blazed. "If you do not shoot them, they will give the alarm."

Doc moved to the disarmed soldier's side, rendered him unconscious. The procedure was repeated on another man who was unarmed. Doc had to catch him first, for the man lunged blindly for the door. But it was soon done.

"No need to shoot," Doc told Fiana.

The woman sneered, "Shooting is final. If we let them live, they will hunt us down like wild wolves."

"No time to argue," rapped Doc, urging her out of the room. He paused to lock the door, after first dousing the room's light.

Retracing his steps, Doc reached the spot where he had left Simon Page.

Two sad grass-green eyes fell upon Fiana Drost.

"Hello, Fiana."

Fiana looked around wildly. "Who speaks?"

"Me. Simon Page."

Her thin eyebrows shot up in surprise. "You live? Where are you, Simon?"

"Here. Right beside you."

Fiana Drost made searching faces. Dark orbs falling upon the familiar green ones that were framed by no face, she became rubbery in the knees.

"Simon…" she breathed.

"Time for talk later," said Doc. "We are getting out of here."

Doc Savage led them along until they came to a soldier in chartreuse who stood guard at what appeared to be a side door to the castle structure.

Spying them, he brought his rifle to his shoulder and ordered a halt.

Doc obliged. There was nothing else to do.

"Simon," he undertoned.

The green eyes winked out. Consequently the guard failed to notice them advancing. A shuffling of brushy feet caused the man to switch his rifle muzzle this way and that, thinking that someone—or some *thing*—was moving along the corridor.

Seeing no one, he shifted his weapon back to fix the big bronze man in his gun sight.

Abruptly, the muzzle jumped upward, began twisting out of his hands. Grunting, the sentry strove to hold on, but the sheer unbelievability of what was happening threw him badly.

The rifle went flying. Doc Savage captured it in both hands, snapped it around, training the cold muzzle on the dumbfounded guard.

"Shoot this one!" Fiana hissed.

"I have a better idea," called the voice of Simon Page.

The guard wore a steel helmet. It came off his head and without anything seeming to control it, began hitting the top of his skull repeatedly.

This produced painful unconsciousness. The man corkscrewed and flopped on his slack face. The helmet landed on his head with a clunk of a sound.

Doc maneuvered Fiana Drost around the conquered one, saying to the disembodied green eyeballs, "Good work."

"My pleasure."

"I cannot get used to this," murmured Fiana, looking very drained of color now.

THEY emerged into clear daylight. Before them lay a broad expanse of open field, brown with dead grass.

Preparations appeared underway for an incipient war. There were soldiers everywhere. Drilling. Marching in formation. Officers were shouting profane orders.

"The Tazans are mobilizing," Fiana breathed.

Simon Page assessed the situation perfectly. "We would never get past all those soldiers."

Doc Savage directed, "Back."

They slipped inside the castle and Doc Savage went hunting. He found closed doors, signifying more offices, and tried knob after knob until one surrendered.

Slipping within, he found a telephone reposing on a desk. Jiggling the switch hook, Doc got some type of switchboard on the line.

In perfect Tazan, the bronze man began issuing curt orders.

"The enemy spy Drost has escaped. She was seen leaving by the back way, headed into Ultra-Stygia. No doubt she expects to rendezvous with confederates there."

His voice, tone and inflection, was unmistakably that of General Consadinos. Doc Savage was a perfect voice mimic.

"At once, General," a nervous voice returned.

Rejoining the others, Doc waited.

A great stirring came from outside. Shouted orders cracked out. Men and machines were quickly organized for the hunt. Canvas-sided military trucks rumbled into view. The latter carried soldiers in green crouching in the back.

In short order, the assembled forces of Tazan were charging into Ultra-Stygia, in hot pursuit of Fiana Drost, led by a formidable war tank which grumbled along with grim purpose.

"They will not be fooled for very long," Fiana warned.

"The contrary," said Doc. "The soldiers believe themselves to be under official orders. They will comb Ultra-Stygia until you are found."

"I refuse to be found," Fiana said defiantly.

Doc led them back to the empty office, where he placed a telephone call to the Hotel Kronstadt.

"Put me through to the royal suite," he asked in Tazan.

"Yes, General Consadinos."

Fiana Drost stared in amazement at the giant bronze man.

Monk Mayfair answered, "Yeah?"

Doc switched to the Mayan language, to foil any eavesdropper. In quick succession, he explained his predicament, and ordered Monk and the others to slip out of the hotel and reclaim their aircraft.

"I will meet you there," Doc concluded.

"Got it. Where are we goin'?"

"Back to Egallah."

"Is that smart?"

"Smarter than remaining in Tazan, where we are certain to be shot."

"Won't we be shot on sight if we show our faces in Egallah?"

"Conceivably," admitted Doc.

"So what's the difference?" asked Monk.

"The difference," returned Doc Savage, "is that the darkness machine is in Egallan hands, and that is our main objective now that I have collected Simon Page."

"Meet you there!" Monk said enthusiastically.

Chapter XVII

HARPY OUT OF HADES

GETTING OUT OF the royal suite proved more challenging than Monk, Ham and Long Tom Roberts expected.

Two police officers stood outside their door when they attempted to exit the suite. Each wore broad web belts which supported a holstered revolver on one hip and a long ceremonial sword on the other. At the sound of the door opening, hands went nervously to hilts, knuckles whitening.

"You cannot leave," one told them firmly.

"Why the heck not?" demanded Long Tom.

"You are under house arrest."

Ham Brooks stuck his head out and said, "I happen to be an attorney. There has been no formal arrest. Therefore, we are free to go."

The police changed their minds about drawing their swords. Two pistols were produced and aimed at the dapper lawyer's aristocratic nose.

"Consider this official notification of arrest," he was informed.

Ham retreated. There was nothing he could do in the face of the twin muzzles.

"Monk, you reason with them."

Monk emerged next. The sight of the great hairy chemist whose long arms dangled gorilla-like to his knees gave the officers momentary pause. Prudently, they trained their pistols on him.

"We're kinda bumfuzzled," Monk confessed. "Maybe you boys can explain what the charges are."

The other spoke up. "We do not know. We have orders only."

"Do you have orders to shoot us if we escape?" wondered Monk.

The two officers of the local law looked momentarily nonplussed. It was plain that their instructions did not go that far. It was written all over their features.

"Sounds like you boys got hold of a powerful dilemma," suggested Monk.

The American word was unfamiliar to them. They said so.

"A dilemma," said Monk expansively, "is a conundrum with horns."

"What is conundrum?" one wondered.

"Why, it's a— Hold on. I'll show you an example of one."

Monk ducked into the suite only long enough to unship his supermachine pistol from his underarm holster. When he emerged, the spiky muzzle was trained directly on the two police officers, who had crowded a little too close together in their efforts to block the door.

"What is that?" one gulped.

Monk said breezily, "A kind of a conundrum. You have one pistol each. Right?"

"Yes. Obviously."

"I have only one pistol. Correct?"

"That is correct."

"Your pistols are loaded with six shots apiece. That makes twelve, all told."

"Yes. Twelve. More than sufficient to shoot you," the other officer reminded.

"On the other hand," Monk said flatly, "this pistol of mine holds sixty shots in the drum and can spit lead faster than a Tommy-gun."

The two police officers did some mental math. It told them

that if the hairy ape of a fellow menacing them so casually should pull his trigger, it would take only four seconds to empty the drum into their unprotected bodies.

"Are you asking us to surrender?" asked one man, thick-tongued.

"Because if you are," said the other, "that is strictly against our orders."

Monk eyed them. "Your orders that don't allow you to shoot us. Is that right?"

The pair exchanged uneasy glances. In that moment, their muzzles wavered.

That was sufficient opening for the hairy chemist.

Monk pulled back on the firing lever of his supermachine pistol and mowed them down with a brief moaning burst.

They collapsed to the carpet, their pistols unfired. Almost immediately, the duo began breathing like men who had fallen asleep. The thin-walled mercy-bullet capsules had broken against their skins, introducing a potent anesthetic into their bloodstreams.

Monk called over his shoulder, "Let's go."

Ham emerged first. "That was easy," he murmured.

"It's all in the buildup," beamed Monk.

They took the elevator down to the lobby and sauntered out the rear exit, unchallenged and unmolested. It was late afternoon, and pedestrians, bundled up in their winter hats and coats, appeared busy rushing homeward.

"This is *too* easy," muttered Long Tom.

"We ain't there yet," commented Monk.

They hailed a taxicab, and directed it to take them to the airport. After going a few blocks, Monk prevailed upon the driver to pull over.

"What for?" the hackman wondered as he slowed down.

"I need to tie my shoe," said Monk, stepping out.

"You need to stop to tie shoe?"

"Humor him, O.K.?" Long Tom suggested.

The driver slewed to the curb. Monk exited.

By main strength, Monk yanked open the driver's door and hauled the hapless hackie out into the street.

"No, I guess I don't after all." He bopped the driver on the top of his head, then as an afterthought, stuck a ten-dollar bill into his open hand. "That's for your trouble, guy."

Leaving him on the sidewalk, Monk pulled the door shut and took the wheel. He sent the cab hurtling away.

"Couldn't very well have him blabbin' our destination to the local cops," explained Monk.

THEY made the airport in good time. Apparently, no alarm had been given.

They rolled into the place unchallenged. It was not very busy. A plane had just taken off. No others crowded the tarmac.

"Where's our bus?" asked Long Tom, scratching his pale locks dubiously.

Monk replied, "Probably in a hangar. Look for one with a lot of guards."

Ham Brooks spotted the hangar in question. A large structure of corrugated sheet steel tucked away in one corner of the large flying field.

"Only three guards," he said. "Even odds."

Monk waggled his supermachine pistol. "I don't need you two to handle only three guards."

Long Tom objected, "Shouldn't we wait for Doc to show up before we start trouble? Be pure hell getting off the ground if we're in the middle of a ruckus."

Ham said, "Long Tom makes sense. I vote we wait."

Monk latched the safety of his superfirer and looked disappointed. "O.K. We'll hold off until Doc shows."

They hunkered down in the cab to await the bronze man.

They did not have to loiter very long.

Long Tom happened to be glancing in the direction of the guarded hangar. One of the sentries suddenly wilted at his post. Then another. The third joined him. It was as if tall corn stalks were being scythed down, one at a time. Not a sound reached their ears.

Elbowing Ham beside him, Long Tom said, "What got into them?"

Ham started to exit the vehicle, peering about thinly.

"They dropped."

"I can see that!" Long Tom said peevishly. "What dropped them?"

A moment later, a resonant voice spoke at their side. It had a quality of restrained power they all knew.

"Come on. The others are already on board."

A colossal figure towered in the darkness. There was no mistaking him.

"Doc!" cried Monk. "Where'd you come from?"

The metallic giant pulled open the door. "Just arrived. We have no time to waste."

The trio piled out and followed the bronze man to the formerly guarded hangar. They entered through a side door and Doc led them to the open aircraft.

Once on board, their eyes fell upon Fiana Drost, seated quietly. No one looked surprised or, for that matter, appeared very pleased to see her.

She looked away guiltily.

Long Tom dropped into an apparently empty seat, gave a howl of surprise followed by a nimble jump, landing back on his feet.

"What did I sit on?" he complained. "A pincushion?"

"Me," a disembodied voice murmured. "Sorry."

"Who are you?"

"Simon Page."

Long Tom's jaw sagged. The others goggled.

"Where are you?" Ham wondered, swishing his sword cane about the apparently empty seat. The stick encountered an obstacle. He could now see that the cushions were mashed down under the weight of something that could not be discerned. "Jove!"

"What the heck happened to you?" Long Tom asked thickly.

"I am a victim of Ultra-Stygia," Page said, pushing the cane aside.

"Take seats," ordered Doc Savage. "We will go over developments in the air."

They grabbed seats while Doc warmed up the motors. This was a risky thing to do. Planes of this size are normally pulled from hangars by tractors, but there was no time for such formalities. They had to risk raising an alarm.

Propeller blades churned, rattling the thin walls of the hangar. Radials spilling bluish exhaust, the amphibian gave a forward lurch, began rolling.

Long Tom got out and pushed aside the hangar doors, then scrambled aboard.

Props howling, displacing cold air, the aircraft inched ahead, blunt nose emerging from the open hangar. Doc turned toward the runway, advanced the throttles. The air wheels began rumbling along.

In the gathering dusk no one seemed to notice this unusual event for the longest time.

When an alarm was raised, it was smothered by the charging plane as it fought to get into the air. The wheels soon left the asphalt, clawing skyward.

Banking, Doc turned the aircraft north.

"Smooth," complimented Ham.

"Yeah," seconded Long Tom. "No one noticed until we were up in the air."

"We are not out of danger yet," warned Doc.

Sure enough, less that a minute later, a trio of warplanes took to the air. They fell in behind Doc's charger, propellers snarling like spinning swords.

Gun muzzles mounted in the wings began turning red. Tracer slugs went shooting past Doc's plane, becoming visible from the control cabin. Spent, they fell to earth harmlessly.

The next burst of rounds made hammering noises against the amphibian's tail section. It sounded like rivets being driven into sheet metal.

"Want me to open the door and blast 'em out of the sky?" offered Monk.

The bronze man shook his head in the negative. "No need." Doc instead reached for a set of levers that were not part of the ordinary aircraft controls. He yanked one, then another, and finally a third.

"What are those?" asked Fiana Drost, curiously.

Monk explained, "There's a tank of chemical in the tail. Doc is releasing the stuff. It will be sucked into the motors, and choke 'em good."

"What if it does not? What then?"

The question proved premature.

Behind them, the trio of warplanes slammed into the hazy cloud and their air-greedy engines gulped the stuff in.

It was not long until the engines began missing, propellers faltering in their swift revolutions.

One by one, they ceased spinning.

Thrown into confusion, the pilots hastily sought clear spaces for landing. All thought of pursuit fled their consciousness. Preserving their lives and their winged steeds was all that mattered to them.

They soon fell behind.

"That settles that," said Monk, pleased with himself.

Fiana commented dryly, "You sound as if you were the one who defeated our pursuers."

"I helped formulate the concoction," Monk admitted proudly.

Silence fell as Doc Savage sent the amphibian winging north over the desolate frontier that was Ultra-Stygia. It had a cratered look that might have been the dark side of the moon. Here and there, sunset reds shimmered where frost clung.

"Back over this forsaken place again," grumbled Ham. "I don't like it."

"It is Hell on Earth," sighed Simon Page.

The others turned in their seats to get a good look at the rescued journalist.

All they saw was a pair of tired green eyes, which blinked every so often, like an owl hiding in a dark tree. The odor of rankness emanated from unseen fur. Fiana pinched her nose shut with two fingers to keep out the offensive aroma.

"Perhaps you should put on some clothes, fellow," suggested Ham.

"Have you any to spare?" asked the unnaturally round green eyeballs.

Monk went in back, rummaged around, and produced some extra stuff.

"Try these duds. Might fit you. They belong to Renny."

Renny was Colonel John Renwick, the civil engineer of Doc Savage's group of adventurers. At present, he was sojourning in France, there lending his expertise to the construction of a network of advanced flying fields large enough to accommodate transport planes. With archeologist William Harper "Johnny" Littlejohn—himself busy plumbing the moldy entrails of a lately-discovered Pharaoh's tomb in Egypt—Renny had been alerted to watch for any signs of the missing and believed-dead John Sunlight.

Simon Page accepted the commodious items of clothing. The others watched in amazement as the clothes floating in the aisle between seats, jumped and jerked, seemingly wrapping themselves around a semi-human form.

Semi-human, because once they were buttoned in place, they seemed to envelop a body whose outlines appeared more bear than man.

Curious, Ham Brooks reached over and encountered stiff bristles.

"Jove! This man is hairier than even you, Monk."

His own curiosity aroused, Monk felt about the clothing.

"*Ye-o-w-w!* What happened to you?"

Page gulped, "This—fur has been growing every day, ever since I woke up in that castle dungeon. I have no idea why."

"Perhaps you are cursed," suggested Fiana dolefully.

"No such thing!" barked Long Tom.

"Then you explain it," retorted Monk. "He's as bristled as Habeas here."

The pig had been watching with fascinated eyes all through the proceedings. Now he jumped up and began sniffing Simon Page. Evidently, he did not like what his snout took in. Hackles rose up along his skinny back, and the shoat began backing away.

"Even animals fear me," moaned Page. "Perhaps I *am* cursed."

In the cockpit, Doc Savage asked, "It is time to hear everyone's story in detail. Miss Drost, to whom do you owe allegiance?"

"I was born in Egallah," she returned sullenly. "I admit this now."

"Then why did the authorities there attempt to execute you?"

"For this reason: I was instructed to assassinate you."

"Blazes!" exploded Monk.

"It was my duty to liquidate you," Fiana continued. "But after you rescued me from the auto wreck, I found that I could not. So instead, I injected you with a sedative designed to put you to sleep."

"What good did you expect that to do?" challenged Doc.

"The sedative was formulated to plunge a man in a coma for three weeks—no less. I thought this would be enough. I do not know how you escaped that fate."

Doc Savage said only, "My constitution may be more tolerant than the chemist who made the stuff expected."

This was an understatement. Doc Savage was inured to colds and other physical ills. He also made it a practice to imbibe antidotes to many of the more pernicious potions that an enemy might employ to overcome him. Conceivably, his trained physique simply shook off the preparation much faster than any ordinary mortal might.

Doc passed over this. "Why did Egallah want me out of commission?"

Fiana admitted, "I was not told. Only that they feared you for some reason."

Simon Page spoke up. "Fiana, you mean that you aren't from Tazan, after all?"

She shook her luxurious hair. "No, I was a spy. Now I am a woman without a country. Both nations would shoot me on sight."

"Perhaps," suggested Ham Brooks, "due to your unsavory profession, you had that coming to you."

Fiana compressed bloodless lips. There appeared to be nothing to say; it was the truth.

Long Tom said, "I think we all know what the dictator of Egallah was worried about, Doc."

Ham nodded. "Prime Minister Ocel was expecting you, Doc."

No one offered a further explanation. They did not wish to talk about the darkness machine. It was a secret they hoped to keep from the world. Doc Savage especially did not want it to be publicly known that a menacing war weapon had been stolen from him, only to fall into dangerous hands.

Before anyone could question the logic of that, Simon Page said, "Of course, Doc Savage has a reputation for stopping wars before they start."

That satisfied the concern.

"It is clear," Doc imparted, "that Simon Page was subjected to a process that rendered him invisible."

"Obviously," said Fiana Drost dryly. "But what about the horrible hair which is growing on his body?"

"The answer to that will have to await further investigation," said Doc. "Unquestionably, this is connected to the one-eyed ogres which are roaming Ultra-Stygia." Doc turned his head. "Miss Drost, are they creatures of Tazan or Egallah?"

"Neither. They are monsters of blackest Ultra-Stygia."

Which, while it was hardly a satisfactory answer, smacked of the truth.

"Tell us how you survived the fall from our plane," invited Doc.

Fiana was a long time in answering. "I transformed into a winged bat and glided safely to earth."

Doc eyed her steadily. "Just like that?"

"You are familiar with the legend of the *vampiri*—vampires? Need I say more?"

"Fiana," blurted Simon Page in a shocked voice. "What are you saying?"

The cold-blooded woman eyed him unflinchingly. "That I am—how do you say?—one of the Undead. A creature of midnight."

Floating green eyeballs goggled. "Great stars! What have you become?"

"You should speak!" she hissed back. "Look into a mirror, Simon Page. Tell me what you see there."

Simon said nothing. Fiana turned her head and stared out the window. All were silent for a very long time.

Long Tom broke the thick gloom by saying, "I, for one, take no stock in vampires."

"You have nothing to worry about, scrawny one," said Fiana. "You are too pale to contain very much red blood. No one would want you."

"I resent that!" snapped Long Tom.

"I'm with Long Tom," said Monk. "Vampires are the bunk."

"You also need not worry, for you possess no neck to fasten teeth upon," Fiana said frostily.

Ham started to laugh at that, but subsided when he discovered Fiana Drost looking at him with undisguised interest. He adjusted his cravat nervously.

NIGHT was falling over the bleak, broken barrenness that was Ultra-Stygia. Long evening shadows were crawling along the wasteland, like advancing monsters.

Ham addressed Long Tom. He used Mayan, for privacy.

"Earlier, you mentioned that your Egallan captors desired that you work on a defense against the inexplicable darknesses that have been plaguing this region."

"Yeah. But they didn't exactly come out and say that. They were cagey about the whole thing."

"The reasons for that are obvious," inserted Doc Savage. "Operation of the darkness device has no doubt incited terror within Ultra-Stygia. And the Egallans would not wish to admit that it failed to fall into their hands after Baron Karl acquired it."

"I could tell that they were confused on that score," said Long Tom, still speaking in Mayan. "I got the idea they weren't quite sure who had it. But they called him—or it—the Dark Devil."

Doc nodded. "Someone appears to have been tinkering with the device," he said. "When it was turned on us during our entry into the region, its range appeared to be several miles. It had not that capacity when it was first stolen."

"Well, whoever has it sure knows how to use it," said Monk. "My peepers are still achin' from that last dose of blindness."

Ham added, "I wonder how the darkness ties in with the devilish music we heard over Ultra-Stygia? They seemed to go together."

"What language is this?" Fiana suddenly demanded. "Why are you speaking this way?"

"We are wondering about that infernal music we keep encountering," Ham mused, switching back to English.

Fiana fell silent. It was clear that her firmly sealed lips meant that she knew more than she was willing to say.

"What can you offer to shed light on that mystery?" Doc asked steadily.

"I have nothing to say."

"You have no loyalty to give any longer," Doc Savage pointed out.

She shook her dark-haired head firmly. "That is for me to decide."

Turning her face to the window, Fiana Drost stared out at the rising moon, ebony orbs bleak, and fell to studying the cloud scud.

THEY flew along for a time, no one speaking, when Doc Savage noticed something in the sky to the west.

A shadowy shape was gliding along, an indistinct black harpy of a thing silhouetted against the moon rising up between two sharp mountain peaks.

Doc Savage spoke up. "Monk."

"What is it?"

"Train your binoculars on that object yonder. Ham, get on the radio and listen."

Ham replied, "Sure. For what?"

"Anything."

Monk grabbed field glasses and trained them on the spot where Doc Savage indicated. His low brow beetled in perplexity.

"Where is it?" he grunted.

"Look for two glowing red spots," apprised Doc.

"Red—?" Then Monk saw it. "Blazes! It looks like a bat fresh out of Hades!"

"Describe it," Doc requested.

"Big as a barn, maybe bigger. I see black wings, a head. It's got fox ears and a ratty snout. The eyes look like coals burnin' to beat the band."

From the radio cubicle, Ham Brooks called, "Listen to this."

He yanked out the jack that connected his headset to the receiver. Over the cabin loudspeaker came the undisciplined music they had come to know—eerie, wild in its cadences, uncanny in its effect upon the nerves.

Doc said, "Ham, see if you can locate the spot from which this transmission is coming."

"Righto," said Ham, engaging a loop antenna, which connected to the ship's direction finder.

"Let me do that!" snapped Long Tom, rushing up to the radio cubby. "This is my specialty."

The dapper lawyer surrendered this seat. Long Tom began spinning knobs with practiced fingers. Changing wave coils, he began tuning his way through the spitting carrier waves he encountered on the band.

In the cockpit, Monk was describing what he saw.

"It's a bat. A big leather-winged bat," he decided.

"Take the controls," instructed Doc.

Monk did, handing over the binoculars to the bronze man.

Doc Savage trained them on the darksome apparition.

"What do you see?" asked Ham, leaning his head into the control cabin.

"It appears to be a monster bat as large as a small aircraft."

"Bats never grow that big!" snapped Ham tartly.

"I don't think that this is an ordinary bat," offered Monk. "It's got eyes just like the portholes of Hades."

Ham Brooks turned to accost Fiana Drost, sitting in back.

"What do you now about this?" he demanded.

"It has begun," said Fiana dully.

"What has?"

"The opening of the doors of Hell. The Dark Devil is loose upon the world."

"You might explain what you mean," suggested Doc Savage.

"I refuse to do so!"

Ham Brooks interjected, "You probably know Doc Savage has means of making you talk. Truth serum is only one of them."

Fiana Drost sneered, "Precious good his truth serum will do the bronze one."

"It's potent stuff," warned Monk.

Fiana cast a cold eye upon the hairy chemist. "It works through the bloodstream, does it not?"

Monk met her unfathomable regard. "Yeah. So what?"

"So it cannot have any effect upon me." Fiana drew in a great shaky breath. "I no longer have any blood running in my veins."

"Anyone can see that," said Long Tom flatly.

Chapter XVIII

THE DRACULA TRAIL

GRIPPING THE CONTROL yoke, Doc Savage sent the mighty amphibian into a sharp, stomach-wrenching turn. The shadowy harpy of a thing became framed in the windscreen.

Monk asked, "Gonna chase it, Doc?"

The bronze man nodded. His flake-gold eyes were very active now.

From the radio cubicle, Long Tom reported, "I think I have a fix on the location where the mad melody originates. Due north of here."

"From Egallah?"

"Egallah—or the part of Ultra-Sygia that borders Egallah."

"Same difference," suggested Monk, training his binoculars on the bat-winged thing skimming silently along over the bare, broken treetops.

Doc Savage set the nose of his bronze bird on a point just in front of the bat's flight path and gave the twin radials all the power he could. The amphibian lunged ahead, propellers screaming. The cabin shook under the strain.

It became obvious that Doc Savage was attempting to intercept the ebony-winged bat with the burning orbs.

"You will never catch it," said Fiana coldly.

"You ain't seen Doc jockey a bus like this around," Monk retorted confidently.

But Fiana Drost proved to be prescient.

Doc's plane continued to gain speed and looked to slam down just ahead of the gliding thing.

Abruptly, the bat executed a maneuver that smacked of a living creature, and nothing else. It suddenly began rising in a way that was supernatural. Straight up.

"Lookit!" exploded Monk.

"I have never seen a hawk do that, much less a bat!" Ham exclaimed.

When Doc's plane shot into the spot where it would have intercepted the mammoth bat, the apparition was no longer there. Instead, the thing was winging high above them.

Booting rudder, Doc hauled back on the control yoke. He side-slipped, then stood the laboring amphibian on one wing briefly. Everyone grabbed for their seats—or anything solid and handy.

The commotion continued until Doc Savage had once more righted the aircraft, and went climbing for a look at the evasive winged thing.

As it happened, the bronze man fell in behind it. Doc began gaining on the bat. The gap closed steadily.

Settling on an altitude and heading which matched their weird quarry, Doc advanced the throttles again. The engines responded, props clawing air faster.

Ham was training his binoculars on the monster's tail.

"What does it look like from this vantage?" Doc asked him.

"A bat. Posterior view."

"Too bad we ain't got wing-mounted machine guns on this bus," said Monk grimly. "We could shoot it down and see what it's made of."

In the next instant, they received an inkling of the substance comprising their quarry.

A sudden spatter of jet began coating the windshield. It issued from the bat's tail.

Doc Savage engaged the wipers. They began rocking back

and forth lazily.

But the blades only made the stuff worse. It smeared and ran thickly.

Monk grunted, "What is that goop—India ink?"

Doc Savage increased speed, hoping that air friction would help dispel the sepia stuff. While it helped somewhat, visibility was becoming a concern.

"We will have to land," he announced firmly.

"Drat it!" said Ham angrily. "We are almost upon the bally thing."

Doc glanced out the side windows, saw a patch of scorched and blackened earth that looked promising and overflew it twice. Handling of the craft was becoming unnerving, due to the sticky coating on the windshield.

Landing a flying boat on unpaved ground is not an advisable course of action, but as a defense against infiltrators, the Tazans had leveled this segment of Ultra-Stygia of standing trees and burnt all other dead growth, grooming the charred remains until the flat ground resembled a shallow charcoal pit. There were absolutely no rocks or other obstructions, Doc saw.

Finally, the bronze man decided to attempt a landing.

It went well enough. The amphibian jounced only twice as it bumped along. Long Tom and Ham were certain that a crackup was inevitable, and braced themselves for a disaster.

But the miraculous skill of Doc Savage brought them to a safe stop. Doc cut the engines and leaped for the cabin door.

OUTSIDE, the bronze man first inspected the boat-like hull and landing struts. All looked fine. Had the hull been breached, any future water landing would be out of the question.

Monk, Ham and Long Tom clambered out next.

Staring upward, they began searching the night sky. Eagle-eyed Ham spotted it first. He pointed.

"There!"

The great winged monstrosity was sweeping along to the west, a macabre master of the night sky.

They took turns watching it with the binoculars.

"It's just scudding along at treetop height," said Long Tom.

"Look at them eyes!" exploded Monk.

They could see the skeletal crowns of the trees swaying as the black-winged thing swept by.

"It's big, all right," decided Long Tom, getting his first real look at the ebony apparition.

Suddenly, the thing gave a weird twist and cartwheeled above. Abruptly, fiery red eyes were glaring at them, coming closer by the minute.

"Quick. Inside!" rapped Doc.

No one questioned the order. The urgency in the bronze man's voice seized them all, fixing their attention.

Doc Savage pulled the cabin door shut, locked it.

Everyone rushed to the windows, began craning their heads, trying to get a good look at the approaching creature.

Great wings passed over them like the shadow of death itself. Their beating made a great commotion, stirring dead grass and equally dead tree branches farther away.

Only seconds did it linger, then continued on, where they could not follow it because there were no ports in the rear of the plane permitting viewing.

After a few seconds, Ham Brooks noticed a rank odor.

"What is that stench?"

Monk sniffed, made a face that would have done a bulldog proud. "Blazes! It smells like brimstone!"

"I detect sulphur, too," insisted Long Tom.

Everyone grabbed for handkerchiefs to place over noses and mouths to keep out the horrible stink. Habeas the pig began squealing in fright.

But Doc Savage was already handing out gas masks, for he had scented it first.

They donned these. They were compact devices of the bronze man's own invention. Consisting of a nose clip and chemical filter which fitted into the mouth, they were good for over an hour. There was also a canister-style custom job designed for Habeas Corpus. Monk fitted the elongated contraption over the shoat's inquisitive snout.

They got them on, including Fiana Drost, who had become terror stricken.

Long Tom suddenly asked, "What about Page!"

Only then did they remember their largely-invisible passenger. It was not a surprising thing. For except for his green eyes, Simon Page was hardly noticeable—the hairy man having divested himself of his borrowed clothing after complaining about the cabin's sultry warmth.

Doc Savage felt around the cabin.

"Gone!" he concluded.

Monk squeaked, "Blazes! He musta slipped out when we did, and we forgot to check for him."

Doc Savage opened the cabin door and began a reconnaissance of the immediate vicinity, Monk and Ham following close behind.

The metallic giant immediately spotted fur-fringed footprints, followed them a ways. There they collapsed into a disturbed blur in the cold dry soil of Ultra-Stygia. The trail petered out. Careful searching failed to pick up any spoor.

As luck would have it, Ham Brooks was shifting his cane before him, like a blind man. He encountered something obstructing his path, prodded it and called excitedly.

"Located the beggar!"

The others rushed over. Kneeling, Doc used his hands to feel for a body, encountered a man-sized bristled form and got his great cabled arms around it. The bronze man then gave the impression of a man lifting something imaginary.

Bearing the unseen form back to the aircraft cabin, Doc set it in a chair.

"Is he—dead?" asked Fiana quietly.

Doc felt around, encountered what he determined to be the chest, but the thick, coarse hair defeated his every attempt to detect a beating heart. He transferred his attention to the limbs and encountered hairy wrists. A thready pulse was detectable.

"Alive," he pronounced.

"Musta wandered off and gotten knocked out by the fumes," Monk hazarded.

"Evidently, they are not always fatal," Ham suggested.

Doc got another gas mask and after discovering the mouth and nose by touch, affixed it in place. It was like trying to muzzle a great wolf.

"He should come to in time," Doc said, straightening.

Long Tom turned to Monk and quipped, "Well, you called it."

"Huh?"

"A bat out of Hades, brimstone breath and all."

Fiana Drost remarked, "Such is the true nature of Ultra-Stygia. There are many entrances to Hell here. And many kinds of devils that emerge from the dark bowels of the earth below."

The mournful timbre of her voice made the flat pronouncement sound like a knell of doom.

DOC began issuing new orders.

"Monk, your portable laboratory, please."

"Gotcha."

Going to the back of the plane where metal storage containers were racked, the hairy chemist removed a large one that contained as complete a chemist's laboratory as was possible to assemble in one receptacle.

Taking this outside, he threw it open, began collecting samples of the air, which he captured in glass bottles.

At Doc's command, Long Tom returned to the radio cubicle to continue monitoring the broadcast transmission that carried the music of the lower regions, it seemed.

Outside, Doc borrowed some tools from Monk and began taking soil samples.

"What's that for?" asked Ham, who hovered about, having nothing otherwise to do.

"Two nations are contesting to dominate this land, barren and blighted as it is. There must be a sound reason."

"You are thinking minerals. Or gold. Maybe uranium."

"Land is usually valued for what lies in it, or how it can be developed."

Ham prodded the rocky soil with his slim stick.

"Doesn't appear to be suitable for farming, I would judge."

"Therefore, the soil contains a thing of value," said Doc.

Ham offered, "It is certain that this pocket of godforsaken turf is not coveted because it is crawling with unclean and unnatural things."

The dapper lawyer grew thoughtful. He had something on his mind, which was puzzling him.

"Doc, do you suppose the 'Dark Devil' that Emile Zirn spoke about is John Sunlight?"

Doc Savage shook his head slowly. "The Dark Devil is not a human being."

"How do you know?"

"By looking into the crystal," Doc said slowly.

His reply caused Ham to look extremely disappointed. Doc's answer was not serious. He could not tell any more than the next man by looking into a soothsayer's crystal ball.

Because of Doc's uncanny ability at reading clues and drawing conclusions from them, someone had once accused him of having the power of a seer.

The dapper lawyer wanted to ask the bronze man for more, but knew that Doc Savage only spoke of his conclusions when he was ready, not before.

Doc finished his analysis.

Ambling up, Monk asked, "Discover anything, Doc?"

"Nothing of consequence. And you?"

"A gas of some kind."

"Man-made?"

"Either that, or like nothing that was ever found before now."

"That hardly answers the question," sniffed Ham.

"Maybe you can find this stuff down in the hot place," Monk agreed. "Could be that big bat-monster brought a dose of it up from down below. But unless you want to be the first lawyer to go to Hell without dyin' first, my expert opinion is the best you have."

Doc climbed onto the wing and worked his way to the window, balancing himself atop the aircraft's roof. He had a chemical sprayer in one hand and a wad of waste rags in the other. Lying down on his stomach and applying the stuff to the windshield liberally, he began making inroads on the black stuff. It had begun to thicken. He took out a pocket clasp knife and did some scraping.

Monk watched this operation with gimlet-eyed interest.

"That sure ain't engine oil," he remarked. "Petroleum products don't harden up that fast."

"It appears not," agreed Doc, finishing the job and climbing back down to the ground.

He toted a sample of the sepia matter to Monk's portable lab and subjected it to a battery of tests. When he was done, his trilling sound issued forth from somewhere deep in his pulsing throat. It struck the ears surprisingly like a whistle of puzzlement.

"What is it?" Ham asked.

Doc replied, "There are several natural substances mixed in, including mucus, but the primary ingredient is an unusual one."

Expectant eyes regarded him.

"Octopus ink," said Doc.

Uneasy glances were exchanged. No one knew quite what

to say to that.

"Now what?" wondered Long Tom.

BEFORE anyone could answer, a flock of the huge black harpies flew overhead, elongated, rat-like snouts pointing south, toward the Tazan border.

Everyone looked up, following them with fascinated eyes.

"Look at the size of them!" Long Tom exploded.

"There must be a dozen of the devils," breathed Ham.

No expression crossed Doc Savage's face. "We will take to the air," he decided.

They climbed back on board. Doc Savage got the engines going, threw the craft around by releasing only one brake and, after releasing the second, threw the aircraft into a headlong sprint over the same patch of cinder-strewn ground on which he had landed.

They were aloft very quickly.

Doc climbed to an altitude that placed him considerably over the formation of harridan creatures.

"Figurin' to dive bomb them, Doc?" asked Monk from the co-pilot bucket.

Doc Savage shook his head. "I want to observe them carefully first."

Trailing the unearthly flock proved a simple matter. They did not appear to notice the big bronze bird flying along in the darkness. The wing-mounted motors could be silenced by the throwing of a cockpit lever. Doc engaged this. Operation of the silencer cost the engines some fuel efficiency, but Doc was more interested in stealth than speed.

Monk had his field glasses pointed downward. Ham was using a second pair plucked from a starboard seat pocket.

It was difficult to make out much. Black wings flowing over dark terrain. The moon lay behind a range of mountains. The twinkling of scattered starlight was of no help.

Ham was saying, "Those great wings appear to be... beating."

"So?" retorted Monk. "Ain't that what wings are supposed to do?"

"They are ribbed exactly like bat's wings," the dapper lawyer added. He sounded skeptical of his own words.

"Whatever they are," said Long Tom, taking his headset off for a moment to contribute to the conversation, "the things are flying in formation."

"Birds do that," Ham reminded.

"Bats don't," pointed out Long Tom.

That put an entirely different complexion on it.

Doc Savage trailed the chevron of monster bats as they approached the border with Tazan.

Up ahead, a contingent of soldiers and their vehicles were charging about, raising Cain.

"This appears to be the bunch that went searching for us after our escape from Jagellon Castle," said Doc Savage.

Approaching the steel-helmeted detachment, the bats broke formation, diving and swooping with grisly intent.

A coiling gray mist began filling the air. Trucks ground to a halt, and men piled out, fleeing in all directions. Scattering soldiers clutched at throats, began crumpling.

"Want to bet it smells of brimstone and sulphur?" remarked Long Tom.

No one took him up on that wager.

It was the matter of a few minutes before the black bats had finished with their awful activities.

When it was over, soldiers in uniform—their color was impossible to ascertain in the evening air—lay in heaps and clusters where they fell.

"What's goin' on?" blurted Monk.

From the rear, Fiana Drost intoned, "The legions of Hell are attacking Tazan."

"Will you knock that off?" snapped Long Tom. "You are

giving me the creeps with that kind of ghoul talk."

"You'd get bigger creeps if you ever saw her fly through the air like one of them midnight rodents," Monk muttered.

Their fiendish work done, the black bat-things wheeled about and, regaining altitude, flew back toward Egallah. They did not fly in formation this time, but went singly, as if once their dreadful deeds were accomplished, they had relaxed all discipline.

Their red eyes, skimming over the earth, were horrible to behold. They painted the surroundings with a lurid light.

DOC SAVAGE suddenly sent the aircraft screaming earthward. Wind in the wing braces began howling in sympathy with the powerful radials.

"What's going on?" demanded Fiana.

"It is my intention to throw a scare into these things," said the bronze man.

"Are you insane?" blazed Fiana. "They are devils. Things from earth's underbelly. You cannot—"

Doc Savage snapped the amphibian's wings about, lining up on the things until they were directly ahead of the discolored windshield.

With a bronze hand, he turned on the powerful wing-mounted flood lamps.

This illuminated the oncoming monsters. It also had an immediate effect upon them.

They began scattering. It happened very quickly, and perhaps only Doc Savage got a good look at the many-winged commotion. Abruptly, they were gone.

The bronze amphibian shot through the space where they had been, bore on.

"Man alive!" enthused Monk. "You spooked 'em good!"

"Did you see them more clearly?" asked Ham.

Monk replied, "Yeah. They looked like big bats with devil-eared heads and burnin' coal eyes. Nothing else."

"Impossible!" snapped Ham.

"I saw what I saw," returned Monk. "Don't say I didn't!"

Doc was maneuvering the amphibian about, attempting to find the bat squadron once more.

It took some doing. Doc spied no smoldering red orbs to help pick them out of the increasing dusk, but in time he found two that were flying close together.

Once he had the ugly pair in view, he snapped off the flood lamps and asked Monk Mayfair to fetch a pair of scanning binoculars. Monk came back with two sets.

Doc took his in hand. Monk lifted his, too. These ingenious devices were sensitive to so-called "invisible" light and enabled the viewer to see in absolute darkness.

Engaging an ultra-violet light projector mounted in the nose of the great aircraft, Doc Savage fell to studying the thing via "black light." Photofluorescent images began parading before his eyes, each one produced mechanically.

The world thus depicted had the qualities of a black-and-white movie, but with stark contrasts. In this uneven illumination, the two bat apparitions looked even more eerily alive.

"Glidin' home to roost somewhere," Monk decided.

"Bats live in caves, don't they?" asked Long Tom.

"Mostly," agreed Monk. "Caves or the hollows of trees and attics—when they can find their way in."

This particular species of bat proved to live in a cave—or rather several of them.

For as Doc Savage flew along, he spotted one of the harpy-like pair fluttering down into the mouth of a cave set in the side of a hill and vanish within.

"There he goes!" yelled Monk.

The other one selected an entirely different cave.

As they watched, additional bat monsters began arriving. Each selected a cave—the hills seemed to be honeycombed with them—and slithered in. They did not even tuck in their wings, but settled down in an uncanny way that appeared to defy gravity.

"We found their rookery," decided Monk. "What next?"

"We will continue on while seeking a suitable landing spot," said the bronze man without outward concern.

Chapter XIX

STRANGE CAVE

FOR THIS ONCE, Doc Savage proved to be a hopeless optimist.

No suitable landing spot could be found. True, the growing darkness made it harder to find any such flat locality. But this limb of Ultra-Stygia proved to be the hilly portion. Flat swatches were rare, and unsuitable due to craters, tumbled boulders, lightning-blasted dead trees and other natural obstructions.

By now the moon was up and they could see the spectral starkness of it all.

"This place was well-named," Ham opined. "Gives one the shivers."

"We will have to change plans," said Doc. "Monk, you will fly."

The apish chemist seized the controls. "What you got in mind, Doc?"

Instead of answering, Doc Savage went to the back of the aircraft and began donning a parachute pack. It was the last one in the remaining store. He wore his leather equipment vest, whose pockets were stuffed with myriad devices.

Long Tom, the electrical wizard, spoke. "I've got an angle to work on, Doc."

"You mean the mysterious music?" Doc asked. "That was the angle I intended to put you to work on. See if you can locate its source. But do not intervene."

"Got it."

"Isn't this one time it is too dangerous to go it alone?" asked Ham.

Doc replied, "Whatever impends, it seems to be concentrated in this region of Ultra-Stygia." The bronze man directed his steady gaze toward Fiana Drost. "What can you add to this?"

"Below is the Marea Negra," she said. "What the Tazans call Monti Alb. The most desolate and disputed pocket of Ultra-Stygia."

"Why is it so valuable?" asked Doc.

"Look below you," Fiana said dryly. "Obviously it is not. No?"

Doc Savage finished buckling the web harness and completed his instruction.

"There is no point in flying on to Egallah, or back to Tazan for that matter," he said. "We have no friends in either country. Return to the safe place where we last put down. I will join you there."

"But that's fifty miles back as the bat flies!" exploded Monk.

"I will find you," repeated Doc, who wasted no time in throwing open the cabin door and leaping out into space.

Ham rushed to pull the door shut, almost falling out himself because he neglected to abandon his stick while doing so, and it entangled with the door frame.

But the dapper lawyer got it shut. The air was very cold. It was winter, after all. Even if the early snows had yet to arrive.

Everyone settled down. The fact that their bronze leader had elected to go it alone was no surprise.

"He is a very foolhardy man, the bronze one is," intoned Fiana Drost, apparently unmoved by the display of courage Doc Savage had shown. "It is a shame that he is now doomed."

"If you keep up that funeral talk," Long Tom said sourly, "I am going to march back there and plug your tonsils with a vacuum tube."

Fiana looked indignant, but kept silent. Long Tom was no special gentleman when it came to difficult and possibly unsavory women. Such as Fiana Drost.

That caused the electrical expert to remember his shipboard encounter with the mystery woman.

"Know anything of a Countess Olga?" he asked Fiana.

Fiana Drost showed her first warm-blooded reaction.

"Who—what did you say?" she stuttered.

"You heard me. She called herself Countess Olga. The more I see of you, the more you remind me of her."

"You are not accusing me of being the notorious *Contesa* Olga Davour, are you?"

"You don't look much like her," admitted Long Tom.

"I thank you for the inadvertent compliment," said Fiana Drost coolly. "And to answer your question, Countess Olga is well-known in the upper circles of the Tazan leadership. One might venture to say that she is a personal pet of General Consadinos."

"Another spy, eh?"

Her voice became thin. "Possibly. One never knows about such persons."

"Well, she's dead anyway. Say, does the name Emile Zirn ring a bell?"

"It is a common name in my country, nothing more. Rather like Bill Smith or John Jones."

"Never mind," said Long Tom. "I didn't think you knew anything."

At that implied slight, Fiana Drost folded her arms and looked once again indignant. She took to staring out the window, as if wishing that she were anywhere other than in an aircraft hurtling over the grim desolation that was Ultra-Stygia.

DOC SAVAGE landed in the solitude of a copse of broken trees. These showed signs of having been shattered by a shell long ago, during the Great War, and left to be gnawed by insects. There were signs of frost heaves, which warped the landscape as if an earthquake had struck.

Shedding his parachute and pack, Doc made a bundle of both and shoved them into the dead part of a hollow tree, where they would be unlikely to be discovered.

There was no telling whether he had been spotted in his descent. His parachute was a neutral gray color designed to be visible in daylight, but less detectable at night. So the odds were in his favor.

Still, the bronze man dared not remain in one spot for very long.

Doc moved toward the cluster of caves into which the evil-looking black harpies had disappeared so incredibly.

He carried no weapon in the conventional sense, preferring to rely on his wits and the special equipment he toted in his carry-all inner vest which was filled with devices and implements sure to come in handy in a variety of circumstances.

Despite the fact that Doc had invented the supermachine pistols and was proficient in their use, it was not something he normally carried on his person. Long ago he had learned that a man with a weapon was easily disarmed and that weapon just as easily trained on the former owner.

So the bronze man went bare-handed.

By this time, there was an ivory moon hanging high in the sky. This washed a startling effulgence over everything, throwing deep shadows that were like inky pools in which dark devils might dwell.

From one of these to another, the bronze man made his stealthy way. He had learned the art of stalking from a number of experts, ranging from an Apache warrior to a Zulu tribesman. All of them had to be adept in negotiating their home turf. But Doc Savage's work took him to all parts of the globe and he needed to be prepared for outdoor activities from the Arctic to the Equator. So in combining these skills, the bronze man had become the greatest woodsman of them all.

Although the woods hereabouts left a lot to be desired in

terms of concealing properties, and nothing existed to permit the bronze man to leap from tree to tree as he liked to do, jungle-style, Doc made his silent way to a mouth of one of the caves.

Entering said cave might be another matter entirely.

Hunkering down behind a boulder that was balanced in an unnatural way, Doc studied the mouth of the place. It looked natural enough. It was stony, which suggested that these hills were more rock than soil.

The thought passed through the bronze man's mind that such a network of caves, whether connected or not, might have been worked as mines in the past. Sometimes even exhausted mines could be reopened to advantage.

He searched his retentive memory for what metals were common in this part of the Balkans, or had been in historic times. Gold and silver, certainly. But Ultra-Stygia had never been a gold field of any consequence. Other metals, of course, possessed commercial value, copper for example. Platinum was possible, too. Coal was common as well.

Dismissing that subject from his consciousness, Doc began creeping up on the yawning cave.

He decided that the best approach was to climb the overhanging hill to a point just above the cavern mouth and peer down from safety.

He did so.

Ironically, this put him in the position of hanging with his head down, rather like a bat. Bats prefer to sleep in an upside-down position, hanging by their feet, head downward, wings tucked in.

Lowering his head, Doc peered into the cave.

All was dark. The smell coming from the opening was earthy, unpleasant. It smelled like the den of something. He saw nothing. From his equipment vest came his spring-generator flashlight. He dared a quick flash ray.

It disclosed nothing more interesting than the interior gullet of a cave.

Rolling down from his perch, Doc became suspended by his fingers. He let drop to the earth and began inching forward, using his flashbeam sparingly, turning it on and off, giving the generator a wind now and then.

The earthen floor became moist and slippery the farther in Doc went. Directing the ray to his feet, he noticed a coating of slime. Grayish stuff. Splashing the ray along the walls, Doc saw more of the same. Some of it had hardened to a grayish-white crust, like dried toadstools.

This was the source of the earthy smell the bronze man had first detected.

Proceeding cautiously lest he slip, Doc Savage worked deeper into the cave.

It had some qualities of a mine, but of an older sort, hewn from rock long before modern equipment was devised. Nothing he saw gave any hint as to what had been mined here in olden days.

After a while, Doc detected a familiar sound.

It was the mad funeral melody again!

He paused, attempting to find the insane sound with his acute ears. It was definitely coming from within the deeper recesses of the cave, or mine, as it were.

From a pocket, Doc extracted two objects. One looked like a camera, but with a dark lens. The other was a pair of thick goggles. He put on the goggles and pressed a switch on the camera-like device. The thick-lensed goggles operated on a principle similar to that of a fluoroscope.

This was a more compact and correspondingly less powerful edition of his big ultra-violet projector. Good for only a few rods. The goggles translated the invisible "black-light" ray into visual images. This was done electrically. These goggles were more compact than the binoculars, and again were less acute. The pictures tended toward distortion.

Still, this allowed Doc to move ahead without betraying his

presence by employing any detectable light sources.

UP ahead, the cave entrance split into two forks, a greater and a lesser. The unearthly music appeared to be coming from the lesser. That was the fork Doc Savage chose.

Proceeding down this, he entered an area of hideous stalactites and stalagmites. Like closing fangs, these grew in great stony profusion. Under the shifting black light, they were shadowy and stark.

In the interstices between these, hung limp membranous forms. *Bats!*

These were the normal-sized variety. Evidently, they did not see him, for they slumbered on undisturbed, huddled in their enwrapping wings.

After a bit, Doc Savage grew curious. The bats should have stirred by now. And since they are creatures whose eyes are not very good, they should have smelled him. Their lack of stirring was also unusual.

So Doc took a chance and pegged a small stone in the direction of one cluster.

He managed to strike a bat in its brown-furred body. It fell from its perch, landing on its head. It did not rise or otherwise flap its folded wings.

Going to the thing, Doc nudged it with a toe. The curled-up bat did not respond. It had been alive once, but was now dead. Examining the claws, the bronze man saw signs where glue had been used to affix the animal to its anchorage. There were clear signs that this had once been a live specimen that had been stuffed by a taxidermist.

Doc's trilling coursed briefly, but he got hold of it. Evidently, these bats were affixed to the cavern walls to discourage exploration.

Moving along, Doc came to an area that was widening and heard something that sounded like footsteps, accompanied by a leathery rustling and flapping. These were no natural sounds, so Doc Savage prudently hung back in concealing shadows.

Voices began speaking. They were excited. He could not distinguish individual words, and the accents were strange. But this was a land of unusual accents, at least to American ears.

Pressing his great body between two stout stalagmites, Doc made himself immobile.

The excited chattering continued. Intermixed with it was a noisy clattering, as of a typewriter. Remembering Long Tom's description of a monotonous typewriting sound in cabin B-12 of the liner *Transylvania,* Doc listened carefully.

He could make little of the sounds, which might have been produced by a very skilled typist working an electric typewriter with smooth, steady precision.

At length, the clicking paused. A hurried series of movements suggested bodies racing about with urgent alacrity.

Doc waited. The mad footsteps were rushing his way.

Remaining immobile in the clotted darkness, Doc watched unseen as a cluster of upright beings charged by.

They looked leathery, their heads furred, black eyes goggling in a strange way. Arms pumping as they ran flapped grotesquely, due to membranes stretched between them and their unwholesome-looking bodies.

They resembled upright human bats racing by!

Doc allowed them to pass. Then he eased out of concealment, making his way toward the source of the music, which continued uninterrupted, accompanied by the robot-like clicking of keys.

As it happened, a straggler came into view.

He—or it—spotted Doc Savage. Atop its head, pointed devil ears seemed to become erect. Heels going into a skid, the creature gave out a very bat-like squeak. Arms to which were attached membranous wings flapped, windmilling frantically.

It appeared that the thing wanted to take flight. A moment later, it became obvious that it was only trying to regain its awkward balance.

This failed. The thing landed on its leathery tail.

Doc Savage pounced, found the thing's furry jaw, and stunned it with one bronze-knuckled fist.

The human harpy subsided; its smoky black eyes remained open and staring, however.

Giving it very little attention, Doc Savage moved to the source of the disturbing sounds.

He discovered a room carved out of the stone of the hill. A wooden door hung ajar. Doc opened this further, entered.

A droplight illuminated a small desk surface. There were chairs. Ordinary wooden chairs, as might be purchased in any furniture store.

Doc doused his black-light projector and doffed the fluoroscopic goggles.

In one corner sat a console radio receiver, no different from any that might dominate a living room in Manhattan or Pristav. The glow of the dial told Doc Savage that it was tuned to a commercial radio station.

ON the table reposed a machine which resembled an electric typewriter, except that it was mounted on a very thick base. Otherwise, it appeared to be an ordinary typewriter.

The keys were clicking busily. But there was no person seated in the chair, and no fingers typing away! Just the phantom action of the keys.

A continuous sheet of paper rolled up from a cardboard box into the platen of the device as the keys continued typing uninterrupted words onto the moving roll.

Doc Savage examined these lines as they were typed. The language employed was the national tongue of Egallah. The words were crisp, and efficiently composed. They had the quality of a military directive.

Reading along, Doc comprehended a great deal after very little effort. He transferred his scrutiny to the device itself, attempting to understand the nature and construction of the thing.

After a bit, he walked over to the radio and shut it off. The weird music instantly ceased. The miniature teletype machine—for that was what it appeared to be—also stopped working.

Doc turned on the radio set once more. Music again poured forth from the speaker grille. The typewriter keys resumed clacking away.

When Doc returned to read more, he noticed that a sentence or two was missing from the trend of the report.

Another paragraph of this intent perusal and Doc Savage was suddenly plunging out of the room and down the corridor.

The bronze man moved with the blinding speed for which he was famed. But the slippery floor defeated him somewhat.

Still, he made it to the place where the cavern forked and this time he whipped up the other way.

This fork was much wider. The way was not so slick underfoot. The farther he penetrated, the dryer it became. The way was crusty with the gray matter that might have been petrified toadstools.

This did not surprise him, although no trace of emotion touched his metallic features.

Doc had his goggles on and black-light projector working again.

They almost undid him.

Had he not been encumbered by them, Doc Savage might have paid more attention to his hearing. It is an interesting quirk of the human brain that when one focused on seeing, one pays much less attention to what reaches one's ears.

Doc was not paying sufficient attention to sounds reaching his ears.

So the roar that started rolling toward him was not detected until two great burning eyes came scooting his way!

Doc reversed direction. Whipping off his goggles, he sprinted toward the exit.

Pouring on speed, he reached the place where the cave forked, ducked around, reaching safety.

Just in time to see a great black bat of a thing go hurtling past him.

Another followed. Two more!

They tore by with a brisk beating of wings, making the cavern walls glow with their fiery orbs. Their long snouts brought to mind those of vicious hunting rats.

After the last of them passed, Doc raced toward the cave mouth in pursuit.

The bats were climbing into the sky, rising in a way that was unusual even for winged things. They seemed to possess the ability to rise almost vertically, as opposed to climbing in the natural fashion of such creatures.

Standing at the cave mouth, Doc watched them ascend.

As they climbed into the moonlight, the last to leave chanced to bank, as if taking a different course than the others.

This brought the ugly furred head swiveling around and the great fiery eyes seemed to fall on the Man of Bronze.

Suddenly, the foul-looking thing changed course again, and began coming at Doc! Beneath its body, great bony talons began clacking, opening and closing greedily.

The bronze giant decided not to retreat into the cave where he might be cornered. Instead, he flung himself to one side and raced into the desolate landscape.

An unholy red glow began pursuing him through the night. It lit up the surroundings, making them hellish and weird.

Behind him, Doc Savage detected the faint but ominous odor of brimstone, pressing closer and closer....

Chapter XX

TERROR IN THE SKY

THE BRONZE AMPHIBIAN volleyed along through the uncanny night of Ultra-Stygia, throwing a ground-traveling shadow ahead of it resembling a pursuing eagle.

Monk was flying. Ham Brooks had the co-pilot's seat.

The dapper lawyer was hectoring the hairy chemist on the subject of Habeas Corpus, the pig.

"One of these days I'm going to tie that insect's long ears into a knot and hang him on my Christmas tree for an ornament!" fumed Ham.

He was fuming because the pig had slipped up from his sleeping perch in the rear and made off with Ham's sword cane, which had been lying behind Ham's seat.

Ham had discovered this only after going to the rear of the aircraft and tripping over the strategically positioned stick. Ham had accused Monk of teaching Habeas to do that. Monk had denied everything, saying, "Habeas knows that you've been threatening to carve him with that fancy pig sticker of yours, so he was just protecting himself."

"If my Chemistry was here—"

Monk snorted, "If that mangy baboon of yours *had* tagged along, we'd probably still be cooling our heels in that clammy cell."

From the radio shack, Long Tom called, "Will you two pipe down? I think I have a fix on the radio station transmitting that music from the Netherworld."

"Is that so?" asked Monk. "Close to here?"

"Not sure. Can you swing around to the west?"

"Sure." Monk sent the big aircraft lumbering about.

Ham remarked, "Doc wanted us safely on the ground by now."

"We're gettin' there," said Monk. "It won't hurt to get a radio bearing on that broadcastin' station. Doc just don't want us to land there."

"It's on the commercial band, so there must be a pirate station or repeater out here," Long Tom mused. He was busy plotting lines on a chart.

Monk ran the amphibian back and forth in a pattern while Long Tom called out instructions.

"I think we just overshot it. What's below, anything?"

Ham pulled out a map and consulted it.

"A small town, or hamlet. Nedavno."

"I will lay odds that the music is being broadcast from Nedavno," Long Tom decided.

"Too bad we can't mosey down and take a looksee," murmured Monk, who was not looking forward to cooling his heels out in the wilds of Ultra-Stygia.

"Nedavno would be your undoing," said Fiana Drost from the rear of the plane, where she sat across from the slumbering form Doc Savage had deposited in the seat opposite. The green eyes of Simon Page had not opened once since take-off.

"You," grumbled Long Tom, "give me a sharp pain between my ears."

"Then you should cut them off. They are too big for your head."

Long Tom ignored that insult. The truth was that his ears were very generous. He was not particularly sensitive about it, but being reminded of the fact did not add any cream to his sour disposition.

"If we had any parachutes left," Monk noted, "you could drop in on them, Long Tom."

"An idea."

Ham complained, "Are you encouraging him, ape? Doc wants us to stay out of trouble until he returns."

"That don't mean we can't meet trouble if it comes after us," Monk pointed out.

Ham swallowed further protest. He knew that they had the latitude to follow their own judgment. But this was one time he felt that disobeying the bronze man's orders would lead to disaster.

As it developed, matters were taken out of their hands.

It happened this way:

THE night was far along; midnight drew near. It had never more the semblance of a witching hour than over the vast desolation of Ultra-Stygia. Even the clouds marching along around them appeared sinister, like hump-backed monsters on the prowl.

There was a stirring in the rear.

Fiana Drost was the first to notice this. Her dark orbs went to the seat into which Doc Savage had placed their invisible passenger. The cushions were dented. Now these indentations began to shift of their own volition.

"He is waking," she said almost without interest.

Then came a sharp intake of breath as Fiana saw a solitary eye pop open. It roved about, shot in her direction, focused angrily. The orb was not the cat-green she had expected.

An unladylike scream issued from her red lips.

"His eye! *It is black!*" she shrieked, retreating to the rearmost portion of the cabin.

Long Tom was the first one out of his seat. Ham uncoiled not a step behind him.

They rushed down the narrow aisle. Long Tom spotted the floating orb first. It glared like an animated 8-ball.

"Trouble!" he rasped.

"Where is my stick!" Ham cried.

It was nowhere to be seen, so Ham made his hands into fists and prepared to wade in behind Long Tom.

The problem was, they could see the floating eye of the opponent, but nothing more of him. This presented a problem in tactics.

Unseen hands reached out, and as it happened, grabbed Long Tom by one oversized ear, twisted painfully.

Seeing stars, he was hurled back at Ham. The latter dodged, tried to work around the flailing electrical wizard.

The dapper lawyer half succeeded. Stepping over Long Tom, he managed to position himself for the attack.

As Fiana watched, horror written all over her face, Long Tom's head and Ham's skull suddenly weaved apart, only to come crashing together with an audible *bonk!*

The two would-be combatants collapsed, knocked senseless.

At the controls, Monk roared. He was in the act of setting the robot pilot—which would allow the craft to fly itself for a time—when something big and heavy lumbered up behind him. He felt the cool edge of Ham's sword cane resting just beneath his unshaven jaw.

"If I slice, you die," a growling voice warned.

"If I die, we crash," Monk pointed out.

"I am prepared to die for the glory of my nation," the other countered.

"Yeah. What nation is that?"

"The nation that lies beneath the crust of the earth. You know of it. The country of the damned called Hell."

"Now that you mention it, I do," said Monk, stalling for time. "Back in Sunday School, they talked it up somethin' powerful."

Then he seemed to have trouble with his throat.

"What is that you said?" demanded the unseen one.

"Just clearin' a clog in my throat," explained Monk. "Where

do you want me to set down?"

The sword cane left his Adam's apple, and the tip pointed off to starboard.

"Turn around. West. I will direct you."

"Sure. Anything you say."

The growling voice warned, "No tricks."

Monk made his voice innocent. "Tricks. Me? I'm no magician."

The simian chemist noticed the reflection in his windscreen. One ebony eye floated directly behind him, staring like a reverse-hued 8-ball.

Just then, the hairy thing gave out a yelp of pain and began dancing on one foot. Or so it sounded to Monk Mayfair as he popped out of his bucket seat and began jabbing hairy knuckles at the spot where he believed the thing's invisible skull was. His first swing missed. The second connected. There was the audible crunching sound of a broken jaw, but it might have been a neck bone.

In either case, the unseen creature began falling backward, detached black orb careening madly.

Habeas the pig, having nipped the thing's ankle unexpectedly, hastily retreated, lest he be trampled by the toppling brute. It slammed to the floor, its noisy fall the only evidence of its defeat.

That grisly black eye goggled upward like a moist billiard ball. Boar-bristled paws grabbed for Monk's ankles, squeezed hard.

Monk let out a war whoop that would have done credit to a Comanche. The apish chemist executed a two-footed jump that landed on the prostrate chest of his assailant. Breath gushed out of the foe's lungs. That took the fight out of the beast.

Reaching out, Monk found Ham's sword cane and used it to prod at the body of his fallen foe. The anesthetic-coated tip did its work. All activity subsided. Normal breathing returned. The black eye stared up blankly, and did not move.

Monk grinned. "Good thing I taught you the Mayan word for 'bite.' Right, Habeas?"

The ungainly shoat squealed happily, but maintained a respectful distance.

Returning to the pilot's seat, Monk regained control of the aircraft.

Fiana Drost crept forward, eyes stark.

"It is one of the *Ciclopi*," she breathed.

"We musta retrieved the wrong guy," declared Monk. "Now we gotta find Simon Page again—if we can."

"I doubt that we will ever see Page alive, again," Fiana said dolefully.

"To talk so cheerfully all the time," muttered Monk, "you musta had a rough childhood."

"I am speaking truth."

"Well, I, for one, could stand to hear less of it," growled Monk. "Now simmer down, you gloomy Garbo. I gotta find us a landin' spot."

Fiana withdrew to sulk in her seat.

Monk concentrated on his flying, paying little attention to anything else. He listened for any sign of Ham and Long Tom coming back to life, but all he could detect was their monotonous breathing. Years in the company of his two comrades had familiarized him with their distinctive breathing. Long Tom snored. Ham rather whistled.

After some time, a new sound came to his ears.

At first, it came as a ripping, followed by an unpleasant noise as if someone was choking, or perhaps drowning noisily.

"What the heck's goin' on?" asked Monk, screwing his apish head around.

He was just in time to spy Fiana Drost stand up from the spot immediately behind the pilot compartment, where that gruesome ebony eye stared ceilingward.

"It is nothing," she said. "I have merely cut the worthless

brute's throat."

"You did what!"

"He is an enemy, and therefore deserving of his fate."

Setting the robot pilot, Monk pounded out into the aisle. He all but tripped over the hairy heap that obstructed the forward portion of the aircraft.

Reaching down, he felt around the thing, encountered stiff bristles. The impression of a hulking hedgehog was created in Monk's mind.

As he did so, he could see the hackles on the back of Habeas rise in a startling fashion; the pig's beady eyes looked unnerved.

Locating the head, Monk probed for the throat. He encountered a wet slick of moisture. It ran warm and thick.

Leaping to his feet, he stared at his fingers.

They looked dry, but felt wet. Monk sniffed. The metallic tang of blood filled his apish nostrils.

"Ye-o-o-w!" howled Monk. "Throat cut!"

"Did I not tell you this?" returned Fiana coolly.

Wiping his hands on a rag, Monk returned to the controls, feeling his own blood run cold in his veins.

"Lady, I don't know what Doc will do with you when this is all over, but I think he's gonna have to find a special place for you."

"There is no place for me," said Fiana Drost dolefully. "On this Earth, or elsewhere. Not any more."

LONG TOM ROBERTS was the first to awaken. He shook his head and climbed to his feet.

Feeling of his bruised skull, he asked, "What happened?"

"The black-eyed Cyclops knocked your heads together," explained Monk.

Long Tom looked around wildly. "Where is it?"

"On the floor right in front of you."

Blowing on one fist, Long Tom said, "I'll teach it to smack

its betters."

"Don't bother. It's dead. Fiana cut its throat."

Long Tom looked less surprised than he should. "Why?"

Fiana answered that. "I wanted to drink its blood, but since decided against it. The brute smells like a skunk. No doubt its blood would taste putrid on my tongue."

Long Tom looked as if he didn't know whether to believe the dark-haired woman, so he concentrated on getting Ham Brooks roused. He brought some cold water from the lavatory and splashed it in the dapper lawyer's patrician face. That did the trick.

Coming to, Ham asked the same questions. When Long Tom explained what had happened, Ham's alert eyes went to Fiana Drost, then his manicured hands felt of his own throat.

"I will consider myself lucky that I did not fall victim to the same fate," he gulped.

"Perhaps next time I feel thirst," said Fiana disinterestedly.

"Where are we?" snapped Long Tom, jumping to the radio set.

"Almost there," replied Monk.

"Good. Let's see what's coming in over the radio." Clapping headsets to his ears, the puny electrical expert fiddled with the dials.

"There's a lot of chatter on the military band," he said excitedly. "Too bad I don't know enough of the local lingo to follow along."

"Let me hear it," suggested Fiana.

Long Tom unplugged the jack, cutting the transmission into the cockpit.

Excited words spewed forth.

"They are frantic," said Fiana.

"Who is?"

"The forces of Egallah."

"About what?"

"I am not certain. But they are mobilizing. They say that the Dark Devil is loose."

"Loose?"

"Perhaps they mean missing. I cannot follow it. But they are ordering their forces into Ultra-Stygia to recover it. Yes, they are saying 'recover.' The Dark Devil—whatever it may be—is lost to them."

"That means the war is on!" howled Monk.

Ham frowned, "It may be too dangerous to land in Ultra-Stygia now."

"Got a better plan?" snorted Monk.

No one did.

Monk suddenly announced, "Take your seats. Landing coming up."

Everyone settled down. Including Habeas. Ham took the co-pilot's chair again.

Monk overflew the landing spot once, seemed satisfied, and began his approach. The landing wheels came down electrically.

Lining up the plane, Monk's tiny eyes combed the desolate stretch of land being illuminated by the wingtip landing floods.

Suddenly, the lights went out.

At first, Monk and Ham thought that the floods had been hit by gunfire. They would not hear bullets arriving over the howling of wind in the struts. Not in the scientifically sound-proofed cabin.

But after only a few seconds, they realized that they could see nothing at all.

Moonlight turned to jet darkness.

"What black magic is this?" Fiana Drost moaned, clapping hands over suddenly aching eyes.

"The damn *black* again!" Long Tom moaned.

"Pull up! Pull up!" Ham cried out.

"Too late," growled Monk. "Brace yourselves! I'm putting

this baby down—hard!"

The sound of the wheels striking earth was a noise none of them would ever forget. It went on and on for what seemed an unending, nerve-wracking eternity.

Monk cut the motors. After what felt like forever, he thought it safe to apply the brakes. He heard them lock, and the hurtling machine began to slow.

When all motion ceased, a profound silence hung over all. They took stock, first feeling their arms and legs for breaks and other serious wounds. They looked around with eyes that saw nothing. Waving hands in front of their faces produced no sensation other than a fanning breeze.

The world was a deep black pit in which they dwelled in abject, unrelieved darkness.

The peevish voice of Long Tom Roberts broke the silence.

"Talk about pitch black," he clipped.

"Did we make it?" Ham wondered aloud. "I mean, are we still alive?"

"Who can tell in this blasted *blot?*" muttered Long Tom peevishly.

From what seemed to be an infinite distance behind them, Fiana Drost said morosely, "No, we are all dead."

Chapter XXI

MONSTER BAT

DOC SAVAGE RAN as never before. He put all his energy into headlong motion, bending almost double in his urgency to outrace the thing pursuing him.

As he ran, the bronze giant reached into his emergency vest for one item.

Out came a slim case that opened to reveal several glass globes nested in cotton. Doc removed two of these and began pegging them directly behind him.

They broke on the ground, releasing an invisible, odorless gas capable of bringing down a charging bull, once inhaled.

But the bat-thing swept through the gas, unfazed, clacking claws grasping madly. Doc tossed several more. This time, he risked the loss of forward momentum to glance over his shoulder.

The lower jaw of the bat monster dropped, disclosing discolored yellow fangs. Eyes above the flaring nostrils were glowing weirdly. A hungry squeaking issued forth.

Doc threw one grenade into the creature's open mouth. His aim was true. The thin-walled globe broke, releasing its contents, but that was all that resulted.

Nothing seemed to retard the rat-faced creature. The whir of its wings grew louder, nearer, infinitely more menacing.

Recognizing that he had no hope of outdistancing the ghoulish pursuer, Doc Savage dropped to the ground, rolling to one side.

Metallic hands dived into his equipment vest. This time they came out holding steel forms the size of pigeon eggs. He armed these with a flick of tiny levers.

As the thing passed overhead, Doc flung them, then dived for the shelter of a cluster of tumbled stones.

These were explosive grenades. They let go a heartbeat apart, expelling noise, smoke and vicious shrapnel.

Doc's aim was true. One wing came off the winged apparition. Its high-pitched squeal came to the bronze man's ears, where he crouched safely.

Skimming low to the ground, the great bat of a thing careened along, until its surviving wing encountered a dead tree. Tree and wing tangled, with the result that the monster was thrown to one side and landed face-first in the ground, its leathery tail upended and askew.

As if struggling to regain its natural aerial element, the manic beating of wings sounded clearly. Then another noise, as if frantic pinions were flailing themselves to pieces. This cacophony finally ceased.

A silence followed.

PICKING himself up, Doc Savage started in the direction of the fallen monster.

He did not get far when his ears detected a weird whirring sound—and over a rise came another of the mammoth creatures!

This one swooped down at a steep angle that defied belief, claws poised for a grab. A hawk might drop on its prey by such a fierce maneuver. Yet this was no hawk, but a great black behemoth in the form of a bat.

Reversing course, Doc sought shelter. He sprinted with all of his might, but in a contest between man and animal, man often comes out second best.

The whirring of wings told the bronze man that it was almost upon him. A great shadow overhauled him, intercepting the lunar light.

In the act of twisting to one side, Doc felt something clamp him about the head and shoulders!

Struggling against what felt like the jaws of a steel vise, the metallic giant found himself being lifted into the air. Straight up! With a mad beating of wings, the awful creature was lifting him off the Earth!

Bronze fingers reached for purchase, encountered talons that felt hard and horny. Using this as leverage, he twisted, attempting to break free.

Doc Savage might as well have battled the hand of a colossus of steel. The talon refused to relinquish its obdurate grip.

In his equipment vest was a small bundle, a folding grappling hook and knotted cord, the latter very strong.

Doc got this out, flicking it open. He swung the tiny grapple in a tight circle several times and let go.

The sharp tines found purchase in the wing bones above, caught and held fast. Doc next wound the cord around one wrist, made it secure.

It was wise that he did so, for another fifty feet of vertical climbing later, the claw clamping the bronze man so tightly abruptly let go!

Doc dropped free—*but the cord held!*

Grasping it with his other hand, he released his wrist and began climbing the cord two-handed, using the knots for handholds.

This brought him up to the furry belly of the behemoth bat. The scent of the monster was suggestive of a tomb, smacking of something long dead.

The bronze man could see little at first. Then he spied what appeared to be the creature's talons hanging on either side of him. They were as large as shovels, nails sharp in the manner of pitchforks.

Doc began swinging his muscular body. Like a pendulum, he swayed, rocking the bat in flight. There came a precarious wobbling, followed by an abrupt reaction, until the thing righted itself.

At the apex of one swing, Doc grasped a claw-tipped leg, clamped it firmly. He transferred, and managed to cling with both hands. This brought him close to one great webbed wing, whose skin he could see flap and chatter as the wind and slipstream worried it. It was held stiffly rigid as it swept over the fierce terrain below.

The bronze man's muscular strength could impress a person as prodigious. But Doc Savage was no mere muscle-bound exhibitionist. Great effort and attention had gone into other aspects of his physical training. He could have worked as a professional gymnast or circus acrobat if he so chose.

Doc Savage demonstrated his acrobatic skills now.

First, he kicked off his shoes. Then, employing agile toes, he removed both socks. Tucking his legs under him, with the wind whipping his face, Doc executed a snapping maneuver that drove both feet through the flapping wing surface. The stuff was tough, but the power of Doc's kick was greater still.

He was soon hanging by his amazingly prehensile toes, levering his upper body until bronze digits found suitable purchase among the splayed wing ribs. He scrambled over.

Soon Doc was lying along the wing, which remained stiff as the thing glided along. Curiously, the beating and whirring sounds of its flight came from above the outflung wings.

But the bronze man gave that curious phenomenon no attention.

Instead, he crawled toward the great bat-eared head. And there encountered a ghastly sight.

There, like a baby clinging to its mother, a smaller bat head turned and snapped at him with smoky black eyes.

For back of the head was a cockpit, and seated within was one of the bat-men he had earlier encountered.

Doc Savage moved toward the human bat, intending to grasp it by the neck in order to overpower the being.

The other reached for his throat, and fur-trimmed hands

came away with a sharp object—a medallion in the shape of the spread-winged bat. It glinted viciously.

Standing up in the cockpit, the bat-man made a sudden lunge with the throat-ripping tool.

A bronze hand flicked out, tore it free. It went overboard.

Smoky eyes goggled. The strength and speed of the bronze man was dazzling. The creature emitted a cry of undisguised fear and leaped from his perch!

Out he went. The body of the great bat monster began tipping, veering out of control.

Doc hastily jammed himself into the vacated seat. He instantly familiarized himself with the controls before him. They resembled those of an autogyro, but much more complicated.

Testing the cant lever, he got the thing under control and sent it winging in the direction of the spot where the bat-man had bailed out.

Peering down, Doc saw a manlike black shape, arms and legs stretched outwards, and in between, a leathery webbing. The creature employed these membranous wings to catch updrafts and air currents, which created a remarkable braking effect that slowed its descent. Once, it executed a looping turn that actually caused it to glide. The effect was of human flight, but the bronze man recognized these acrobatic maneuvers as techniques employed by the barnstorming stuntmen known as delayed parachute jumpers.

Doc circled, watching and waiting.

He almost missed the parachute bell when it finally blossomed like a black mushroom, but moonlight dusted it sufficiently to disclose that the pilot had cracked silk.

After determining that the bat-man had landed safely, Doc sent his strange steed northward, to the spot where Monk, Ham, and the others should be waiting for him.

A light snow began to fall.

As if the swirling precipitation portended something sinister, Doc Savage advanced the throttle of the macabre bat-ship.

Chapter XXII

OGRES IN THE NIGHT

IN THE INTENSE, irredeemable darkness, Long Tom was saying, "If you were a man, I would sock you good."

His bile was being directed at the unseen Fiana Drost.

"If you feel teeth upon your throat," returned the woman, "they will be mine. Then it will be too late for you."

"I've had enough of your brand of sunshine," Long Tom gritted.

"And I, of yours," Fiana flung back haughtily.

They were picking their way through the amphibian cabin, feeling for the cabin door. Ham found the door handle first, yanked and threw it open.

"Drat!" he exclaimed upon poking his head out.

"What now?" groaned Long Tom.

Ham sighed, "I suppose it was too much to hope for. Seeing moonlight. But it's just as black out there as it is in here."

"Let's step out anyway," suggested Monk.

They tumbled out, Monk last. He shut the door before Habeas Corpus could escape. Retrieving the shoat, should he become lost in the seemingly infinite dark, would be a near impossible task.

The apish chemist squinted around with eyes that saw nothing. The effort to perceive any particle of light made them throb.

"Black as a bat's nightmare," he decided.

"We are not dead?" demanded Fiana Drost from nearby.

"Don't be such a problem child," sulked Long Tom.

"The way Doc explained the how this darkness-marking machine works," Monk was saying, "is that it creates an electronic field, causin' the rod-and-cone mechanism of the eyes to stop workin'. Any light gettin' to our retinas won't be turned into pictures in our brains."

"That shouldn't bother you any," Ham said unkindly. "You have hardly any brains to begin with."

Long Tom was moving about the aircraft's exterior by feel, seeking the landing gear. Condition of the struts and tires would tell him how rough the landing had been.

"Everything checks out O.K.," he reported.

Monk said, "Not a bad landing—if I do say so myself."

Ham scowled. "Let's wait for light before you start boasting. We don't know if the wings are still attached."

But Monk had already clambered up on the high wing and began bouncing along its length like a boisterous bull gorilla demonstrating his strength.

"Feels solid," he pronounced.

The other side of the wing proved to be intact, also, from the whanging sounds it made under Monk's tramping feet. Satisfied, the hairy chemist leapt to the ground and, guided by voice sounds, joined the others.

They sat down to wait for Doc Savage, no better course of action suggesting itself. Walking around the plane had caused them to bump into one another repeatedly and this was becoming tiresome.

As Monk put it, "If we wander off, no tellin' how hard it'll be to get back."

A steady wind began blowing. It made a low keening, as of lost souls in search of home. A wintery chill touched their exposed flesh, prompting shivers. The air was filled with the smoky scent that overhung parts of Ultra-Stygia, owing to the burning of dead vegetation. This made throats scratchy, and clogged nostrils, which accounted for what happened next.

Fiana Drost suddenly gasped.

Ham demanded, "What?"

"I hear something."

"Probably a bad dream you had once," said Long Tom sourly.

"No!" Fiana dropped her voice. "I hear footsteps."

Monk had excellent hearing, and cocked his nubbin of a head this way and that, ears hunting sounds.

"I ain't hearin' anything but the dang wind."

"I believe fresh snow is falling," suggested Ham.

Monk reached out an apish hand in the painfully-intense darkness and scooped up some of the cold precipitation. Tasting it, he pronounced, "Snow all right. Heavy stuff, too. We may have to move back into the plane."

It was a good idea, but they got organized too slowly for it to pay off.

First, Fiana Drost stood up. They could hear her unfold herself, but that was all.

"I *smell* them," she breathed anxiously.

"Who?" asked Long Tom.

Sniffing the air, Monk Mayfair suddenly shot to his feet.

"She ain't kiddin'. I smell polecat, too!"

"What?" wailed Ham.

Monk bellowed, "It's them invisible hedgehog things!"

WITH that, everyone found their feet. The natural instinct was to make a circle, with their backs to one another. They did that in a rough fashion, by feel, but by the time they managed it, the foul odor was unmistakable in their recoiling nostrils.

"Everyone back into the plane," ordered Ham, waving his sword cane about commandingly. Unfortunately, it was a poor idea because in doing so, he conked Long Tom by accident.

Thinking an unseen foe had struck him, Long Tom lashed out with a bone-hard fist and knocked the dapper lawyer off his feet, with the result that Ham saw stars and lost consciousness. Long Tom packed dynamite in his fists.

Monk hissed, "What happened?"

"I think I socked Ham by accident," said Long Tom.

"You shoulda been more careful," Monk gritted.

"He started it."

Monk gathered the unconscious barrister in his burly arms and bore him toward the open cabin door. The hairy chemist advanced three paces before he encountered something as hairy as himself. The sensation was of a great invisible porcupine obstructing his path. It smelled rank, beastly.

"Uh-oh," undertoned Monk.

"What is it?" hissed Fiana sharply.

"One of them blasted ogres. Right in front of me."

"Where?" demanded Long Tom. "I can't see a blamed thing!"

No one could. It was maddening. The effort to see through the impenetrable darkness made their eyes ache like diseased teeth.

Gingerly, they began backing away.

This time, Fiana Drost ripped out a scream that might have brought some of her soul coming up through her throat.

"There is one here... beside me..." she husked.

"Where?" yelled Monk, jumping around in place and making furry fists.

It was at that point when they realized that they were helpless. Helpless and surrounded by the unseen things whose invisibility was made more distressing due to the baffling influence of the darkness maker.

"Wait a minute," mumbled Monk. "If we can't see them, they can't see us. Right?"

"I don't know," admitted Long Tom doubtfully.

Abruptly, Monk dropped Ham Brooks to the ground and felt about for Ham's dropped stick. Monk used his foot, encountered the barrel, and reached down without hardly having to bend. His apish arms were exceedingly long.

Separating the thing, Monk whispered in Mayan, "Hit the ground." He waited for the sound of dropping forms. Then he began flailing the supple blade around in wild circles.

The hairy chemist was no swordsman. He jabbed, stuck and plunged the blade into any hairy form he encountered. He encountered many.

Hands clutched at him, seized, but suddenly relaxed as the potent anesthetic daubed on the sharp point worked its chemical magic. Merely a scratch introduced the quick-acting stuff into the bloodstream.

"If Ham ever finds out I had to use his overgrown pig-sticker," Monk muttered darkly, "I'll never live it down."

"Are you beating them?" Long Tom demanded, head swiveling in futile anger.

"They keep coming!" complained Monk, swinging wildly. "And this sticky dope don't last forever."

It was the truth. Monk stabbed and jabbed again and again. But although he laid a stack of the coarse-coated monsters at his feet, others moved in with grasping paws that triggered acute terror in the unrelieved darkness.

Suddenly, moonlight washed over all. Just like that.

It had the effect of harsh sunlight on their unprepared optics.

Bellowing, Monk threw a hirsute beam of an arm across his deep-set eyes to protect them.

A great unseen paw swept in and relieved him of Ham's stick.

Seeing this, Fiana screamed, then choked back all further outcry. All of her cool self-possession had been stripped away by the hideous combination of frustrating darkness and unseeable foes.

Lowering his arms, Monk peered around, heavy jaw slack, seeing nothing. The former impression of many forms crowding him was suddenly no longer there.

Instead, Monk saw that he was surrounded by a veritable wall of eyes. Separate, varicolored orbs regarding him with cold, inimical intent. It was as if some species of otherworldly bees were harassing them. Their unremitting stares were something to remember.

"You will all surrender," a firm voice ordered.

Monk looked around, seeking the source of that commanding voice.

A green-uniformed man stepped forward. General Basil Consadinos!

MONK exploded, "What are you doin' here?"

"Preparing to launch a war that I cannot lose," said the general, smiling under his pointed mustaches.

While that was sinking in, a new figure stepped forth.

Alone of all of them, Long Tom recognized the smooth features of the new arrival. He was a wolfishly lean man.

"Emile Zirn!"

"That ain't the Emile Zirn we met," Monk muttered, squinting at the man.

"It's the one from the *Transylvania*," explained Long Tom.

Monk asked, "The gink who went up in a cloud of smoke back on that liner?"

"The very same," said Emile Zirn proudly. "It was a very smooth trick, I might add."

Long Tom eyed the other narrowly. "I had my doubts about your story," he said.

Zirn executed a polite bow. "It was sufficient for me to cover all tracks and return to my homeland with my prize."

"Prize?"

"I might have lost it to certain Egallan spies," Zirn offered, "but they fell upon you instead. Or so I am told. Your misfortune became my salvation, you see."

"The typewriter case you carried to the hotel," Long Tom growled. "What is it?"

"Never mind," snapped General Consadinos. "For we have just acquired a newer prize. A glorious trophy of war." He seemed very pleased with himself.

The war minister lifted a heavy hand and made a gesture.

All light vanished. Their eyes began hurting, it was so dark.

"The blasted *black*," muttered Long Tom.

They stood in the smothering grimness for less than a minute before the general called, "Light, please."

The world returned to normal—or as normal as the spectral weirdness of Ultra-Stygia could seem.

A soldier in green was crouching there, closing a heavy steel box which sat on the ground. The darkness-making mechanism was apparently housed within.

The general smiled at them. "We have lately acquired this from our national enemy, Egallah. Now we may proceed with the annexing of the Marea Negra region of Ultra-Stygia as a first step toward hurling the enemy far from our present frontier."

"Blazes!" Monk said. "How'd you get it away from them?"

"Our Elite Guard has the ability to go anywhere in Ultra-Stygia—and Egallah, for that matter—to spy and pillage at will."

General Consadinos gestured toward the numberless orbs that surrounded them. They blinked as lightning bugs might, one at a time, no two exactly matched. It was unsettling.

"You control these things!" blurted out Long Tom.

"They are our secret weapons. Not monsters, but men. Loyal soldiers of the Tazan nation."

"There's been talk about your nation conducting scientific experiments with invisibility," said Long Tom.

The general nodded in acknowledgement. "Experiments which have succeeded—but not without peculiar side effects. Hair on men is one of them. But we discovered that this could be put to good use. Instead of invisible spies, we had produced invisible creatures. Hair growing so profuse that it covered the eyes. So we instructed our Cyclops Corps to cut back the hair over one eye only. That made what remained half as visible, and produced a very shocking effect. No?"

"Not Cyclops after all," muttered Monk. "Just hairy men with one eyeball covered."

"This preyed upon the animal fears of the Egallans, who are a very superstitious people. For this land is said to abound with *varcolaci*—werewolves to you."

Monk said, "Wait a minute! What about that big monster that pulled the other Emile Zirn apart? The thing with a dozen heads and twice as many paws. Ham and I saw it."

"Or thought you did," purred General Consadinos. He snapped his fingers once.

Suddenly, Monk was surrounded by a half a dozen unmatched eyeballs. Heavy hands took him by his wrists, elbows—everywhere. He felt them rather than saw them. Hides so hairy they scratched his rusty skin.

Monk lunged forward in the middle of the grunting commotion. His rusty-knuckled fists began popping about him. They smashed faces—or what felt like faces, producing the sounds of very satisfying grunting and pained exclamations of surprise. Encouraged by this, Monk's big feet began to stamp. This, too, brought reactions. Howls of agony accompanied the crunching of toe bones. The press of unseen hairy bodies seemed to retreat.

"Boy oh boy, am I hot tonight!" Monk said gleefully.

Monk's foes were tough. Moreover, there seemed an unending supply of them. Others rushed in, took fresh hold. Monk wrenched, fought back. With each move, he emitted a whooping howl or bellow of wrath. But the supply of unseen combatants appeared inexhaustible.

Soon, Monk was overwhelmed. Before he knew it, the homely chemist was lifted into the air and pulled in several directions by strong pairs of bristling but irresistible hands.

"Ye-o-o-w!" he hollered. "Leggo of me, you hair-coated goons!"

Monk's strength was prodigious. He pulled one hand free and lashed out. Four more paws seized his furry wrist, arresting it. It was impossible to fight the unseeable. But Monk gave it his all. He tried biting. Twisting his bullet head, his great teeth snapped in vain. Something slapped him in the face. He roared. Feet kicked out. Monk's ribs took a pounding. He kicked back.

In the end, he had to take it. Growling, Monk gave up.

"Do you understand now?" asked the general. "You saw only eyes, nothing more. The rest was your imagination attempting to cope with what you perceived. Thus do we of Tazan control and guard Ultra-Stygia."

Long Tom had attempted to intervene, but something that felt like a bear tripped him so hard he landed on his stomach. A heavy foot reminiscent of a barrel cactus set down on his back and kept him flat to the cold ground.

After a bit, the foot withdrew and Long Tom was allowed to stand up. He looked like a man spoiling for a fight, but the wall of staring orbs which closed in from all sides dissuaded the slender electrical wizard.

MONK began floating away. Another one-eyed ogre picked up Ham Brooks. The elegant barrister was promptly carried off, shouldered, to all appearances, as if by a playful winter wind.

Long Tom and Fiana Drost fell in line, shoved along by the rude porcupine things.

"I am to be executed," Fiana said unhappily.

"You should be used to it by now," grumbled Long Tom, becoming even more sour than usual. But the bleak circumstances justified his lack of sentimentality.

"You will doubtless face the same fate," Fiana pointed out.

"There isn't a bullet in Ultra-Stygia with my name on it," Long Tom said confidently. He made an elaborate show of expectorating into the snow.

But inwardly, the electrical genius had his doubts. None of them were carrying their supermachine pistols. They had neglected to collect them upon exiting the plane, because they knew they would be useless without the faculty of sight. And their pockets were likewise bereft of useful devices.

They were marched some distance to a military truck. This was painted, of all colors, black. Somehow it seemed to fit the surroundings, if not the circumstances.

In the back of the truck lay a man they knew.

Long Tom was the first to recognize him.

"I'll be damned! Baron Karl himself."

The baron sprawled in the flatbed of the truck. He was spread-eagled, as if his ankles and wrists were tied to separate cords and these stretched in four directions, anchored to the wooden sides of the open truck. But they were not.

The baron groaned. His face was ghastly, a combination of lunar-painted pallor and exquisite agony. His trademark monocle was missing.

Upon closer inspection, Long Tom noticed that his physical condition suggested that his arms and legs had been pulled from their sockets and he had therefore lost all power over them.

"Just desserts," pronounced Long Tom.

"The good baron came to us, offering to come over to our side," explained the general. "But we would have none of this traitor to his own nation. We seized him instead. He resisted our interrogation techniques." Consadinos smiled thinly. "For a time. But when the pain grew too great, he told us where to locate the machine which produces darkness."

"Figures," said Long Tom. "The chiseler probably never turned the darkness maker over to his leader."

"Precisely," confirmed General Consadinos.

They were forced at rifle point to climb into the truck bed. Ham was tossed in without ceremony. Monk was dumped in last, like a sack of russet potatoes. Released from the multiple grips, he bounded to his feet, bearing ferocious teeth, fists bunching up.

The clank of rifle bolts being thrown by soldiers of Egallah caused the hairy chemist to rethink his tactics. Grimacing like a frustrated gorilla, he sullenly sat down instead.

The truck's engine gave a grunt and started off, fat tires struggling through squeaking snow.

"Where are we goin'?" Monk wondered.

"Is it not obvious?" said Fiana gloomily. "To be shot as spies."

Monk eyed the woman a long time. "I think Long Tom had the right idea about you," he decided.

Fiana shrugged nonchalantly. "I think this time I will accept the offer of a last cigarette. This night has frayed my nerves."

And that was all the cold-blooded daughter of Egallah would say.

No one noticed a pair of footprints which followed the slushy ruts made by the military truck's winter tires. No apparent body appeared to be making these tracks. But floating almost six feet above these tramping, invisible feet were a pair of eyes the dappled hues of a spring forest....

Chapter XXIII

BAT BARRAGE

DOC SAVAGE SOON caught up with the advance guard of bat-shaped autogyros. For that is what they were. In actuality, they were an advanced type—more along the lines of a gyroplane. The ribbed bat-wings were stiff. They did not flap. That illusion had been created by the rotating windmill-style vanes that whirled above the pilot's head, which provided aerodynamic lift, when viewed from certain perspectives by night. Motive power was supplied by a pusher-type propeller cleverly mounted in the bat's tail section, out of plain view.

The noses of the aircraft were cunningly crafted to suggest a bat's unlovely countenance. Scarlet-lensed headlights gave the effect of the supernatural eyes. Doc found a lever in the cockpit which, when he threw it, caused the long, rat-shaped lower jaw to drop. This prompted a mechanism that produced convincingly loud bat-like squealing. Doc shut this off.

Experimenting with another lever, the bronze man discovered a glass porthole on the floor at his feet. This permitted the pilot to see the claw-like landing gear which hung beneath the furry fuselage of the craft. Operation of the lever caused the mechanical talons to open and close. By this means, he had been snatched up by the agile gyro. No doubt other victims had been carried off in the identical manner, only to plunge to their deaths from a punishing height when the mechanism released.

Nearby, a petcock connected to an arrangement of tubing. Doc left this strictly alone. There was also a choke, pulling of which appeared to release the octopus-ink spray designed to discourage pursuit by faster aircraft.

Other controls allowed the gyroplane to rise almost straight up in the air. This feat was many years in advance of the present generation of autogyros. Doc himself had been experimenting along those lines, so the operation of the weird aircraft was more understandable to him than it would have been to an ordinary pilot.

It was obvious to the bronze man that use of these bat-ships was calculated to invoke terror in the citizens and armies of Tazan by playing upon local legends of vampirism and the Undead who walk by night, seeking the blood of the living. At night, seen from below, the illusion of monstrous vampire bats was nearly perfect.

Doc fell in behind the trailing bat-planes.

They were headed toward the Tazan border, looking like vicious winged rats. A barrage of them. A bat barrage.

Below, snow was accumulating on the rugged terrain of Ultra-Stygia, transforming it into a bleak, leprous landscape. The coating of night frost did not improve the scenery; instead, it painted everything ghostly and unreal in the moonlight.

The combination of endless snow and spectral lunar light made spotting movement on the ground easier than it had been, even an hour previous.

Golden eyes roving, Doc Savage noticed footprints appearing in the wintery turf. Many of them. What was remarkable about these tracks is that no visible agency was apparently creating them!

When the pilots of the other planes began noticing these lines of centipede imprints, they went into action.

Swooping low, waves of bat-planes began corkscrewing into the concentration of enemy forces. Bat jaws dropped and, feeding from steel tanks slung under each wing, a vapor began spewing, funneling back by the pusher props' slipstream. These were laid down in foggy trails over the magical footprints.

Doc Savage drew a small chemical gas mask from his vest, donned it hastily. The bronze man watched tensely as the first waves fell upon the invisible beings—spraying them just as a crop-dusting pilot would do.

When the ghastly gray vapor settled, the footprints grew frenzied and confused.

Unseen forms collapsed and threshed, as evidenced by great disturbances in the snow. This activity persisted for only a minute or so. Then the stricken forms ceased all animation.

Poison gas!

A grimness settled over Doc Savage's cast-in-metal features. There was no telling if the gas was lethal, or merely designed to incapacitate. Not from this height.

The flight of bat-gyros made two passes, then peeled off to the southwest, possibly in search of other victims.

Doc Savage declined to follow them. He brought his weird craft down into the welter of disturbed snow. The talon-shaped landing gear had good springs; they bounced only once before settling. There were no wheels, none being needed.

Cutting the overhead windmill, the bronze man vaulted from the cockpit and extracted a small glass bottle from his equipment vest. He waved it about, capturing fumes, capped it again. If time permitted, he would analyze the stuff later.

Moving among the fallen, Doc Savage used his bare feet to feel around for signs of life. He found none. The invisible creatures had all succumbed to the deadly vapor that was redolent of brimstone and sulphur.

Returning to his craft, Doc Savage engaged the windmill arrangement of vanes, which was powered by the same ingenious engine that drove the rear-mounted propeller. Grasping the throttle, he sent the bizarre craft leaping into the air.

Aloft, Doc employed the dash transceiver to communicate with his amphibian. The bronze man switched to the frequency they all used for communicating by radio.

Several minutes of this produced no results, prompting Doc

to push the ungainly gyroplane as fast as he dared.

IT took the better part of an hour to reach the designated landing spot. The bat-ship proved nimble, but not terribly fleet.

A survey from the air told Doc a difficult landing had ensued. He saw no sign of footprints around the craft. A flicker of alarm touched his otherwise metallic features.

Settling the bat-gyro nearby, he jumped free and pelted toward the deserted craft.

Reaching the bronze flying boat, Doc noticed for the first time the line of footprints leading away from the amphibian.

These had not been visible from the air due to the rapidly accumulating snow. But the faint impressions of tracks leading away told the tale.

Doc was an expert at reading sign. He recognized the furry nature of some footprints, as well as others. Madly disturbed snow suggested a fight. Capture. Men made prisoners. Ham's sword cane stuck up from a drift, the tip coated with frozen gore.

In a very short time, Doc had mentally reconstructed the chain of events. Monk and Ham had been carried off, possibly wounded. Long Tom and Fiana Drost were on foot, prisoners for certain.

The trail led away to the south, in the direction of Tazan.

Men on foot cannot travel far, so Doc decided to follow in that fashion.

But first he entered the aircraft. Halted. The metallic scent of blood came to his sensitive nostrils.

Habeas Corpus crawled out from under a seat. Doc knelt, gave him a brisk rubbing, and found a green apple, which the shoat accepted happily. The bronze giant noticed that the hog's hackles were erected, as if in fear.

Golden eyes roved the cabin interior. In the direction of the cockpit, Doc Savage spied a black object resembling an 8-ball hovering several inches above the floor. He went to it.

Exploring hands told him that the corpse of one of the invisible Cyclops men blocked the aisle. It was no longer warm.

Hefting the hairy thing, Doc carried it from the plane, then returned to the cabin, where he began replenishing his many-pocketed vest, changing some of the contents, discarding others. It was evident that the bronze man had a plan of action in mind. He was going into battle well prepared for what he expected to encounter.

Discovering the bottled sample of poisonous air he had acquired after the aerial attack by bat-gyroplanes, Doc subjected it to a chemical test, swiftly determining that the noxious mixture consisted mainly of carbon monoxide exhaust produced by the weird aircrafts' engines, which was made more concentrated and therefore doubly lethal by injection of sulphurous chemicals. No doubt these latter were contained in the pressurized cockpit tank whose petcock the bronze man prudently declined to open.

Doc filled a packsack with supermachine pistols for his men, along with extra drums of ammunition. He had brought along Ham Brooks' abandoned sword cane from the snow, but this he placed on a seat for retrieval later.

One last precaution was to don a suit of metallic alloy mesh. This covered his entire body, like a suit of flexible armor. Once he donned matching gauntlets and a transparent globe of a helmet made of a glassy material similar to that which composed his Fortress of Solitude, Doc Savage was wholly impervious to bullets, not to mention protected from poison gases. The suit was lined with rubber and carried its own oxygen supply in the form of tablets which, when taken into the mouth, introduced oxygen into the blood without the need for respiration.

Doc shrugged into his equipment vest last. Normally, he wore it under his clothing. But owing to the enveloping armor, that would not be practical. There was also a belt whose pockets were filled with extra gadgets and other useful devices.

Exiting the amphibian, Doc pushed south.

As the bronze man mushed through the snow, he saw, on the horizon where the wildly fierce black mountains of the Marea Negra region loomed like sharp fangs, flights of bats.

They might have been ordinary night-hunting bats, but for their size, which even at this distance impressed one with their uncanny precision flying.

They swooped and arose again into the air, in a macabre midnight dance of death.

The eerie trilling sound of Doc Savage lifted into the night. Since he was alone, Doc did not attempt to repress it, but rather allowed it to have free rein.

It was an unearthly sound, fully in keeping with the desolate surroundings. It might have been the wind wailing through the dire desolation of Ultra-Stygia, making skeletal music in the dead tree branches.

Chapter XIV

SINISTER SNOW

THE TRUCK CARRYING Baron Karl, Doc Savage's men and Fiana Drost lumbered through the night, escorted by other machines, including a modern military tank, which joined them en route.

Spidery snow fell steadily, coating everything. There seemed no end to it.

The wet stuff pelted Ham Brooks' exposed face, waking him. He blinked, saw white flakes swirling over his head, then asked a natural question.

"Where are we?"

"Prisoners," said Long Tom Roberts in a disgusted tone.

"It's worse than that," offered Monk.

"What could be worse?" asked Ham, sitting up.

Fiana replied to that. "We are to be shot as spies."

Monk said, "That wasn't what I was gettin' at. But that part may be true, too."

"What could be worse than being shot?" wondered Ham, shaking snow out of his hair.

"We lost your cane back by Doc's plane," Monk elaborated.

At first this did not sink in, but when it did, various expressions played along the dapper lawyer's handsome face. Finally, he began swearing.

Normally, good breeding prevented the elegant barrister from resorting to profanity. But the loss of his prized stick brought forth a stream in bitter maledictions.

Fiana Drost, surprising them all with a sudden display of primness, inserted both fingers into her ears to keep out the bad language.

When Ham had exhausted his spleen, he noticed Baron Karl sprawled beside him, in obvious discomfort, looking like a crippled starfish.

"Where is your monocle?" asked Ham, recognizing the man at once.

Baron Karl merely groaned. He was very pale. All of his former suaveness had departed, along with his Continental dignity.

Ham sputtered, "Jove! This man looks as if he fell into a nest of those were-men!"

"He did," said Monk. "They practically pulled him apart until he told them where the darkness machine was at."

Stabbed by the memory, Baron Karl squeezed his eyes shut in pain. He was gnashing his thin lips with his teeth, fighting agony in every joint.

"Who has it now?" asked Ham.

"General Consadinos."

"And there's another surprise," added Long Tom. "Emile Zirn is here, too."

Ham blinked. "Which one?"

"The one who was supposed to have evaporated on the *Transylvania.*"

"Queer," mused Ham, rubbing his chin thoughtfully.

"Next thing we'll know," Long Tom observed, "Countess Olga will rise from the dead."

"Do not mock that possibility," inserted Fiana Drost. "In Ultra-Stygia, anything is possible. Even *that.*"

No one had the energy to argue the point, so they lapsed into silence as the snowy landscape reeled past. Even with the white stuff covering all, the terrain looked dark and disturbing.

"What happened to Habeas?" asked Ham.

"Left behind," said Monk morosely.

Ham looked around and seemed surprised at how much snow had piled up in such a short interval. It lay over the terrain in mounds and sharp, wind-sculpted drifts.

"Any idea as to our destination?" he inquired.

"What does it matter?" sniffed Fiana. "One stone wall is the same as any other."

Which comment prompted Long Tom to fashion a snowball and pelt the morose woman with it.

"Next time it'll be my foot," Long Tom added warningly.

Fiana only glared at him, brushing caked snow off her shoulder.

ANOTHER few minutes of lumbering along brought them to a small town. A military barracks town from the looks of it. Green-clad soldiers marched everywhere. They wore strained faces. No one paid the new prisoners any heed.

A makeshift air field of sorts stood nearby. Warplanes sat idly, knife-like wings collecting heaps of snow. Only a glimpse of these could be seen as they rushed past them. But they counted three aircraft.

Out of the lead vehicle came General Consadinos. He began issuing curt orders, whereupon the activity grew more alarmed.

An orderly raced up, snapped off a brisk salute, and chopped out his report.

Fiana translated it for their benefit.

"Great vampire bats have been harrying the troops of Tazan," she repeated. "Men have died of asphyxiation. Poison gas, they are saying it is."

"Then war has started in earnest," breathed Ham Brooks.

Fiana made an impatient gesture for silence. She listened intently, pulling dark hair off one cocked ear.

"The general is giving the orders to counter-attack," she

translated.

Monk's eyes widened. "No kiddin'?"

"He is ordering warplanes into the sky. He is telling his men to fight back with snow."

"Snow?" said Long Tom.

"He is telling them to unleash what he is calling 'the Snow of Silence.'"

Ham frowned. "What could that mean?"

"I do not know," admitted Fiana. "But the orderly who accepted this order has turned very white. Like a ghost."

"More mystery," muttered Long Tom. He was looking around. "I don't see any sign of that Emile Zirn."

"Small potatoes in this witch's brew," grunted Monk.

Soldiers in Tazan green came forward and escorted them to a long barracks-like building. Hard rifle barrels prodded them along. To a few were affixed bayonets.

There they were placed in a basement that had but one entrance and only a single light—a feeble bulb in a lamp stand without a shade. It sat on a wooden box, of which there were many strewn about. They had the look of rough coffins. All empty.

"At least it's not another cell," said Long Tom. "I'm mighty sick of them."

They were locked in, and left to consider their fate. Scratching sounds in the cobwebbed corners suggested rats at work. So they stood around instead of sitting.

"Doc oughta be findin' our plane by now," reminded Monk.

"That doesn't mean he will find *us*," Long Tom said pessimistically.

Ham turned to the puny electrical wizard. "Has the company of that bloodless woman been rubbing off on you? You sound like her long-lost brother."

Long Tom opened his mouth to assert the contrary opinion, but decided against doing so. The dapper lawyer's verbal barb had stung. Ham turned to fussing with his clothes and fretting over his missing cane.

Then, Long Tom began fooling with one sleeve of his shirt. Out popped a small item.

"What's that—another trick coin?" asked Monk.

"No, a crystal rectifier." Another device came from the opposite sleeve.

"That's an electrical meter, isn't it?" asked the hairy chemist.

"Quiet."

Long Tom began hooking these up to a thin wire that led from his vest. It was an ordinary looking vest. But obviously it was not. Vests are not usually wired for electricity.

"Mind explaining what you're up to?" asked Ham.

"I put this on back in the plane. It's a radio direction-finding vest. Government men use them to locate pirate radio broadcasting stations. A directional loop is woven into the lining of the back of the vest. I just connected it to the crystal rectifier and meter. If we bust out of this dump, I can trace that radio transmitter that's been broadcasting the queer nightmare music."

"What possible good will that do?" asked Fiana.

Long Tom ignored her. He went on, "I have an idea that the music is some kind of clever carrier for coded messages. I don't know how it works, but if we find the source of the broadcasts, we'll get to the bottom of whoever issued the orders that nearly killed us a time or two."

"You're thinking that the music started the first time we tried to land, and that infernal darkness clamped down," suggested Ham Brooks.

"Exactly. That was when the darkness-making weapon was in Egallan hands. Now it belongs to Tazan."

"Speaking of the Devil," said Monk. "What happened to Baron Karl? They didn't haul him off the truck with us."

A moment later, a volley of rifle shots cracked out.

"I think that was your Baron Karl," said Fiana Drost dryly.

"Encountering his destiny."

"Isn't he *your* Baron Karl?" wondered Ham. "Your country-man?"

"I have no longer any country," Fiana Drost reminded.

A thick silence followed as the severity of their situation sank in.

Booted footfalls came tramping up to within earshot. A lock grated. The door opened and a body was tossed in without comment. It landed heavily. And did not move.

The wan light disclosed that it was Baron Karl. Of that, there was no doubt. His face was a bloodless mask of horror.

"Good riddance to bad rubbish," pronounced Ham.

The door closed again with an awful finality.

Not long after, the sound of aircraft warming up their engines came through the fieldstone basement walls.

"Warplanes, I'll wager," said Ham.

"Yeah," said Monk. "Gettin' ready to counter-attack. It's gonna be a pretty big show, and here we are sittin' on the sidelines."

One by one, the warplanes moaned up into the sky. Soon, their sound began to recede.

WHILE Long Tom was experimenting with his vest rig, Monk and Ham examined the cellar for another exit. There was only the locked door.

"This bouncin' from one hole to another is startin' to get me down," Monk complained.

"You should talk!" Ham snapped. "Look at my clothes!"

"At least," Monk returned, "you'll be buried in style."

"You two give me a swift pain," said Long Tom peevishly. "Pipe down!"

A while later, a tentative sound came from the direction opposite of the locked door. All eyes veered to it.

There, a crate of some kind began opening. In the gloom, it might have been a coffin lid rising. With a slow creaking of hinges, the top lifted with hair-raising fascination.

No one blinked as the operation continued with drawn-out slowness.

Then, a bulbous-shaped head began lifting up from the coffin-shaped box.

It was round in an odd way, uncanny in its inhuman aspect. It might have belonged to some hairless vampire from the Netherworld.

A sinuous body followed it and this slipped silently from the coffin, made its careful creeping way toward them in the dark. The thing was almost soundless.

Not until it came under the weak radiance of the standing light bulb did they behold the new arrival clearly.

When they did, pent breaths escaped open mouths in a great rush.

Fiana gasped, "You!"

Ham blurted, "Who?"

But it was Long Tom Roberts who gave the apparition its identity.

"Countess Olga," he breathed. "Back from the Other Place."

The elegantly tall emerald-turbaned countess placed a long carmined fingernail to her rouged lips and said, "Hush! I am here to succor you."

"Aren't you dead?" asked Long Tom.

"Many times over. But never mind that now. Come!"

They were not bound, so she gestured them to the long box from which she had emerged.

Monk looked within. A grin wreathed his wide features.

"An escape tunnel! We're as good as out of here, brothers."

"No!" said Fiana Drost sharply. "Do not trust that witch! She is not what she seems."

"You should talk," sniffed Ham.

"Yeah," added Monk. "You she-bat."

Olga hissed, "Quiet, all of you! Escape or talk. But not both."

They hesitated. Long years walking the paths of danger invested Doc Savage's men with great caution. On the other hand, they expected to be stood before a firing squad by dawn—if not before.

Invariably impressed by nobility and position, Ham offered gallantly, "I feel we can trust this woman."

Because he was always contrary in the face of Ham's opinions, Monk snapped, "Wait a minute! Could be Fiana is right. All we know about this woman is that Long Tom saw her disappear in a puff of black smoke back on that ocean liner."

All eyes fell on the pallid electrical wizard, who was expected to cast the deciding vote.

"I saw no such thing," Long Tom reminded. "It was Emile Zirn who claimed that she did. And neither of you two have shown a lot of brains when it comes to trusting strange women."

Monk and Ham clamped their mouths shut. Long Tom had them dead to rights.

"On the other hand," added Long Tom, "anything's better than a firing squad. Let's go!"

Suiting action to words, the slender electrical expert went first.

"I refuse!" snapped Fiana Drost.

Ham said coolly, "Very well. Remain here. We will return for you later."

"If there is a later for you," added Countess Olga pointedly.

Fiana Drost flinched at the sound of that. Various conflicted expressions troubled her drawn features. She waited until the others had clambered into the coffin-like crate, then followed with undisguised reluctance.

The lid closed with a dull clap, after which the cellar became silent except for the industrious rustling of rats in a corner.

Chapter XV

HELL'S LID LIFTS

THEY FOUND THEMSELVES in a long tunnel of packed earth. At intervals, wood rafters shored it up. The floor had the hardness that comes of human tread tamping down dirt over generations.

Countess Olga led the way with a blazing flashlight. Its backglow made shadows leap and flutter. This did not make for comfortable feelings. The way slanted downward, going deeper and deeper into the ground.

Eying the gloomy cobwebbed ceiling, Ham murmured, "Any bats down here?"

Countess Olga spoke up. "Bats are the creatures of Egallah."

"You are not Egallan?"

"No."

"Tazan, then?"

"Not that either."

"Where is your allegiance?"

"It lies vith the destiny of Ultra-Stygia," Countess Olga intoned.

"Do not believe her!" hissed Fiana Drost from the rear. "She is a creature of Tazan."

"Your own credibility, young lady, is hardly exemplary," sniffed Ham Brooks.

Fiana said nothing to that.

On they marched, not appreciating the noisome smells of

255

the earth. Broken bones poked up from the dirt here and there, making them think that they were crawling through catacombs where the ancient dead were interred.

A long claustrophobic march ensued. It took them deeper and deeper into the earth—and then they came to a wooden ladder. It looked new.

Pointing the flashbeam upward, Countess Olga invited them to climb it.

No one looked pleased at the prospect. They were deep under the pocked and pitted surface of Ultra-Stygia.

Long Tom went first. He used his fist to knock a trap door out of his way, poked his head up and then called down.

"Looks like a mine or a cave," he said slowly.

"It is a cavern," corrected Countess Olga.

They took turns climbing it. Olga motioned for Fiana Drost to go ahead, before following last.

Standing on solid rock, Olga motioned for silence, then gestured for the others to follow. They did so, picking their way carefully along. Here, bare light bulbs were strung at well-spaced intervals, providing zones of light between long passages of gloom.

Strange, pungent odors came to their noses. Ham used thumb and forefinger to close off his aristocratic nostrils.

"Smells like chemicals," suggested Long Tom.

Monk began sniffing vigorously. "I don't recognize the stuff, but it sure smells like something is brewing."

"They are making monsters here," intoned Countess Olga. "Come. I vill show you."

They were led upward along a stony path until they came to a gray rock wall pierced by a rude iron grille, evidently for ventilation purposes. Light bled through this.

Gathering close, they took turns peering through the close-packed bars.

Below, in a great shallow stone depression, three large rock vats bubbled with a greenish-yellow chemical stew. It smoked faintly, or seemed to.

Long Tom said, "Monk had it right. Looks like a witch's brew!"

Shoving him aside, the hairy chemist got a good look.

"Blazes!" he squeaked. "I see men jumpin' right into them vats."

It was fact. Men were filing in from feeder tunnels, one leading to each vat.

As they approached, the men removed every stitch of clothing until they stood as nature made them. They closed their eyes tightly, then employed adhesive tape to seal them. Each took great care with that part of their preparation.

Then, one by one, they leapt into one of the chemical mixes, began cavorting within like seals, or mermen.

As they bathed, their skins gradually grew transparent. Muscles showed like squirming red animals. Skulls were revealed. Ribs. Other bones. Organs. Pumping hearts. Then even these gradually melted from sight, until only their frisking movements in the waters showed that they were still swimming therein.

When the transformed men emerged, their eerie eyeballs alone showed. From this distance, it was as if very round paired gems were going about.

Leaving shapeless wet footprints behind them, they marched off, disappearing into gloomy tunnel mouths, like nocturnal creatures returning to their lairs ahead of the rising sun.

"This is how Tazan creates its so-called *Kuklopsz* Corps, the spies who cannot be seen or stopped," explained Countess Olga. "*Kuklopsz* is their vord for 'Cyclops.'"

"What's your role in all this?" snapped Ham, not liking anything of what he had thus far witnessed.

"She is a betrayer," reminded Fiana Drost.

Monk asked, "Then why is she showin' us all this? This is a state secret of Tazan."

Fiana again had nothing to say in response. So she looked away, eyebrows knitting together.

Monk Mayfair put in, "I dunno. None of this looks good to me."

"I have something to show you all," Countess Olga announced. "But because of the grave danger, I must do so one at a time. Who vill accompany me first?"

Bowing, Ham Brooks said, "Lead the way, *Contessa.*"

"It is a trap," warned Fiana.

She was ignored.

Ham followed Countess Olga to a place far from the spot where men were being turned into the disembodied brutes that did General Consadinos' dirty work.

"A terrible thing is about to transpire, Mr. Brooks," she was whispering.

"Tell me," Ham said eagerly.

"Now that he has acquired the terrible veapon belonging to Egallah, General Consadinos is about to unleash his most fearsome terror plot. Only Doc Savage can stop it."

"Granted," declared Ham worriedly. "What is this scheme?"

She stopped, turned, faced him, eyes imploringly earnest. "First, vere is Doc Savage?"

Ham hesitated. "I confess that I do not know. When we last saw him, he was searching Ultra-Stygia for—"

"For vat?"

Ham hesitated, set his lips firmly. "I am sorry. But Doc Savage does not like us to disclose his movements. You must understand."

"Yes," said Countess Olga. "I understand perfectly. Now come. There is something I vish to show you."

She led the dapper lawyer—hardly dapper now—to a room hewn out of solid rock. She unlocked it.

Ham entered first.

Countess Olga stepped in and closed the door behind her,

softly, carefully, placing her sinuous back to it.

The turning as of a key in a lock came to Ham Brooks' ears as a short squeal of a sound, like a rat being stepped on.

He whirled. Ham's hands fluttered aimlessly. The absence of his sword cane flustered the dapper lawyer.

Countess Olga was looking at him with a definite intensity. Ham swallowed. Something in that look struck him as weird, almost wolfish.

Countess Olga smiled sinisterly, eyes narrowed like a cat spying a mouse.

"Velcome to my sticky veb," she said.

Ugly rage gleamed in her eyes. A moment before, she had seemed a mild woman. Now she was glowering, ferocious.

"Have you ever heard the legend of the Medusa?" she asked. "She of the serpent locks?"

Unexpectedly, the countess removed her elegant green turban, revealing her hitherto-hidden hair—and Ham Brooks let out a scream of sheer horror.

THAT piercing shriek—no other descriptive fit—echoed down smoky tunnels and impacted upon the battle-battered ears of Monk Mayfair.

"Ham!" he squawled. "He's in trouble!"

They raced in the direction of the sound. The stony course twisted wildly, maddeningly, and Monk might not have found the source of the dapper lawyer's outcry but for the singular fact that billowing gray smoke rolling out of one side tunnel drew his attention. Instinctively, he veered in that direction.

The apish chemist blundered through the pale, ghostly stuff, coughing, until he discovered its source.

It was vomiting out of an oaken door that was ajar.

Out of this stumbled a man, also coughing.

Long Tom, pulling up behind Monk, identified him.

"Emile Zirn!"

Monk grabbed Zirn, flung him into Long Tom's arms, then pushed through the coiling stuff to the chamber beyond.

Beating at the pall with his hairy arms, Monk encountered nothing at all.

"Ham! Ham!" he yelled. No response was heard.

Finally, Monk tumbled out into the corridor, and sat down to cough his lungs clear. His barrel chest worked like a bellows.

Long Tom was interrogating Emile Zirn, who wore a shocked expression on his smooth face.

"Where's Ham?"

Zirn gulped out, "He—he was in that chamber. I heard a scream. When I arrived, I threw open the door. Just in time to see... *it*."

"It?"

Emile Zirn seemed to have trouble with his words, as if a fishbone was caught crosswise in his throat. Long Tom shook him vigorously.

"Spill!"

"The—the one called Ham and Countess Olga stood inside. They had turned dark as coal. Like statues they were. Frozen immobile. Their expressions were fearsome to behold. As I watched, they turned... into smoke."

Emile Zirn waved his hands wildly.

"This foulness that you see about you here... is all that remains of them!"

Hearing this, Monk Mayfair gave forth a howl of rage and jumped up on bandy legs. He reached out and seized Emile Zirn, pulled him out of Long Tom's tight grip.

Monk growled fiercely, "Are you sayin' we're breathin' all that's left of him!"

"This I saw with my very eyes," said Emile Zirn, pointing at his smarting orbs. The evil, oppressive smoke was bothering him, too.

Long Tom grated, "This yarn is starting to sound familiar."

"Ain't this what happened back on that liner?" Monk questioned.

Long Tom nodded. "Exactly. Countess Olga disappeared, and I found this bird was hanging around. Then he vanished, and all that was left was smoke—just like now."

Monk looked around, tiny eyes narrowing.

"Before, when people were killed by the death-dealin' machine, they turned black and the smoke that they turned into was black as well."

"That's what I was just thinking," Long Tom said skeptically. "But this smoke is gray. Now that I think of it, so was the stuff on the liner—that I saw anyway."

It was also beginning to thin. Monk raced back to the chamber and fished around in the thick stuff, which resembled soiled cotton.

He came back bearing a fired-clay crock that still smoked faintly.

Long Tom gawked at it. "What's that?"

"Miniature stove filled with coal oil. They probably use them for clearing the air of pesky insects and vermin."

"Suspicious," decided Long Tom.

Monk demanded of Emile Zirn, "If Ham and that Olga turned to smoke, what's this doin' here?"

"You will have to ask them, if you can find them." Abruptly, Emile Zirn straightened his thin shoulders, eying them with a growing animosity.

"As for you all," he sneered, "I denounce you as spies who have somehow managed to escape. For this, you will be shot dead."

Monk jutted his brutish jaw belligerently. "I don't see anyone steppin' up to do the job," he growled.

Zirn snapped two fingers sharply. At that, rifle barrels came charging around the corner, borne by soldiers wearing Tazan green. One was promptly trained upon each of them.

"Stand as you are," a Tazan officer ordered.

Emile Zirn plucked Monk Mayfair's hairy fingers off his coat lapel and displayed an unctuous smile.

"As I was saying," he purred, "your fate is very clear." Turning to the soldiers, he barked, "Take them to the execution chamber!"

"Here we go again," said Long Tom glumly.

Chapter XXVI

PERIL'S DOMAIN

THE FALLING SNOW made tracking Monk, Ham and the others a comparatively simple matter.

Doc Savage kept his attention on his surroundings, knowing that the one-eyed were-men called *Ciclopi* were abroad in the night. Their footprints, larger than an ordinary man's due to the fringe of coarse hair surrounding the bottoms of their bare feet, made them relatively easy to discern.

The bronze man made a strange apparition moving through the Ultra-Stygian night. Moonlight painted a spectral sheen on his helmet, picking out star points on the alloy mesh that protected his Herculean form.

Despite the weight he was carrying, Doc's passing was ghostly. He might have been one of the legendary creatures that are said to haunt Ultra-Stygia, a monster of mailed metal rather than flesh and blood. His flake-gold orbs moved ceaselessly, ever restless in their eerie animation.

The trek through the falling snow was uneventful for a time.

Before long, bats began wheeling in the night sky.

Doc looked up. At first, he spotted the ordinary variety of bats, out hunting for moisture. It was too cold for insects. These made rat-like squeakings.

Then a flight of the eerie bat-gyroplanes passed overhead, all but silent.

One spotted him and peeled off from the rest, making a run for the solitary mailed figure moving through the swirling whiteness.

The macabre aircraft passed low overhead, and from its furred tail issued a long plume of exhaust.

Doc Savage knew this was not ordinary exhaust.

Sure enough, a few moments later, he came upon a spot in the snow where bats flailed and writhed in their death agonies. Their squeakings came unpleasantly to the ear, even muffled as it was by the glassy globe protecting Doc's head.

As the grim bronze man moved through them, they began expiring, leather wings wilting, curling inward.

The batship came around again, attempting to spray the indomitable figure moving through the zone of death. A long serpent of gray vapor settled dismally.

When this pass also failed, the ship did something remarkable.

It lined up in front of the armored giant, hanging there like an ornament on a string. The pilot—his goggled-eyed head gave the impression of a baby bat peering over the devil-eared head of its mother—lined up a spike-snouted pistol and this began snapping and sparking.

Bullets skimmed past Doc Savage, making sounds in the clear night like glass rods breaking. This is the distinct cracking noise a passing bullet makes.

One slug caught Doc in the shoulder, throwing him half about.

Undeterred, the bronze giant straightened, resumed walking.

Another bullet struck him in the chest and Doc staggered back. The weapon must have been of small caliber, because even with the mailed suit, the bronze man should have been hurled off his feet by the impact of powder-driven lead.

Yet, Doc Savage continued striding forward, face resolute.

The pistol snapped a few more times to no avail. Every shot missed. The hand that held the gun was trembling now.

The pilot evidently decided that he was facing a foe who

could not be struck down. Taking hold of the controls with both hands, he sent his weird craft shooting straight upward. It was a maneuver no autogyro had ever achieved.

The bronze giant watched this with interest. The batships had been perfected to a degree that impressed even him. And Doc Savage was considered a living genius in the field of aeronautics.

The bat craft reached a safe altitude, then hurled off to the north, flying normally.

Striding ahead, Doc next encountered a place where the snow was depressed in several spots. He gave these some attention.

It was as if someone had scoured out hollows with a great broom. The snow was feathered strangely about the edges of these depressions.

Moving toward one of them, Doc discovered the reason why.

Staring up from one hollow were a pair of brown eyes. They were open and glassy, fixed in a way that suggested death.

Exhaust from the batships had gotten to some of the night-prowling ogres. They had succumbed. Even in death, all that could be made out were their staring, sightless eyes. The still corpses remained invisible.

Returning to the road, Doc resumed his advance.

Ahead, he could spy the batplanes dancing over the near horizon. They cavorted for a time, then flew off, heading south back to the bat caves whence they had originated.

The trail of footprints eventually came to a line of tire tracks. This, in turn, led to a garrison town not far away. Here, Doc began to employ greater stealth, lest he be seen.

It proved to be an unnecessary precaution.

For as Doc drifted up to the edge of the town, he discovered that nothing lived within.

Soldiers lay sprawled in death, rigid fists still clutching their useless firearms. Their dusty green uniforms told that they were men of Tazan.

Many had attempted to flee the death exhaust, only to skid onto their faces, where they died in the snow, or curled up in doorways, like insects sprayed by chemical insecticides.

It was a grisly sight. A town of corpses. Here and there lay a dead animal, dogs and cats predominately, slack tongues lolling out of gaping mouths.

Concern for his missing aides caused a flicker of emotion to whip across the bronze man's normally impassive features. He searched the streets and byways, seeking any signs of their footprints. Particularly were Monk Mayfair's feet distinct.

Doc soon found a series of footprints answering to those of Monk's oversized feet, accompanied by Ham's slender footprints. And with them the unmistakable tracks of a woman's heels. Fiana Drost.

Doc followed these to a hovel of a barracks building and to a cellar door. It was locked with a common padlock.

Picking it could be done, but time was of the essence.

Grasping the padlock in one mailed fist, Doc Savage twisted and gave a wrench.

What transpired next would have impressed a circus strongman.

The padlock, along with retained hasp, came off the wood like a rotted tooth. Doc tossed it away and flung open the door. He entered.

WITHIN, the cellar was sparsely illuminated.

Doc immediately discovered the body of Baron Karl. He examined it briskly, quickly determined that the man was deceased. All signs pointed to his having been executed in the customary fashion—a single rifle bullet to the heart.

Moving on, Doc found signs that drew him to foot marks clustered about an elongated box. The dusty floor told the story.

Lifting the lid, the bronze man spiked the ray of his generator flashlight, which disclosed a ladder leading down into an earthen tunnel.

It was a close fit, but Doc climbed in successfully. He moved down the protesting ladder, which gave near the bottom, two rungs splintering.

Doc landed on his feet, looked both ways and selected a direction that appeared promising. Discovering a ladder, he climbed it, continued on.

He had not progressed very far when a pair of Tazan soldiers in muted green came trooping around a bend, and reacted with appropriate shock to the unexpected sight of the fantastic Man of Bronze encased in mail. Eyes under helmet rims got very round.

For a moment, they looked uncertain as to whether to turn and flee, or raise rifles and begin firing at the colossus in metal.

Doc Savage helped with their deciding. He wrenched back, ducking around a rocky bend.

Crying out, the soldiers charged after him. Rounding the turn, they skidded to a boot-heeled halt, looking every way but up. For the metallic intruder had vanished! Only a long tunnel, interspersed with lights, lay before their perplexed gazes.

While they were deciding what next to do, one soldier chanced to step on something underfoot, which broke with a glassy crunching. A strange slumber swiftly overtook them. They fell in a slack heaps of green, entirely dead to the world.

Doc Savage climbed down from the high rafters into which he had concealed himself, reached down and emptied the rifles of ammunition. After scattering the shells, he broke the rifles in two with his bare hands.

Stepping over the fallen, Doc moved on. The bronze man had deposited a globe of his special anesthetic gas which he had palmed from his equipment belt onto the dirt floor. During the confused soldiers' moment of indecision, one had stepped on it, releasing the odorless concoction. This had been inhaled with instantaneous results. Doc's helmet had protected him from the fumes.

The passageway wound and twisted, and many times Doc

Savage had to bend to negotiate a stretch where the ceiling was too low. From time to time, dirt sifted down from the rafters, disturbed by his passing.

Doc was not greatly astonished when he suddenly came upon a pair of disembodied eyes blocking the way. He had expected the one-eyed creatures to be guarding the place.

What did bring a gleam of surprise to Doc's flake-gold orbs was the fact that these optics were a familiar forest-green.

"Page!" Doc said sharply. "What are you doing loose?"

"It's a long story," came the seemingly sourceless voice. "I'll explain later. But I followed your men here. I know where they are. I can take you there."

"Lead the way then," said Doc.

Simon Page turned and trooped away.

Doc had to remind him that seen from the rear, his eyes were no longer visible, and following him was not an easy thing. It was uncanny the manner in which his floating orbs vanished and reappeared each time Page turned his head. Evidently, the weird invisibility had the property of making anything behind it unseeable as well. This explained why whenever one of the ogres closed an eye, that orb appeared to vanish from sight.

As they worked forward, Simon Page told Doc of how he had exited the aircraft upon landing and, after exploring for a bit, had been overpowered by something as hairy and invisible as himself.

"I think I was chloroformed," Page concluded. "When I woke up, the airplane was gone."

Doc told him, "Your assailant must have laid down and played possum, hoping that he could slip on board the plane, unsuspected. He succeeded in this, but met with misfortune."

"What happened to him?" asked Page.

"Slain," Doc admitted uncomfortably.

"That reminds me. I've been lurking around the caverns, waiting for a chance to rescue Fiana. I overhead talk that Ham Brooks is dead."

"Are you certain?" Doc asked with low urgency.

"That is what I heard. There was talk he and another person turned black and blew away in a gust of smoke."

This information seemed not to perturb the big bronze man as much as it might. His whirling eyes visibly relaxed.

"Take me to the other prisoners," said Doc.

They moved on. The way twisted and seemed to double back on itself. The place was a labyrinth of hewn rock. The work had been going on for some time, Doc saw.

Far ahead, there seemed to be great commotion.

"The Egallan forces are attacking," Page explained. "I think the Tazans are preparing a counter-attack."

No sooner had Page spoke than a pair a soldiers in Tazan green came around a bend, accompanied by a single floating eyeball. The latter was a milky blue.

The startled soldiers frantically reached for sidearms.

Compared to Doc Savage, they appeared to be moving in slow motion. Doc's hand flashed to his gadget vest, plucked a cartridge grenade. Priming it, he pitched the device ahead of him, then reversed course, hauling Simon Page with him.

Came a roar. Black smoke gushed, filling the corridor with eerie sullenness. The bomb Doc had thrown did not depend on flames consuming a substance for its smoke-making properties, but upon the combination of chemicals released and intermingled when it was shattered. The smoke had a dense purple quality, and that made the soldiers think of poison gas, if their excited cries were any indication.

Prudently, the Tazans went into full retreat. They neglected to do any firing. The twisting tunnels made that effort pointless.

"I know another way," Page told Doc as they ran. "Follow me."

Working along the tunnels, they circled around until they got back on track. The hideous-looking smoke had thinned appreciably by that time. There was no sign of any uniforms, nor phantom eyes for that matter.

IT did not take long to reach their destination. The place where the prisoners were kept was a strange room barred by iron. It was unguarded.

Doc strode up, saw Monk and Long Tom—but no one else.

"Doc!" Monk exclaimed, seizing the bars. His grin split his broad face like a suddenly-sliced melon.

"Any of you hurt?" asked Doc, throwing back his spherical helmet.

"Not bad," Monk replied. "They gave us the works a time or two, trying to find out where you were. Once, they fed us some kind of truth serum, and it made us sick as dogs. Lucky we didn't know where you were."

Doc Savage's metallic features were grim. His practice of failing to disclose his plans or his movements to his own associates, whenever the procedure did not interfere with his own operations, had paid off upon other occasions. Monk, Ham—none of the others—could not be easily tortured into disclosing knowledge, but of course they had no more defense than the next man against some forms of truth serum.

Long Tom put in, "They made a big show of hauling us to an execution chamber in order to scare us into talking, but we didn't scare worth mentioning."

Monk called out, "Say, Doc, something's been worryin' me. What became of Habeas?"

"Hiding in the amphibian," Doc advised. "He is all right."

Something resembling a pair of matched cue balls materialized in the gloom beside Doc Savage.

"Where is Fiana?" blurted the voice of Simon Page, his steadily staring eyes switching from face to face in the ghastly manner of a mechanical puppet.

"She slipped away before we were captured," said Monk, suddenly startled. "How did you get here?"

Doc Savage interjected, "What became of Ham?"

Long Tom answered that. "We were lured down here by that Countess Olga. Ham went off with her, the fool."

Monk interposed, "Not long after, the shyster let out a yell like he had happened upon Old Nick himself. Next thing we hear, that slippery Emile Zirn is tearin' around, claimin' they'd both turned black and the oily smoke boilin' about the tunnels was them."

"But I figured out what really happened," added Long Tom. "It was—"

"Time for talk later," admonished Doc.

Doc reached into his equipment vest and removed a thing like a flare candle. He smeared some of the gooey end onto the lock and hinges of the strange gate.

Next he applied another substance, this one powdery in form. This came from a glass tube.

"Cover your eyes," he warned, turning away and restoring his helmet.

Everyone clapped hands over optics. The looming orbs belonging to Simon Page retreated, then winked out.

The three points Doc had daubed began a violent sparking and hissing. The patches of metal turned molten and after a few moments of pyrotechnics, the gate simply fell forward with a clang, there being nothing substantial to hold it in place.

Monk and Long Tom stepped out over the grate, taking care to avoid the molten portions.

Doc handed them superfirers and extra ammunition drums from his packsack, saying, "Follow me."

Monk examined his weapon eagerly, seemed vaguely disappointed when he discovered the drum was charged with mercy bullets. "Where to?"

"To locate Fiana and Ham."

"I can do without finding that female ghoul," Long Tom muttered.

"Watch what you say about Fiana," Simon Page warned.

"For two cents," Long Tom retorted hotly, "I'd blacken both your glims, but no one would know the difference."

They failed to find any trace of Fiana Drost, however.

Instead, they came upon the great stone vats where more soldiers of Tazan were shedding their uniforms and diving into the chemical soup. They watched the men turn transparent by stages and vanish altogether—all but the weirdly staring disembodied orbs.

"This must have been what they did to me when I was out cold," Simon Page said dully. "Do you think I can be cured?"

Doc pointed to one individual—a rather hairy fellow—who was preparing to jump in. "Observe how some of his limbs are semi-transparent. He has been invisible before, and is going in for a second treatment."

A gleam jumped into Page's looming orbs. "So this wears off!"

"Apparently," said Doc.

Long Tom suddenly exploded, "There's that slippery Emile Zirn!"

All eyes followed his skinny pointing finger.

"High time we shake some unvarnished truth out of that guy," Monk muttered.

Long Tom said, "That's good enough for me."

Rolling up his shirt sleeves, he waded in.

It was an article of faith among Doc Savage's band of adventurers that each man had his specialties. Monk was a great chemist. Long Tom, a first-class electrician. But apart from their professions, each possessed other special qualities.

While Monk might be conceded the most ferocious in a fight, this was a result of his brutish strength, which was more simian than human. Ham was the most nimble in action, especially with his sword cane.

On the other hand, while Long Tom Roberts would be classed a bantam weight fighter, pugilistically speaking, he more than made up for his lack of bulk in fighting ferocity.

By his fierce temper, a trait that caused even Monk Mayfair—

who outweighed him by over a hundred pounds—to avoid tangling with him, Long Tom had the edge over all. Rarely did he meet his match.

Emile Zirn had no such luck.

Long Tom strode up to him, grabbed him by the collar and began applying knuckles to nose, jaw and other suitable spots in a drumming barrage. His fists became trip-hammer blurs. None missed their mark.

Zirn was not unversed in the art of fisticuffs. He got in one good punch. It rocked Long Tom back three paces. But that blow only made the puny electrical wizard all the madder.

He charged back in with a tigerish expression, and it was all Emile Zirn could do to keep his nose from being smeared across his face, and retained some teeth in his mouth.

Zirn went down and Long Tom stood white-knuckled over him as if wishing the fallen one would rise for more.

Zirn would have none of it. He threw up helpless hands in abject surrender.

Doc Savage strode up and got between the two. For Zirn's safety, it was evident. He eyed the other.

"You are Emile Zirn," Doc said.

"One of them," the man said shakily, feeling of his askew jaw. One bruised eye was turning purple. He expelled a tooth.

"Explain yourself."

A female voice came out of nowhere to say, "Allow me to do that."

Simon Page's detached voice gasped out, "Fiana! You're safe!"

FIANA DROST stepped out of the cobwebbed shadows. She had found a black cape somewhere and was wearing it wrapped tightly about herself. It gave her the funereal aspect of a female Dracula. Lifting an accusing hand, she pointed one tapered finger at Emile Zirn.

"That man is a secret agent of Tazan," she accused.

Emile Zirn began hissing like a snake. He glowered at the sable-cloaked woman.

"What about the other Emile Zirn?" asked Doc.

Fiana curled one lip contemptuously. "Secret agents of Tazan all call themselves by that name. It is one way to confuse the enemy and also conduct their espionage with impunity. Whenever one Zirn is captured or killed, the others continue in his place, making it seem as if a single resourceful man were perpetrating wonders, thereby adding to their legend."

Monk asked, "You mean that other Zirn was a Tazan spy!"

"Yes! Of course!"

"Then why did the invisible thing kill him out there in Ultra-Stygia?"

"That is easily explained," said Doc Savage. "Zirn parachuted from our plane. The Cyclopes did not know him by sight. So they assumed he was a Egallan agent infiltrating Ultra-Stygia, and fell upon him, unaware of the truth."

"What about the bat medallion we found on him?" wondered Monk.

Fiana Drost reached into the neck of her blouse and pulled out an identical emblem on a silver chain. "You mean like this one?"

"Uh-oh," said Monk. "You have one, too?"

Fiana nodded. "We of Egallah carry them as a means of identification. They are also excellent tools for cutting of throats, or inflicting punctures that make it appear as if vampires have bitten a victim." She demonstrated this by snapping the chain and applying the points of two steely bat ears to Emile Zirn's pulsing throat.

Zirn's eyes became sick. A touch of green came to his smooth cheeks.

Fiana said bitingly, "Doubtless the Tazan dog took one of these from an Egallan loyalist, intending to employ it to pass as fellow countrymen if ever caught."

Monk let out a great gusty breath.

"All this double-crossing stuff has got me dizzy."

Doc Savage said, "We will sort this out later. Zirn, where is the darkness maker?"

"I do not know." Zirn's tone was thin and unconvincing.

Doc Savage reached down, effortlessly lifting the hapless man to his feet. Removing one mailed glove, he began applying chiropractic pressure to the man's neck.

Doc Savage's greatest skill was surgery. He had learned to do many things well, but nothing more expertly than to deal with the human body in all of its intricacies.

It was a simple thing for the big bronze man to render a foe unconscious by applying these skills. But Doc had also managed, through experimentation and long practice, to produce other results. He did this now.

When Doc was through, Emile Zirn stood rigid, body paralyzed, eyes very wide. These latter were all that were capable of movement, for they wheeled about in their sockets.

Doc began saying, "I can release you from this paralysis at any time. If you are willing to talk."

Zirn's eyes ricocheted back and forth in his head wildly.

"If you are prepared to talk, move your eyes over to the right and I will release you," Doc offered.

Emile Zirn's eyes went so far to the right they almost hopped into his right ear.

Doc made further manipulations, and mobility returned to the man's stiff form.

"What is the counter-attack plan?" he demanded.

Zirn's mouth formed strange shapes. He was evidently torn between his national loyalty and his sense of self-preservation.

A bullet came out of nowhere and made a tiny black hole in the center of his forehead, settling his dilemma for all time. Zirn toppled forward, smashed onto his face, soon quit quivering.

Doc Savage whirled.

Standing a few yards behind them stood General Basil Consadinos, jet eyes aglow.

Fingering his neat mustache points, he said, "Allow me to answer that question for you."

Chapter XXVII

THE TRUE DARK DEVIL

ON EITHER SIDE of General Basil Consadinos hovered uniformed riflemen, faces seemingly cut from stone under their steel helmets.

The muzzles of their rifles were trained squarely upon Doc Savage.

The general's right arm was raised. He brought it down in a sharp chopping motion.

In unison, the rifles discharged, making tremendous noise and echoing in the close confines of the dim-lit cavern. Stabbing flame spurted from each gun barrel.

Two high-powered bullets struck Doc Savage in the center of the chest. He tumbled backward, went down hard.

Bellowing his rage, Monk got his superfirer up and picked off the two soldiers with a pair of short bursts that felled them instantly, the potent mercy slugs doing their usual quick work. Their eyes rolled up in their heads and they corkscrewed at the knees.

Long Tom rushed in to take charge of the general. Consadinos attempted to resist. Long Tom kicked him in both shins, a tactic that was neither expected nor preventable. The general grabbed at his legs and started hopping, testing each one for support. Neither could quite accomplish the job properly.

Long Tom dragged the surprised general back to the others.

Doc Savage was getting to his feet. The bronze man was coughing hard. Two modern military rifle bullets are nothing to laugh at, not even when one is protected by alloy-mesh armor. But the bronze giant was not injured, merely bruised.

When he got control of his breathing, Doc addressed the stiff-necked general.

"Your counter-attack plans."

"—Are a secret you will never pry from my lips," returned Consadinos stiffly.

"In that case," inserted Fiana Drost, "let us cut his throat now and be done with it."

The general flinched visibly.

"The darkness device," pressed Doc. "Where is it?"

General Consadinos' mustached mouth curled into a sneer. "You will never find it."

Doc Savage regarded the general steadily in silence.

"You are our prisoner," he said at last.

"Preposterous! Utterly! You are in *my* country. It is *you* who are *my* prisoners."

By way of showing him the error of his thinking, Doc marched the general on a tour of the winding catacombs that lay under Ultra-Stygia.

The sparsely-illuminated passageways were all but deserted. They soon discovered why.

One great tunnel led north, in the direction of Egallah, as the crow flies. It was filled with the steady *pad-pad-pad* of heavy feet. The rafters shook in sympathy.

Monk peered around a corner. He saw only eyes. Processions of round, staring varicolored eyes. An eerily undulating wave of them.

"Doc, they're marchin' them invisible nightmares straight to Egallah!"

Doc demanded of the general, "That is your counter-attack?"

"One portion of it, perhaps," Consadinos admitted, fingering his mustache points.

Long Tom said, "We overheard them talk about unleashing

'the Snow of Silence' on Egallah."

Suddenly, Doc Savage's trilling rose in the tunnel, becoming a chilly thing that chased itself around the overhead rafters. He fixed General Consadinos with his eerily active flake-gold eyes.

"General, how did you plan to deliver the anthrax spores?"

"Anthrax!" gulped Monk.

Long Tom snapped his fingers sharply. "The Snow of Silence!"

The slack expression on the general's face told plainly that Tazan's war minister understood that the jig was up.

Monk made a fierce face. "Say, if he's usin' anthrax on Egallah, that means...."

Doc Savage nodded grimly. "He is the one who tried to assassinate me by mailing those infected items to Pat—the raccoon coat and the ring-tailed monkey."

The general paled. He saw the accusing looks in the eyes of Doc Savage and his men. Their faces had turned to hard bone.

Monk laid a heavy paw on braided shoulder boards and shook Consadinos vigorously, all but loosening teeth.

"Out with it, guy! We don't take kindly to assassins."

"It was Emile Zirn who was the actual agent of death," Consadinos bleated.

Long Tom demanded, "Which one?"

Their tour of the catacombs had brought them back to Emile Zirn's inanimate corpse. The general pointed to the dead man with the purplish-red smear on his forehead, the result of a bullet-split skull.

"That one."

"On your orders?" pressed Doc. A frost had come over the bronze man's ceaselessly whirling flake-gold optics, congealing them.

Consadinos nodded somberly. "I admit this. Zirn perpetrated this act before leaving New York. It was revenge for the slaying of our king, whose corpse your man Roberts caused to be delivered to our embassy."

Long Tom countered, "Doc had nothing to do with that! It was John Sunlight."

A gasp erupted. It sounded so shocked that all heads turned to fix it.

The sound had come from Fiana Drost. Her natural pallor was a bloodless white now.

"What—? How did—?" she managed weakly.

"What is the matter?" asked Doc, looking at her strangely.

Then she spoke the words that chilled their very marrow.

"Why do you speak of my father?"

A shocked silence hung in the clammy claustrophobic air. Doc Savage broke it.

"John Sunlight is—*was your father?*"

Fiana Drost lifted her chin defiantly. "I am not proud to admit this, but yes. He raised me. I have not seen him in years."

"You are the offspring of the terrible Sunlight?" said General Consadinos, himself shocked white.

Doc turned, asked, "You know of Sunlight?"

The general shrugged. "Who does not? Sunlight is well known in this region. Or was until he vanished. He goes by many names. Janos Nepfeny. Ioan Soarelui. Jan Slunce. It is all much the same. The Devil incarnate—John Sunlight."

Fiana spoke up. "My father—is a very evil man. I know this. But well did he teach me the art of espionage. I am my father's daughter. I admit this. I never knew my mother and have long feared that my father killed her when he was done with her."

Shocked, Doc asked, "Done?"

"I suspect that once he had a daughter to rear, my father had no use for my mother. He—he did away with her." Fiana hung her head sadly. "I could never learn the truth from him."

The stunning confession held them rigid. Silence froze their tongues.

"You say you have not heard from your father in years?" asked Doc Savage finally.

"Yes. Is he—dead?"

"We believe so," said Doc.

Fiana looked deeply shaken. She ran disturbed fingers through her dark hair. "That is almost a relief. But I do not know what else to tell you."

"We will attend to that angle of this affair later," decided Doc.

The bronze man turned to General Basil Consadinos. A little of the animation had returned to his metallic eyes.

"The darkness machine and the anthrax. Tell us everything."

Whether it was the weird revelation, or his perilous situation, General Consadinos suddenly appeared to turn a trembling new leaf. He began unburdening himself.

"The devil's device is stored in my headquarters office. As for the counter-attack—" He consulted his wrist watch. "It is en route to the capital city of Egallah even as we speak. It is far too late. You cannot stop it."

"Where is this office?" asked Doc.

Consadinos jerked his head. "South of here, in the tunnels."

"Thank you," said Doc, who then knocked him flat with his fist.

The crunching of jaw against knuckles spoke eloquently of the fact that the bronze man did not pull his punch in the slightest. Thus was the general repaid in full for his attempt on Pat Savage's life.

Doc turned to the others. "I will seek the darkness machine. Locate Ham, if you can."

Monk grinned. "Gotcha, Doc."

They moved in different directions, Simon Page trailing along, a strange apparition of haunted green eyes, and seemingly nothing more.

In their search for Ham Brooks, no one noticed Fiana Drost double back to the spot where General Consadinos had fallen. In her bloodless fingers, she clutched the enameled black medallion in the form of a sharp-winged bat.

Kneeling down beside the unconscious man, she calmly inserted the bat's needle-like ears into his jugular vein, and yanked them out swiftly.

Crimson cascaded out, bubbling merrily.

Fiana Drost stood up, kicked the dying man in utter contempt, and hurried back to the others.

AS it happened, the efforts of Monk, Long Tom and the others were an exercise in futility. Doc Savage discovered Ham and the darkness machine in the same place.

General Consadinos' "office" could hardly be dignified with the term. It was a cave of sorts, rather modest, and carved out of the living rock. Lacking even a door, a curtain was draped before it for privacy purposes.

Coming upon it, Doc swept the brocaded hanging aside and found Ham Brooks tied to a chair. There was a roll-top desk and another chair, both unoccupied.

Entering, Doc cut Ham loose with a blade he took from his belt. He then went to a corner where a bulky steel box sat unguarded. Doc knelt, threw it open and inspected the contents. Satisfied, he quickly sealed it again.

In one corner a radio was playing orchestral music, low and softly.

Doc noticed the cumbersome electric typewriter squatting on a plain deal table nearby. A long roll of paper sat in the platen. It was blank.

Ham yanked off his gag and asked, "Where is Monk?"

"Searching for you. Safe."

Doc seemed distracted. He found a military radio transceiver in the roll-top desk. Warming this up, the bronze man began listening to words coming from the speaker grille.

The talk was in the heavy-accented language of Tazan. Doc listened intently.

"Let's find the others," he said at last.

As they turned to go, the other radio began playing the nerve-affecting medley. It began on a glum note, and proceeded to unravel in dismal chords that strained for the effect of making the listener want to cut his own throat, seemingly.

And on the table, the bulky typewriter began clacking of its own volition. Inked words started appearing on the paper, forming lines. It was as if a ghost were taking dictation from the otherworldly music.

Halting, Doc paused to read the paper rolling out of the platen.

What he read caused his weird trilling to issue forth, haunting and ethereal. It mixed with the discordant melody, battled it briefly.

Hovering nearby, Ham observed that the lines being printed out suddenly became brokenly spaced, as if words and letters were missing.

"What is this?" he asked, scowling.

"The music coming from Egallah is a kind of a code," explained Doc. "Beat notes actuate the printer mechanism, which translates the message into readable words."

"Rather like a bally teletype machine," remarked Ham. "Can you make it out, Doc?"

The bronze man nodded. He was fluent in almost all spoken languages. Then he made his trilling sound again, apparently deliberately. This time, it overpowered the weird tones emanating from the radio.

Once again, the words coming from the device began to miss, letters spacing apart in a way that suggested interrupted words.

Ham exclaimed, "Jove! It appears as if your trilling is interfering with the machine's ability to decode that deuced melody!"

Curious, the dapper lawyer picked up the device and examined it from several angles. It appeared to run off storage batteries. There was no sign of a microphone, by which the mechanism must somehow "hear" and translate the unpleasant melody that actuated it.

Suddenly, Ham felt Doc's viselike grip on his arm and he was being pulled along. In the bronze man's other arm was the bulky steel box. The dapper lawyer held tight to the typewriter, which continued clattering until they had put the general's office well behind them.

They raced along tunnels remindful of earthy entrails until they found the others. The reunion was brief and memorable.

"I knew you weren't dead," Monk said upon spying Ham.

"How so?" Ham blurted.

Monk grinned. "If you were a goner, you'd have been hauntin' me already," explained the simian chemist.

"Come on," said Doc, guiding them out.

As they rushed along, Ham made explanations.

"When that damnable Countess Olga took me into a chamber, she attempted to gull me for information on Doc. When that failed, she claimed to be the Medusa—the mythical woman whose stare turned men into stone. Removing her turban, she underwent a horrid transformation."

"That's when you screamed, correct?" said Long Tom.

"In all my days, I never beheld anything so shocking," admitted Ham. "It was horrible—ghastly."

"You're just saying that because she flashed her eyes at you and you fell for her, hook, line and sinker," snapped Long Tom. "Then she showed you her true colors."

The dapper lawyer colored angrily. The expression on his aristocratic face told that he was torn between biting his sharp tongue and divulging the truth. The truth won.

"Yes, she—I mean he—did exactly that," Ham fumed.

"He!" exploded Monk, eyes widening.

Avoiding Monk Mayfair's gimlet gaze, Ham turned even redder. "Countess Olga was nothing more than an alias for Emile Zirn," he reluctantly admitted.

Doc Savage inserted, "It became obvious that the three persons who vanished aboard the liner *Transylvania* were in fact one individual. Countess Olga alias Emile Zirn, and the unidentified witness to the apparent demise of the first two. The latter two offering testimony that one of the others had vanished in black smoke before himself disappearing. In truth, one clever quick-change disguise artist was concocting lies designed to make it appear as if the electron-stopping machine had survived."

Monk piped up. "I get it now! Baron Karl knew that John Sunlight sold the electron-stopper to Tazan at the same time the Egallans got the eye-paralyzing gimmick. The Tazans were tryin' to make it sound as if they still had it. That way the balance of power would be maintained."

"You mean the balance of *terror*, don't you?" inserted Long Tom.

"I was never so mortified in my life," sputtered Ham. "Fooled by that—that—"

"Spy," spat Fiana, who had caught up with them. "I have suspected for some time that Countess Olga was a man. A woman can sense such things," she added.

"When I was reeling from the shock," Ham elaborated, "she—I mean he—brained me with something."

Monk guffawed loudly. He knew he now had something with which to ride the fastidious barrister for months to come. Ham was forever ribbing him about his chorus cuties. Now Monk had a perfect retort.

"Let that be a lesson to you, you skirt-chasing discredit to the ambulance-chasing profession," Monk chortled.

Had he possession of his cane, the dapper lawyer would surely have brained the hairy chemist right then and there.

Their headlong running took them to the body of General Consadinos, his jugular vein still bubbling, albeit in a less lively manner.

Doc gave a quick glance and saw that life had all but ebbed from the Tazan leader.

"What happened to him?" asked Ham, aghast.

Long Tom cocked his head toward Fiana Drost. "A she-vampire got him."

No one said anything. They ran on until Doc Savage led them to the escape tunnel that brought them back to the cellar through which they had escaped what seemed like an eternity ago. His astonishing memory allowed him to backtrack through the underground labyrinth without error.

They entered into the night, moving past the dead bodies splayed about until Doc Savage located a military truck. It refused to run until Doc exposed the engine and did something to the wiring.

"All set," he said, slamming down the snow-dusted hood. Doc took the wheel. Monk got in with him. The others piled in back.

Pressing the gas to the floor, Doc sent the truck careening out of the town of the dead and through the rapidly accumulating snow.

Here and there they passed patrolling one-eyed Tazan were-men who had become a ludicrous sight, coated in heavy snow.

"Like snowmen from Hell!" Monk muttered.

They were not molested by the roaming monsters. The latter appeared to be unarmed, there being no practical method of arming them that did not betray their presence.

Watching the prowling Cyclopes, Monk unlimbered his machine pistol, took aim and began peppering the lumbering were-men. He had set his weapon to fire single shots.

Mercy bullets struck, knocking snow from the ambulatory hulks, sending the creatures staggering slightly. But they did not go down. Making raging fists, they attempted futile pursuit. As they ran, more snow fell off their forms, until only angry eyeballs chased after them.

"Figures," grunted the hairy chemist, changing drums on his superfirer.

"What does?" demanded Ham as he watched the monsters fall behind.

"Their hair is so dang thick, the mercy bullets break against the bristles, not the skin. The chemical dope can't get into their bloodstreams like it's supposed to."

Ham said, "This explains why we failed to fell the multi-eyed group that seized the first Emile Zirn after he parachuted from our plane."

"Watch this," Monk said, aiming his machine pistol at the strange patrol stranded in the snow, glaring one-eyed fury at them.

A long burst ripped out, sounding like a deep-voiced monster burping. The hairy chemist hosed his spitting muzzle about.

The results were comical. As if strings were cut, the floating eyeballs began dropping in bunches. They landed in the snow, winked out.

"What ammo did you use?" wondered Long Tom.

"Anesthetic gas shells," grinned Monk, holstering his weapon. "One whiff and they're out cold."

AFTER some amazingly skillful driving on Doc's part, they reached their plane and Doc Savage rushed them inside. The snow had piled all about the amphibian, covering the charred ground on which they had landed. The snow cover reminded them of the anthrax spores of death.

"How are we gonna get off in this stuff?" Monk complained, as he slammed and locked the cabin door.

Getting the engines turning took only seconds. Exhaust stacks coughed smoke and sparks. Doc advanced the throttles. Props began swirling airborne snow. Then they were trundling along as the propellers dragged the air wheels forward through treacherous drifts. A few rods of this and the tires began dragging. Then they squealed briefly, jarred to a halt—held fast in a high drift, motors straining.

"Tough break," muttered Long Tom.

"I'll say," grumbled Monk. "We're stuck, but good."

Doc Savage then did an unexpected thing. He snapped a

switch that caused the wheels to retract into the boat-shaped hull. The big plane settled into the snow crust. They could hear the drifts creak and grunt under its crushing weight.

"What good will this do?" demanded Fiana sharply.

Doc Savage jazzed the throttles, endeavoring to push the big plane forward. Surprisingly, the craft responded. It lurched, wallowed a bit, then started gaining momentum, the way it might on water. Momentum increased. Before they could absorb this, the amphibian was skimming along, hull drumming beneath them.

Everyone looked to the bronze man in astonishment.

"New hull design," Doc explained. "The front portion acts as a snowplow. The keel is flat, waxed thoroughly to double as a long ski runner."

Monk grinned broadly. He was looking forward to a fight; now he would get one.

Scenery rushed past in a blur. Wing-tip floats had been dropped. These also acted like skis, keeping the wings from catching in snow banks. The tail picked up, and they were airborne.

Only then did Monk jerk a thumb at the large container Doc had brought on board. "What's in that box?"

"The sight-stealing field generator."

"You found it, huh?"

Doc nodded. "It is our last hope," he said gravely.

Chapter XXVIII

BEDLAM

DOC SAVAGE RAN the leviathan flying boat with both powerful engines pushed to their performance limits. Often, he batted at the throttles, as if he could wring more might from the laboring motors. His metal face was grave.

"It stands to reason that the Tazan aircraft carrying the anthrax spores would not be flying a direct route to their target," Doc was saying. "Egallan anti-aircraft guns ring the frontier and every large city. We therefore have a chance of overhauling them."

Ham interjected, "Consadinos admitted that they are planning to hit the capital city, Glezna—a fair distance from here."

"We never got a good look at the kinda ships that took off back there," admitted Monk Mayfair from the co-pilot's seat. "So what do we search for?"

"Given the distances involved, it stands to reason light bombers would be employed," Doc said, golden eyes scanning the skies.

But the night sky ahead was crammed with gyroplanes in the shape of mammoth bats. They were dimly visible through the grimy windshield, which was still smeared with the dark substance which consisted of octopus secretions.

Doc made explanations. "The Egallans have perfected an advanced type of gyroplane, one capable of perfect vertical ascension and hovering in place. They built these craft to resemble giant bats, the better to prey upon the superstitions of the Tazan folk."

"Why?" questioned Ham. He had found his lost sword cane. Possession of it seemed to settle his frayed nerves. The ordinarily unflappable barrister was still shocked by his unnerving encounter with the pseudo Countess Olga.

Doc continued, "In the caves south of here, I discovered the underground hangars for these bat-ships. And in one cave, a substance that could explain much."

Ham's dark eyes glowed with interest. "What kind of substance?"

Before the bronze man could reply, three spread-winged bat-ships came wheeling out of the lunar light to harass them.

Doc executed a flashing chandelle, then a sideslip that put the nimble whirling craft behind him. With their underpowered pusher-type propellers, the gyroplanes were no match for the two-motored amphibian.

Ham had brought along the strange combination teletype-typewriter machine. Long Tom was studying it in his radio cubicle.

The dapper lawyer remarked, "If that is an Egallan apparatus, how did it get into the hands of General Consadinos?"

"No doubt it was pilfered from Egallan secret agents in New York," ventured Doc. "Countess Olga—the first Emile Zirn—was conveying it back to Pristav, where he employed it to eavesdrop on secret messages passing between Prime Minister Ocel and his operatives."

"I see," said Ham. "So when the music started that first time we flew over Ultra-Stygia, it was a signal to activate the darkness machine, hoping to cause a crash landing?"

"Baron Karl feared we would reclaim the device," said Doc, "so naturally he desired to thwart our arrival in the region. Doubtless the music commenced due to Egallan agents reporting that our plane was spotted over Ultra-Stygia. Karl assumed that we would intervene in their plot, and reclaim the blinding ray."

Ham asked, "Is that the Dark Devil everyone feared?"

Doc nodded. "So it would appear."

Monk Mayfair groused, "My head hurts from tryin' to make sense of all this."

"It's elementary, simplewits," declared Ham. "Both sides were using the superstitions of the region to frighten the other nation into staying out of Ultra-Stygia."

"That, I get," said the homely chemist. "But what flummoxes me is what all the fuss is about. Anyone can see that Ultra-Stygia is a barren wasteland. Fit for a bone yard, but that's about all."

Doc called back to Long Tom, "Did you bring your special vest?"

"I'm wearing it," said Long Tom.

Doc nodded. "We may need it later."

"If there is a later," murmured Fiana Drost disconsolately.

In back, she and all-but-invisible Simon Page were seated apart. They were not speaking. The wire-service reporter still smarted from the sharp words Fiana Drost had inflicted upon him. It was clear that Page's ardor for the mysterious woman with ice water running through her veins had cooled considerably.

"It is very unpleasant to be seated next to such a malodorous monstrosity," Fiana remarked carelessly at one point. "Do you others not agree?"

"Invisible men are old stuff to us,"* boasted Monk, "but I'll admit the last bunch we fought didn't need baths."

Pained green eyes squeezed shut, and remained that way.

"So these midnight rodents and their octopus-ink discouragers are just some Balkan inventor's notion of a terror weapon," Monk was musing.

"It would appear so," agreed Doc. "The pilots are garbed to resemble human bats, even to leather flying suits equipped with

---

* *The Spook Legion.*

underarm membranes that allow them to glide for brief periods in the fashion of delayed parachute jumpers. Fur-and-leather flying helmets replete with squirrel ears and smoked goggles completed the illusion."

Ham glared back at Fiana Drost. "So she was only wearing a trick suit under her coat to make us think she was a vampire. You," he accused, waving his cane at the woman, "are nothing but a patent fraud."

"I am suddenly overcome by an urge to taste your neck, fastidious one," Fiana drawled back.

"You might dispense with the bloodthirsty act," Doc suggested. "It has worn very thin."

Fiana shrugged elaborately. "What can I tell you? I am the daughter of my father."

Which reminder of her unholy parentage caused a hush of unease to settle over the plane cabin. Fiana still wore the sable cloak wrapped around her person, which brought difficult memories rushing to their recollection. The evil John Sunlight had often cloaked himself thus.

No one spoke again until Doc Savage overhauled the warplanes carrying the anthrax. There were three of them, flying in squadron formation, their wing lights resembling fast-traveling stars. Twin-engine jobs.

"Long Tom, tune in to the Tazan military frequency," instructed Doc.

Long Tom dialed the receiver below two hundred meters until he found it, swiftly displaying an uplifted thumb.

Doc Savage engaged his own microphone. His lips parted.

Out of his mouth issued a familiar voice. It was known to them all. But now it sounded ghoulish, for these were the living tones of a dead man.

"Consadinos!" Fiana gasped out.

Doc spoke at great length in the exact voice and manner of the late Tazan war minister. Urgent words crackled back. Doc responded crisply.

There was a brief silence. Static hissed.

Then, one by one, the three Tazan bombers broke off and started to circle back.

"What's going on?" asked Ham, head swiveling between windows.

"They are returning to their country," explained Doc. "I just ordered the counter-attack canceled."

Monk whistled admiringly. Behind them, Ham and Long Tom exchanged congratulatory handshakes.

Then, another voice blistered from the radio speaker. It was an unfamiliar one. It rattled out harsh words in the thickly-accented language of Tazan.

Doc attempted to interject. But the other voice kept talking, shouting him down. Some of it had the vehemence of profanity.

Ahead, the trio of night bombers again altered course. This time, they returned to their original heading.

Jaw dropping, Monk demanded, "What just happened?"

"A high official in the Tazan government has informed the bomber pilots that General Consadinos is deceased," Doc informed them. "The anthrax attack is back on."

"Obviously someone found his corpse," Ham said unhappily.

"It is the will of the Devil," commented Fiana Drost.

Long Tom removed a shoe and hurled it back, barely missing the woman's ducking head. "Did you have to cut his throat!" he snarled.

A gloomy funk filled the cabin.

Doc kept the thundering amphibian following in the wake of the bomber trio. They were approaching the area of the caves, now white with snow.

Strange activity could be discerned below. Dead trees, stumps and boulders had toppled here and there. As they watched, others followed suit. The ground seemed to be convulsing in scattered spots, exposing black holes in the earth. Burrows.

Amid the snow cover, strange footprints began appearing magically. They formed snaky lines, as if an invisible centipede were progressing through the drifts. Every line of tracks progressed outward from one of the newly-exposed holes.

Monk yelled, "A lot of them stumps and things are fake! Hairy goons are crawlin' out of trapdoors everywhere!"

So it appeared to be. Each fresh disturbance in the snow moved toward a cave mouth. And there were scores of these tracks. It was an eerie sight, down there in the frosted expanse of Ultra-Stygia.

"We're too high up to spot their eyes," Ham observed. "But it appears that the forces of Tazan are invading the Marea Negra pocket."

"Won't take long till we see fireworks," Monk added.

Nor was it. No sooner had the first bare footprints trickled into one cavern, then the inhabitants began reacting. Footprints which had disappeared into one entrance, came scrambling out, pursued by men garbed in the regalia of human bats. Gunflame stabbed sporadically. The bat-men were firing pistols and rifles. The ogres had arrived unarmed, apparently preferring to rely upon their invisibility to provide the element of surprise. The attack became a rout.

From every other cave, waves of great black-winged bat-ships began rushing out into the night to meet the onslaught in full force.

The harridan craft lifted, canted around, and began laying down long gray worms of vapor. The footprints of the invisible ogres of Tazan began scattering in confusion. Hollows began making themselves in drifts, signifying the fallen. These churned briefly—only briefly. Then they were still.

Over the radio, a frantic bomber pilot was reporting that the tide of battle was turning against the legions of Tazan. Fiana translated this for them.

"Big battle brewing," Monk warned. The homely chemist

turned anxiously to his bronze chief. "What do we do, Doc?"

"Brace yourselves," warned the bronze man. And reaching down, he lifted the darkness machine onto his lap. It still reposed in its heavy steel container.

Monk eyed it warily. "You gonna turn it on?"

"No choice in the matter," Doc said firmly.

The thing was in the manner of a great coil—the operating principle being primarily short electrical waves mixed with sonic vibrations, which paralyzed the light receptivity of the optic nerve and thus cause the eye to see no light at all—in other words, blackness. Storage batteries powered it. There was a lot of black insulation visible on its bulky steel housing.

Doc slanted the amphibian upward, gained as much altitude as possible in the night-time sky. He turned off all lights in the cabin. It became as thrilling as riding a roller coaster skyward while blindfolded. Fear of falling became uppermost in their minds. But this prepared them for what came next.

A bronze finger snapped a switch.

A humming was the only preliminary sign of the device warming up.

Then the *black* clamped down.

No matter how many times they were exposed to its awful influence, it remained a terrible thing to experience. All light ceased. It was as if the world had been folded up and put away by a sinister something that controlled all illumination.

But the truth was much simpler. Their eyes no longer worked. They could move them about in their eye sockets, but that was about all. It was impossible to see, or focus, or perform any act that included processing light rays. The rays were still there, of course. It was just that the eyes could not receive them. They might as well have been blind.

Fiana moaned, "The Dark Devil is loose again!"

"Feeling blind as a *bat?*" sharp-tongued Ham accused.

"Don't sweat it," Monk reassured her. "Doc invented this gimmick. He can turn it off any time."

"Quiet," rapped Doc Savage.

From the sound of the radio chatter, panic had overcome the bomber pilots. They did not know what to do. It became clear that they had no idea what had taken all sight away.

"They are requesting permission to bail out and ditch their planes," Doc related.

Another exchange crackled through the ether. Doc listened intently.

"That permission has been denied," he reported. "They have been told to dump their loads onto the bat caves."

"Good grief!" Ham croaked in horror. "Doc, if they do, it will contaminate this entire area with anthrax!"

"But if they don't," interjected Long Tom, "the bombers will fly on to a big city and spread their pestilence there. Thousands will perish."

All understood what that portended. The tiny white spores were fatal if inhaled. And should one enter the bloodstream through a break in the skin, the awful black sores would soon appear, signaling imminent, horrible death....

IN the dark, with laboring engines making the still-climbing amphibian vibrate, no one spoke. Doc Savage was obviously considering options.

Snapping the master switch, he turned the device off. Moonlight filled the cabin. They looked out every available window. Doc helped by tilting the plane.

Below, bat-ships were careening around crazily. Some had already crashed. Others simply hovered in place like dark hummingbirds, awaiting developments.

The three bombers began dropping their noses in a power dive.

Several bat-gyros rose to greet them. Now that they understood what the ugly craft actually were, Doc's men were able to distinguish in the dark the whirling vanes mounted over the fixed bat-shaped glider wings.

Frantic exchanges between the bomber pilots and their Tazan leader volleyed back and forth.

Fiana said, "The pilots are saying that they are under attack, and outnumbered. The leader is telling them to crash their aircraft, if they must."

Doc turned on the darkness machine, ending the argument.

Throwing the aircraft into another steep climb, Doc said, "This should not take long."

It did not. Reaching the amphibian's service ceiling, Doc waited for the engines to begin coughing from lack of air. This they soon did. Then he let the ship slide off one wing. A jarring drop followed, eliciting grunts of surprise.

That was when the bronze man turned off the darkness machine for the last time.

Doc leveled off. Below, the three bombers had already impacted the ground. One had the misfortune to strike a cave, turning its entrance into leaping flame.

The others had made tangles of burning duralumin metal here and there. In the natural darkness, they resembled smoldering witch cauldrons. Beyond any doubt, their deadly cargoes had been violently expelled into the surrounding terrain.

The bat-ships had fared better, some of them. They were settling down to the ground to investigate.

One by one, the bomber pilots began landing via parachute. They were immediately set upon. Watching with a pair of binoculars hastily clapped to his eyes, Monk reported, "Looks like the man-bats are slashin' the bomber pilots' throats with their trick medallions."

Doc rapped out, "Long Tom. The Egallan military frequency, please."

"Go!"

Immediately, Doc began warning the Egallan high command that the Marea Negra region had been infected with anthrax bacteria and was too dangerous for habitation. He repeated this several times in their language.

Word must have gotten though to the bat pilots because several took off hastily and winged in the direction of the Egallan frontier proper.

Doc circled. Worry etched his normally composed features, stabbed deep into his flake-gold eyes.

Below, all was a weird pale panorama in the moonlight. It was exactly the hue of anthrax spores—except that the latter were too small to be visible. Still, the suggestion that doom lay like a leprous blanket over the Marea Negra impressed itself strongly upon their minds.

"Whatever's down there worth fightin' over," opined Monk, "nobody will be able to claim it for a very long time."

Long Tom suddenly snapped his fingers. "I get it!"

"What?"

"Uranium is what's down there!"

"I say it is gold," insisted Ham Brooks. "Only gold motivates men to wage war."

"No," said Doc Savage. "Another substance entirely."

"What is it?"

Instead of explaining, Doc said to Long Tom, "Time to ferret out that secret radio broadcast station."

Long Tom spun the receiver dial and found the frequency once more.

The uncanny music began flowing out. It filled the cabin like a funeral march— which is what it was alleged to be, of course. These mordant strains took away any feeling of victory that was rising in their spirits.

"I guess our job ain't done here," Monk decided.

"My country will surely respond to this provocation," intoned Fiana Drost. "I imagine that it will be very satisfactorily bloody."

She ducked another of Long Tom's shoes. This time Fiana flung it back, missing the electrical wizard's pale locks completely.

Ham suddenly had a question. "If these secret broadcasts

were coming from Egallah all along, why did the Egallans broadcast the funeral march of the Tazan monarchy as a means of conveying their messages?"

Doc Savage offered, "To further disguise the true nature of this means of communication, by sowing confusion as to its origin. You will remember the pirate radio station employed a commercial frequency owned by Tazan."

To which Fiana Drost retorted, "You must remember that the Tazans had unleashed their evil ogres upon Egallah. This was seen in my country as another provocation. The Tazan dogs have been squatting upon our sacred land, tarnishing it with their filthy tread, for a generation. They have been spoiling for a war. Now they have one."

No one disputed her assertion. Nor did anyone think it necessary to mention that the late monarch of Tazan was no model of kingly decorum—not to mention the fact that, just as Baron Karl had, the former playboy prince paid millions of dollars to John Sunlight for a death-dealing device whose sole purpose was the slaughter of innocents.

Ham cast a challenging eye toward Fiana Drost.

"Do you realize that this conflict which both sides seem to desire so much, very nearly resulted in horrible death for thousands?" he demanded. "Do you no longer care about your own people?"

Fiana Drost favored Ham with a withering stare. She opened her mouth, seemed about to speak, then closed it tightly. Wrapping her sable cloak about her, she seemed to lose herself in her own dark thoughts.

After a while, she could be heard murmuring, "Death comes to us all. In due time."

Grimly, Doc Savage pointed the great bawling amphibian due north.

Chapter XXVIX

FUNERAL MUSIC

DOC SAVAGE WAS unusually tight-lipped. His metallic countenance was etched in grave lines; the aureate flakes of his eyes resembled dull mica.

Ham Brooks looked to him. "You're thinking that none of this would have happened if it weren't for John Sunlight," he suggested in low tones.

Doc shook his head. "None of this terror would have transpired had I destroyed those infernal death-dealing machines, rather than storing them in my Fortress vault."

"But who woulda thought anyone would get way up in the Arctic to find 'em?" countered Monk.

"I should have foreseen the possibility," admitted the bronze man wearily. "And there is still the matter of the missing cache of weapons."

"Probably still back in the ice pack, since we're pretty dang sure Sunlight got eaten by that polar bear," Monk opined.

By this time, they had lapsed into speaking Mayan for privacy.

Monk suddenly thought of something. "Say, Doc, why did you invent that blinding gimcrack in the first place?"

Doc Savage grew reflective. "Blindness is a terrible scourge," he replied thoughtfully. "If an electrical ray could be devised that would restore the impaired rod-and-cone functions, permitting sight for the sightless, it would be a boon to mankind. My original researches were along that line."

"Instead, you got the opposite effect, huh?"

"Exactly."

Long Tom stuck his head out of the radio cubby. "Doc, I found it!"

Doc turned. "Yes?"

"We passed over this sector before. Directly ahead is Nedavno. A frontier town. The radio transmission's coming from there."

"We will land," Doc decided, throwing the bawling plane downward so rapidly that the others had to hang on for dear life.

The town of Nedavno showed up in the moonlit snow not long after. It was a modest hamlet, and probably had been standing on the same spot for centuries. The bell tower of an old stone church peeped up from among the low housetops arrayed around it in no particular configuration.

Doc flung the amphibian around the spot, seeking a safe landing place. He found none. Nor was he surprised. This was rugged country.

"Looks like we're out of luck," Monk muttered.

"We will chance a landing in the snow," decided the bronze man.

Doc picked a pasture that was an undulating expanse of snowdrifts. He dragged it only once, once because he realized that it would be impossible to tell what snags—tree stumps and whatnot—lay beneath the innocent-appearing white crust.

Doc slanted the amphibian out of the sky.

"Here goes," warned Long Tom.

Doc took the plane in along a shallow glide path. He did not drop the landing wheels. Everyone expected that.

The ground hurtled up like a looming shroud. Landing was such an unsettling prospect that even Fiana Drost's morose tongue remained still. She closed her eyes. Her lips moved, as if in praying. No one noticed this.

The flat keel of the pontoon hull touched, bounced, and a long scraping sound filled the cabin, making their teeth clench.

The flying boat jarred only once—a fair result under the circumstances.

Doc hauled the protesting engines into reverse. This had no immediate effect.

The amphibian banged along, slewing to starboard. Doc held the controls in place, but everyone understood that there would be no controlling the great hurtling aircraft should she start careening in any direction.

Providence—or luck at any rate—was with them. The big bronze bird eventually scraped to a slow sliding halt. Doc cut the engines. The silence that followed was an eerie thing.

Doc jumped from his seat. "Come on, Long Tom."

"What about the rest of us?" asked Ham, worried that he would be left behind, and miss a good fight.

"You and Monk must remain behind to guard the plane. We will need it for our escape. Technically, we are spies in wartime."

"I will go with you," Fiana offered.

"Not likely!" Long Tom snapped. "You'll lead us into another trap."

"I would prefer to lead my nation out of war," she returned. Her voice had undergone a profound change. Gone was its former coldness. There was pain deep in her dark eyes.

"Why the sudden change of heart?" asked Doc.

"I have had no change of heart," she snapped. "But I have been thinking. My thoughts have run to what would have befallen my beloved nation had you not stopped the Tazan bombers carrying their loads to the cities. For the same reason that I could not liquidate you, I cannot bear to see innocent persons suffer and die. Soldiers are another matter. Their sacrifice is their glory. Spies such as myself, we court death knowingly. But the people… that is another matter altogether."

Doc Savage regarded her for a long interval, in which the only reaction lay in his ceaselessly whirling golden eyes.

"You will remain close at all times," he directed at last.

"Of course."

"Doc!" Ham protested. "You cannot trust her. She's—"

"—coming with us," the bronze man said firmly.

And that was the end of that.

Doc divested himself of his alloy-mesh armor, and handed Long Tom and Fiana chemical gas protectors, should they become necessary.

"In case of attack by the bat-ships," he explained.

They exited carefully, began trudging through the snow. Drifts were piled deep enough that they soon sank to their knees. Doc glanced back and saw that the amphibian had been undamaged by their rough landing. It had been designed for just such circumstances, but that did not mean it was foolproof. The compromise between boat hull and ski runner meant that the ship was not ideally suited for either water or snow landings.

They moved on, stealthy as the noisy snow crust permitted.

NIGHT reigned. The moon was rather high, and correspondingly it looked very far away now. That meant it shed a weaker light than before. This suited their need for concealment.

Soon, they came to the hamlet. All seemed still. The only activity was wind snatching at the smoke arising from ancient chimneys, whose slanting roofs were whitening with each passing minute.

They slipped in between two darkened houses that belonged to another century. The town folk appeared to be sleeping, for the hour was now very late.

Overhead, a bat flapped along, sounding like ghoulishly soft applause.

"Ordinary bat," Long Tom observed. He rarely took his eyes off the meter that attached to the special vest in which a radio-direction loop was woven.

"North," he decided.

Doc looked at the meter. "Northwest, perhaps."

They moved northward, creeping along like careful cats. Draped in funeral black, Fiana Drost stayed close. Her eyes were hollow from lack of sleep, and their hollowness brought to mind the sunken eyes of the sinister John Sunlight, her acknowledged male parent.

"What are we going to do with her when this is over?" Long Tom whispered in Mayan.

"Send her to the college," returned Doc.

Long Tom muttered darkly, "Too good for that murderess."

Doc made no reply. His eyes were scouring the way ahead.

They made good progress. The town was a haphazard thing, with dwellings arranged here and there, streets and lanes growing up naturally between them in the manner of cow paths. Only when they reached the town square did they see signs of planning and organization.

The town square was not much. A simple tree-lined park. The stone church they had spotted from the air overlooked this blanket patch of smooth, undisturbed ivory.

Fat flakes of snow were still falling and Long Tom shivered, thinking of the anthrax spores, which were white as snow, but silently deadly.

"We're close," he hissed.

Doc squeezed Long Tom's slender shoulder for attention, pointed toward the church bell tower. A single window showed, shuttered tightly.

"A radio set-up could be secreted in that hollow space," he said quietly.

"My idea, too."

They advanced on the church, taking care not to make any sounds. But cold night air was already hardening the snow, which made it crack and groan under their feet.

Still, the town of Nedavno seemed to slumber on, oblivious to their presence.

They reached the stone entrance steps. The ancient church

was fronted by a large door, painted gray. Opening it without producing noise was out of the question. Doc moved around to the side, looking for another way in.

A hatch in the rear suggested access to a cellar. The hatch was covered in an inch of fresh snowfall.

Doc knelt, smoothed away this accumulation and found a handle. He pulled. It refused to budge. There was no hasp or other fastening.

"Locked from inside," hissed Long Tom.

Doc nodded. From a pocket of his equipment vest, the bronze man removed a case that contained an insulated handle and several steel shafts that would fit into it. Selecting one shaft, he inserted it and created a serviceable screwdriver, which he used to unscrew the hinges on one side of the hatch.

When he had made a pile of screws, Doc separated the hinges from the hatch door and placed the latter carefully against the church wall. They went down onto cobwebbed steps.

"Is there any place around here that doesn't lead down to depths where they bury people?" complained Long Tom.

Doc used his flash ray to examine the cellar. Except for fiery grates of a coal furnace, there was nothing remarkable to be found.

Doc led them to a set of plank steps. They mounted these, up to an unlocked door, and into the church proper. It was a gloomy place, vaulted, but rather modest. The pews stood empty as tombs.

From above their heads, they could hear the strains of ethereal music. It seemed a fitting place to hear it.

Long Tom suddenly hissed, "That's not coming from a radio speaker!"

Doc touched him for silence. A bronze digit indicated a set of circular steps in a dim corner alcove. They climbed this—or started to, rather.

A mammoth bat came flapping down at them.

Recoiling, Long Tom choked back an outcry of surprise.

Lunging, Doc Savage reached out and seized the thing by its throat. The bat fluttered and flopped wildly, flailing and stamping its booted feet. For it was one of the human bats who piloted the grotesque gyroplanes of Egallah.

The bat pilot was a man of fair size, but Doc overpowered him easily. After a moment's pressure on spinal nerves, he went limp in the bronze man's terrible fingers.

Doc set him aside and waved Long Tom and Fiana up the steps to the upper regions of the old church.

Long Tom's eyes went back to his meter one last time, then evidently satisfied, he pocketed it. Out came his supermachine pistol.

The stairs corkscrewed up to the bell tower—it was hard not to think of it as a bat's belfry. The plank risers groaned at every step. They came at last to a closed door.

Doc tested it, then eased the panel open.

The place was a circular affair. On one side stood a makeshift broadcast booth. In the booth sat a man. He was hunched over an electrical instrument consisting of an upright wooden box resembling an oversized country telephone, from which two antennae jutted upward. Moving his hands between these posts in the manner of a wizard conjuring up a demon, the operator somehow managed to produce wild tones. The chords being strummed to wavering life were eerie, unnerving, but perfectly in tune with the mordant surroundings.

Doc recognized this as the invention known as a Theremin, sometimes referred to as an electric harp. The antennae were in reality two heterodyne oscillators. Proximity of the operator's ever-moving hands controlled pitch and amplitude, which together created the uncanny chords. These were amplified and transmuted to a loudspeaker.

Radio broadcasting apparatus nested nearby. It was necessarily compact, but looked powerful. This conveyed the wildly discordant bars into the ether, for reception through any radio receiver.

Pushing in behind Doc, Long Tom indicated with a pointing finger an aerial snaking up to the inner apex of the bell tower.

Doc Savage strode up, and from his lips issued his trilling sound. Normally, it started softly, building in volume. Here, it surged out strongly, swiftly building to an arresting crescendo.

The man at the harp looked up, and his long face broke into lines of shock. Elongated fingers ceased strumming.

The individual stood up. He was very tall, cadaverous of face the way undertakers are often pictured as being, but rarely are in life. A bony beak of a nose dominated his features.

"Prime Minister Ocel," breathed Fiana Drost.

"At your service," said the leader of Egallah in an unflappable tone.

Long Tom trained his supermachine pistol on the man.

"Stay away from that thing," he clipped.

Ocel threw up long-fingered hands. He stood to his full height, which was considerable. With his bony nose, he gave the impression of a carrion bird.

"I would never dream of disobeying you, my dear sir." His snapping eyes fell on Fiana Drost. "I know you. Drost, is it not?"

"Yes. Your signature condemned me to undeserved death."

Ocel's head inclined in the direction of Doc Savage. "The proof of your perfidy stands before us, does it not?"

Fiana swallowed her hot retort. Instead, she met the other's eyes fiercely.

"This American saved Egallah from the deadly scourge of anthrax," Fiana pointed out.

"You have interrupted my playing," Ocel told Doc Savage. His face and voice were glum, like a person roused from an afternoon nap. He looked quite put out, but not really angry. His utter calm was disturbing.

"You were giving the order to attack Tazan," Doc accused.

"Counter-attack," corrected Ocel smoothly.

"Liar!" snapped Long Tom. "Your poison gas started everything!"

Prime Minister Ocel looked pained. "War between Egallah and Tazan has been a constant that has endured over many centuries. To talk of starts. Pah! That is nothing." He lifted an imperious digit skyward. "Finishing this conflict— Ah. That is everything."

Doc Savage said firmly, "Your orders will be countermanded. Immediately."

"No need. You have spoiled them with your interfering whistling." He spread open hands. "Now what do we do?"

Doc revealed, "I have reclaimed the darkness-making machine from the Tazans. You no longer need fear it."

"Very good. But that is but one thorn in our side. And there are so many that I have run out of fingers on which to count them." Ocel smiled thinly.

"If you have not yet heard," advised the bronze man, "three Tazan bombers have contaminated the caves south of here with anthrax. Many of your gyroplanes and pilots have been lost."

For the first time unhappiness traced the features of Boris Ocel. "The sacred caves!"

Doc nodded. "And all that is locked within them. It will be years before they can again be inhabited, much less mined."

Ocel's shoulders sagged. His voice creaked like an old door closing. "Then it was all for nothing...?"

"What was?" asked Fiana sharply. "What has this war been about?"

"Why, a very valuable commodity which will turn Ultra-Stygia into an Egallan paradise," Ocel purred.

Fiana looked blank. Her questioning eyes went to Doc Savage.

"What is this man saying?"

"The caves of the Marea Negra," explained Doc Savage, "have been the home for generations of bats over hundreds, if not thousands, of years. Roosting there by day and flying out at night."

Fiana grimaced impatiently. "Yes, yes. Of course. Every schoolchild knows that. What of it?"

"During their roosting period," explained Doc, "they naturally produced considerable quantities of guano."

Fiana Drost blurted, "Guano? I do not know this word...."

"Bat droppings," supplied Long Tom laconically.

"Thousands of tons of the stuff," explained Doc, "suitable for processing into commercial fertilizer. Enough to turn this desolate region into arable land capable of feeding both nations for many years to come."

Ocel made a dismissive gesture. "Both! *Tch-tch.* My good fellow. One nation. *Egallah!*"

Fiana Drost took a stunned step backward.

"I—we have been fighting a senseless war for—for *bat* droppings!"

"Fertilizer," corrected Ocel. "Highly valuable indeed. Wars have been fought over much less. Our spies recently discovered this treasure. Thus it became imperative to reclaim those caverns before the Tazans learned of it."

Doc Savage interjected, "You neglected to mention that the stuff contains nitrates—a key ingredient in making gunpowder. Perhaps that is the real reason you covet the bat caves."

Fiana Drost looked stricken. Her knees appeared to have turned to water. She staggered back, weaving.

Long Tom demanded, "Why are you conducting operations from this place?"

"He is too much a coward to do otherwise!" spat Fiana.

"Nonsense!" Ocel retorted. "Only I know how to operate the electric harp that whispers the orders of Egallan glory. Where better to broadcast them than from a quiet little church in an obscure hamlet unlikely to be infiltrated by the Tazan Elite Guard, whose eyes and ears, it seems, have penetrated every fortification in Egallah."

"As I said," sneered Fiana, "a coward."

Prime Minister Boris Ocel made a shape with his mouth preparatory to flinging back a counterargument. Not a syllable escaped his lips.

Just then windy, whispering sounds filtered through the bell tower's stone blocks.

"What's that?" asked Long Tom, shifting his supermachine pistol about.

"Warbats!" crowed Ocel. "My flock has returned to deal with you. Did you really think that I was so lightly guarded?"

Outside, they heard the sounds of the grotesque bat-ships dropping from the night sky. Sharp-tined talons landed with a succession of thuds. Next came running feet.

Boris Ocel smiled complacently. "I believe the English phrase for your plight is 'hopelessly surrounded.' No?"

Long Tom eyed Doc. "We can fight our way out."

Doc Savage strode up to the prime minister and made the man unconscious with a painful squeeze of his spinal centers. Ocel collapsed into his arms.

"He deserves to die," said Fiana solemnly.

"No more killing," said Doc, eyes flashing with a rare anger.

There was a shuttered window on one side of the bell tower. It was shaped like a church door, and consisted of two wooden shutters. Doc went to it and threw the leaves open.

Below, human bats were converging on the church, creeping through the snow like furtive ghouls out for a night of grave robbing.

Doc whispered, "Long Tom. Here, please."

The puny electrical wizard joined the bronze man and trained his compact weapon on the advancing creatures. In the moonlight, it could be seen that they wore leather aviator helmets trimmed in squirrel fur, and smoked goggles that helped create the unpleasant aspect of human bats. Their webbed limbs shuffled as they came.

Long Tom pulled back on the trigger. The weapon hooted, ejector mechanism shuttling busily. Mercy bullets began striking their leathery forms. The hide might have been good for fending off the cold in the open cockpit of a gyroplane, but it provided no protection against the chemically-charged hollow slugs. They stitched sudden holes, and the bat-men fell in dark heaps of hide.

"Got them all," Long Tom said with satisfaction.

But that comment was premature. Others were sweeping around and coming in through the front door and the cellar hatch. They could hear their flap-limbed commotion plainly.

"We can hold the stairs until I run out of ammunition," Long Tom stated.

Doc shook his head. "No need."

Striding to the door, Doc removed a handful of grenades from his vest. These were of several varieties. First he lobbed some of the thin-walled anesthetic globes. They landed at the bottom of the spiral staircase, broke.

Human bats began dropping where they encountered the invisible, odorless stuff. There was no protection against it, short of not inhaling.

When he exhausted those, Doc went to the tower door, tossed out a steel grenade, which he first armed by flicking a tiny lever.

It sailed down the stairs, bounced several times and stopped. Doc retreated.

Detonation came. The old staircase became a splintering ruin, which collapsed in on itself. Smoke boiled up, filling the gloomy space beneath the tower ceiling.

Long Tom took his fingers out of his ears. "They can't climb up, but we can't get down. Or can we?"

Doc turned to the broadcast booth containing the uncanny-sounding electric harp and the broadcasting apparatus. He had another device, this one a canister of some type. It was equipped with a timer. He armed it and tossed it in, closing the booth.

"Let's go!" he urged.

Hefting Boris Ocel over one shoulder, Doc Savage joined Long Tom at the window, saying, "The bat-men are all inside the church now."

Stealthy whispering movements below seemed to confirm this supposition.

Doc said, "We will jump outside and outflank them."

Fiana flung back defiance. "I am not jumping."

Doc eyed her, hesitated. "Very well. You will be safe here, if you stand as far from the booth as possible. We will return for you. There is more to say on the subject of John Sunlight."

"I know no more about his fate than you. It is the truth."

"We will discuss that later," returned Doc.

"And after that, what will become of me?"

"We have a special place to which you can be sent."

Fiana's eyes narrowed to dark slits. "I do not like the sound of that."

"It is a good place," Doc assured her. "You will have a new life."

Fiana said nothing to that.

HOOKING one leg over the sill, Doc Savage slid out, dropped. His mighty leg muscles cushioned his fall. He did not lose his balance, even with Ocel as burden.

Long Tom followed, landing cat-like on both feet. He swept his superfirer muzzle about, found no targets. Disappointment sucked in his sallow cheeks.

"Now what?" he breathed.

Doc went to the great front portal of the church and slammed it shut.

That was when the grenade went off. It was not a powerful thing, but it made the old stone edifice tremble briefly. Smoke spurted from the solitary tower window.

In reality, Doc had unleashed a grenade that sprayed a strong acid over the broadcast booth. A modest concussion was necessary to spread the stuff. The smoke was the result of the acid rapidly consuming the apparatus.

A lone bat flew out. A real one. Evidently, it had been roosting in some chink within.

The detonation was very noisy and this caused the bat-men to come rushing out in panicky arm-flapping confusion.

Between them, Doc and Long Tom overcame their leathery foes without having to exert any great effort. They used their fists for the most part. Cracking jaws, Doc and Long Tom laid them out in untidy piles.

When they were done, Long Tom spanked his hands together. "They look kinda scary, but they're not much."

"Pilots," agreed Doc. "No more, no less."

When the smoke began to clear, Doc Savage entered the sanctuary and went to the ruined staircase. He called up.

"Miss Drost. You may come down now."

Silence.

"Miss Drost."

"Maybe her eardrums got ruptured when the grenade let go," Long Tom suggested.

Doc said, "The booth appeared bulletproof. Otherwise, I would have forced her to follow."

Doc Savage decided he could scale the rubble and transfer to the stone inner wall. He did this, climbing the last part like a spider. Then he disappeared from sight.

The haunting trilling sound, which was a thing unique to Doc Savage, wafted down shortly thereafter. It possessed a marked quality of sadness this time. The sound went on for an unusually long time, as if Doc failed to realize that he was making it. Eventually, it trailed off, although ghostly echoes of it continued to persist in the bell tower's peculiar acoustics.

The bronze man remained out of sight for so long that Long Tom began to worry.

"Everything O.K. up there?" he called out.

Silence.

Long Tom cupped his hands around his mouth and tried again. "Doc. What are you doing?"

"Cutting her down."

"Cut—"

When Doc Savage reappeared, he was bearing the limp form of Fiana Drost. She was enwrapped in her black cape. A ragged-ended segment of it was wound around her neck, unpleasantly knotted and remindful of a hangman's noose.

Long Tom made an awkward sound. "Ahr-r-r."

Doc lowered her down, employing his grapple and silk line, which he had wound about her black-shrouded body. More than anything, Fiana Drost resembled a bedraggled bat huddled in its own ebony wings.

Long Tom caught her, saw the bloodless pallor of her face and knew the awful truth.

"Suicide!" he gulped.

Doc dropped beside him, face grimly metallic.

"Evidently, she did not wish to have a better life," he said quietly.

THEY interred her in the graveyard behind the old church, smoothing over the spot with new-fallen snow. Neither man spoke over the little mound. No one knew quite what to say. Nothing seemed appropriate for the troubled daughter of the wicked John Sunlight.

By the time the simple ceremony was finished, Prime Minister Ocel began stirring. Doc Savage helped him along by releasing him from the spell he had inflicted. Ocel looked around him dazedly. Dark eyes blinked.

"Where are my men?" he croaked out.

"Indisposed," replied Doc. "And if you are wise, you will dismantle your warbats. You have nothing more to battle over. Peace is your only sane alternative."

Prime Minister Ocel looked crestfallen. He collapsed into a shrunken shell of his former self. Then, mustering the last remnant of his will, he squared his bony shoulders.

"I will defend Egallan sovereignty with my last breath," he creaked. "Ultra-Stygia will never be Tazan! It belongs to us!"

The night wind carried his words away. There was no other response. Ocel looked around, as if in anticipation of rescue. None materialized. He blinked. His mouth squeezed shut.

"Your war appears over," Doc Savage told him.

"What am I to do now?" Ocel squeaked thinly.

"Here's a tip," said Long Tom. He reached into his pocket and tossed the man a half-dollar. When Prime Minister Ocel caught the coin, Long Tom clicked his heels together.

The result was that the cadaverous man had a taste of what sitting in an electric chair must feel like. He danced a jig that was painful to behold. Contortions threw him to the ground. There, his long limbs jerked and twitched. Boris Ocel found himself unable to release the electrified coin until Long Tom separated the copper contacts on the inner sides of his shoes.

"Keep the change," finished Long Tom.

They left him there, returning to their plane. No alarm was sounded. No one attempted to intercept them.

THE bronze amphibian stood in the snowbound pasture unharmed. A few warbats lay scattered in the crust of snow, damaged beyond repair. They had fallen out of the sky. All signs pointed to the ferocious action of superfirer rounds.

"We had us a little fracas," Monk explained when he threw the cabin door open.

"Miss any?" inquired Doc.

Monk grinned broadly. "A few got through. But it was like shootin' bats in a barrel. The pilots bailed out and ran off like the Count Dracula himself was chasin' 'em."

Doc closed the door, saying, "We are taking off at once."

From his seat, still utterly invisible, Simon Page's forest-green eyes searched their faces. "Where is Fiana?"

Doc told him, "Miss Drost has elected to remain behind, for good."

The emerald orbs squeezed shut. "I—I can't blame her. Look at me."

"Your condition will wear off, as you know. As for the coat of hair, it can be shorn."

Page's voice seemed to grimace. "Like a damn sheep."

Doc pointed out, "Electrolysis treatments should ensure that none of it grows back. That may not even be necessary, however."

Doc dropped into the control bucket, and started the engines. Taking off was an exercise in nail-biting, but once again the bronze man's consummate flying skill lifted them safely into the sky.

Back in the air, Ham Brooks asked several questions about what had transpired. He did not get all the answers he sought. Doc Savage was unusually tight-lipped.

Finally, Ham inquired, "What about the darkness machine?"

"We will dispose of it over the ocean," said Doc. "It is too dreadful to be allowed to exist."

Once they reached the Black Sea, the bronze man was as good as his word. Monk took the controls, while Doc Savage carried the bulky device to the cabin door. This he knocked open. Without hesitation, he flung the thing into the darkling waters. It struck, disturbed the shimmering moonglade briefly, then was lost.

The scientific secret of generating blindness would thereafter survive only in the bronze man's amazingly retentive mind.

Regaining the controls, Doc Savage pointed the amphibian west, toward Europe and America.

An hour along, Long Tom turned from the radio to say, "All seems quiet. I think the appetite for blood has left the war makers."

Doc nodded. "It is over," he said quietly.

Monk spoke up. "Say, now that we've cleared this up, should we check in on Pat?"

"Pat should be fine," Doc advised.

"Won't hurt to hear her voice after all this. We haven't exactly come across a lot of babes on this trip." Throwing a knowing glance in the direction of Ham Brooks, he added, "Unless you count Ham's latest flame, Countess Olga."

Ham Brooks purpled, but refrained from offering a rejoinder. He looked as if he might explode. When he wasn't looking, Habeas the pig stole up and made off with his cane, entirely unnoticed.

Taking over the radio, Monk dialed around until he got Pat on her private radio set. He put her on the cabin speaker.

Pat greeted cheerily, "I hear you boys found yourself a nice little war."

"And how!" Monk enthused.

"It's over now," Doc told her. "You sound well, Pat."

"The doctors gave me a clean bill of health. I've been home for over a day."

Grins of relief broke out over that welcome bit of news.

Pat's pleasant voice crackled across the ether. "Say, Doc, exactly how much fun did I miss out on this time?"

The bronze man was a long time in responding.

"On this trip," he said somberly, "we met with no fun whatsoever."

About the Author
LESTER DENT

LESTER DENT HAD the good fortune to write his early Doc Savage novels during the period of classic movie monsters. The original *King Kong*. Boris Karloff in *Frankenstein*. Bela Lugosi as Dracula. *The Mummy*. No doubt he saw them all during their first runs. For some of Lester's earliest pulp stories, such as "The Sinister Ray" and "The Mummy Murders," belonged to that pulp sub-genre called "menace," which was nothing more or less than a reflection of Hollywood's fascination with malevolent monsters during the Great Depression.

Knowing that his readers expected similar thrills in the pages of *Doc Savage Magazine*, Dent and his editors pitted the superhuman Man of Bronze against some of the most monstrous foes imaginable. Out of the Dent typewriter came such fearful fantasies as *The Sargasso Ogre, Brand of the Werewolf, The Squeaking Goblin, The Thousand-Headed Man*, and what may be his masterpiece of menace, *The Monsters*.

In the scientifically-based world Doc Savage inhabited, he never encountered a real vampire, or battled an actual werewolf. But that was the point of his adventures. Science was the greatest weapon against the mysteries of the unknown, and with the right tools, mankind could overcome any foe, no matter how supernatural he seemed.

This theme threaded through the 1930s and '40s, until in Doc's final adventure, *Up From Earth's Center*, the Man of Bronze was unexpectedly plunged into Hell itself, emerging unscathed, if not victorious—which puts him in the same company as the great heroes of legend and myth, going back to Gilgamesh, Osiris, Orpheus, Hermes, Hercules, Dionysus and Odysseus. Nice company for a 20th century pulp hero.

About the Author
WILL MURRAY

WILL MURRAY'S FIRST brush with monsters came when he took in a double-feature of *Mr. Roberts* and *Gorgo* back in 1961—keeping one anxious eye on the darkened orchestra pit where *things* were said to lurk. Not long after this, he began devouring the four-color creatures offered in comic books such as *Tales to Astonish, Journey into Mystery, Amazing Adult Fantasy, Strange Tales, Tales of Suspense, Strange Adventures, Strange Suspense Stories, My Greatest Adventure, Tales of the Unexpected, House of Secrets, Adventures into the Unknown, Forbidden Worlds, Unknown Worlds, Mysteries of the Unexplored, The Incredible Hulk, Konga* and, of course, *Gorgo. Famous Monsters of Filmland* was in its glory. *Mad Monsters, Horror Monsters* and *Castle of Frankenstein* soon followed. Classic Science Fiction films saturated television, as did *The Twilight Zone* and *The Outer Limits*. It was the Age of Monsters.

It was during that wonderful time that the Aurora Plastics Company began releasing their model kits based on the old Universal monster movies. Murray loved the atmospheric box art as much as the cool kits themselves. A few years later, he again encountered the anonymous artist behind those masterful illustrations. By that time, artist James Bama was signing his work on Doc Savage covers as memorable as his moody monster work. An interest in the adventures of Doc Savage superseded—but did not replace—Murray's fascination with monsters. It made perfect sense. The Man of Bronze was a monster fighter of epic proportions.

Murray never lost his love for creatures of the unknown, and it was with great pleasure that he wrote *Death's Dark Domain,* a Doc Savage novel that revisits those wonderful legends—with a Kenneth Robeson twist!—and is graced by a fantastic cover that evokes those Aurora kit boxes of yore.

About the Artist
JOE DeVITO

FEW THINGS BRING back memories as fun and as thrilling as good old-fashioned monsters, science fiction and adventure. Whether in a book, a movie, or—perhaps especially—a story told at night with a bunch of childhood friends, it's part of being a kid.

The classic Universal monster movies are well known. I particularly love The Creature because of its Devonian Period overtones. And has anything ever bettered the Atomic Age flicks of the 1950s, such as *The Day the Earth Stood Still, War of the Worlds, The Thing From Another World, Forbidden Planet,* or *Invasion of the Body Snatchers?*

The Aurora kits released in the 1960s are beloved by an entire generation. All of us who grew up during that period (at least the guys) would be rich if we had a dime for every bottle of Testor's red paint bought during those years. I still remember serious discussions regarding final details to be put on the monster kits. They inevitably got around to: "…Yeah, it's looking great, but it needs more blood!"

But creatures of the COLLOSAL variety have always fascinated me most. As a boy, dinosaurs were the first giant "monsters" I encountered. I think seeing a *Tyrannosaurus rex* skeleton for the first time by a three year old would certainly qualify, don't you? The granddaddy of all colossal monster movies, the original *King Kong*, still has a grip on me a half century after my first viewing. *Mighty Joe Young;* the Rhedosaurus, Ymir,

Cyclops and Talos from Ray Harryhausen's oeuvre; Bert I. Gordon's giant humans in *The Cyclops, Amazing Colossal Man* and *War of the Colossal Beast; The Giant Behemoth, Godzilla,* all the giant bug movies et al.—were an integral part of my fantasy formation.

For me, the cover to *Death's Dark Domain* is a visual homage to all of the above. Combining a Doc Savage adventure with gigantic bat creatures and other quintessential SF/Fantasy details would paint quite a picture in anyone's imagination. I hope I caught a piece of it.

About the Patron

MARK O. LAMBERT

MARK O. LAMBERT has been a Doc Savage fan since 1975, discovering the movie edition of Bantam's *The Man of Bronze,* and later many other Doc novels, on the paperback shelf of the small-town pharmacy where he regularly bought comic books. This was about the same time that Marvel Comics was publishing its *Doc Savage* comic, and the Doc movie was released.

Lambert has always had a fascination with monsters—he was and is a fan of horror comics, *Famous Monsters of Filmland* magazine, and the classic Universal monster movies, and while his brothers were building model cars, he was building the Aurora monster models. Owning an original of a Doc Savage cover painting is a dream come true for Lambert, especially since it has a monster element to it that evokes the feel of the Bama paintings on those monster-model boxes!

Lambert is an attorney and has worked as a lobbyist, public-policy consultant, state utilities commissioner and most recently as an Administrative Law Judge. At the time of this writing he lives in Polk City, Iowa, with his two daughters.

Lambert has visited Lester Dent's hometown La Plata, Missouri, dozens of times, and has made it a point to place flowers on the graves of Lester and Norma Dent every time he visits. Lambert's activism as a Doc Savage fan has included publishing a small book about Lester Dent, *Lester Dent: The Man, His Craft and His Market* in the early 1990s, and later publishing an anthology of short stories, set in Lester Dent's hometown, entitled *Two-Fisted Tales of La Plata, Missouri.* He also produced a documentary film about one of his other obsessions, the comic-strip caveman Alley Oop. This was a biography of Oop's creator titled *Caveman: V.T. Hamlin & Alley Oop;* the documentary has aired on PBS stations.

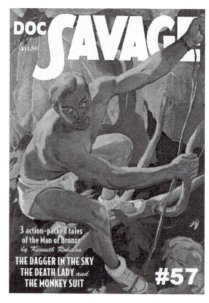

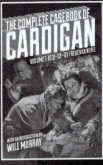

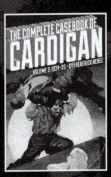
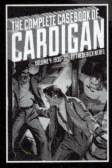

Robeson, Kenneth.
Death's dark domain

APR   2017

Made in the USA
Lexington, KY
19 March 2017